DREAMS THAT VEIL

An evocative and charming Edwardian family saga

DOMINIC LUKE

The Brannans Family Trilogy Book 3

JOFFE
BOOKS

Revised edition 2021
Joffe Books, London
www.joffebooks.com

First published in Great Britain by Robert Hale in 2015

© Dominic Luke 2015, 2021

Cover art by Jarmila Takač

ISBN: 978-1-78931-837-1

... *No wishes and no cares, almost no hopes,*
only the young girl's hazed and golden dreams
that veil the Future from her . . .

A Castaway
Augusta Webster

CHAPTER ONE

'I don't like this photograph.'

Eliza Brannan aged twelve was standing in the middle of the day room in the nursery with her back to the barred window.

'What photograph?' Her cousin Dorothea Ryan, eight years older and seated by the fire, looked up from her sewing.

'This photograph.'

Eliza tilted the silver frame first one way then the other. Cold December light glinted on the glass. Her brother Roderick stared back at her, a cryptic expression on his face. In the picture he was wearing a cap and gown. He was a fresher — whatever that might mean.

But what did any word truly mean, thought Eliza: not just *fresher* but *brother*, as well? *Brother, brother, brother:* if you repeated a word too often, it shook itself free of all meaning and became just a sound, like a dog's bark or a cat's miaow.

My brother.

It meant nothing.

Eliza lowered the photograph to find Dorothea at her side.

'That's the photograph from the parlour, isn't it? You'd better take it back before Aunt Eloise misses it. What do you want with it, anyway?'

'I wanted to remind myself what Roddy looks like.'

'You can't have forgotten already! He's only been away since September.'

'But I wasn't sure that the way I remember him is the way he really is.'

Dorothea laughed. 'What odd ideas you get in that head of yours!'

'I can't help it, Doro. Ideas just pop up without my asking.' Eliza held the picture up at arm's length, looking at it critically. 'I don't like this photograph,' she said once more.

'It isn't the best likeness, I agree. The photographer hasn't captured Roddy's . . .' Dorothea hesitated.

'His swagger?' Eliza suggested.

'His vim and vigour, I was going to say.' Dorothea returned to her chair. 'Take the picture back now. It's not as if you need it. The real Roddy will be here before you know it.'

Eliza sighed and turned to go but at that moment the nursery maid Daisy came into the day room, staggering under the weight of the coal scuttle.

Eliza held out the picture. 'Oh, Daisy, take this back, will you?'

'No, Eliza,' said Dorothea, 'you must take it back yourself. Daisy has enough to do without running round after you.'

Eliza wrinkled her nose. Roderick, were he here, would have said that running round was exactly what Daisy was *for*. He would also have called her Turner, as Mama did, and not Daisy. But spending so much time with Dorothea, Eliza had picked up Dorothea's habits.

Eliza decided that she might as well return the photograph as not. Apart from anything else, it would give her a legitimate excuse for what Mama called 'rampaging round the house'. Mama held the firm opinion that children should be seen and not heard. A child's place was in the nursery, Mama said. But one always took Mama's opinions with a pinch of salt.

Swinging down the stairs, Eliza turned her thoughts back to her brother (*brother, brother, brother*). He would not be arriving alone. He was bringing guests with him, four new friends from Oxford. It was just like Roderick to make *four* new friends in *one* term and then to persuade them all to come for Christmas (not to mention persuading Mama to invite them). Roderick never did things by halves.

One of Roderick's new friends was a boy called Milton, a member of that immense tribe of Miltons, many of whom lived not far away at Darvell Hall. There were two girls coming as well. One was a cousin of the Milton boy, the other a friend of this cousin. They too were students. Eliza had been taken aback to discover that there were *women* at the university. And yet why not? Why should boys like Roderick have all the fun? In this day and age — it was 1911, after all — sisters ought to be treated the same as brothers.

'I shall also go to university when I am older,' she had announced.

But Mama had said it was unnatural for women to be undergraduates. It only encouraged loose morals. Female students were dry sticks for the most part and never got married in later life.

Eliza was in two minds about whether she ever wanted to marry but she was quite certain that she didn't want to be a dry stick. She'd decided against university.

All of which didn't say much for Roderick's guests: two dry sticks and a ten-a-penny Milton. But there was a fourth guest. And the fourth guest was a Russian — a real live Russian!

Eliza shivered with excitement as she jumped the last few steps to land in a heap on the black-and-white tiles of the hallway, only just saving the photo frame from extinction. Just think! A Russian at Clifton Park! It was too thrilling for words! She couldn't wait! But what would he be like? Russians, Eliza knew, were numerous, barbarous and perfidious. People spoke of 'the Russian menace' and 'the great Russian bear' — not that Russians had fur (did they?). Russia

3

was ruled by an emperor called the Tsar who was forever plotting to invade Turkey and Persia and India (but the King was in India just now, he'd put a stop to that). Russia in the map book looked quite big enough already, which only went to show how greedy Russians must be, wanting more, more, more. To think of a Russian coming here, to Clifton Park in the heart of England, was rather disturbing. Might he not be part of a secret plot to add Northamptonshire to the oversized empire? Would Roderick's friend be a savage, menacing brute? Would he growl like a bear and help himself to the whole of the joint at dinner?

Dorothea was keeping an open mind. There was nothing wrong with foreigners as a rule, she insisted. Just look at the mam'zelle (the mam'zelle, now back in France, had once been Dorothea's governess). And what about those German gentlemen they had met on holiday in Switzerland last year? No one could have been nicer, kinder, friendlier.

Eliza had all but forgotten the German gentlemen. The holiday seemed such an age ago now. She had grown up immeasurably since then.

Mama took a rather different attitude towards foreigners. She was not as trusting as Dorothea. Secretly, Eliza wondered if Mama might have a point. Dorothea never saw bad in anyone. But there had to be bad people somewhere or else why was there so much wickedness in the world? Not that there was any wickedness at Clifton Park, nor in the nearby village of Hayton. In fact, there was probably no real wickedness anywhere closer than — say — the little market town of Lawham three miles away. But what went on in Lawham was anyone's guess.

Bursting into the breakfast room, Eliza skidded to a halt by the big round table. She cocked an ear. There were voices in the next room, the parlour. Mama, of course. And, by the sound of it, Mrs Bourne.

The thought of Mrs Bourne made Eliza reconsider the idea of wickedness at Clifton. Was the housekeeper wicked? Perhaps not. But she was certainly rather terrifying. To come up against both her *and* Mama at the same time was more than anyone ought to be expected to cope with.

Eliza placed the photograph face down on the sideboard. Someone would find it eventually and put it back where it belonged. Dorothea would be none the wiser.

As she waltzed back up the stairs, curtseying on the half-landing to the portrait of the red-faced man in the white wig, Eliza turned her thoughts from Roderick and Russians and the wickedness in the world to the more immediate and important question of what sort of sandwiches and cakes Cook would send up for tea.

* * *

As it turned out, Eliza that day took tea not in the nursery but in the drawing room: a special treat. This was no doubt Dorothea's doing. Mama would not have thought of it, would probably have argued against it. But Mama on occasion deferred to Dorothea, especially on nursery matters. No one apart from Dorothea could work this magic with Mama. Eliza knew. She'd tried — and failed.

Mama this afternoon was being what Roderick called 'the Perfect Hostess'. It was a persona she slipped on when guests called, in the same way that she slipped on her best tea gown. The advantage of having the Perfect Hostess in the room was that all attention was turned to Mama. One could watch and listen without much danger of being caught staring.

From her place on the couch by the french windows, Eliza took stock. Her eye was drawn first — naturally — to her brother, who was standing by the piano drinking his tea. He was rather tall, rather handsome (much more handsome in the flesh than in the photograph), and he had that look on his face which Dorothea called 'cat that got the cream' and which Eliza called 'puffed up' and 'insufferably pleased with himself'. She could tell that Mama wished he would sit down. This was probably because of some rule to do with good manners. There were lots of rules of that sort. One could not hope to remember even half of them — unless one was Mama. But even if Roderick was breaking the rules, Mama would not tell him off. She never told Roderick off.

Mr Milton and the two girls were sitting in a row on the settee on the far side of the room. Mr Milton was dull. He stammered and blushed and was not worth bothering with. The two girls were of more interest. They were cool and reserved and rather intimidating. There was no hint of loose morals that Eliza could see. They wore button-up blouses, long narrow skirts, and shiny boots. They sipped their tea and took bites from their cakes and looked incredibly sophisticated. Eliza felt a positive child by comparison.

Sitting apart was the Russian. Eliza's heart beat fast. She hardly dared look. But when she finally plucked up courage, he proved something of a disappointment. He did not look in the least barbaric. He looked, in fact, rather ordinary. He had an ordinary face, rather round, rather pale, with a nose that was neither one thing nor the other and a mouth that was just a mouth. His hair was sort of blond and sort of wasn't, and it was cut quite short but not very. He had an odd accent and his clothes looked slightly shabby (Mama would have noticed this), but apart from that he could easily have come from the village or Lawham or just *anywhere*. In actual fact he came from a place called Petersburg and his father was a professor (these were the sort of facts the Perfect Hostess elicited from her guests almost by sleight of hand). The Russian was studying at Roderick's college in Oxford which was how they had met. Eliza wondered why he couldn't study at his own college. Perhaps they didn't have colleges in Russia.

The Russian was looking round with keen interest. This room, Eliza realised, so familiar to her, would be wholly new to him. What did he think of it? What did he think of the delft vase and the Chinese fan on the sideboard, of the tea things on the low table, of the landscape painting on the wall? What did he think of Mama — and of her, Eliza Brannan?

She shivered. His eyes, a sort of translucent grey, had seemed at first just as ordinary as the rest of him. But as she watched him looking round the room, she got the uncomfortable impression he could see into things, that he could see their very essence, as easily as reading the pages of a book.

She dismissed the idea. It was probably her imagination. It usually was.

Mama had switched her attention to the dark-haired girl, the one whose name Eliza had forgotten but who wasn't Mr Milton's cousin. The dark-haired girl was being inter-rogated under the guise of what the Perfect Hostess called 'polite conversation'.

'There are three of us, Mrs Brannan: my brother, my younger sister, and myself. We have a house in Bloomsbury.'

'In Bloomsbury? How interesting. I believe Bloomsbury has become quite respectable recently.' Mama tilted her head a fraction, as if she still harboured doubts about Bloomsbury. (Where was Bloomsbury?) 'What about your parents, Miss Halsted? Who are your parents?'

'Both my parents are dead.'

'How sad. I am so sorry.' Mama did not bat an eyelid. She was never caught off guard. Whatever else one might say about Mama, no one reigned over a drawing room in quite the same way.

Mama turned to the other girl, the Milton cousin. 'I knew your mother quite well at one time, Miss Ward. We came out in the same season. She is a widow now, I believe — as am I, of course. Tell me, do you see much of your Uncle Philip these days?'

Eliza sensed that this for some reason was a trick ques-tion. The girl did not seem to notice.

'I've never met Uncle Philip, Mrs Brannan. He is *persona non grata* at Darvell Hall — isn't that right, Gerry?'

'Oh . . . er . . . yes . . . rather. Grandpa won't speak of him.'

Interesting, thought Eliza, taking up the mystery of Uncle Philip and just as quickly dropping it: there was simply too much else to think about. (*Persona non grata*: was that the way dry sticks always talked?)

'Another of your uncles, Mr Giles Milton,' Mama continued, 'is — I'm sure you know — in charge of the BFS showroom in town. My late husband, Albert, built up the BFS Motor Company from nothing. I don't pretend to understand the ins and outs of it, but I'm told that BFS motors are now amongst the most popular in the country.'

Eliza wondered if, despite Mama's smile, mention of the motors and the showroom was a subtle way of putting Mr Milton and his cousin in their place. Their grandfather at Darvell Hall was a millionaire — so the story went — but their Uncle Giles was, to all intents and purposes, a mere employee: Mama's employee, for the BFS Motor Manufacturing Company had passed to Mama when Daddy died two-and-a-half years ago. Mama, of course, had little to do with the day-to-day running of Daddy's factories. The fact that they were as far away as Coventry meant that one forgot all about them most of the time.

Mama now got to her feet. Afternoon tea was over. There was a bustle of movement in the drawing room. The little gathering dispersed.

Led back upstairs by Dorothea, Eliza could not stifle a sense of disappointment. She had looked forward to meeting the new guests but they were in their way just as dull as the boys Roderick used to bring home from school, boys who had either been as timid as church mice or insufferably full of themselves. Those boys had often taken up much of Roderick's time during school holidays. Would the new guests do the same? If only one could have Roderick all to oneself! But there was time for that yet, weeks and weeks until Roderick had to go back to Oxford. The guests would not stay that long. In the meantime, afternoon tea in the drawing room was quite enough excitement for one day.

* * *

8

A dinner party was arranged for Christmas Eve. Everyone was to be there. Everyone, Eliza learned, except her.

'You are too young, Elizabeth, to eat with the grown-ups,' Mama said firmly, not to be budged. Even Dorothea could not change her mind this time.

To add insult to injury, the nursery maid Daisy would be at the dinner too: she was going to help out downstairs for the evening. It was an affront! It was an outrage!

Eliza began to make plans.

* * *

'My hair!' sighed Dorothea, fingering her dark curls as she looked at her reflection in the three-folded mirror on the dressing table in her room.

Now that she was grown up — as old as twenty — Dorothea by rights should have moved to a bigger room on the floor below, leaving the nursery behind as Roderick had done. But Dorothea preferred to keep her old room. Eliza was glad. Together they made a little colony of their own, separate from the rest of the house.

But why was Dorothea worrying about her hair? It was quite out of character.

Standing behind her cousin, Eliza said, 'Your hair is lovely, all those curls. You are beautiful: much nicer than the dry sticks.'

Dorothea smiled at her in the mirror. 'You do exaggerate, Eliza. I am not beautiful. I have never been beautiful.' The smile faded. She sighed again. Then she gathered herself, turned on her stool. 'Now, you will be good, won't you, while I'm downstairs? You'll eat all your supper and won't stay up late? Promise me.'

'I promise.' (*I promise to do whatever I choose.*)

Eliza waited until Dorothea was safely out of the way before leaving the nursery. She ran along the corridor to the far end where the servants' rooms were. It was better to use the back stairs this evening. One might meet anyone on the main stairs, with the house so busy.

She hurried down, trailing her hand on the wall. It was a rather grubby wall. The paint was peeling. But that didn't matter because only the servants ever saw it.

There was a whirl of activity downstairs, guests arriving, servants flitting back and forth. Eliza made a dash for the dining room. As she'd expected, it was all in readiness and for the moment deserted. She closed the door and circled the room, drinking it all in: the leaping fire; the glowing lights; the flickering candles in the candelabra, centrepiece of the long table. The table itself was covered by a vast white cloth, pristine. Eighteen places were set. Each place had a napkin in a sliver ring and a menu card. Cutlery gleamed, glasses shone. There were vases on the cabinet and on the mantelpiece, each crammed with flowers: half the contents of Becket's greenhouses by the look of it. There were Christmas decorations, too, green and red and silver-sparkly. It all looked so lovely, so perfect, that it made Eliza's mouth water. To spy on such a dinner as this — for that was what she intended — would be just as much of a treat as sitting down herself: better, in a way, for she would not have to make polite conversation and remember which knife and fork to use. There was a peephole in one of the dining room doors, a tiny crack in the wood. It was Dorothea who'd once pointed it out. She'd used it herself, she'd said, when she was a little girl. Roderick had used it too. 'Now,' said Eliza, 'it's my turn.'

She had to go. Someone might come. To be discovered at this juncture would be a disaster.

She slipped across the corridor and waited in the morning room. A distant bell tinkled. Footsteps sounded, the unobtrusive but unmistakeable tread of the butler, Mr Ordish. He must be about to announce dinner.

Taking her life in her hands, Eliza ran pell-mell to the hallway where she ducked behind the coat cupboard. From here she could peek out and see right along the passageway that led from the front of the house to the back.

Three-quarters of the way along this passage, a door opened. The grown-ups emerged. Two-by-two, they crossed from the drawing room to the dining room. Roderick led the way, Mrs Somersby of Brockmorton Manor on his arm. Roderick was tall and handsome, his slicked-back hair dark and shiny. Mrs Somersby was incomparably glamorous and very old: fifty at least. The others followed in order, the ladies in their finest frocks and bedecked with jewels, the gentlemen scrubbed and polished and debonair. The Russian, Eliza noted, was wearing one of Roderick's jackets. He was taking Miss Cecily Somersby in to dinner: she was a terrible wallflower. The dry sticks were accompanied by Mr Charles Harding — a silly man — and Mr Mark Somersby, who Roderick called 'the Boer War War-Bore'. Mama and Colonel Harding brought up the rear. Mama was in black, her skin porcelain white. Mama always wore black, since Daddy's death. Black did not suit her. It made her look cross.

All nine couples had gone in. The dining room door was closed. A maid came scurrying, went into the drawing room, reappeared with a tray of glasses. She pulled the door to with her foot, hurried off towards the basement. The passageway was now empty. No one would need to use it for ages and ages. Dinner would be taken in through the other door. Emerging from behind the coat cupboard, Eliza made her way along the passage and put her eye to the crack in the door.

Eighteen people were arranged around the table eating anchovies and drinking sherry. Roderick sat at one end with the curtained window behind him; Mama presided at the other, regal as a queen. Dorothea was half way along with her back to the door. She had the village doctor on one side, the War-Bore on the other. Conversations were sprouting like new shoots in spring. Mrs Somersby, to Roderick's left, was debating the merits of Christmas decorations. She herself found their prevalence these days somewhat vulgar. What did Roderick think?

Eliza, uninterested in Roderick's (or anyone's) opinion of Christmas decorations, found her eye drawn inexorably towards the Russian in his borrowed jacket. He was opposite Dorothea, talking to the wallflower. The wallflower, to Eliza's disdain, was blushing bright red. 'But would I,' she asked herself, 'be any braver, sat next to a Russian?' She had her doubts.

The conversations were blossoming, the noise increasing. Loudest of all (he was always the loudest) was Colonel Harding, seated on Mama's left. His voice echoed round the room: '. . . when I was in India . . . the British raj . . . those sepoys, not worth a . . .' Mama was smiling her 'very interested' smile. But how could anyone really be interested in anything the boring Colonel had to say?

Mr Ordish in the background made a sign. The servants began to clear the plates, the footman, Basford, tall and deliberate, the maids brisk and nimble. Eliza wrinkled her nose, remembering how smug Daisy had been at the prospect of waiting on at dinner. But Daisy's pinafore was coming undone. It would serve her right if it fell off altogether.

The soup arrived. Eliza sniffed. Could it be — was it possible — Cook's mulligatawny? Cook's mulligatawny was the finest soup in the world! But there was no time to dwell on the injustice of missing out. Colonel Harding's voice had risen another notch. The whole table was agog as he butted in (he always butted in) on a disputation between his son and one of the dry sticks: the dark-haired dry stick whose name was Miss Halsted.

'You are wrong, my dear girl, quite wrong. Women don't need the vote. They don't *want* the vote. There are ladies present. Let us ask them.'

'The vote!' exclaimed Mrs Somersby. 'Oh dear me, no! Please don't give me the vote! I shouldn't have the first idea who to vote *for*!'

'Of course you wouldn't!' boomed the Colonel. 'And that is just as it should be! Politics is men's business. There's nothing in it for ladies to worry their pretty heads about.'

But Miss Halsted had more to say. It was, thought Eliza, rather reckless of her. Perhaps she didn't realise that the

Colonel, when crossed, had been known to become almost apoplectic, going red and purple in the face, his eyes popping out of his head: terrifying.

'Are women, then, to have no influence in how the country is governed? That way of thinking is, if I may say, typical of a man. Mr Asquith opposes the unearned privilege of the House of Lords but does nothing about the unearned privilege of men!'

'Asquith?' growled the Colonel ominously. 'Asquith is—'

Mama interrupted, smoothing things over. 'The question is academic, I feel. Women won't get the vote in my lifetime.'

'But Mrs Brannan!' cried Miss Halsted eagerly. 'In New Zealand women have the vote already!'

'New Zealand?' boomed the Colonel. 'New Zealand! My dear girl, that's the colonies! There's no accounting for what goes on in the colonies!'

'Even in this country,' Miss Halsted persisted, 'there have always been women in positions of power. Take Queen Victoria. She ruled the British Empire. She was the most powerful person in the world. If a woman can rule an empire, then surely she's capable enough to vote!'

'You've got things rather muddled. Queen Victoria didn't have the *vote!*' The Colonel guffawed. He seemed to think he'd scored a resounding success.

Eliza let out her breath. Miss Halsted had got off lightly, her act of defiance laughed away. But how brave she'd been, standing up to the bullying Colonel! Perhaps she wasn't such a dry stick after all. Certainly she looked quite different this evening with her hair up and wisps of it hanging down, and candlelight reflected in her wide brown eye. Her rather olive skin gave her an almost exotic appearance, so different from the other ladies round the table. Even Roderick seemed to have noticed and he didn't have much time for girls, he was always saying so. He was watching Miss Halsted with a fierce look on his face, as if he was angry.

What did it mean? Had the idea of votes for women given him indigestion? But no one really cared about votes for women. Dorothea said it was a fuss over nothing.

The quenelles had been eaten. The quails were brought in. Course followed course. The once immaculate table was now littered with breadcrumbs and spilt salt. Menu cards had been laid aside higgledy-piggledy; the cutlery was askew; wax ran in rivers down the smooth sides of the candles.

Eliza yawned. Grand dinners went on so long! It was impossible to keep up with all the separate conversations. Grown-ups laced their words with so many different meanings.

There were invisible threads, she said to herself, running from person to person, criss-crossing the table like a cat's cradle or a spider's web, the pattern growing ever more complex as the dinner wore on. Every glance, every movement, every word added yet another gossamer thread. Some threads were brittle and easily snapped (Mrs Somersby, dabbing decorously at her mouth with her napkin, glanced at Mr Milton then looked away, dismissive). Some threads vibrated like violin strings (the Russian and Miss Ward were debating some arcane point across the table). The thread that linked Roderick and Miss Halsted was taut like steel wire as if holding them against their will; whereas a soft and caressing thread ran from Dorothea to the wallflower, Dorothea taking pity as she always did and trying to ease Cecily's discomfiture. 'In Germany on Christmas Eve . . .' But why was Dorothea always talking about Germany these days?

At last it was time for desert. The crumbs were swept away, the dirty glasses and the salt cellars removed. Fresh glasses were put out. The dessert wine was handed round. Mr Ordish in the background inspected every detail with a critical eye. Finally he nodded. He ushered Basford and the maids out of the room. The babble of voices now rose to a final crescendo. Faces were flushed, arms were waving; ties were askew and hair out of place. Only Mama was unchanged, a velvet spider sitting at the heart of the web, aware of every thread, aware of every tremor and vibration.

The Colonel began to dominate once more. He was railing against 'all this new-fangled rubbish, science and technology, the work of the Devil', a favourite theme.

Mrs Somersby smiled a mischievously. (Mrs Somersby, mischievous?) 'What about Crippen, Colonel? Crippen would never have been caught but for new-fangled radio signals.'

Mama stepped in, keeping the peace. 'What happened to Crippen in the end? I never heard.'

'Bally fellow was hanged, I should hope,' said the Colonel.

The Russian spoke up. 'Hanging is barbaric, the practice of savages!'

'I agree with Kolya!' cried Miss Halsted. 'One can't really talk of civilisation when we still employ the methods of the Dark Ages!'

The Colonel growled threateningly. Eliza prepared for a purple-faced explosion of the most devastating kind. Shock waves could already be felt, radiating round the table. But Mama brought a lightness of touch which stilled the quivering threads, glancing at the Colonel with a raise of her eyebrows, the merest hint of a smile, thereby averting disaster.

She turned to the Russian. 'Surely, Mr Antipov, you can't defend a man like Crippen? Surely you can't argue that he didn't deserve to die?'

'Life is precious, Mrs Brannan: most precious possession we have. It should not be taken away for punishment or revenge.'

Colonel Harding snorted. 'And what do you do with your criminals in Russia? Drown them in vodka? Haw, haw, haw!' His rollicking laughter jolted the invisible web; he nodded and winked at Mama.

Eliza's hands strayed to her neck. What was it like to be hung? It *did* sound barbaric. Yet perhaps Mr Crippen deserved it. Who was Mr Crippen? Everyone seemed to know — everyone except her.

Mama gave a little sign and got to her feet. It was time for the ladies to withdraw. They would be leaving the dining room by this very door.

Eliza abandoned her post, scrambled across the passage, dashed across the drawing room and the breakfast room and into the parlour. She would be safe in the parlour (or *Mother's Lair*, as Roderick called it). Once the ladies were settled and the coffee had come, she could make her way back to the nursery.

She yawned, settling herself on the sofa. It was peaceful in here, the only light coming from the glowing embers of the fire. If she closed her eyes just for a moment . . . just a moment . . . just . . . just . . .

* * *

She woke with a jerk. The fire had gone out and it was pitch dark. How long had she been asleep? She must get back to the nursery before Dorothea came up — if it wasn't too late already.

She jumped up, ran into the breakfast room. This too was now in darkness — someone had turned off the lights — but there were slivers of brightness under the doors. There was no sound from the drawing room but a murmur of voices came from the hall. Outside, carriage wheels were crunching on the gravel. A horse stamped impatiently.

Eliza pressed her ear against the hall door. She could hear Colonel Harding, grumpy-voiced, slurring his words, and Mr Charles, yawning loudly: the last to leave as they always were. Mr Ordish must be helping them on with their coats, hats and scarves. If only they'd hurry! She was trapped where she was until they moved. But it was probably too late in any case. Dorothea would be back in the nursery by now. The only hope was that she hadn't looked in on Eliza's room and seen that the bed was empty.

At last the front door banged shut. The sound of the carriage faded into the night. Eliza slipped out from the breakfast room. As she ran on light feet across the hall, the grandfather clock began to strike the hour. 'One, two, three

. . . ,'she counted under her breath, '. . . ten, eleven, twelve. Gosh! Midnight! How thrilling!'

In her excitement she almost trod on the book before she saw it. It lay face down on the bottom step where someone had dropped it. What an odd book it was, full of lines of print that didn't make sense. Some of the letters were quite ordinary. Others were mysterious symbols of unknown meaning. They were all jumbled up together. Someone had gone through the book underlining passages in pencil and writing notes in the margin: desecration, Dorothea would have called it. Eliza could not imagine how anyone would have time to pause and write down their thoughts. All she ever wanted of a book was to rush to the last page to see how it finished.

'I see you have found my book.'

The unexpected voice made her heart stop. She had not heard anyone come. Slowly she looked up. There he was, looming over her on the stairs like a giant: the Russian. She could feel her cheeks burning. She must be as red-faced as that wallflower Cecily Somersby. How shameful, how humiliating, to be no better than Cecily Somersby!

'I . . . I . . .' *Oh, stupid girl: speak, speak!* 'Your . . . your book.' She held it out with a shaking hand.

He ran down the last few steps, took the book slipped it into his jacket pocket. '*Spasibo.* Thank you.'

He was now very close. They were face-to-face in the hallway. He had seemed very tall on the stairs. He was still taller than she was. But he was not as tall as Roderick, nor as imposing.

She lowered her eyes, too shy to look at him.

'I am always losing my books, Miss Brannan. I put them down and forget them. They drop out of my pockets. I leave them on trains and in other people's houses. So I am grateful to you.'

He had a deep voice despite his slim frame. He had a most peculiar accent. The familiar hallway seemed suddenly like a wild and uncharted land at this late hour with this stranger before her.

'I . . .' She swallowed, forced herself to speak. She didn't want to be a wallflower. 'I shouldn't be here. I should be in bed.'

'Ah, I see. Then your secret — is that right word, *secret*? — is safe with me.'

'Yes. Yes.' She was overcome with confusion. 'Good . . . goodnight!'

She fled. She did not have the courage to look back.

Safely in bed, she pulled the covers close around her. The night light glowed on the bedside table keeping the dark at bay. What an evening! The excitement of the dinner party, and then an encounter with the Russian. She had been alone with him, completely alone. Anything might have happened! He might have kidnapped her and carried her off to Russia!

What eyes he had, looking at you as if he could *really* see you, as if you weren't just part of the furniture. But she had avoided his eyes. She had stared at his hand instead, the hand that had taken the book from her: the long bony fingers, the pared nails, the red knuckles. His shirt cuff sliding out from the sleeve of Roderick's jacket had been frayed at the edges.

She tried to remember his name. It began with an A. And what was the name that Miss Halsted had called him during dinner: a different name, a nickname perhaps?

Eliza snuggled down in bed, trying to find words to describe the mysterious Russian. He was like a deer. Or a rabbit. Or . . . or—

Her mind fumbled. The words *deer* and *rabbit* didn't fit. The Russian was like nothing except himself. Maybe all Russians were the same, beyond words, unimaginable.

She hugged herself under the bed covers, feeling that she'd had a lucky escape: for if he had kidnapped her and carried her off, would anyone have even noticed?

* * *

Roderick looked very dashing astride his tall horse Conquest, impeccably turned out from his black silk hat down to his polished black boots, more handsome even than usual. He appeared much older than his nineteen years.

'And he's my brother,' thought Eliza. 'My very own brother.'

The word *brother* had regained its meaning on this blustery Boxing Day morning. It was a dynamic word, a weighty word, ambivalent too: it summed up Roderick completely.

Eliza had come to Lawham to see the hunt off. Dorothea and Miss Halsted were with her in one of Clifton's motors (Mr Milton and Miss Ward had gone that morning to Darvell Hall to pay their respects to their many relatives). There were one or two other motors on Market Place, several carriages as well, and a large crowd of onlookers. The huntsmen and women (there were half a dozen women) were resplendent in their coats of scarlet or black, polished buttons glinting in the grey light. Their horses — bays and greys and roans — were fidgeting and dancing, striking sparks off the cobbles with their hoofs. The hounds were everywhere, yammering and slavering and showing their teeth. Smoke rose from the chimneys of the houses lining the square. The tall, pointed spire of the church tapered into a leaden sky. There was rain in the air.

Roderick was peerless. No one could match him. Some of the riders, indeed, looked rather ridiculous in comparison, with their great paunches and their spindly legs. The Russian was awkward and ill-at-ease. His borrowed clothes did not quite fit. He was pulling at the reins of his prancing horse, frowning. His name was Mr Antipov. Eliza had memorised it at last.

She had learned something terrible about Mr Antipov. He was an atheist. An atheist was someone who did not believe in God — unlikely as that seemed.

'It's pure affectation.' Dorothea had been unusually scathing. 'And I do think — it would only have been polite — that he could have made the effort to come to church yesterday morning.'

'Russians are Orthodox, Doro, not C of E,' Roderick had said. 'They have Christmas on a different date. So Antipov would not have gone to our church even if he did believe in all that stuff.'

Mr Antipov must do as he chose, Mama had averred. He was a guest and guests could please themselves.

But Eliza could not help but worry. 'Will Mr Antipov go to hell when he dies?'

'Oh, I shouldn't think so,' Roderick had replied cheerfully. 'He's not a bad sort. God, I'm sure, will forgive him. God is like that — or so Doro tells me.'

But why worry about Mr Antipov? She would probably never see him again. Roderick during his school days had often invited boys who came once and once only. Her brother had exacting standards when it came to friends. All the same, as she sat in the motor on Market Place, Eliza could not help but feel sorry for the Russian. He had no God to protect him. All he'd got were borrowed clothes and a horse which Roderick called 'an old nag'.

The hunt was off at last. Horns blared. Horses charged. The hounds went streaming down Priory Street between the rows of terraced cottages. Roderick and Mr Antipov disappeared into the melee.

'Now we can go home,' said Dorothea, 'and not before time. It looks like rain.'

'Oh no, please, not yet!' cried Miss Halsted. 'Couldn't we follow them, Miss Ryan, just a little way? I'm starting to enjoy myself!'

The chauffeur Smith twisted round in his seat to look at them. 'If we head down London Road, miss, we can meet up with the hunt again on the other side of Barrow Hill. I've heard that they're going to draw the coverts between Bodford and Newbolt.'

Dorothea did not care for hunting. She'd said to Roderick that morning as they were all preparing to leave, 'What a bloodthirsty lot you are! The poor fox!'

'Poor fox, my eye!' Roderick had scoffed. 'Why did God make foxes if not to be hunted?'

Roderick was all for hunting. Smith was too, even if he never rode. And now Miss Halsted was enthusiastic as well. Dorothea, therefore, gave way: more for Smith's sake, Eliza felt, than for Miss Halsted's.

They left Lawham and drove out past Barrow Hill. Smith turned off the main road onto a cart track which wound its way towards the village of Newbolt hidden somewhere ahead amongst the wintry fields and leafless hedges. To the left the land rose in steep slopes to the long, flattened summit of Barrow Hill. Rooks flying high were black dots against the scudding clouds.

Smith brought the motor to a halt and turned off the engine. In the sudden silence Eliza could hear, carried on the gusting breeze, the faint yammering of the hounds.

'They're coming this way!' Smith jumped down from his driver's seat. 'And they've found a fox by the sound of it!'

He turned up the collar of his long chauffeur's coat, gazing out across the fields. Miss Halsted joined him, slim and stylish in her three-quarter coat and large hat. Her interest in the hunt seemed somehow unladylike. Eliza wondered what Roderick saw in her. Would she too pay one visit to Clifton and then disappear?

Red and black blobs appeared in the distance, the riders in all their finery. They seemed to be moving without purpose, spread higgledy-piggledy across the fields. The noise of the hounds grew louder, blown on the wind. A far-off horn wailed.

'They've lost the scent.' Smith was disappointed. 'The whole field is strung out.'

One of the black blobs detached itself and began to head in their direction. The blob soon became recognisable as Colonel Harding, his horse picking its way across a ploughed field.

'Hoi there! Miss Ryan! There's been an accident! Your cousin, I'm afraid: young Brannan. He's taken a tumble.

Nothing to worry about. But he's a little winded and his arm is giving him pain. It could have been worse, of course. When I was in India—'

Miss Halsted interrupted. 'Where is he? We should go to him!'

'It might be an idea, Miss Ryan, if you were to take him home in that *contraption* of yours.' The Colonel curled his lip. His hatred of motors was notorious. 'You take him back and my man will bring his horse. Follow me.'

The Colonel led the way, tugging sharply on the reins of his big horse as it pranced and bobbed along the cart track. The motor juddered behind, Smith manhandling the steering wheel. Eliza's heart was beating fast. Roderick was alright, the Colonel had said. But to a man who'd been in the army, anyone would be alright who wasn't stone dead.

The worst of Eliza's fears abated as they reached Roderick waiting by the side of the track. He'd lost his hat, he was covered in mud, he was clutching his arm, but he certainly wasn't dead. He let rip in true Roderick style as they drew near. 'That absolute ass Charles Harding! He's nothing but a prize idiot!'

'Hush, Roddy,' murmured Dorothea. 'The Colonel will hear you.'

'I hope he does! He ought to know what a fool he has for a son! Charles Harding is the biggest fool that ever drew breath! He headed the fox, rode over the hounds, made his first horse lame. And then, to top it off, he jinked right in front of me at a hedge and I went head-over-heels. I was lucky not to break my neck!'

'That's awful, that's terrible!' cried Miss Halsted. 'But you've no serious injuries? You aren't badly hurt?'

'Only my arm. It's throbbing like Hades.'

'And you're shivering, and covered in cuts and grazes. You poor thing! I expect you're suffering from shock. Here, let me help you into the motor.' Miss Halsted took charge, bundling Roderick into the car, wrapping him in rugs. His teeth were chattering. 'That'll be the shock, making you feel cold. You must have the chauffeur's coat. We'll put the roof up too. Now, Miss Ryan, if you sit this side and I sit the other, together we can keep him warm. The little girl can sit in the front.'

Little girl! Eliza was seething as she got into the front passenger seat. Anyone would think that Roderick was Miss Halsted's brother, the way she was carrying on! Even Dorothea had been pushed aside. Why was Roderick just sitting there letting her pet and pat him? Usually he hated fuss. Usually he bit your head off if you tried to smother him (as he called it).

Smith finished fixing the roof and set the motor going. Eliza sat stiff and formal in the front seat all the way home.

* * *

Roderick was helped into the house and laid on the couch in the drawing room. Quite a congregation gathered. Mama was there, of course, and Dorothea and Miss Halsted. Mr Milton and Miss Ward were back from Darvell Hall. At a respectful distance Mr Ordish, Mrs Bourne, Basford and two of the maids looked on; Cook peeked round the door. Eliza found herself thrust to one side and ignored.

Mama wiped the mud off Roderick's face and mopped his brow. Dorothea eased off his jacket. Miss Halsted removed his boots. Mrs Bourne and the maids hastened to fetch pillows and blankets. Basford heaved the couch nearer the fire. A glass of water was thrust into the patient's hand and then a glass of brandy. The best linen was torn up without a murmur to make a sling or bandages, depending on who one listened to.

Finally, Dr Camborne arrived hotfoot from the village. He ushered everyone out of the room. Eliza sat glumly on the stairs. No one told her to go back to the nursery. No one took any notice of her at all.

She cocked an ear. There were voices in the passage, Miss Halsted and Miss Ward whispering together. They must be waiting outside the drawing room door as if they could not tear themselves away.

'Rosa, I'm disappointed in you!' hissed Miss Ward. 'How can you say you *enjoyed* the hunting?'

'I didn't *enjoy* it exactly. But there is something rather . . . exciting about it. There's a sense of tradition, of Merrie Olde England.'

'It's cruel. A cruel sport. Not a sport at all. "The unspeakable in pursuit of the uneatable." Oh, why did we ever come here? It's everything we abhor!'

'We came because Roderick invited us.'

'Oh, well, Roderick!' Miss Ward's tone suggested that she did not think much of Roderick.

'He's not so bad, Maggie, he really isn't, once you get to know him.'

'That's not what you used to say. You used to call him a hidebound chauvinist.'

'I may have been a little . . . hasty. One shouldn't be too judgmental. One should always give people the benefit of the doubt. And you have to admit, Maggie, here in his own setting he is rather magnificent — heroic, almost.'

'You've lost your head, Rosa. All men are the same, you should know that. All men are the enemy.'

'Oh, Maggie, don't be so obdurate! Not all men are—'

At this point, the conversation came to an abrupt end. The doctor had finished with Roderick, was saying his good-byes. Everyone gathered once more in the drawing room.

'What did Arthur Camborne say?' asked Mama.

'I've a broken bone. I could have told him that. He's put this splint-thing on. He seemed to take great delight in twisting my arm about until I was in the throes of agony. He's something of a sadist on the quiet.'

'That's rather unfair,' said Mama, gently chiding. 'It was good of him to come so quickly.'

'Yes, of course. He's an angel form heaven, is dear old Arthur.'

From her vantage point by the piano, Eliza studied her brother. Was he really *heroic* as Miss Halsted said? He'd looked very dashing that morning sitting tall and straight-backed on Conquest. But now he was ashen-faced, dishevelled, covered in cuts and bruises. His poor arm, too! How fragile people were! What had Miss Ward meant by calling him 'the enemy'? The fact that Miss Halsted had defended him set Eliza's teeth on edge.

'Does it hurt very much?' asked Eliza when at last she was able to get a word in edgeways, daring to touch — very gently — his arm in its sling.

'Not much,' he said. 'Not at all.' He laughed but his voice did not have its usual swagger. 'What are those tears for? I'm not dead yet, you silly goose. My arm will mend. Give me your hand. You can help me up and see me to my room.'

Her heart swelled as she pulled on his good arm so that he could get to his feet. He had asked *her* to help, not Mama or Miss Halsted or even Dorothea! Oh, she did love him so! But he'd only laugh all the more if she told him.

* * *

'Where is your hat, Eliza?' said Dorothea in the nursery after tea. 'It needs mending. There's a ribbon loose.'

'Oh—' Eliza looked round, then remembered. 'I left it in the drawing room on the piano. I'll fetch it.'

She ran helter-skelter down the stairs, arriving in the hallway just as the front door opened and Mr Antipov let himself in. He was wet, mud-spattered, limping. His fingers were white from the cold, his face streaked with blood.

'You're hurt! You're bleeding!' The meeting was so unexpected, he looked so bedraggled, that she forgot that she was shy of him.

'Not my blood. The fox. Is old English custom on first hunt, they tell me, to wear the blood of the fox. Do you think they have joke on me, about fox's blood?'

'Then they found the fox after all? They killed it?' It seemed all the more real, seeing the dried blood on the Russian's pale, ordinary face.

He looked in this state like the barbarian she'd first imagined he would be. But oddly his eyes, which she'd been rather afraid of before, now belied his gory appearance. They were not savage eyes. Just the opposite. The fear she had felt the other evening, that he might kidnap her and carry her of to Russia, now seemed quite absurd.

She thought of the fox, *the poor fox* as Dorothea had called it. She found herself, most disconcertingly, agreeing with Miss Ward of all people, that hunting was cruel.

'Do . . . do you hunt foxes in Russia?'

'In Russia we hunt wolves and bears.'

'Wolves! Are there really wolves in Russia?'

'Yes, of course.'

'Have you ever seen one?'

'One time, at our dacha—'

At that moment the door to the breakfast room opened and Mama appeared. She took in the scene, poised, impassive.

'Ah, Mr Antipov, you are back at last. You will want to get changed, I expect, and to bathe. There is plenty of time before dinner. I shall send the footman up.'

'Thank you, Mrs Brannan.' The Russian gave one of his little bows which, if anyone else had done it, would have looked silly. But with him — and when it was Mama he was bowing to — it seemed strangely in keeping.

As Mr Antipov made his way upstairs, Mama cast a glance at Eliza. 'What are you doing out of the nursery, Elizabeth? Please return there immediately.'

* * *

The guests departed. Mr Milton and Miss Ward were to see in the New Year at Darvell Hall; Miss Halsted was off to visit some aunts in Tonbridge; and Mr Antipov had an appointment with an émigré friend of his father's. It wouldn't be long before Roderick was off too, heading back to Oxford for the Hilary term. Then, at last, life at Clifton would get back to normal.

To her surprise, Eliza found this thought not in the least comforting. The days had flown by with the house so busy. The old routine paled by comparison. And the thought that she might not see Mr Antipov again for a long time — if ever — filled her with an entirely unexpected sense of desolation.

CHAPTER TWO

'Such a day! I'm quite exhausted!'

Mama had just got in. She sank onto the settee giving the impression of being flustered, though of course there wasn't actually a hair out of place. She still had her hat on and, as Eliza watched from the window seat, began to reach round for the hatpins.

'London is so much more crowded than it used to be and people nowadays have such bad manners. The shops are not half as good as I remember, either. I can't think why I let you persuade me to come, Dorothea.'

Dorothea, who had not just her hat on but her coat as well, had sat down in the chair by the door. Mama's remark seemed to pass her by, which was most unusual. Mama obviously thought so too. She gave Dorothea a quizzical glance but let it pass.

Still searching for the hat pins, Mama continued, 'It's remarkable how few horse buses one sees these days. But there are motors everywhere. We saw — how many was it, Dorothea? — so many BFS machines, getting on for half a dozen, Albert would be astonished. When I was young—' Mama broke off, exclaimed irritably, 'Oh, this hat! What is wrong with it?'

Dorothea looked up at last. 'Shall I ring for Sally, Aunt?'

'There's no need. I've done it.' Mama removed the last pin with a flourish, took off her hat, laid it on the settee. Patting her coiffure, she got to her feet. 'I think I'll take a little rest now. I shall go up. What time is Roderick due?'

'Just after five, Aunt.'

'I shall be sure to be down in plenty of time.' Mama swept to the door, looked back. 'Do sit up straight, Elizabeth. You will get a curved spine if you slouch like that.'

Eliza pulled a face as Mama left the room. She would die of boredom long before her spine ever became curved. It was Tuesday today. They'd arrived in London last Friday. She'd not been allowed on any of the shopping trips: she would only get in the way, Mama said. Not that Eliza particularly wanted to go clothes shopping with Mama. But it would have been nice to see the crowds, the shops and the many BFS motors for herself. Instead she spent her days looking out of the window at the neat square with its railed garden and the trim terraces of white-fronted houses. Nothing much ever happened. People passed by on the pavement below. There was an occasional motor car, a handful of four-wheelers, delivery boys on bicycles, the butcher's van, the baker's cart. At times, a maid from one of the houses opposite walked back and forth with a perambulator in the garden. The leafless branches of the plane trees swayed in the breeze. The drab sky threatened rain which never came. It was all very dull. London — the real London — was out there somewhere, just out of reach: round the corner, down the next street.

They had not visited their home at 28 Essex Square for three years, since before Daddy died. But now that Mama was out of mourning she had decided she needed some new clothes and Dorothea had suggested London. Here Roderick was to join them today. Since the end of term, he'd been visiting yet another new Oxford friend. Eliza counted off the weeks since she'd last seen him. Almost three months. It was April already.

The last time they'd come to London, Eliza remembered, Daddy had promised to take her on their next visit to a place called the Crystal Palace. It was a name that had stirred her imagination. She had looked forward to it so much. But Daddy had failed to keep his promise. He had died instead.

The ticking of the clock on the mantelpiece was loud in the silence. The seconds slid slowly by. Dorothea sat with a faraway look in her eyes. Eliza shrank from disturbing her.

At length, Dorothea sighed. She grew suddenly agitated, wringing her hands. It was as if she'd woken from a long sleep.

'Oh, Eliza! I simply *must* tell someone or I shall go mad!'

'Tell someone what?' asked Eliza, apprehensive.

'About the letter. The letter.'

This was not much help. Letters often came for Dorothea. There were letters, for instance, from Mrs Carter in Coventry who'd once been a nursery maid at Clifton; there were letters from abroad with strange stamps. Eliza had grown to recognize the different writing on the envelopes: Mrs Carter's laborious hand; the flowing script with little flourishes that belonged to the former governess Mlle Lacroix; and the neat, compact penmanship of the German boy they'd met on holiday in Switzerland nearly two years ago.

Now that she came to think about it, Eliza remembered that it had been a German letter that had arrived at Clifton on the day they departed for London. There had been so much going on that morning that she hadn't given it another thought.

'The letter——' Eliza prompted.

'I don't know how to tell you. I don't know where to start. He said . . . he wrote . . . he's asked me to marry him!'

Eliza reeled with shock at Dorothea's words. Marriage? To the German boy? But that was impossible, unthinkable. One might as well marry Polly the Parrot. Eliza could not even remember the German boy's name. He had been quiet and shy. He'd not climbed up mountains like his companion (his cousin) because he'd been convalescing. There had seemed nothing remarkable about him — although Roderick, for some reason, had disliked him.

'But Doro . . . you can't . . . you *mustn't* . . .'

'Mustn't?' Dorothea stared at her with wide eyes. To Eliza's dismay, tears began brimming and coursing down Dorothea's cheeks. 'But you're right, of course. I can't possibly marry him. I can't marry anyone. How could I, plain old Dorothea? I am nobody. I have nothing.'

'I don't think you're nobody, Doro! You're . . . you're *everything*! And . . . and . . . and he must think so too or he wouldn't write so many letters!'

'He's so kind, so thoughtful. He said I must take as long as I like to make up my mind.' Dorothea took a deep shuddering breath and wiped the tears from her cheeks with her hand. 'I'm sorry, Eliza. I shouldn't have burdened you with this. You won't say anything, will you? You won't say anything to anyone? No, of course you won't! I know I can rely on you!' She gave a tearful smile and then got to her feet, patting her hair in an unconscious imitation of Mama. 'I must look a fright. I will go and tidy myself straight away.'

Left on her own, Eliza felt weighed down by the secret she had to keep. Even if Dorothea said no to the German boy and it all blew over, the secret would still be there. Dorothea would say no, of course — wouldn't she? What would Mama make of it all, if she knew? And Roderick?

Roderick! She had quite forgotten Roderick! He was due at any moment!

She flew upstairs to get ready for her brother's arrival.

* * *

They heard Roderick before they saw him. His voice came echoing up from the hallway, laying down the law, ordering the servants to watch what they were doing with his valise. Next moment he came breezing into the drawing room, taller, louder, more alive than ever. His sling was gone and his arm to all appearances as good as new.

'Hello Mother, Doro. Hello, kiddo. Here I am at last. The train took an age and the crush at Paddington was

31

beyond belief. There wasn't a porter to be had for love nor money.'

He had plenty to say for himself. He'd had the jolliest time with his friend from university, a rather upmarket sort of boy — an honourable — who lived in a vast house with hundreds of servants. A week really wasn't long enough, but never mind, there'd be other visits. In the meantime, he had a few days in London to look forward to. And were they all heading back to Clifton for Easter, was that still the general idea? Travelling by train, though, was becoming such a bore. Mother really must consider buying him a motor of his—

He broke off, held up his hand. 'I say, was that the door-bell? I rather think it was, you know!' He sat up, watching the door with an eager light in his eyes.

'How very odd,' said Mama. 'We're not expecting anyone.'

After a moment the door opened and Sally came in. 'Excuse me, ma'am, there's a Miss Halsted—'

Roderick interrupted. 'Show her up, Kirkham. Show her up at once.'

Sally's eyes flicked from Roderick to Mama. Mama gave no sign. Sally curtsied and went out.

'By the way, Mother . . .' Roderick sat back, picking his nails. 'I wrote to Miss Hasted, invited her to dinner. I thought, as I'd be in town and as Miss Halsted lives here . . .' He shrugged, as if inviting Miss Halsted was an obvious corollary and didn't need to be spelled out.

'You might have given us some warning, Roderick,' Mama reproached him. But there was no mention of the inconvenience or the extra work in stretching dinner to five. Daisy often said that Master Roderick was allowed to get away with murder and, just then, Eliza was inclined to agree.

Dusk was falling outside in the square but the drawing room was brightly lit and the fire blazing. From her place in the window seat, Eliza watched as Miss Halsted was shown in and stood a little awkwardly looking round at them. In one hand she held her hat trimmed with fake roses; in the other hand was a bunch of real flowers.

Roderick jumped up. 'Miss Halsted! So glad you could come! You're staying to dinner, I hope? Of course you are!' He took her hat, passed it to Sally Kirkham; took the flowers too, looking at them with a curl of his lip. 'From an admirer? From Antipov?' He handed the flowers to Sally, ushered Miss Halsted towards the settee. 'Sit here, Miss Halsted.' He placed her next to Mama, sat down beside her.

'The flowers are not from Mr Antipov,' said Miss Halsted. 'Why would you think that Mr Antipov would give me flowers? They are, in fact, a gift from one of my students.'

'One of your *students*?'

'I do some lecturing in the vac. There's a college for working men in the East End—'

'Philanthropy.'

'Philanthropy is not a dirty word, Mr Brannan. I find the work very rewarding, if you must know, and my students are all very eager to learn. A boy gave me these flowers. He is unemployed, so you see they are worth their weight in gold.'

'Very profligate of him, not to mention presumptuous. You told him so, I presume?'

'Well, of course I didn't! That would not have been very gracious.'

Eliza wrinkled her brow. What was philanthropy? And why was Miss Halsted here? She looked rather out of place, sandwiched between Mama and Roderick on the settee. She looked like she *felt* out of place. Eliza, who had looked forward to dinner with Roderick and just Mama and Dorothea for company, rather resented Miss Halsted's intrusion.

* * *

Dinner ran smoothly, of course. It would take more than one unexpected guest to throw Mama off her stride. In London, Eliza ate with the grown-ups. The normal rules did not apply in London. Roderick spent most of the meal disputing with Miss Halsted.

33

'You must face facts, there will always be rich and poor, it's a law of nature. The strong prosper while the weak go to the wall. It's called survival of the fittest.'

'We humans have risen above the motivations of animals, Mr Brannan. We have the ability to change: to change ourselves and to change the world we live in.'

'Sentimental humbug! There's no room for sentiment in the real world!'

'You take such a *pessimistic* view of life, Mr Brannan. I can't think why I associate with you.'

Eliza wondered if they always carried on like this. They seemed to disagree on everything. Why invite Miss Halsted only to quarrel? Mama listened with an air of disapproval. Dorothea seemed barely to be listening at all.

After dinner, Mama despatched Eliza to bed. Eliza was too shy to argue in front of Miss Halsted.

'I'll come and tuck you in by-and-by,' smiled Dorothea.

In her room, Eliza began to brush her hair, counting towards a hundred, but she soon lost interest. She yawned, put the brush aside, crossed to the window, looked out between the curtains. The square was quiet and empty. The skeletal branches of the plane trees were etched against the grey-dark sky. There were pools of light beneath the street lamps. Lights showed in many windows. She wondered what people were doing in all the different rooms. She wondered, for that matter, what was happening downstairs. She yawned again and let the curtain fall back into place.

On her way to the closet, she hesitated at the top of the stairs. She could hear voices below: Roderick's voice (unmistakeable) and Miss Halsted's. They had just emerged from the drawing room by the sound of it. Eliza in her stockinged feet inched down first one step then another, listening.

'I shall walk you home,' Roderick was saying.

'I shan't walk,' said Miss Halsted. 'It's too far to walk. I shall catch an omnibus on the Fulham Road.'

'Then I shall catch it with you.'

'Whatever for? I am more than capable of seeing myself home.'

'In other words, you don't need the help of a *mere man*.'

'That's it. That's quite right. You are beginning to learn, Mr Brannan.'

Miss Halsted's mocking voice faded. Roderick's reply was all but inaudible. They must be going downstairs, Eliza realised. She debated, looking back up at the landing. How long before Dorothea came to tuck her in?

Curiosity got the better of her. She ran quickly to the first floor landing and turned the corner, following her brother and Miss Halsted down to the ground floor. She moved slowly, soundlessly, hugging the banister as Roderick's voice came into earshot once more.

'. . . and Mother *doesn't* dislike you, that's just her way. She's the same with everyone. You are using Mother as an excuse to leave.'

'I don't need an excuse. It's quite late enough. Mrs Hammond will be wondering where I am.'

'Never mind Mrs Hammond. She's only your cook.'

'Cook, housekeeper, spy: she spies on Leo and Carla and me and reports back to the Aunts in Tonbridge.'

'Then you should get rid of her. Get someone else.'

'We can't afford anyone else. The Aunts pay Mrs Hammond's salary. You wouldn't understand. You never have to worry about money.'

'How you go on about those aunts of yours!'

'They interfere and they're frightfully old-fashioned — but they do love us in their own way.'

'And you love their money.'

'What a horrid thing to say! Why must you be so disagreeable, Roderick? You make it very difficult for people to like you. Now please fetch my coat. I'm going home.'

Eliza with infinite care had edged down the last few steps as she listened. She now held her breath and peeped round the corner. Roderick and Miss Halsted were by the front door with their backs to her. Roderick was helping

Miss Halsted into her coat. It seemed a terribly inappropriate thing to do, at once menial and intimate. Why had they not rung for Sally?

Miss Halsted began buttoning her coat. Roderick, instead of stepping back, moved closer. He put his arms round her from behind. Far from objecting to this treatment, Miss Halsted seemed content to lean back against him and rest there. They stayed like this for what seemed to Eliza an age.

At length Roderick said, muttering into Miss Halsted's ear, 'I am sorry for being disagreeable. I wanted to be alone with you, like in January. It was hell not having you to myself this evening.'

'January was pure luck,' said Miss Halsted. 'We'd never have the house to ourselves like that a second time. Which is just as well when you think of . . . of what happened. It mustn't happen again.'

'Don't say that! I shall go mad, wanting you!'

'Then you must go mad. Please let me go.'

'I shan't. I shall keep you here forever.'

Miss Halsted twisted round in his arms. She was facing him now — but also facing Eliza. Eliza shrank back but Miss Halsted only had eyes for Roderick. She gazed up at him, a smile playing on her lips.

'I preferred it when your arm was broken,' she murmured. 'I could get away from you then.'

'But you didn't get away from me. Just the opposite, in January.'

'I think you broke your arm on purpose, so that I would feel sorry for you. You are a very bad influence, Roderick Brannan.'

'What about *your* influence on *me*? You don't know what it was like, having you sit there all evening calling me "Mr Brannan". You don't know how much it made me want to do this—'

Roderick leaned down and kissed her.

He kissed her!

It was too ghastly for words, lips-to-lips, brazen and savage, in this very house, in the hallway, with Mama upstairs and Dorothea—

They broke apart. Eliza ducked back, more afraid than ever that they might see her. She heard Miss Halsted's plaintive voice: 'Oh *why* do I like you so much? I wish I didn't!'

'You don't mean that,' said Roderick.

'I don't know *what* I mean. I get so confused when I'm with you, I start to think that white is black. But I really must go or else I'll miss my omnibus.'

They were opening the front door, they were saying their last goodbyes. Eliza turned to go before Roderick came along and caught her. She had to cling to the banister as she climbed up and up, round and round. Her legs were like jelly.

The door to her room was ajar as she'd left it. Had Dorothea been yet to tuck her in? Had she found her gone? But what did that matter!

Eliza closed the door, got into bed, pulled the covers up to her chin. She couldn't get it out of her head, the picture of Roderick kissing Miss Halsted. He'd always been a hot-headed sort of boy but to kiss Miss Halsted as if it was nothing seemed reckless beyond measure. Why had Miss Halsted let him? Why had she seemed to want it, and yet not want it too?

Then there'd been all that talk about January: they'd met in January. Had they kissed then as well? Eliza remembered now that Roderick had departed Clifton earlier than expected in January, before the beginning of term. He had to meet a friend in London, he'd said, someone he'd known at school.

'You can't possibly travel in your condition, Roderick,' Mama had said. 'Your arm is in a sling.'

'Don't fuss, Mother. I'm not a cripple.' Roderick had been determined. He'd got his own way.

But what if there'd been no friend, just Miss Halsted? Roderick wouldn't tell fibs — would he?

Eliza shivered, suddenly wondering if she really knew her brother at all. She wished Dorothea would come quickly to tuck her in and send her off to sleep in peace. But Dorothea also seemed different this evening, was wrapped up in that German boy and his letter.

It was London, thought Eliza. London changed people, bewitched them. She wished she wasn't in London. She wished she was back at Clifton, safe, with everything as it should be.

If only she was back at home!

* * *

In sure and certain hope, Eliza read, *of the resurrection.*

She picked the moss off the crumbling gravestone. *Died 28 November 1745, aged 38.* Who had died? Someone called — it was just possible to make out the name — *Maria Adnitt.* She'd been the *beloved wife of* — somebody-or-other (the name had quite worn away). What had she looked like, Maria Adnitt? Why had she died? Did anyone now remember?

Turning away from Maria Adnitt's last resting place, Eliza threaded her way between the gravestones of Hayton churchyard, her skirts trailing through the long grass, the tips of her fingers brushing against the tallest stems. What would the resurrection be like? Would all the graves crack open and the dead people come climbing out? Would Maria Adnitt come back to life? Would her husband somebody-or-other come back to life too, even though his name had worn away?

But how dull, how boring, to lie in a coffin for hundreds of years waiting for the resurrection! Jesus had not had to wait. Jesus had been resurrected almost at once. But Jesus was special. That was what the old vicar had said in his Easter service last week. Jesus was special whereas Maria Adnitt was unimportant, had been all but forgotten.

Skirting round the grey church under the blue sky, Eliza took a detour to avoid Daddy's grave (she didn't like to look at Daddy's grave, it gave her a funny feeling in her tummy).

She had come full circle now, she could see Dorothea once more standing by another grave, Richard's grave. Dorothea's head was bowed, she was lost in thought.

Eliza watched from a distance, ringed round by the long grass. Birds chirped. A bumble bee lazily buzzed. The spring sun shone brightly. Why had they come to Richard's grave today? It wasn't his birthday or the anniversary of his death. Why, for that matter, had they taken their walk this morning instead of in the afternoon as they normally did? Everything was topsy-turvy. If Eliza on returning from London had hoped to get back to the old routine, she had been disappointed.

A visit to the village always took longer than expected when you were with Dorothea. There was always someone wanting to stop and talk; there was always a quick call to make. Dorothea was popular in the village. The villagers laid claim to her. But Eliza felt that, as Dorothea's cousin, she had a greater claim: she was able therefore to bask in reflected glory.

Today, after calling at the shop for a length of ribbon and some Fry's chocolate, they had stopped off at the carpenter's house opposite the burnt cottages in School Street. A new baby had recently arrived at the carpenter's.

'Our little miracle.' Mrs Keech, the carpenter's wife, had proudly cradled her grandson. 'We thought we'd lost him, Miss Dorothea. We thought we'd lose out poor, dear Milly, too. We had the doctor as well as the midwife. They were here half the night.'

Poor, dear Milly was Mrs Keech's daughter-in-law, who at other times was said to be *not quite good enough for our Nolly* and who *led him a merry dance*. Eliza did not much care for the carpenter and his wife, nor their son Nolly who made it obvious he thought a lot of himself. Milly, by contrast, always seemed rather downtrodden. Dorothea got on with them all equally and they all got on with Dorothea. But that wasn't very surprising. Probably there was no one in the entire world who disliked Dorothea.

Leaving the carpenter's, Eliza had walked with Dorothea down School Street then up Back Lane, stopping on the way to pass the time of day first with old Mother Franklin sitting wrinkled and toothless outside her daughter's front door (the way she chewed her gums turned Eliza's stomach), and then with white-whiskered Mr Lee working on his bit of land (his beady eyes missed nothing; Eliza was rather scared of him). Dorothea had knocked in vain at the door of the Carters' cottage (Nibs Carter was one of Dorothea's special friends; Eliza found him rather surly) but Mrs Turner had answered the door of the cottage opposite and invited them in for a cup of tea. Mrs Turner by her own admission could 'talk the hind legs off a donkey', but Eliza rather liked her: she was plump and jolly and made a fuss of her. When they'd finished their tea, and as they were taking their leave, Mrs Turner had followed them out and cut some flowers from her garden for Dorothea. She always gave flowers to Dorothea.

'What a glorious day, Miss Dorothea! Not a cloud in the sky!'

'Oh Mrs Turner! Dear Mrs Turner! How I'd miss you if I went away!'

'I'd miss you too, bless you! But why would you ever want to leave Clifton? Where would you go?'

Mrs Turner's flowers now rested against Richard's grave which was neither crumbling nor moss-grown. Dorothea stood there, silent and solemn — or not quite silent, for Eliza thought she could make out some murmured words.

'. . . ye now therefore have sorrow, but I shall see you again and your heart shall rejoice, and your joy no man taketh from you . . .'

It was something the vicar had said during the Easter service. Why was Dorothea repeating it now? Was she thinking of a time when she would see Richard in heaven?

Eliza barely remembered her cousin Richard who had died years ago aged fourteen. She knew by heart, however, the story of how Dorothea and Richard had first met: how Dorothea had heard a voice in the corridor and had gone to investigate, and the voice turned out to be Richard's. Dorothea at that time had been newly arrived at Clifton but this was something Eliza had no memory of at all. She couldn't imagine Clifton without Dorothea.

Dorothea turned, caught sight of Eliza, held out her hand, smiled. It was the old, familiar smile that had mostly been missing these last few weeks. Eliza ran to her joyfully, took her hand.

'It is time to go back,' said Dorothea. 'We don't want to be late for luncheon.'

They let themselves out of the churchyard by the side gate, set off across the fields taking the short cut to Clifton.

Eliza ventured to say, 'Were . . . were you *talking* to Richard, Doro?'

'Yes. Sometimes I do. I feel that he can hear me.'

'Does he ever . . . talk to you?'

'Not with words, of course, but . . .'

Eliza shuddered. The thought of talking to the dead — the thought of the dead answering — made her come up in goose pimples. It seemed to her that a shadow had fallen. The brightness of the morning had suddenly dimmed.

Dorothea seemed to feel it too. 'There must be a storm on the way. We shall get home just in time.'

But when Eliza looked at the sky there still wasn't a cloud in sight. All the same, her feeling of unease grew as they climbed the last stile and made their way through the Pheasantry. It was decidedly gloomy beneath the trees but did not seem much brighter as they emerged into the open once more. There before them was the great grey facade of the house with the wide space of gravel in front encircling the cedar tree. The gloom was now so intense it was like seeing the house through a film of dust. The tree cast deep shadows. The air had grown decidedly cool.

Eliza's heart raced. What did it mean? Had the day of resurrection come? The thought of all the graves opening and the dead people climbing out filled her with horror. She felt giddy.

'Hello, you two!' Roderick was standing on the gravel in his shirt and waistcoat. He had a piece of glass in his hand. 'What do you think of this? Isn't it extraordinary!'

Eliza ran to him. 'Oh, Roddy, what is it? Why is it going so dark? Is it the end of the world? I don't like it!'

'Of course it's not the end of the world, you goose. It's an eclipse. Didn't you read about it in the newspaper? I thought Doro made you read the newspaper every day for your edification.'

'Well, yes, we always read the paper.' Usually they read it together. But that morning Dorothea had been more pre-occupied than ever. Eliza had skimmed through *The Times* to show willing. There had been a report about the first woman to fly across the Channel. Eliza took a great interest in flying machines though to her chagrin she had never seen one. But in the next column, impossible to ignore, had been the latest news about the sunken liner. Eliza did not like to think about the sunken liner, all those unfortunate people drowned in the cold Atlantic. She had quickly folded the newspaper and put it away in a drawer. Dorothea had not noticed.

To be reminded now of the sunken liner only added to her feeling of doom.

'Roddy, what's an eclipse?'

'It's when the moon passes in front of the sun and blocks out the light. Here, you can see for yourself, but you must use this piece of smoked glass or you will go blind.'

Eliza looked. 'It's . . . it's *horrible*! The sun is being *eaten*! Will it be dark forever now?'

'Not forever.' Roderick leaned across to re-appropriate his piece of glass. 'It only lasts a few minutes.'

'It's a sign,' said Eliza solemnly.

'Yes: a sign for you to sharpen your wits.'

'But Roddy, don't you feel it too, that something *terrible* is about to happen?'

'I feel nothing of the sort. Nor do you. You really must learn to rein in that unbridled imagination of yours.'

Dorothea joined them. She was looking up at the darkling sky in wonder. 'Just imagine if it *was* the end of the world,' she murmured. 'Just imagine all the things one would regret never having done.'

Roderick looked at her in disgust. 'Not you as well, Doro, going off on these flights of fancy. Honestly, the female mind! This is a remarkable natural phenomenon, not a portent from the gods. Nothing terrible will happen. Nothing will happen at all. Nothing ever does at Clifton.'

* * *

Roderick was right. Nothing exciting ever happened at Clifton. The house seemed even more dull and commonplace than ever after the disturbing experience of the eclipse. But then—

'Daisy says that Mr Antipov is coming! He's coming today! He's due this evening!'

Dorothea looked up in some surprise from the letter she was writing as Eliza stampeded into the day room, all agog with excitement.

'Well, yes, of course he's coming. You must have known.'

'I didn't. Nobody told me. Nobody tells me anything.'

'I don't think that's quite true. But why are you so interested in Mr Antipov?'

'I'm not. I'm not interested at all.' Eliza feigned indifference, not sure if it was seemly — not sure if it was sensible — to show such enthusiasm for the Russian. She could not decide if the shiver of anticipation was entirely pleasant. Perhaps if she was to see him, to speak to him, she might be able to make up her mind about him. 'Couldn't I eat dinner downstairs just this once? Oh please say I can, Doro!'

Dorothea worked her magic with Mama. Permission was granted. Eliza was soon hopping up and down with impatience. When the gong finally sounded, she couldn't contain herself.

'You go down,' said Dorothea. 'I think I'll just change my blouse.'

She had already changed it twice. Anyone would have thought it was *her* first grownup dinner at Clifton. What was wrong with her? There was no time to puzzle it out. Eliza was far too eager to get downstairs.

She raced down the stairs and burst breathlessly into the drawing room. She skidded to a halt. Roderick and Mr Antipov were already there dressed for dinner, standing by the french windows. They both turned to look at her. Eliza was overcome with confusion. She felt her cheeks burning. Oh treacherous, treacherous cheeks!

'*Dobryy vecher*, Miss Brannan. We meet again.'

She had forgotten quite what he was like, slim and flaxen-haired with the surprisingly low-pitched voice and the strange Russian accent. His eyes, too: she had forgotten his eyes. He gave her one of his little bows, very formal yet somehow subtly mocking. Mocking her? Or himself? Or could it be that he was mocking it all, dressing for dinner and making polite conversation in the dull Clifton drawing room where nothing ever happened? His presence upset the balance of things. It was deeply perturbing.

She forced herself to speak. She was determined not to be a wallflower. 'How do you do, Mr Antipov. Please carry on, don't let me interrupt.' It sounded polite. It sounded like something Mama might have said. Eliza was pleased with herself. 'May I have one of those drinks, Roddy?'

'No you may not. You're enough of a handful as it is. Heaven knows what you'd be like intoxicated.' He turned back to the Russian. 'Now look, Antipov, what you're saying is complete rot—'

They'd obviously been in the middle of a heated discussion which now resumed. Eliza sank down onto the settee, happy not to be the centre of attention anymore.

'What I say is truth!' cried Mr Antipov. 'Englishman is died-in-the-wool, is blinkered like a horse. When subject races rise in rebellion, Englishman will honestly believe them ungrateful!'

'There won't be any rebellions, don't be absurd.'

'What about Ireland?'

'Ireland's different. It's a special case. The Irish aren't a subject race, they're British. Besides, it's only the Catholics who make trouble.'

'In Russia we have our Ireland too: it is called Poland. Poles also are Catholic. But these sects, these factions, they are not important. Religion is not important. It is opium for the people.'

'Poppycock! The Church provides moral guidance, it keeps up standards of behaviour, it—'

'It keeps people in their place. This is hymn you sing, yes? *The rich man in his castle, the poor man at his gate.* You tell poor, "Accept your lot. You will be rewarded in heaven." Is a fraud! There is no heaven! Only heaven we can have is what we build for ourselves, here and now!'

'Heaven on earth?' scoffed Roderick. 'Now who's being fraudulent? You can't change—'

He broke off as the door opened and Mama came in soon followed by Dorothea. The conversation at once took a different turn. It became ordinary. The eclipse was discussed and the sunken liner. Dorothea talked of the Keech baby in the village who'd nearly been lost. Mama reported on a visit to Newbolt Hall where there was much excitement over the forthcoming marriage of Colonel Harding's younger son. Eliza stifled a yawn. She found herself thinking about heaven on earth. Impossible, Roderick said. But Mr Antipov thought differently. Eliza's mind galloped. She pictured golden sunshine and silver fountains. She pictured people dressed in togas holding heroic poses. Was this what heaven on earth would be like?

Mr Ordish appeared. It was time to go through.

* * *

Sometime later, Mama got to her feet. Dinner was over already. Eliza reluctantly followed Mama into the passage with Dorothea bringing up the rear, leaving Roderick and Mr Antipov to their cigars or whatever it was gentlemen did when the ladies left the room (what *did* they do?).

Mama hesitated, one hand on the drawing room door. 'You may return to the nursery now, Elizabeth. It's quite late enough.'

The door was shut in her face.

Eliza was nettled. Late enough? It wasn't much after nine! Why was she treated like a baby? Why did she always miss out? She wouldn't stand for it anymore! She wouldn't meekly accept her lot like the poor waiting for heaven.

In a spirit of mutiny, she walked back into the dining room. Roderick was pouring something from a decanter. He paused, staring at her. Her mutinous spirit drained away. She had just enough aplomb to take her seat. She would only go if he told her.

He didn't tell her. He finished pouring (wine? port?), filling Mr Antipov's glass then his own.

The Russian put his cigar aside and raised his glass. 'A toast. Down with the Emperor of All Russia!'

Roderick rolled his eyes as he put the stopper back in the decanter. 'Honestly, Antipov, you're impossible.'

The Russian looked pleased. 'I offend your royalist soul, yes?'

'What's the emperor ever done to you?'

'Perhaps you do not know of atrocities — that is good word, I think, *atrocity* — perhaps you do not know of atrocities committed in Emperor's name? When I was fifteen years old, one thousand men, women, children were shot dead by Emperor's soldiers outside Winter Palace. This happened in city where I live, in Petersburg.'

There was a sudden steeliness in the Russian's eyes that made Eliza shiver. The Winter Palace. It sounded like something out of Hans Christian Andersen but the thought of all those dead people disturbed her. What would happen to

46

them all on the day of resurrection? It was one thing for Maria Adnitt to wake up in sleepy Hayton where nothing much had changed in half a thousand years; it would be quite different if you'd been shot by the Emperor's soldiers. Would you still have the hole where the bullet went in? Might you not be angry? Might you want revenge?

Roderick glanced at her in a way that made her feel he knew very well what she was thinking (she knew that he was all too aware of her vivid imagination). 'You will give the child nightmares, Antipov, with all your gruesome—' He stopped abruptly, cocking his head. 'Hark. What's that?'

It was the sound of raised voices coming from the drawing room. But it couldn't be Mama and Dorothea. Mama never raised her voice and Dorothea was the most even-tempered girl in the whole world.

Eliza found that Roderick was looking at her with suspicion, reading her mind again. 'I don't suppose you have any idea what this is about?'

Eliza shook her head. But even as she did so, everything seemed to slot into place: the letter from Germany and the proposal, the visit to Richard's grave, Dorothea saying to Mrs Turner how much she'd miss everyone if she went away. Even the dreadful portent of the eclipse took on a new meaning now. Dorothea must have made up her mind. That letter she had been writing before dinner: could it be a letter of acceptance?

Roderick's eyes narrowed. 'So you *do* know something! Well, out with it!'

'It's . . .' Eliza hesitated. Had she not promised to keep Dorothea's secret? But her resolution crumbled under her brother's stern gaze. 'It's the letter!'

'Letter? What letter?'

'The letter from Germany.'

'Ah. I see. Another missive from that Teuton, the pasty-faced convalescent we met in Switzerland. What did he have to say for himself this time? You must know, Eliza, you and Doro are as thick as thieves.'

Eliza wished now that she'd obeyed Mama and gone up to the nursery. Instead, faced with Roderick at his most implacable, she knew she had no choice but to betray Dorothea.

'He . . . he . . . the German boy . . . he asked Doro to . . . to marry him.'

'He did *what*? Are you sure you've got this right, Eliza? You're not making your usual muddle?'

'It's true, all true,' Eliza gabbled. 'The German wants to marry Doro but Doro didn't know what to do, "Plain old Doro," she said, but then today she changed, she was different, she talked to Richard and—'

'What on earth are you blithering about? Richard is dead. The dead don't hold conversations.' Roderick got to his feet. He seemed taller and more intimidating than ever. 'I see I shall have to get to the bottom of this myself.'

He crossed the room, flung open the door. Eliza had her back to it. She didn't dare look round. She sat rigid, watching the smoke curl up from Roderick's abandoned cigar.

After a moment, Roderick's voice was added to the heated discussion in the drawing room.

'Mother? Doro? What on earth . . . ?'

'. . . and I do wish you'd make her see sense Roderick . . .'

'. . . feel that it's right — I *know* that it's right . . .'

Eliza became aware that Mr Antipov was watching her as he slowly smoked his cigar. What right did he have — a stranger — to sit there listening?

Eliza slipped from her chair. She wanted to run and hide — to hide from the Russian's curious eyes, to hide from the raised voices in the drawing room that were tearing her to pieces. In the passage, however, she hesitated. She didn't want to hear the voices but she couldn't help it. She was rooted to the spot, her stomach clenched in knots. The drawing room door was ajar. She could hear everything clearly.

'. . . and after all we have done for you, Dorothea!' Mama's displeasure was plain to hear. 'To throw yourself away like this!

To even *think* of accepting a proposal made in a *letter*! We don't even know this young man. He's a foreigner, too. Why won't you listen to sense? Why must you be so stubborn?'

'Mother's right, Doro.' Roderick sounded very calm, persuasive, apologetic. 'You've only ever met him once. You can't make a decision based on that.'

'I wouldn't expect you to understand, Roddy,' said Dorothea. 'You didn't like Johann. You took against him from the start. But don't you see, it doesn't matter how many times I've met him. What matters is to do the right thing.'

'Foolishness!' cried Mama. 'Albert must be turning in his grave!'

'At least Uncle Albert would have *listened* to me! Uncle Albert always listened!'

'But he would never have allowed you to make a mistake like this! He always did everything he could to look after you, to take care of you. That is why he took you in when your father abandoned you. That is why he had you live with us here at Clifton. That is why he burned those letters—'

Mama broke off. There was a sudden awful silence. Eliza trembled. She pressed herself against the passage wall, holding her breath.

At length Dorothea spoke. Her voice was quiet, barely audible. 'What letters?' There was no reply. 'I wrote letters,' she continued, as if talking to herself. 'I wrote lots of letters to Papa. He never wrote back.'

'Mother?' Roderick's voice was questioning, also a little unsure. 'Are those the letters you're talking about?'

'Those letters were never sent—'

'Never sent!' exclaimed Dorothea. 'What do you mean, they were never sent?'

'You'd best explain, Mother.'

'It was for the best. Your father, Roderick, decided. He made up his mind that Dorothea would stay with us. And when letters came from Frank Ryan—'

'Letters from Papa? Letters for *me*? But why did I never see them?'

'Albert burned them.'

'Uncle Albert burned them? He burned letters that were meant for me? He burned letters from Papa?'

'You were living with us. It had all been decided. There was no going back, Albert said.'

'But what was in those letters, Mother? What did Frank Ryan have to say for himself?'

'I don't know, Roderick. I never read them. All I know is that your father burned them. He did what was necessary, what was right. He always did what was right. I am only sorry that I mentioned them after all this time. They are best forgotten.'

'Doro, you do see I hope that Mother is—'

'How could you! How could you — all of you! How could you *lie* to me all these years! Papa *didn't* abandon me. He *wrote* to me. But he must have thought that I'd abandoned *him* when he didn't receive a reply! Oh, I can't bear it! I can't *bear* it!'

Without warning, the drawing room door was flung wide open. Dorothea came running out. Eliza, flattened against the wall, had a brief glimpse of her cousin's wild eyes and pale, tear-stained face; her head of curls seemed almost preternaturally black just then.

In an instant she was gone. Footsteps sounded on the stairs then faded.

Mama and Roderick began to talk in low voices in the drawing room. Eliza did not want to hear. She stumbled to the foot of the stairs. Here her strength failed her. She sank down onto the bottom step. She held her head in her hands. What had happened? She tried to piece it all together.

It had started with the German boy: the German boy and his proposal. But the German boy had been overtaken by events. Something to do with letters. Something to do with Dorothea's papa.

Eliza had heard the story many times, how Dorothea had turned up at Clifton out of the blue, brought from London by her papa who had then gone off, never to be seen again. Having no idea what Dorothea's papa looked like, Eliza had come to picture him dressed in flowing robes with a long beard, like a saint in a painting; she pictured him with a halo offering up a baby for Daddy to look after. But that was silly. Dorothea hadn't been a baby when she came to Clifton. She'd been a little girl of seven or eight.

Where had Dorothea come from exactly? She must have been a baby once, she must have been *delivered* as babies were: delivered to their new home in the doctor's black bag or the midwife's. Eliza frowned, remembering Mrs Keech's words that morning concerning her grandson: 'our little miracle . . . we thought we'd lost him . . .' How did that tally with babies being delivered? Could babies sometimes get lost in transit, like letters in the post?

Letters! The thought of letters was like a dose of salts, clearing her head. Dorothea had been upset about the burnt letters. Eliza remembered the brief glimpse of Dorothea's tear-streaked face. Dorothea might need her and here she was, dithering! It was Dorothea that mattered. Dorothea mattered more than Mama or Roderick, more than anyone. She must go to Dorothea at once.

She raced up the stairs. In the day room the lights were on, the fire glowing, Polly was biting the bars of her cage, but there was no Dorothea. There was no Dorothea in her room, either. But what a mess! Drawers were open, the wardrobe too; clothes were strewn on the bed. Dorothea, who was always so tidy, so scrupulous!

A cold hand seized hold of Eliza's heart. She was sure that Dorothea had packed a bag. Dorothea must be going away. But it wasn't too late to stop her. No one had come down the stairs all the time Eliza had been sitting there.

Like the clanging of a bell, the thought came to her: *What about the back stairs?*

The back stairs! Quick, oh quick!

She flew along the corridor, plunged headlong down the back stairs. In the ground floor corridor she hesitated. Faintly up the basement steps came the sound of crockery, of voices, of laughter: life going on as normal. It seemed incredible that Dorothea would leave without a word. Where would she go? But just to be sure, Eliza opened the door by the stairs. A short, dark passage led to the outside door. She stepped into the stable yard. She was in one corner, near the water pump. It was cold, dark, there was a smell of horses. On the far side of the yard, a glimmer of light was coming from inside the old coach house which now served as a garage for the motors.

At that moment something brushed against Eliza's skirts. Her heart stopped. She was too terrified even to scream. And then—

'Miaow! Miaow!'

'Oh, Pandora, it's you!' Shuddering with relief, Eliza scooped up the cat into her arms, hugging the warm body tightly against her. 'You *did* give me a fright, you naughty girl! I'm looking for Doro. Have you seen her?'

Pandora's eyes glinted, she wrinkled her nose in displeasure. Wriggling free, she jumped down and went stalking off into the shadows with her tail in the air: she was a very independent cat. As Eliza watched Pandora disappear, bubbles of laughter suddenly burst out of her for no reason she could think of. It sounded horribly loud in the quiet of the yard.

Forcing the laughter back down, she made her way to the coach house. The fold-back door was ajar. Light spilled out onto the cobbles. She could hear voices inside. She peeked through one of the grimy windows set in the door panels. She saw an oil lamp hanging from a hook and the three Clifton motors lined up side-by-side. Dorothea was there with her coat on and holding a little bag. Smith the chauffeur was in his shirtsleeves, a chamois leather in his hand.

'London, Miss Dorothea?' He sounded doubtful. 'London's a long way at this time of night.'

'Please Stan, I must go at once, I *must*. Too much time has been wasted already.'

'Does it mean that much, miss?'

'More than anything.'

'And it can't wait until morning?'

'I can't bear to lose one more second!'

Eliza had no doubt that Smith would allow himself to be persuaded. People did things for Dorothea. They put themselves out. It was part of her magic.

'I'll need to put a clean shirt on, miss, and fetch my coat.'

'Hurry, please hurry.'

Eliza with infinite care had edged round the door as they were speaking and she now ducked down behind the nearest motor. Just in time. Smith passed within inches of her, went running off to his billet up in what had once been the coachman's rooms. His boots rang on the cobbles, echoed up the stairs, faded. Silence fell.

Eliza's heart sounded in her ears like galloping hoofs. She wanted to rush out and throw her arms around Dorothea but something held her back. All she knew was that she didn't want to be parted from her cousin. Where Dorothea went, she must go too. But she couldn't risk asking permission and being refused.

Eliza peeped out. Dorothea was standing by the open door, looking out. Seizing her chance, Eliza quickly debated: which motor would Smith take? Not this old landaulet, the one they'd used to follow the Boxing Day hunt. He would take the new four-door Mark IV saloon, his pride and joy. He'd obviously been polishing it even at this hour when Dorothea found him.

Eliza crept round behind the motors. She eased open the back door of the Mark IV, crawled into the foot space, pulled a rug on top of her. Almost at once came the sound of the garage door being rolled back and the voices of Dorothea and of Smith.

'I'll sit in the front with you, Stan.'

'Right you are, miss.'

The engine coughed, spluttered, came to life. The motor began to move. They were inching out into the stable yard. Next came the sound of the tyres crunching over the gravel in front of the house. Before long, the motor swung round.

They must have turned onto the Lawham Road. Soon they would be passing through the village. A mile or so further on and they'd come to the crossroads and the way to London. Eliza wondered if anyone at home had noticed yet that they'd gone. Were Mama and Roderick still talking in the drawing room? Was Mr Antipov still sitting at the dinner table, forgotten?

The motor gathered speed. The engine began to purr like Pandora when you tickled her behind the ears. Eliza felt a thrill of excitement. She hugged herself beneath the rug, eyes wide and heart beating as the motor sped into the night.

CHAPTER THREE

Eliza woke with a start. She looked around wide-eyed. She'd been having such dreams, the most uncomfortable dreams. But here she was safe and sound in her own room at 28 Essex Square.

She lay listening to the muffled sound of passing hoofs clip-clopping outside, the whistling of a delivery boy running down some area steps. How long had they been in London now? Mama had been shopping, Roderick was expected, it would soon be Easter.

But no. There was something wrong. She frowned, looking round again. The curtains weren't closed, for one thing. Sunshine was slanting in through the window. And she had been sleeping in her clothes. She was wrapped in an old rug with just the bare mattress beneath.

Her mind raced. It all came back in a rush. They'd returned to Clifton weeks ago. Easter had come and gone. Yesterday morning, she'd walked to the village with Dorothea. There'd been an eclipse. Mr Antipov had arrived. She'd been allowed to eat downstairs with the grown-ups. And then—

She tried for a moment to blank it out as she lay watching the shadows on the ceiling, the sunshine fading in and out. But there was no getting away from it, everything that had happened, ending with her stowing away in the motor unseen by Dorothea or Smith. They'd set off for London in the dark. It had seemed such an adventure.

Time had passed. She'd grown weary. Incredible to think, but she'd actually fallen asleep. How many hours had passed before she woke, muzzy, cramped and aching, chilled to the bone? The motor had been still and silent, the darkness oppressive. It was as if they had entered an endless night leaving daylight behind forever. Were all adventures like this? If so, she'd said to herself, shivering, then she wanted no part of them.

She had scrambled up onto the back seat, afraid they'd abandoned her, afraid she was all alone. But Dorothea at least had still been there, asleep in the front seat, her chin on her chest. The driver's seat had been empty. Eliza remembered hearing a faint sound like trickling water, the only sound in all the silence. Looking out, she'd seen that the motor was parked by a gate in a hedge. The road had run on into the dark, arrow-straight and deserted, with fields deep in shadow on either side. The black silhouettes of trees had been etched against a moonless sky. It had been an alien landscape, utterly unknown.

The trickling sound had stopped. Smith in his long chauffeur's coat had stepped away from the hedge. She had realised that he must have been passing water.

In her bedroom at 28 Essex Square, Eliza shuddered with revulsion. Men were so coarse, so crude, Smith with his spots and crooked teeth peeing up a hedge in the open like a dog. Even her own brother was little better. In this very house Roderick had put his arms round Miss Halsted and kissed her as if it was nothing. Watching the shadows chase each other across the ceiling, Eliza recalled how she'd ducked down as Smith walked back to the motor fastening his trousers. He'd been puffing and blowing from the cold as he got in. Dorothea had stirred.

'What time is it? Why have we stopped? Is something wrong?'

'Nothing's wrong, miss. I couldn't keep my eyes propped open, that's all. I had to stop and stretch my legs.' (He'd not mentioned the peeing.)

Dorothea had sat up, yawning and rubbing her eyes. 'Where are we?'

'Somewhere near Dunstable, I think, miss.'

And then—

'*Ah — ah — atchoo!*'

Eliza cringed, remembering her sneeze, loud enough to wake the dead. There'd been nothing she could do to stop it.

Smith had pulled the rug away. He and Dorothea had peered down at her, craning over the backs of their seats, their faces strange and pale in the dark. Dorothea in particular had looked drawn and haggard.

Eliza must be taken back immediately, Dorothea had said. This was not a game. Eliza would only get in the way.

Eliza in her room at Essex Square relived the utter misery of that moment, being rejected by Dorothea. She remembered the rage and despair which had built up inside her as Smith was explaining why it would be more trouble than it was worth to go back.

The rage and despair had finally erupted. 'I don't want to go anywhere with either of *you*! You're both horrible! I hate you! I never want to see you again!'

She had thrown the car door open and wriggled free. Unhitching the rickety wooden gate, she had pushed it aside and gone running across a big dark field with no idea where she was going. Almost at once she had tripped over a tussock or a molehill and gone sprawling on her face. The shock of the fall had knocked all the anger out of her. As she lay there breathless and shivering on the grass, the faint screech of a barn owl had sent a shiver up her spine.

Smith had loomed over her. 'Don't lie there in the dew, miss, you'll catch your death.' He had helped her to her feet. 'That's the way, up you come. You've not hurt yourself, have you? Can you walk? I'll put my coat round you, to keep you warm. Off we go, miss.'

Smith's coat, she remembered, had smelt of leather and of Smith himself, but it had been comforting somehow to have it wrapped around her. She had pulled it close, letting herself be guided back to the motor car.

The rest of the journey was hazy in her mind. She had slept in fits and starts on the back seat. Her waking moments had been cloaked in misery. Dorothea, she'd felt sure, had washed her hands of her. The words, *I wash my hands of you*, had echoed over and over in her head. It was silly, because it was not a phrase that Dorothea would ever use. It was something Daisy was in the habit of saying: 'Oh, that Sally Kirkham, who does she think she is? She's only a housemaid but she goes around like she's Lady Muck. I wash my hands of her.' Or, 'Our Billy, he's nothing but a great lummock! I've never known such a misery in all my life! I wash my hands of him!'

They had reached Essex Square at last. It had been silent and deserted, ghostly, the street lamps feebly glowing, a hint of dawn in the sky, cold and pallid. Shivering in the frosty air on the front steps of number 28, Eliza had stood with Smith watching Dorothea fumble in her bag. A moment later Dorothea had turned to face them with a look of defeat.

'The keys — I completely forgot — we can't get in — oh, Stan, it's a disaster!'

'Don't you fret, miss. I'll get us in, you'll see.'

And he had. He'd disappeared down the area steps to reappear moments later, opening the front door from inside and grinning at their astonished faces.

Eliza had stared at him in wonder. 'How did you do it?'

Smith had laughed out loud, as if the dark and the silence didn't daunt him in the least. 'I'm a man of many talents, miss. We didn't always live in the most select parts of town when I was a nipper and Dad was on his uppers. I had some right old mates in those days. They taught me a lot. Not that Dad was impressed. He used to box my ears for hanging round with the wrong sort.'

It was easy to forget that the chauffeur's 'Dad' was Mr Smith the motor designer. Mr Smith had been a sort of protégé of Daddy's and was now general manager of the BFS Motor Company. Indeed, the 'S' in the company name stood for 'Smith', a junior partner. But despite his elevated status, Mr Smith liked his children to 'work their way up' just as he had, hence his son's position as chauffeur at Clifton. Roderick scoffed at such a high-minded attitude. Had he been in Smith's shoes, he said, he wouldn't have stood for it. But would Roderick have been able to break into Essex Square like a burglar?

Eliza had been dead on her feet as she stumbled up the last few steps and crossed the threshold. Smith had scooped her into his arms and carried her upstairs. He was thin as a rake but stronger than he looked. He must have wrapped her in this rug, must have taken her boots off too. She'd fallen into a deep and dreamless sleep to wake hours later in the fitful sunshine. And so here she was lying on her bed in 28 Essex Square on the morning — was it still morning? — of Thursday 18 April. She was in a house with no servants and no Mama, and with the whole of London just the other side of the front door. The thought filled her with a strange, nervous excitement.

But how could she bear to face any of it if Dorothea would not take her back?

* * *

Dorothea was downstairs in the drawing room, sitting in the window seat. The room was completely familiar and yet subtly different; dust sheets covered the chairs, the fire grate was raked and empty, the carriage clock silent. Smith was flat out on the settee, his coat spread over him, his legs sticking out, feet dangling, holes in his socks. He looked different asleep, younger perhaps: even his spots served only to add to his air of innocence. His unkempt hair looked like an unruly boy's.

Eliza hesitated in the doorway. Dorothea looked washed out, a pale copy of the real Dorothea. Eliza was shy of her. To be shy of Dorothea was awful, not right, a travesty. But then Dorothea smiled and it was the same dear smile. She held out her arms and Eliza ran and stumbled to be enfolded, embraced, comforted. It was alright. It was alright. She hadn't lost Dorothea after all.

'Are . . . are you mad at me?' Eliza ventured to ask at length, snuggled next to her cousin in the window seat. 'You . . . you said you didn't want me, that I shouldn't have come.'

'I don't remember what I said. I was tired, overwrought. But I could never be mad with you, Eliza.'

'Why have we come?'

'To find my papa,' said Dorothea calmly, confidently, as if it was easy, as if her papa was out there somewhere just waiting for her. But it was all so long ago, twelve years since Dorothea had been brought to Clifton as a little girl: a lifetime to Eliza, who had been no more than a baby when Dorothea came. Was it possible after so long to find someone who'd not been heard of for years?

'We can try,' said Dorothea. 'We can start by going back to the places where I used to live — to Stepnall Street.'

Stepnall Street. Why did the name sound faintly sinister?

Eliza thrust this question aside as Smith showed signs of life at last, yawning and rubbing his eyes. He sat up, stretching in his shirt sleeves. His long coat slid off him and onto the floor.

'Morning, Miss Dorothea, Miss Eliza. How long have I been asleep?'

'Ages and ages,' said Eliza. 'I've been awake for hours. I'm going to help Doro look for her papa.'

'I'll help too. But what about a bite of breakfast first? My stomach thinks my throat's been cut.'

'Breakfast!' exclaimed Dorothea. 'I never gave a thought to breakfast — or lunch or dinner, for that matter. I packed a few clothes and nothing else. I didn't even bring any money. How could I be so stupid!'

'I've a few shillings in my pocket, miss, enough to tide us over. We can buy some grub. We can send a telegram too. They'll be wondering what's become of us back at Clifton.'

60

He was pulling on his knee-high boots, buttoning his jacket, picking up his peaked cap. 'Now then. Where might there be some shops in these parts?'

* * *

The street ahead was clogged with traffic. The omnibus had come to a halt. Eliza looked out from the top deck, overawed by the tall and daunting buildings on every side, defying the sky. There were countless windows; there were sloping roofs; there were tall, pointed spires. Big brash letters were perched high on the eaves of a corner building spelling out the word *BOVRIL*. Looming ahead — immense, imposing — was a vast dome. Dorothea called it St Paul's. A flower girl was sitting on the steps with a basket. Next to a red pillar box, a man was feeding the birds, throwing out handfuls of bread — or was it seeds? Pigeons wheeled and flocked and swooped suddenly down. Sparrows darted in and out. Swirling traffic, meanwhile, coming the other way, passed in endless procession. The sun shone in fits and starts. Eliza's hair blew in the gentle breeze. She had not brought a hat.

Already it seemed an age since they had eaten bread and boiled eggs sitting at the kitchen table in the basement at 28 Essex Square. They had walked afterwards almost merrily in the spring sunshine to catch an omnibus on the King's Road, setting out on the first stage of the quest to find Dorothea's papa. Eliza was somewhat familiar with the sedate streets around Essex Square. She knew the King's Road and the Fulham Road, she knew Exhibition Road with its museums, she'd often been in Hyde Park and Kensington Gardens, she had a passing acquaintance with Oxford Street and Piccadilly and Euston station, and she had even been once or twice on an omnibus. But as they'd travelled further and further from the places she recognised, as they'd got off one omnibus and onto another, she had begun to feel giddy. Smith had summed it up best. 'Big place, this London,' he'd said in his matter-of-fact voice, staring out at the passing streets. Yes,

London was big. It was immense. It made her head ache to think about it. The traffic was never-ending. And the people — she would never have guessed there were so many people in the entire world, let alone one city.

Now she was sitting next to Dorothea on the top deck of an omnibus stuck in traffic. She was trying to be as quiet and inconspicuous as possible. When she spoke, she spoke in a whisper, covering her mouth with her hand. The other passengers were not so reticent. Several had begun to lean out, trying to find the cause of the hold-up. Many were talking at the top of their voices as if they didn't care who was listening.

'It's a horse. A horse has gone mad and blocked the street.'

'They can be brutes, horses. I shall be glad when we're rid of 'em.'

'I've seen one kick—'

'One bit me once—'

'All the same, there are some jobs where only a horse will do.'

'What's taking so long? I shall miss my appointment.'

'I tell you, it would be quicker to walk—'

The omnibus at last got under way again. It paused for a moment by St Paul's then swept on, leaving the great dome behind. Eliza reminded herself of the quest. They were looking for Dorothea's papa. 'Quite a short man,' Dorothea had said, 'slender and dark-haired with brown eyes and a small moustache.' But that might describe any number of men, thought Eliza. That man there, for instance, with the bowler hat and an umbrella, looking in at the window of a shop. Or that man in the long overcoat forging through the press of people on the pavement. Or that man on the street corner who had stopped to buy a paper from a newsboy. These figures were glimpsed for a moment then disappeared as the bus rattled onwards.

Dorothea got to her feet. Eliza followed, running down the stairs as the omnibus slowed and stopped. She jumped from the platform onto the pavement. The omnibus moved off. Eliza quickly lost sight of it, found herself caught up in the hustle and bustle of the street. She was glad to have Dorothea on one side, Smith on the other; otherwise, she felt, she would have been carried off in the press of people like a leaf in the current of a swollen stream.

Before long they came to a junction. 'This way,' said Dorothea. But as she picked her way, turning this corner then that, she seemed unsure, looking all around. 'It's been so long,' she murmured, 'since I was here last.'

Eliza allowed herself to look around too. Was this still London? If it was, it was a far cry from the swept pavements and spotless facades of Essex Square. There were lots of shops but they were very different to the shops on Oxford Street: Selfridge's, and Marshall and Snelgrove, and Peter Robinson. There were tailors and haberdashers and drapers. There were teeming coffee rooms and tiny tobacconists. Butchers had racks of meat outside and joints in their windows hanging from hooks. Hawkers had spread their wares on the pavements. A woman was selling fish from a barrel. There were carts with little stoves, on this corner offering hot pies, on the next, roast chestnuts. People swarmed in every direction, spilled out across the roads. Dirt and rubbish choked the gutters. The noise was unrelenting.

'This way.' Dorothea turned to cross a street. Eliza hurried to keep up, skipping over the tram tracks, dodging the horse manure on the cobbles, Smith striding beside her.

''Ere, lanky, lost yer motor, have yer?'

There was laughter. Heads turned. People stared, pointed. Eliza hung her head. She would have liked to hold Dorothea's hand, or even Smith's.

They left the shops behind. Dorothea seemed more assured now, seemed to know the direction she wanted to take. They walked along run-down streets between rows of houses. The brick fronts were blackened with soot; the windows were grimy, the glass often cracked or broken, sometimes missing altogether, the holes stopped up with paper or bits of cloth. There were fewer people and no traffic. Here and there, women stood in the narrow doorways or sat on the door-steps: sly-looking women, Eliza felt, and belligerent. Children ran back and forth dressed in what Eliza thought of as rags: many had bare feet, some had snotty noses; they looked dirty. Scrawny dogs nosed at piles of rubbish, lapped at the effluent in the gutters or at the foetid pools in the road where chunks of cobbles were missing. If Eliza had thought herself grubby, still wearing yesterday's clothes — the clothes she'd slept in — she now felt, after walking these streets, as if she was covered from head to foot in something like a film of grease.

Dorothea came to a stop. They had reached a place where a side street led away to the right. On the opposite corner was a man with a barrel organ. Above him on a blank brick wall was a sign, black letters on white — or grey, as it was now, a mucky grey: *STEPNALL STREET.*

'There,' said Dorothea, pointing down the narrow street. Her face was pale. Her hand trembled.

'Are you sure, miss?' Smith was dubious. 'Are you sure you want to go down *there?*'

As they hesitated, the three of them, Eliza found herself mesmerised by the barrel organ. The old man turning the handle had a lined face and untidy whiskers. The jolly, plinky-plonk music sounded out of place in these grim surroundings, like a shower of rain in a desert, futile.

The organ grinder caught her eye. He grinned. His mouth was a miry slit. From somewhere Eliza summoned courage enough to give him a look: the sort of look she imagined that Mama might have given. The organ grinder wasn't daunted in the least. He didn't fawn or doff his cap. His grin grew wider. His cracked lips pulled back over red gums and the blackened stumps of his teeth. Eliza felt queasy and looked away. Almost she felt nostalgia for Mother Franklin's clean, toothless gums in the village far away.

'There's nothing to worry about,' Dorothea was saying, geeing them up. 'This used to be my home.' But she sounded almost as if she was trying to convince herself as much as anyone.

Smith sighed. 'Very well, then, miss. Let's get it over with.'

They ventured into the side street. It seemed to Eliza to take a great effort, as if her legs were leaden. Step-by-step they pressed on. The sound of the barrel organ faded. The air grew thick and gloomy. The narrow street was no wider than an alley, the sky above a thin strip between the sullen, soot-stained walls of terraced houses. Here and there between the squat doorways were arched openings leading to — to where? Eliza shuddered to think. But to her horror, Dorothea turned aside and disappeared into one of those very entrances. Eliza hung back. Surely Smith would protest, fetch Dorothea back?

He didn't. Grim-faced, he ducked under the low brick-work. He too disappeared. Eliza had no choice but to follow. She found herself in a dark, dank tunnel. There was a fusty smell. Somewhere water was dripping.

It came as a relief to emerge into daylight again (or what passed for daylight here). She felt as if she'd been walking in the dark for half her life instead of half a minute. When she looked round, however, she recoiled. She had to stop herself from running back the way she'd just come.

They were in a cramped, irregular-shaped courtyard enclosed by high walls. It was like being at the bottom of a deep well. There were many windows and several blank doorways. The ground was littered with rubbish: bones and scraps and filth. The far-off sky was reflected dully in putrid puddles. Washing hung on a line stretched from window to window. A scraggy chicken pecked in the dirt. Somewhere high above a baby was feebly grizzling.

On one of the doorsteps sat a middle-aged woman with a grubby shawl thrown round her shoulders. She was stuffing a mattress from a sack of rags and straw. Her hands moved in a blur. Her eyes were dark and full of suspicion.

Dorothea was looking round with a strange expression on her face. 'This is the place,' she said. 'This is where I used to live. Our room was on the third floor. We went in by that door there.'

She pointed. Eliza caught a glimpse of a narrow entrance hall and steps going steeply up. The banisters were missing and paper was peeling off the walls.

'Excuse me. I wonder, could you help?' Dorothea seemed fearless in approaching the seated woman. 'I'm looking for someone, a man named Mr Ryan: Mr Frank Ryan. Do you know him?'

'Can't say as I do,' said the woman shortly, not pausing in her work for even a second.

'What about Mrs Browning? Does she still live here? She had two children, Mickey and Flossie. They will be grown up now, of course.'

'Never heard of 'em.' The woman pursed her lips. 'What do yer want wiv 'em, anyway? What's yer game?'

'Frank Ryan was — is — my papa.'

The woman snorted. 'Lorst him, have yer? Careless of yer!'

'He used to live here. *I* used to live here.'

The woman's eyes widened, taking in Dorothea's neat belted jacket, her long, pale blue skirt, her beribboned hat. 'You? Live her? Huh! A likely story!' She turned her head (her hands kept working) and called through the doorway. ''Ere, Mrs Watts, listen to this. *She* says as she used to live here. Have yer ever heard the like?'

A second woman appeared, older, hollow-eyed, her greying hair hanging limp, her dirty frock in tatters. She had no shoes on. It seemed to Eliza shockingly indecent for a grown woman to be standing there with no shoes on.

'*Her*?' said the newcomer, looking Dorothea up and down. '*Her* lived *here*? Get away with you! The likes of her wouldn't live here!'

'But I did, I really did, why won't you believe me!' cried Dorothea. 'It was a long time ago: twelve years. I've come back now and I'm looking for my papa, Frank Ryan.'

'There's no toffs round here.'

'But he wasn't a toff! I'm not one either!'

'Not a toff? Don't give me that! Just look at yer!'

'If she's not a toff then what is she?' said the mattress woman. 'One of them do-gooders, I'll be bound.' She spat into the dirt, contemptuous.

'We don't want no do-gooders round here,' said the woman with bare feet. 'We've no time for do-gooders, have we, Mrs Noakes.' She moved forward, stepping over the mattress. Eliza watched in horrified fascination as the bare feet squelched in the sludge. 'Why don't yer just bugger off? Go on, bugger off, the lot of yer! We don't need *your* sort round here!'

There was a murmur of voices, agreeing. Glancing round, Eliza experienced a catch of fear. Unnoticed, other women had appeared in other doorways; ragged children had gathered; faces were peering down from the upper windows. There was an atmosphere of blatant curiosity, of underlying hostility.

Eliza grabbed hold of Smith's long leather coat, afraid. But Dorothea seemed heedless of any danger. She looked so clean and neat against the dark and shabby court — and when compared to the drab and dirty people — that she seemed almost to shine. It made her horribly visible. She was utterly defenceless.

The onlookers drew near, crowding round her.

'Please — won't you help — if I could just take a look — our old room—'

She actually made a move towards the doorway she had pointed out earlier but Smith now stepped forward and put his hand on her shoulder.

'Come on, miss. We should go.'

'But Stan—'

'You won't find him here, miss. He's not here, he's gone.'

The barefoot woman thrust her face up close to Dorothea's. 'Yeah, that's right. You listen to 'im, listen to that lanky bastard!'

'If . . . if you hear anything . . . about Frank Ryan—'

'Just bugger off! We don't want you here, poking yer noses in! Bugger off and don't come back!'

A chorus of voices rose all round. 'Get on out of it! Bugger off! Fucking toffs!'

In the face of such aggression, Dorothea's shoulders slumped. She allowed Smith to lead her away. Eliza stumbled after them into the noisome tunnel, still clutching Smith's coat tail.

The narrow street seemed like a wide and spacious boulevard after he stifling confines of the court. Eliza gulped air. Now at last they could leave this horrible place and go back to Essex Square.

But Dorothea had other ideas. 'We have to keep looking.'

'Is that wise, miss? We stick out like a sore thumb round here.'

'I have to go on, Stan, I *have* to. You see that, don't you?'

Despite the misgiving in his eyes, Smith said, 'Alright, miss, if that's what you want. Where to next?'

'There's The Swan. Papa used to go there, Mrs Browning too.'

'Who is this Mrs Browning?' asked Smith.

'She is — was — I don't know: the woman whose room we rented. We lived there, five of us in one room: me and Papa, Mrs Browning and her children. But that's not important. The Swan, if I remember, was just down here, by the crossroads.'

Eliza's heart sank into her boots at the thought of going on, but Dorothea was determined and Smith didn't gainsay her. Eliza walked with the chauffeur as Dorothea hastened ahead along the street. Before long they came to a junction where Stepnall Street was intersected by another, slightly wider street. On the far right-hand corner was a pub. It had frosted windows and a door on each street. A battered sign with a picture of a swan hung high on the wall.

Dorothea pressed on, not waiting. She crossed the junction and entered the pub. The door closed behind her.

Eliza and Smith hurried to catch up. As they reached the door, Smith put a restraining hand on Eliza's shoulder.

'Not you, miss. You wait here.'

'Wait here? On my own? Oh, please don't make me!'

'I'll be out again in two ticks. But I must see that Miss Dorothea is alright.'

A small boy was watching them, a scrawny, grubby boy with a tatty shirt and strings for braces. His trousers were too small for him and finished halfway below his knees. His feet were bare. He was lounging against the wall, eyes bright and sharp in his dirt-streaked face.

Smith gave him a hard stare. 'What's your game, then?'

'I ain't got no game, mister.'

'In that case you come here and keep an eye on Miss Eliza.'

'What's it wurf?'

'Never mind what it's worth. Just you up and do as I say or I'll box your ears for you, you little scamp.'

Smith wasted no more time. He plunged into the pub. Eliza got a confused impression of noise and smoke and many shadowy figures, then the door banged shut, cutting her off.

She was alone with the boy. She felt very intimidated. But as she looked desperately round, she realised that she wasn't quite alone: there were people further along the street in both directions, and on the pavement opposite a man was lying face down by the wall (asleep?). The house next to him had a sign over the door:

BEDS
4d a night
SINGLE MEN ONLY

Eliza turned to face the boy. He was a very small boy, very young, although there was a sly and knowing look about him that made him seem older. She drew herself up. She was not frightened of *boys*. She'd never been frightened of Jack Britten or Dixie Carter or Johnnie Cheeseman or any of the other village boys. This boy in fact looked a lot like Johnnie Cheeseman with his bright eyes and his dimples. Johnnie Cheeseman never went barefoot, of course, but there were some in the village at times who did, and several that were almost as scrawny and famished-looking as this boy.

She tried to muster a friendly smile but couldn't quite manage it. The way the boy was staring at her — so bold and bare-faced — gave her a funny feeling inside. They stared at each other.

At length the boy said, 'What's yer name?'

'Eliza Brannan. What's yours?'

The boy ignored her question. 'Got any money?'

'I . . . I might have.' She had a few pennies and far-things left over from the shilling she'd spent yesterday on Fry's chocolate in the village shop. (Was it only yesterday? It seemed like a hundred years ago!)

'Give us some, then. Give us some money.'

She fumbled in her pocket, held out a penny piece. For a moment he didn't move, looking at the coin with mistrust. Then he suddenly snatched it out of her hand. It disappeared into his too-short trousers.

There was no 'Thank you', no hint of gratitude; he just went on staring at her. Eliza felt aggrieved. Johnnie Cheeseman would have said thank you. Johnnie Cheeseman was a quiet, polite boy who called her 'Miss Eliza'. This boy was nothing like Johnnie Cheeseman.

She made one last effort. 'Does it hurt your feet, walking with no shoes?'

'Not so much. I hate shoes. They cramp yer. D'yer like muffins?'

'I . . . I don't know. I've never had a muffin.'

'Coo! Never had a muffin! What kinda girl are yer?' He looked at her sidelong. 'Yer could try one now if yer wanted. There's a muffin man comin'. Look!'

Eliza looked where he pointed but could see nobody, just the man lying on the pavement.

'Where's the muffin man? I can't see him.'

'Are yer blind? There he is, there!'

'But there's nobody there, you must be—'

She turned back to the boy but he'd gone. At once a terrible suspicion took hold of her. She reached into her pocket. It was empty. All her money had gone. Even as her heart sank and a feeling of anguish washed over her, she saw out of the corner of her eye a flicker of movement.

Spinning round, she was just in time to see the boy disappear up Stepnall Street.

Anger flared inside her. How dare he steel her money, how dare he! They needed that money, with Dorothea penniless and Smith's few shillings nearly used up. Without stopping to think, Eliza set off in pursuit.

The boy had a head start. He was running and dodging. She could see his dirty heels, hear his rattling breath. Soon — and to her surprise — she found she was gaining on him. He seemed out of puff already. He was almost within reach.

Just as she stretched out a hand to grab him, he suddenly veered aside and vanished into one of the arched entrances that led to the courts beyond. Eliza followed automatically. Before she realised, she was in a dank, slimy tunnel.

She came to an abrupt halt. The way ahead was blocked. A group of people — boys, she realised — were huddled together in the tunnel, heads down as if engaged in a secret conspiracy. Small and thin as he was, the urchin boy was able to wriggle between them and disappear.

Eliza opened her mouth to say, *Excuse me, please.*

The words died in her throat. A hideous, inhuman shriek echoed along the tunnel. She clapped her hands to her ears, cowering against the slimy wall.

The sound trailed away to a miserable miaowing. Whether the boys had shifted position or whether her eyes had grown used to the dimness, Eliza could not say, but she was now able to see what was holding the boys' attention. They had a kitten, a scrap of a thing with matted fur and spindly legs. They had obviously been tormenting it. It writhed and twisted in their hands, its mouth open showing little white teeth, its eyes—

But there *were* no eyes. There were no eyes. There were just empty sockets dribbling blood.

As Eliza watched, frozen in horror, one of the boys took hold of the kitten's tail in his fist. The other boys drew back. The shape of the kitten for a split second was silhouetted against the bright entrance to the court beyond. Eliza could see its tiny head, could see its mouth moving in a pitiful but now silent miaowing. And then, with a huge swing of his arm, the boy dashed the kitten against the wall. There was a sickening thump as the kitten's body hit the bricks. Eliza heard clearly the crunch of its shattering skull.

Her legs buckled. Everything went dark. Clawing at the greasy bricks trying to stay on her feet, Eliza bent over, retching and retching. There was burning taste of bile in her mouth.

She became aware as if through a dense fog of shadowy figures closing in around her. The boys, having finished with the kitten, were now turning their attention to her. She was completely at their mercy.

Her last ounce of strength drained away as she wondered what was going to happen to her, what tortures and disfigurements. She slipped and slid down the wall, her fingers scrabbling helplessly. It was like falling into a bottomless pit.

'Here! What's going on? What are you doing to her? Leave her alone, you little tykes! Go on, clear off out of it!'

It was a voice out of nowhere, booming and echoing along the tunnel. The knot of boys wavered, broke apart; they fled. In a heap on the floor, Eliza was dimly aware of a pair of shiny black boots looming over her.

'Miss Eliza? Can you hear me? Are you alright, Miss Eliza? If they've done anything—'

'Stan, oh Stan!' She clutched at him desperately, her last tenuous connection with the world. If she let go she'd be lost, she'd fall into the bottomless pit beyond all rescue.

But he was solid and real and immeasurably strong. He was helping her up, he put his arm round her; she was safe.

'Stan . . . Stan . . . the kitten . . .'

If he could just save the kitten too; if he could only save the kitten . . .

She looked up at him, saw him glance over her shoulder, saw his expression change, his mouth fall open, his eyes grow wide.

She buried her face in his chest. She didn't want to see, didn't want to know.

He gathered her up, half carried her out into the street. It seemed like a miracle, to be in the daylight again. Tears were streaming down her face. She was crying with relief; she was crying because of the kitten; she was crying, crying, crying.

Smith put both his arms round her. 'It's alright, miss. I've got you. I've got you now.'

* * *

There was a smell of old leather and cigar smoke. There was a sound of brisk hoofs and a harness jangling. The noise of the city was muffled and muted.

Eliza opened her eyes. She was curled in the corner of a cab. It was rocking and swaying, rattling along brightly lit streets that passed in a blur on the other side of the misted window. Dorothea next to her looked tired and grey as if coated with soot. Young Stan opposite was hunched over his knees, looked thin and drowsy. No one spoke. But that didn't matter, for they were on their way back to Essex Square: at long last they were heading back to Essex Square.

She'd not been asleep long. Before that — well, her mind was a complete jumble. She struggled to put things in order.

'We can't go on with Miss Eliza in this state,' Smith had said in Stepnall Street. Eliza had been faint and dizzy and sick to her stomach. Dorothea had just joined them from The Swan. 'We can't go on,' Smith had said — or Young Stan as Eliza had started to think of him, copying Dorothea and claiming him as their own (he was called *Young* Stan to distinguish him from his father, the motor man Mr Smith).

'But we must — we must —' Dorothea had appealed to them with her eyes.

From somewhere, Eliza had found the strength to carry on. She'd been desperate not to let Dorothea down. But it all seemed like a nightmare now as she sat in the hansom cab remembering — except it was worse than a nightmare because it was real.

They had trudged down one street after another. 'Papa worked here once, for this tailor . . . that is the board school I went to, they may know something . . . I seem to recognise that pawnbroker's . . .' Always the same question: 'I'm looking for Mr Ryan, Mr Frank Ryan, have you seen him?' And always the same reply: 'No, don't know him, never heard of him.'

Daylight had seeped away. A smoky dusk had fallen. Men had come swarming along the streets, heading home. Seeing them, 'The docks,' Dorothea had said, 'sometimes Papa got casual work at the docks.'

Eliza remembered crates piled up and mountains of sacks. The river had been wide and flat in the gloaming with a forest of funnels and masts. There had been much hooting and tooting and a deep, throbbing horn. Smoke billowed, steam rose in clouds. The sky had been streaked with red and purple as the light faded.

At last Young Stan had said, 'We've done all we can, Miss Dorothea,'

'But we can't give up — we mustn't!'

'Tomorrow. We'll come back tomorrow.'

That was when they'd hailed the cab: an old-fashioned cab, rather battered, driven by a battered cabman, pulled by a horse with blinkers.

Young Stan had helped Dorothea and Eliza inside. 'Essex Square, please, mate.'

'Right y'are, guv'nor.'

Essex Square. No words had ever sounded so blessed.

Eliza closed her eyes once more. She was rocked back to sleep by the movement of the cab.

* * *

'Tea, Miss Eliza.'

Stan was shaking her gently. She stirred, yawned, sat up on the settee. He handed her a cup, no saucer.

'The cure-all, my ma calls it.'

The tea was hot, sweet, tasted wonderful. 'And there's a fire, too!'

'I found some coals. And Miss Dorothea is making dinner.'

The room looked different, cosier, with the dust sheets gone and flames leaping in the grate. The electric lights gave out a friendly glow. The curtains were drawn, shutting out the world.

She watched Stan shovel more coal on the fire and prod it with the poker. Where did he find his energy? She felt rinsed out, drained, empty.

But what a nice man he was, Young Stan: rough-and-ready but with what Daisy would call *a heart of gold*. Eliza felt remorse for ever thinking him coarse and crude, for secretly calling him a beanpole and mocking his spots and crooked teeth. When had she learned to be so cruel? What did crooked teeth matter when you had a heart of gold?

She lay back on the sofa thinking of a picnic last summer — only last summer. She had gone with Dorothea and Roderick. Young Stan had driven them and lugged the hamper across the fields. Eliza remembered the heat and the sunshine, the butterflies and the elder blossom. She had pretended to be the Queen of all the Flowers — it made her blush to think of it — but Stan had happily played along. He had knelt in supplication. 'Your Majesty,' he had said.

She had liked him so much that day. What had happened since to make her indifferent? Why must she be so fickle?

Fickle: a word Roderick often used of her. But Stan wasn't fickle, thank goodness. Without him today—

But she didn't want to think about that. She shuddered, thrusting all memories of today to one side.

'Stan?'

'Yes, miss?'

'Won't you be in awful trouble for driving us to London? Won't Mama be cross?'

'I expect so, miss. And if she goes and tells my old man there'll be ructions for sure.' He sounded remarkably cheerful at the prospect. Nothing seemed to dishearten him. 'I don't mind a bit of trouble, miss, not when it's for Miss Dorothea's sake. I've a lot of time for Miss Dorothea. I was homesick like you wouldn't believe when I first came to Clifton. Miss Dorothea was the only one who really spoke to me in the beginning. She helped me settle in. Ah well. That's all done with now. I'll be leaving Clifton soon.'

'Oh Stan, must you?'

'I've had my go at chauffeuring. I've learned how to handle a motor car. Next I'll find out how to build one. I'm for the factory back home in Coventry. It's out Jeff's turn to skivvy. He'll have to learn to mind his P's and Q's for a change!'

'I shall miss you so much, Stan!'

He smiled, showing his crooked teeth: the nicest crooked teeth in all the world. 'It's decent of you to say so, miss. I shall miss you, too, and Miss Dorothea and everyone, all my mates. I've enjoyed my time at Clifton, seeing how the other half live and getting to know the countryside. I've made some good mates, too, Bill Turner for one. We've had some right old times down the Barley Mow, me and Bill.'

Eliza wrinkled her nose. Billy Turner was Daisy's brother. He worked in the stables at home. A rather dour young man, she was always overawed by him if she happened to meet him.

Young Stan laughed at her expression. 'He's alright, is Bill. A man of few words but a fine fellow underneath. But I must go, miss, and give a helping hand with dinner. We can't leave it all to Miss Dorothea.'

Eliza sat up. 'What can I do to be useful?'

'You just rest, miss, and finish your tea.'

'But I want to help. Please let me help.'

'I suppose you could lay the table by-and-by, if you feel up to it.'

She did feel up to it. She felt quite restored. Talking with Stan had helped, and the tea, and the memories of last summer when she'd been so happy. But when Stan had left the room and she was cradling her cup on the settee, she seemed to feel a cold draught coming under the door. The flames in the grate danced and flickered. Her eyes strayed to the window, the closed curtains. Outside it was dark. Outside was London. Outside—

She jumped up. Outside didn't matter. She didn't want to think about outside. She had a part to play here indoors, the table to lay. She would do it right away.

* * *

The sausages were charred, the gravy clotted, the puréed potatoes lumpy.

'Cooks puréed potatoes are so smooth and creamy,' sighed Dorothea. 'I've no idea how she does it.'

But Stan insisted that the puréed potatoes (which he called *mash*) were delicious and the meal every bit as good as his ma's cooking. Eliza thought Dorothea a marvel, able to conjure it all up from nothing. Where did you even begin? Where did sausages *come* from? And gravy: what exactly was gravy?

Back upstairs in the drawing room after dinner, they were snug with the fire glowing and sleepy after the long day and the journey overnight. It was all but impossible to believe they'd still been at Clifton this time yesterday.

'I set out once before to find Papa,' said Dorothea, staring at the fire as if she could see through it into the distant past. 'Twelve years ago, it was. I was only a child. I didn't know what I was doing. I planned to go by train but I hadn't a farthing to my name.' She sighed, looked down at her hands folded in her lap. 'I should never have given up so easily. If only I'd known about those letters.'

'It was Mama's fault! She should have told you!'

'It was Uncle Albert who burned them.'

'Daddy was . . . Daddy . . .' Eliza faltered and fell silent. It seemed improper to talk about Daddy in anything but hushed and reverent tones. But why *had* he burned the letters?

'Did you really live in those places we saw today, miss?' asked Young Stan.

Eliza shuddered. She didn't want to talk about today, she didn't want even to think about it. She wished she could turn the conversation to other matters but her mind was a blank. She came up in goose pimples, feeling that a nameless horror was creeping up on her, getting closer and closer.

'Stepnall Street was my home,' said Dorothea, 'or one of my homes. There were others. But Stepnall Street is the one I remember best. I'd forgotten, though, until today, what it is really like.'

'We lived in some rough places when I was a kid,' said Stan, 'but we were never as poor as all that. Now we live in the lap of luxury. My old ma has a cook and *two* maids, if you can believe it.'

Eliza seized on this subject to keep the nameless horror at bay. 'Roddy says that your ma doesn't exist. Nobody ever sees her so she must be a figment.'

Stan laughed. 'She's a bit shy, my old ma. She likes to keep herself to herself. But she'd never have raised all us kids if she was a figment. There's five of us. Emily's the eldest. Our Michael's just a nipper.'

At length it was time to go to bed. 'We have a long day ahead of us,' said Dorothea. 'You go up, Eliza. I'll finish tidying the kitchen then I'll come and tuck you in.'

Eliza climbed the stairs with a heavy heart. She was not sure she could stand another day like today. And that was not all. In the upheaval of the quest, the German boy and his letter had been all but forgotten — but not for good. He was still there, waiting. Had Dorothea been on the point of telling Mama she had accepted his proposal when the burnt letters had intruded? Did Dorothea really and truly want to marry a German? Did she love him? What *was* love?

There were footsteps on the stairs behind her. 'Not in bed yet, miss?'

'Stan . . . ?'

'What is it, miss?'

'What is love like? Have you ever loved anyone?'

'A girl, you mean? One or two have caught my eye, you might say, but I've never had a proper sweetheart. Then again, I'm only nineteen. There's plenty of time for all that.'

They had reached the landing. Stan opened the door to her room.

'Here you go, miss. Your bed's all ready, Miss Dorothea's seen to it. What's wrong? Don't you want to go to bed?'

'I . . .' She couldn't explain. She couldn't tell him that when the door was shut she'd be all on her own with no defence against the nameless horror. She couldn't tell him about her dread of tomorrow.

'There's no need to worry, miss. I'm right here in the next room and Miss Dorothea's just along the corridor. If you've a . . . a bad dream or anything you've only to call out. Don't go mithering yourself about tomorrow, either. I'm sure Miss Dorothea won't mind if you stay here, instead of coming with us. She's got me to help her, after all.'

Eliza felt a rush of gratitude. He seemed to understand without the need for words.

She smiled, imagining what Mama would say if she knew that Stan was making free with the best bedrooms; Roderick too (*His name's Smith, not Stan, he's a servant*). But what did Roderick know!

She paused before she closed the door. 'Stan . . .'

'Yes, miss?'

'Night-night, Stan.'

'Sweet dreams, Miss Eliza.'

CHAPTER FOUR

Eliza sat in the servants' hall, her head resting on the well-scrubbed deal table. She was alone but quite safe. She had explored every inch of 28 Essex Square over the last two days. Not a mouse, not a cockroach, not even a spider was to be found: only a dead bluebottle lying on its back on the window sill of one of the guest bedrooms.

Having the run of the place while Dorothea and Stan were out continuing the quest, Eliza had thought it would be fun to play at servants. There was no one to stop her trespassing in the servants' domain: the basement, the attics, the back stairs. But when in one of the attic bedrooms she had unrolled a mattress and lain down — pretending to be Daisy — all enthusiasm for her game had slowly evaporated. The mattress was rather thin. She had been able to feel the bed springs. The sloping ceiling had seemed to press down on her so she felt squashed and trapped.

Daisy had not been with them at Essex Square before Easter. She had been left at home. It was just as well. She would not have liked sleeping in the attic, Eliza was sure. Daisy would have grumbled. Daisy always grumbled. She was that kind of girl. 'Daisy Turner should count her blessings,' the housemaid Sally Kirkham often said. 'She gets to go home every evening and see her family. I see my family only once a year on my week off.' But Eliza, while lying on the austere attic bed, had begun to wonder if Daisy might have cause to grumble. She had to get up at five o'clock every morning, she had to trek all the way from the village whatever the weather and in the dark in winter. At Clifton she had a list of duties as long as her arm and was run off her feet all day. She was called 'Turner' and not 'Daisy' (except by Dorothea) and was at everyone's beck and call. Worst of all, she had the house-keeper Mrs Bourne breathing down her neck. Roderick called the housekeeper 'the Dreadnought'. She really was as terrifying as a battleship. Eliza kept out of her way as much as possible.

Getting up off the attic bed, Eliza had gone to the lit-tle window, looking out at all the sloping roofs and rows of chimneys. There were so many houses — so many dif-ferent attics where other Daisys must sleep on equally thin mattresses. The truth was, Eliza realised as she leant out of the window high above the Square, that there were far more Daisys in the world than there were Elizas. But that was not all. There were people even worse off than Daisy, the sort of people who lived in the cramped squalor of Stepnall Street.

Eliza in the servants' hall stared out across the barren surface of the deal table. She did not know what to think about Stepnall Street. She would rather not have thought about it at all. But that was easier said than done. In broad daylight, on this long, slow afternoon with the sounds of the street coming faintly down to the basement, she could keep her thoughts under control. But at night . . . At night she relived in her head every moment of the first day of the quest, tramping the streets as if trapped in an endless maze. Her nights were haunted by all manner of dreams and dark thoughts. The kitten was never far away. She remembered all too clearly its sightless eyes and soundless mewing. She remembered the crunch of its head against the brickwork. She thought of Pandora back home at Clifton. She thought of Pandora's kittens, of little Whisky, the kitten they had kept. What if those boys had got hold of Whisky?

81

She shuddered. Mr Antipov had talked about heaven on earth but what existed on earth was not heaven, it was just the opposite, hell. She had seen it. She would never forget. And that was why she couldn't play at servants anymore. She couldn't play at anything.

A bell jangled.

She sat bolt upright, eyes wide, listening. She must have imagined it. But no, there it was again, harsh, insistent.

For a split second she thought it must be someone upstairs ringing for attention. She had a terrifying vision in which the world had turned upside down, tipping her into Daisy's shoes, as if the game of servants had become horribly real.

But then she remembered that there was nobody else in the entire house except the dead bluebottle. And looking up at the rack of bells on the wall she saw it was the front door bell which was ringing.

There was someone at the door.

Dare she answer it? But the jangling bell was impossible to ignore. She was on her way up the stairs before she realised.

There was a girl or young woman on the doorstep: Eliza could not at first glance guess at her exact age. The girl had half turned as if about to leave. Her clothes were brightly coloured, florid even. They looked rather frayed around the edges. Her hat, laden with fake cherries, had seen better days.

Eliza stared. Momentarily she had lost her voice.

'This is the right address, miss, ain't it?' the girl said. Her accent was the same as the pickpocketing boy, as the women in the court off Stepnall Street: chopped-up words with sharp edges. It was an accent that seemed very out of place in the sedate surroundings of Essex Square. 'This is number twenty-eight, ain't it?'

Eliza nodded.

The girl wrinkled her nose. After a pause she said, 'I was told that someone had been asking after my mother. I was told it might be to my advantage if I came here. I was told wrong, seemingly.'

She took a step back, making her mind up to leave. In a moment's time she'd be gone, lost forever.

Something clicked in Eliza's head. She blurted out, 'Is your mother Mrs Browning?' It was the name Dorothea had used, the name of the woman with whom she and her papa had lived in Stepnall Street. Finding Mrs Browning, Dorothea had said, would be a big step on the way to finding her papa.

Eliza's heart beat fast. Here at last was something she could do for Dorothea. She must keep hold of this girl at all costs.

This sense of purpose gave her a modicum of courage. 'Won't you come in? There's only me at home just now but Doro — Miss Ryan, I mean, my cousin — she'll be back soon and I'm sure she would very much like to meet you.'

Eliza gave the girl no time to think, all but dragging her into the hallway. She closed the front door with relief. The first hurdle was over, the girl netted.

Upstairs in the drawing room, they stood and faced each other by the mantelpiece. Eliza could feel the blood throbbing in her cheeks. The girl fiddled with the buttons on her frock.

'I can't stay long, miss. Ten minutes at most. I've . . . I've an appointment.'

There was no appointment. Somehow Eliza knew this. But knowing that the girl was lying did not help in keeping her until Dorothea got back. They couldn't just stand there staring at each other. What would Mama do? Mama never got flustered or embarrassed. Mama was a match for any situation.

Eliza pointed to the settee. 'Won't you sit down, Miss . . . er . . . Miss . . . ?'

'Oh, call me Flossie, ducks: everyone does.' The girl sat gingerly on the settee as if she thought it might be dangerous; but when she looked up a glint came into her eyes as if she had reached the conclusion that dangerous was something Eliza most certainly *wasn't*.

'Flossie. How nice. A nice name.' Eliza tried to copy Mama's tone, to ape Mama's smile, to be the Perfect Hostess. 'Would you care for a cup of tea?'

'I wouldn't say no, ducks. I'm gasping if the truth be told. And you wouldn't have some bread and butter, would you? Not a morsel's passed my lips this livelong day. I'm fair famished.'

Eliza was already reaching for the bell cord when she remembered there was no one downstairs. She would have to make the tea herself.

'Do excuse me for a moment.' She gave a smile and a nod, just like Mama, at the same time trying not to trip over her feet as she backed towards the door. Mama made it look so easy, entertaining guests. How did she do it?

Eliza dashed down the back stairs and set about making tea. She was all fingers and thumbs. She spilled the tea leaves, dropped the spoons, scattered ash as she stoked the fire, and when she sliced the loaf she ended up with either great door-steps, or slices so thin they petered out half way down. The kettle took an age to boil. She hopped from one foot to the other. Afternoon tea at Clifton required sandwiches without crusts and several kinds of cake but here she had nothing to put in sandwiches and no cake at all. Bread and butter would have to do. And what else? Sugar, milk — there was sure to be something she had forgotten! A simple cup of tea required more effort than she would ever have guessed.

She piled everything onto a tray and set off. It was impossible to hurry. Even taking it slowly she nearly came to grief. The tray tilted first one way then the other. Milk slopped out of the jug. The cups and saucers slid around. Why had she not shown Flossie into the morning room? The drawing room on the first floor required an extra set of stairs. She couldn't begin to imagine how the servants managed. And yet they were so quick and efficient. Trays arrived in the blink of an eye, all in order and not a drop spilt.

She pushed the door open with her bottom and shuffled into the drawing room. Flossie was by the cabinet. One hand held a cigarette; the other was rummaging in a drawer.

'Some pretty things you have here.' She stepped away from the cabinet. 'I was looking for an ash tray.'

Snooping, thought Eliza as she lowered the tray onto the table. She tried to muster a Perfect Hostess smile. 'Milk? Sugar? Lemon?' *Lemon* was a slip of the tongue. There was none. But oddly it made her feel better, saying it. It was what Mama would have said and Mama was not someone ever likely to be daunted by a mere cup of tea.

Flossie pinched the end of her cigarette, put it in her pocket, sat back on the settee, accepted her cup of tea. She must be, Eliza guessed looking at her, about seventeen. With a cigarette in her hand she'd looked older.

'So who is she, ducks, this cousin of yours who's so keen to see me?'

'Miss Ryan.'

'I don't know nobody by that name.' Flossie leant forward, helped herself to more sugar, helped herself as well to two slices of bread and butter.

'I call her Doro,' said Eliza. 'Her name is Dorothea.'

'Dorothea?' Flossie sipped her tea, sucking it into her mouth. 'Well, ain't that queer. I'm sharing lodgings just now with a girl named Dorothea: she's called Dolly for short. I was saying to her just the other day, I said, "Funny you being called Dorothea. I've only ever known two Dorotheas. One is you and the other was . . ." ' Flossie's words dried up. Her eyes widened over the top of her cup. 'Surely it can't be . . . you don't mean to say . . . it's never old Dotty, is it, this Miss Ryan of yours? Get away! It can't be! I ain't seen her in years, wouldn't recognise her now if I did. I was only five or so when she upped and left with her old dad. It can't be the same girl, not after all this time. She wouldn't be living in a place like this, for one thing. Tell me ducks, who is she? Who is Miss Ryan?'

Eliza didn't know where to begin. She was reluctant to begin at all. There was something about Flossie — something sly, sharp, worldly — that made her want to distance herself. She didn't want her dear, familiar Doro to have anything to do with Flossie's 'old Dotty'. Nobody called Dorothea *Dotty*: nobody except her father. That was why she was known as Doro, because Dotty was sacred.

To her dismay, Eliza suddenly realised that she was thinking aloud, that she was telling Flossie all sorts of things about Dorothea that she had not meant to say. She felt she'd been tricked into it. Mama would not have fallen into such a trap. Mama controlled conversations, she didn't have rings run round her. Being a perfect hostess was obviously just as difficult a job as being a maidservant. Eliza now knew she was no good at either. She felt like a fledgling that had fallen out of its nest, unable to get back, unable to fly.

She'd quite lost track of time. She had no idea how long she and Flossie had been sitting there. She heard now — at last — the faint sound of the front door. Relief flooded through her. Rescue was at hand.

A moment later Dorothea came into the room unbuttoning her coat. When she caught sight of Flossie she froze, staring. Stan appeared in the doorway behind her. He regarded the visitor through narrowed eyes.

Flossie was on her feet in an instant, all smiles. 'Well, and *you* must be Dotty — Miss Ryan, I should say. I don't suppose you remember me, Flossie Phillips. I was knee-high to a grasshopper last time you saw me. Fancy you popping up again after all this time!' Flossie's eyes slid round to take in Stan. 'And who's this? Your husband, is it?'

Dorothea, still frozen in the act of undoing her buttons, said automatically, 'I have no husband. I'm not married. This is Mr Smith, a friend.'

'Pleased to make your acquaintance, Mr Smith.' Flossie looked Stan up and down, raised an eyebrow. 'You're a big boy, aren't you just,' she added archly.

To Eliza's surprise, Stan did not make disarming and down-to-earth remark. He simply turned crimson and said nothing.

'Flossie.' Dorothea spoke again at last, letting the name linger on her tongue. 'Flossie . . .'

As if released from a spell, she finished undoing her buttons and took off her coat, putting it aside. She asked Flossie to please sit down and sat on the settee beside her, smiling and making her welcome. Stan was despatched to make tea (more tea) and Dorothea pressed Flossie to help herself to another slice of bread and butter. Eliza retreated to her customary place in the window seat.

It was typical of Dorothea that she should remember her manners and ask all about Flossie first. There had to be a hundred and one questions piled up inside her but she listened patiently as Flossie rattled on. Flossie's smile never wavered, she was very eager to make herself agreeable, but Eliza looking on sensed a certain sharpness beneath like an unblinking eye that missed nothing.

'I get by, Dotty — mustn't grumble — got my health, that's the main thing. I share lodgings just now with a girl named Dolly. A good girl, Dolly. A good friend. Funny she should have the same name as you, Dotty.'

'We shared a room once, you and me,' said Dorothea, edging towards her purpose.

'You, me and the rest: five of us, all told. Do you remember that old bit of curtain we had pinned up to keep us separate at night? You, me and Mickey one side, Mum and Frankie the other.'

'You still remember Frank, then: you still remember my papa?'

'Course I do! I ain't likely to forget old Frankie. Mum had a real soft spot for him. She often used to talk about him after he'd gone.'

'When was the last time you saw him?'

'Well, now, let me see.' Flossie tapped her chin. There was an expression on her face that reminded Eliza of Mrs Keech the carpenter's wife, known round the village for being 'as sharp as a razor': it was not meant entirely as a compliment. 'To tell the truth,' said Flossie slowly (and one *had* to tell the truth when it was Dorothea), 'I ain't seen hide nor hair of him since he upped and left all those years ago, taking you with him.'

Disappointment showed in Dorothea's face. Eliza could see it; she could *feel* it too. She hugged her knees in the window seat, watching and listening. Dorothea and Flossie were turned towards each other on the settee.

'I'm sorry I can't be more help, Dotty, but we never did know what had become of you both. One day you was there, the next you'd gone. Where did you go, Dotty? Where did Frankie take you? Where have you been living all this time?'

'In Northamptonshire with my aunt and uncle, a house in the country. Papa took me there twelve years ago. He took me there and then he went away. I haven't seen him since. But now I'm searching for him. I'm searching as I should have searched years ago. That's why I wanted to find Mrs Browning. I thought she might know where Papa is.'

'Mrs how much?'

'Mrs Browning. Your mother.'

'Oh, her, Mrs Browning.' Flossie laughed, a rather stony sort of laugh. 'She had so many different names, my mum, that I lose track. Mrs Cutler, she was, for a while, Mrs Maclean too. Always Mrs, it was. She used to make out as she was a widow but she weren't no more of a widow than you or me.' Flossie placed an intimate hand on Dorothea's knee. 'She weren't never married at all, Dotty, that's the truth of it.'

'Where is she now?'

'She's as likely down below as up above, if you ask me. Dead, Dotty. She's dead. She's been gone these three years.'

'Oh Flossie — I'm so sorry —'

They were interrupted at this point. Stan returned with the tray. He'd carried it up from the kitchen without slopping a single drop of milk, Eliza noted enviously. Was there nothing he couldn't turn his hand to? Chauffeur, footman, friend, he was only nineteen but seemed so grown up. There was a lot more to him than met the eye, Eliza knew that now. Was this true of all grown-ups? Of Flossie?

Stan poured, bending over the low table. Flossie's eyes repeatedly slid round to watch him. He seemed to be aware of it, his cheeks colouring up again.

Dorothea didn't seem to notice. She was too busy prompting Flossie to talk about Frank Ryan.

'Old Frankie! He was a card!' Flossie furrowed her brow as if thinking hard but her frown turned into a knowing smile as Stan handed her a cup of tea. 'Thanks, ducks.' She grabbed his hand before he could take it away. 'You wouldn't have anything a bit stronger, would you? I could do with a pick-me-up. It might help to jog my memory,' she added, glancing at Dorothea.

Stan snatched his hand away and shook it as if he'd been stung. He looked to Dorothea for guidance. Dorothea gave a distracted nod.

'Well now . . . ,' said Flossie furrowing her brow again as she watched Stan leave the room. 'What can I tell you about Frankie?'

Dorothea, outwardly calm, waited for Flossie to continue. Eliza felt that in some sense Flossie was play-acting — playing a role in the same way that Eliza had played at being a servant. But what role Flossie was playing was impossible to fathom. And Dorothea, preoccupied with her own thoughts, seemed unaware.

Flossie hummed and hawed, not saying anything of import until Stan came back with some brandy. It was the cooking brandy from the kitchen but Flossie didn't seem to mind. As she sipped it, a beatific expression came over her face.

'Well, Dotty, I was saying, my old mum had a real soft spot for Frankie. They were together five year all told. She never forgot him. She used to talk about him a lot near the end. Her *darling Frankie*, she called him. She used to tell me how they first met, the day the bridge opened, the big new bridge with the towers. If I heard the story once, I heard it an hundred times. You'd have thought it was *Romeo and Juliet*, the way Mum used to tell it.'

Flossie sipped her brandy and continued talking. Her mother, known as Mrs Browning, Mrs Cutler or Mrs Maclean, had also been called Madge Phillips, which might or might not have been her real name. Madge Phillips when dying had returned in spirit again and again to that June day when she'd gone down to the river to watch the Prince of Wales open Tower Bridge. The river had been brimming with boats of every sort. The banks had been thronged with people. (Eliza wondered if Flossie's mother had supplied these details, or if Flossie possessed as overactive an imagination as she did.) Dorothea's papa had been a part of the crowd that day. Dorothea had been there too, a little girl, three or four years old. (What had Dorothea looked like as a girl of three or four? Had she been dressed in rags like the children in Stepnall Street?)

'Frankie was down on his luck back then,' said Flossie. 'He'd lost his job-o'-work; he'd got behind with his rent; he'd been kicked out his lodgings. He'd been living on the streets a week or more with no money and nothing to eat and a kid to care for.' Flossie leaned forward confidingly. 'That's how it starts, Dotty, simple as that, losing your bit of work. That's how you start to slip down. It's easy to slip down — don't I know it! It's much harder to climb up again. There's many never make it. They lose heart. Frankie'd lost heart. It were Mum as saved him — that's the way she told it, anyhow. Like I said, she had a soft spot for him. She liked the look of him right from the start. Which is why she took up with him. It certainly weren't for his money 'cause most of the time her never had none. He never had no reg'lar work. A week on the docks now and then, and a bit of dealing. But he never stuck at nuffin for long.'

'Why?' asked Dorothea. 'Why didn't he stick at anything?'

'It was the drink, Dotty. It was the drink what did for him every time.'

'No,' said Dorothea. 'No.' But then she paused. A faraway look came into her eyes. 'I remember the smell of gin . . .'

'Oh, lor, don't talk to me about gin! They were terrible on it, the pair of 'em. Fought like cats and dogs, they did, after they'd been down The Swan of an evening.'

Dorothea shook her head. 'No,' she repeated. 'No.'

'You can't have forgotten how it was, Dotty! I can remember and I were only a nipper. My old mum, she were a demon on the gin and there was no hiding from her. Mickey got it more than you or me, but Frankie bore the brunt. That's not to say he never dished it out hisself, but he weren't a big man, and he didn't have a temper on him the way Mum had, so he often came off worse, a black eye or a split lip or —'

'But that's not how it was! That's not how it was at all!'

'Ah, well, Dotty, it's probably slipped your mind, what with you living the genteel life and all. And 'course Frankie never laid a finger on you. Thought the world of you, he did.' Flossie glanced at Dorothea with something that seemed to Eliza like pity but then she turned away, held out her glass, said to Stan, 'I'll have a drop more of that stuff, ducks, if you don't mind. Slips down nicely, that does.'

As Flossie resumed her story (story?), talking of a time when Frank Ryan, Madge Phillips and their children had lived together in the room off Stepnall Street, Eliza wondered how the she remembered it all when by her own admission she'd only been five or so even at the end, when Frank Ryan took off. Eliza tried to think what she could remember of being four or five. The nursery. Dorothea. Nanny. There'd been a different nursery maid before Daisy, a different one again before that: Daisy's older sister, the one who wrote letters from Coventry. It was all very hazy in Eliza's mind. She was not sure which bits came earlier and which bits came later. But perhaps if she'd lived in one room, perhaps if she'd worn rags and gone hungry, perhaps if she'd had a mother who drank gin and hit her — perhaps she might then have had more cause to remember things clearly.

Flossie, still talking, had moved on. She'd moved to a time when Frank Ryan had gone away, taking Dorothea with him. Madge Phillips had been left to scrimp and save and make ends meet. 'She got on to making matchboxes, tuppence-farthing a gross. It paid for the room but not much else

— and that was working dawn till dusk.' Flossie paused, eyeing the brandy bottle on the table. Stan assiduously avoided her eye. Flossie sighed, continued: 'When Mum got sick the first time, I had to do the matchboxes for her. I weren't much good at first, all fingers and thumbs, I were only a kid. We'd have starved if it hadn't been for Mickey. He was eleven or twelve by then, he could do a man's work. Not that he was much better at holding down a job than Frankie'd been. It weren't the booze with Mickey. It were the scrapping. He'd fight his own shadow, would Mickey. He was light-fingered, and all, but that was a blessing, it kept us going. We was living on scraps, so every little helped.' Flossie paused again. Brazen now, she leaned forward, poured herself more brandy, staring at Stan as she did so, daring him to object. Sitting back, smacking her lips, she went on. 'Things started looking up. Mum got better. She found a new lodger. It was just the three of us by then, with the lodger. Mickey had gone away and —'

'Gone where?' asked Dorothea. 'How is Mickey? I should like to see him again. He always looked out for me when we were children.'

'Didn't he just. Everyone's favourite, you were, Dotty.' For a second there was a flash of something in Flossie's eyes — anger? resentment? jealousy? — but then it was gone, as if a veil had been drawn. 'I don't rightly know where he is. I did hear once that he got himself a job out Romford way, then again someone told me he landed in the Scrubs, which wouldn't surprise me. You lose track, Dotty, when there's other things to worry about.'

Eliza looked at Flossie with surprise. Mickey was Flossie's brother and yet she showed little interest in where he might be or what had happened to him. Imagine losing your brother! Imagine losing Roderick! It was unthinkable!

Flossie picked up the threads of her tale. 'As I said, it were the three of us. Mum was working in a sweat shop, I'd got to be a dab hand with the matchboxes, and we had the lodger's money and all. I say lodger, but he were her fancy man really, the lodgers always were. But he paid his way, which was all that mattered. We lived like royalty for a time. Fried fish twice a week and meat on Sunday. Then Mum got ill again. Scarlet fever, this time. She was dead of it within a week and that was that.'

'I'm sorry,' said Dorothea. 'She . . . she was like a mother to me, really. The nearest I ever had, anyway.'

'She was a hard woman, I'll say that for her.' Flossie, sipping brandy, showed no grief. She too was hard, thought Eliza. The smile, the friendly manner — even her youth: it was like moss on a stone, easily scraped away.

'So there I was,' said Flossie, 'thirteen years old and on my own: no Mum, no Mickey and only what I got for the match-boxes, which wasn't more than a pittance. I set my sights on a job, a proper job. I went for respectable positions at first, the ones that paid well. Then I tried for the ones that didn't pay so well. But no one would have me, not even for a scrubbing maid. I'd no particulars, you see. No one wouldn't take me without particulars. And that was when the lodger — he was still around — the lodger said he might be able to help. He knew just the trade I was cut out for. Offered to get me started. I'd earn good money, he said, with the way I looked and being so young and all. I was only thirteen at the time, Dotty, but I weren't as green as all that, I wouldn't want you to think as I was. But what choice did I have? What else could I have done? I was up a creek and over a barrel and no mistake. And so — well, there's no harm in telling you; you've guessed already, I'm sure. But that's how I got started as a working girl.'

Eliza frowned, puzzled. What was so terrible about being a working girl? Hadn't Flossie been working all along? Wasn't making matchboxes work? But Dorothea took hold of Flossie's hand and stroked it and said it was terrible and she was sorry and she wished she'd come back long ago. 'I might easily have ended up in your shoes, dear Flossie, if Papa hadn't taken me to Clifton, if Uncle Albert and Aunt Eloise hadn't looked after me all these years. I was lucky, that's all it was.'

'I'm glad of it, Dotty. You deserved it. You was always the best one out of all of us.'

'That's not true, Flossie. We were all the same. We all grew up together. You and Mickey were like a brother and sister to me.'

'Not just *like*, maybe,' said Flossie cryptically, gulping brandy and looking sidelong at Dorothea. 'I've often wondered, Dotty, who my dad was. Mum would never say. All I know is that I was born *after* that day by the bridge — *after* Mum met Frankie.'

'That's right,' said Dorothea slowly. 'That's true. I've never thought of it before. And . . . and your name is Florence, which was my mother's name. Papa always cherished mother's memory. Just think, just imagine — you might have been named after her!'

Eliza experienced a sense of panic. She felt that Dorothea was suddenly slipping away from her, being drawn back into the terrible world of Stepnall Street. She'd always felt that she had a greater claim on Dorothea than anyone, being her cousin. But if Flossie was Dorothea's sister . . . It couldn't be true! It couldn't be!

But what if it was?

What did Flossie *want*? Not just bread and butter and brandy, that was for sure.

The sense of panic threatened for a moment to overwhelm her, fragile as she still was after her ordeal the other day. But as she fought against this feeling, something utterly unexpected happened. The door crashed open. A dark figure loomed up. Eliza cowered in terror. Was this the world breaking in, the horrible, cruel, brutal world that she'd been trying so hard to keep at bay?

It wasn't the world. It wasn't even a stranger. Eyes blazing, sweeping into the room like a whirlwind, throwing aside his bag, hat and coat, ferociously angry, it was Roderick, her very own brother Roderick.

What in hell's name did they think they were doing, he demanded: had they any idea how worried Mother had been?

Taking off without a word and only one measly telegram by way of explanation: it was beyond belief! He'd thought Dorothea had more sense, he'd thought she would know better.

'As for you —' Roderick swung round to glare at Stan. 'As for you, sitting there as if you own the place —'

Poor Stan! Eliza's heart bled for him. He was a disgrace, an absolute disgrace, absconding with the best motor: it was tantamount to stealing. He deserved to get the sack. In fact, he *was* sacked. He could leave immediately, right now, this very minute. Goodbye and good riddance.

There was pandemonium. Stan was on his feet, Flossie too, and Dorothea faced Roderick in the middle of the room.

'Roddy, how dare you—'

But Roderick turned aside, fixing on Flossie. Who the devil was this? Who'd let her in the house? (Eliza quailed. What if someone told him it was her, that *she'd* let Flossie into the house?) He'd never seen such a specimen. She was pickled in brandy, she looked like a tramp, she stank.

He grabbed her by the elbow. 'Thank you for calling and all that but it's time you were on your way. Off you go, shoo, shoo!'

'No, Roddy, you mustn't!' Dorothea grabbed Flossie's other arm.

A bizarre tug-of-war ensued, Roderick trying to drag Flossie out into the corridor, Dorothea trying to keep her in the room. But Eliza felt it was she, not Flossie, who was being pulled this way and that, torn apart by the awful madness which had seized them all.

Stan — sensible, dutiful Stan — tried to intervene. 'Mr Roderick, sir—'

'Don't speak to me. I've sacked you.'

'You can't sack Stan!' cried Dorothea.

'I can. I have. He's going. Gone.'

'Will you please leave Flossie alone!'

'She is going too.'

Eliza jumped to her feet. She was aware of what she was doing, what she was saying, but she had no control over it, as if someone else had taken over her body.

'Stop it! Stop it! I can't bear it! Why must you be so horrible, all of you? You mustn't, you mustn't — the world is horrible enough — everything's horrible — it's all horrible, spoilt, ruined — oh, oh, oh—'

Her legs moved of their own accord. She found herself running out of the room, running up the stairs. She went straight to her room and slammed the door.

* * *

A last lingering sob was smothered by the pillow in which her face was buried. She shuddered and lay still. There was nothing left. Everything had poured out of her. She felt as squashed and flat as a flower pressed between the pages of a book.

She was not sure how long she'd been lying there, crying. There was a vivid image in her mind of everyone in the drawing room — Dorothea, Roderick, Stan, Flossie — standing and staring at her open-mouthed as she shouted and screamed and stamped her feet. She could almost imagine that she'd turned them to stone by the force of her rage, they'd been so transfixed. She could hear nothing in the house now but silence. The noises of the street seemed muffled and distant.

She slowly sat up, like Sleeping Beauty waking after a sleep of ages. The bed was a proper bed now with sheets and a counterpane and two soft pillows, Dorothea herself had made it. But Eliza felt an odd, silly nostalgia for the bare mattress and the rug from the motor, which was all she'd had on their first night here.

She waited. After a long, long time, there came a tap on the door. It would be Dorothea, of course.

But it wasn't. It was Roderick.

He sat down on the edge of the bed. His dark eyes watched her, inscrutable. She felt shy of him after what had happened downstairs and avoided his gaze. His hand resting on the counterpane looked big and real and ruthless.

'Well,' he said at length. 'Have you recovered after your extraordinary outburst?'

'I . . . I suppose everyone is laughing at me.' Shame, bitterness, resignation swirled around inside her.

'It is safe to say that no one is laughing.'

'And have they gone, Stan and that girl?'

'Smith is still here.'

'But you sacked him.'

'It proved necessary, as I value my life, to change my mind about that. I found he's rather popular around here.'

'He's been *wonderful*, Roddy. I do like him. He rescued me.'

'Rescued you from what? From all that I gather, the three of you have been roaming the streets of east London as if you were on the Grand Tour.'

'Oh, Roddy, it was horrible . . . the kitten . . .'

'What kitten? What are you talking about?'

But she couldn't tell him. The words weren't there.

'There's no need to look so glum, kiddo,' he said, his voice growing gruffer as he tried to soften it. 'You've just got things muddled in that head of yours as usual.'

'Do . . . do you think that girl is *really* Doro's sister?'

'I don't believe it for a minute. It was just a ploy, a confidence trick. She was trying to worm her way in, telling Doro what she wanted to hear. They don't even look alike.' Which was true, Dorothea with her kind, round face and dark curls, and Flossie thin and hard with lank mousey hair. 'Anyway, she's gone now. Taken to her heels.'

'Is Doro angry?'

'You know Doro. She never stays angry for long. She can see now that the girl couldn't tell her anything she didn't already know.'

'What about the quest, Doro's papa?'

'That girl had no more idea where Frank Ryan is than we have.'

'But she knew so much about him.'

'Rather too much, I think, for Doro's liking.'

'The . . . the way Flossie talked about him: he sounded *horrible!*'

'He was a bit of a wastrel by all accounts and something of a drunkard. Father had no time for him.'

'How could a man like that be Doro's papa? Where did he come from?'

'Ah, well, that's ancient history. It happened years ago, in Coventry, before Mother and Father were married, before they'd even met. You do know, I suppose that Father came from Coventry — that he lived in Coventry until he married Mother? That's where Doro's mother lived, too. Doro's mother was Father's sister. She would have been our aunt if we'd ever known her: Aunt Florence.'

'What happened to her?'

'I don't know the details but, as far as I understand it, what happened was this. Frank Ryan worked for Father. Father back then had just set up his bicycle business (the motors came later, as you know). Frank Ryan was one of the first people he employed. And that was how Frank and Aunt Florence came to meet. Frank turned Florence's head. He was a lot older, you must remember: nine years.'

'Is it bad, then, to be older? Wasn't Daddy older than Mama?'

'Well, yes, he was. But Mother's not someone ever likely to lose her head. Aunt Florence, by all accounts, was just the opposite. She allowed herself to be talked into running away. They eloped, Florence and Frank Ryan. They ran away to get married. Afterwards, they lived in London — at least, that was where they ended up. That was where Doro was born and where Florence, her mother, died. Her mother died in childbirth.'

'What does that mean, Roddy? What happens?'

'Don't ask me. It's women's affairs. I suppose she wasn't strong enough or there were complications. Such things happen, I believe.'

'So Doro's mama died. What next?'

'Frank Ryan tried to raise Doro on his own. He found he couldn't manage it (he was a wastrel, remember). And so he brought Doro to Clifton — to us.'

'I'm glad. I'm glad he did. But he can't have been *all* bad if he did that.'

'I suppose you have a point. We have him to thank for giving us Doro. But that doesn't make him a saint. He had his faults which Doro, being Doro, tends to overlook.'

'Roddy?'

'What is it, kiddo?'

'Do . . . do you think he's still alive?'

Roderick shrugged. 'Perhaps. Perhaps not. We'll probably never know.'

Eliza shivered. 'Just think if he *hadn't* brought us Doro! Just think! Doro said that she would have turned out like that girl Flossie!'

'No!' said Roderick fiercely. 'Doro would never have been like that! No matter where she lived, Doro would never have been less than herself!'

He looked so angry that Eliza was a little afraid of him, afraid of his strength and the way he trampled people. But oddly enough this fear reassured her, made her feel safe. He was her brother, her protector, a bastion against the nameless horror which had been haunting her these last few days.

Acting on impulse, she got to her knees and threw her arms round him as he sat there, hugging him tightly. 'Oh Roddy, I *do* love you!'

'Do you, indeed! That's a turn up for the books.' He patted her back a little awkwardly but then, after a moment, he seemed to relax a little. He said almost gently, 'I don't suppose this means you'll behave yourself in future and do as you're told?'

She smiled into his shoulder. 'I don't suppose it does.'

He ruffled her hair. 'You're hopeless. But I've no other kid sister to pester and plague me so I suppose I must make do with you.' He carefully disentangled himself. 'Come on.

Tidy yourself up then come downstairs. The chauffeur has turned chef. We are to be treated to some sort of sumptuous repast.'

When Roderick had gone, Eliza took up her hairbrush and crossed to the mirror. Her eyes were swollen, her hair tangled; she'd been wearing the same frock for days and it was all crumpled. Slowly she ran the brush through her long locks. Her hair was fair, the same as Mama, but very different to Roderick, who was dark. Dorothea too had black hair. What colour hair did Dorothea's papa have? And the dead Aunt Florence? It was all so odd, brothers and sisters, mothers and fathers: they shared so many traits and yet could be so different. What did it all mean?

She flinched suddenly. She thought she'd seen in the mirror out of the corner of her eye something move: a flicker, a shadow. But when she turned to look there was nothing there.

She flung her brush aside, pulled her frock straight, and ran out into the corridor, leaving her doubts and fears to whisper alone in the empty room.

* * *

They ate sardines on toast served in the dining room by Stan, who ate with them despite Roderick's huffing and puffing. Afterwards in the drawing room with the fire bright and the curtains closed, Eliza curled up on the settee feeling sleepy. The room looked different now. It was difficult to believe that Flossie had ever been there.

'She could be anywhere by now,' said Dorothea. 'If only you hadn't chased her away, Roddy!'

'I didn't chase her anywhere. She couldn't get away quick enough. In any case, you don't know that it was even the real Flossie. She might have been a play-acting impostor. She might have known the real Flossie once-upon-a-time and learned enough to convince you. Besides, she doesn't know where you father is and I thought the whole idea of this benighted expedition was to find *him.*'

'I'll never find him now,' said Dorothea sadly. 'He's gone and I've nothing left of him: no photographs and no . . . no letters.'

'Father only did what he thought was right, burning those letters.'

'I know. I can't criticize him, not really.'

'My dear Doro, you do astonish me at times. Aren't you the least bit angry? You were angry enough at Clifton. How can you be so forgiving?'

'Yes, I was angry. But there's no point dwelling on it. I leave all that sort of thing to you, Roddy, all the fault-finding and the laying of blame.'

'Insults, now, is it? Then you really must be feeling more yourself. I suppose you realise that your father could have come back at any time if he'd wanted? Burning the letters didn't stop him. So you see there's no need to feel guilty about not looking for him. You were only a child, after all. He was the adult. Perhaps he felt a clean break was best. Father thought so.'

'Dear Uncle Albert.' Dorothea smiled. 'How I miss him!' Her smile faded. She sat still and pensive, staring into the fire.

Watching her, Roderick said, 'You have to stop dwelling on the past, Doro. Think about the future instead. There's this . . . this Teuton.'

'Johann,' said Dorothea. 'His name is Johann.'

Eliza had all but forgotten the German boy and his proposal. Why was Roderick bringing it up now? 'Isn't it,' she began hesitantly, 'isn't it against the law to marry a foreigner?'

'You and your mad ideas!' scoffed Roderick. 'Of course it's not against the law! But it rather depends on Doro, whether she wants to accept him or not.'

'I'd made up my mind to,' said Dorothea. 'I wrote him a letter saying yes. It's still on the nursery table, I expect. Oh, but it's impossible! I can't marry him, I simply can't!'

'Why not?' demanded Roderick. 'You can marry him if you want to. You can marry whoever you like. Though how you manage to fall in love in a letter is beyond me.'

'It wasn't just the letters. It was Switzerland. That was when it started. But I don't understand you, Roddy. Why are you so keen all of a sudden that I should marry Johann? You said it would be a mistake.'

'Since when have you ever taken any notice of what I say or think?'

'But you're right, it *would* be a mistake. Aunt Eloise would never agree to it, for one thing. And how could I ever be good enough for him? I have nothing, not even a papa.'

'You do talk rot, Doro. Not good enough for him! Why, you're . . . you're the very *nicest* girl I know, an absolute brick. No one could ever be worthy of you, as I told you once before. But if you've really set your heart on this fellow—'

'I do love him, Roddy: I do. But — oh — how could I ever leave Clifton?'

'We'll always be there, Doro. We won't just disappear into the blue like your father. You can come back as often as you like. As for Mother, she'll come round, you'll see. Don't you realise that Mother thinks the world of you? She won't be able to do enough when it comes to the point. All she needs is to be told a few facts. That's where I come in.'

'You'll help? You'll really help me?'

'Good grief, there's no need to sound so surprised! All I want is . . . is for you to be happy. It's all I've ever wanted.'

'Oh Roddy!'

Eliza saw sudden hope light up Dorothea's face. Roderick was smiling too, his dark eyes shining. Stan was grinning, showing his crooked teeth. There was an air of happiness in the room. But Eliza could not shake a feeling of unease. All too soon it would be time for bed and already in the back of her mind the dark thoughts she'd held at bay were gathering and growing like slow-woven shadows, ready to haunt her dreams.

She dreaded it.

CHAPTER FIVE

Daisy came staggering into the day room. 'The heat, miss! I feel as if I'm melting!'

She did indeed look as if she might be melting, so much sweat was running down her face. Eliza, slouched in her chair, tried to muster some sympathy but it was too much effort, she was too dull and listless. The weather didn't help at all. The windows were wide open but there was not a breath of air.

'I'll swing for that Susie Hobson, doodling about the place!' cried Daisy, leaning against the bars at the window and fanning herself with her cap. 'I swear she hasn't done a stroke of work all day long while the rest of us have run ourselves ragged. All she does is gawp at the guests. "Aren't they handsome!" says she. "Handsome?" says I. "They're Germans, Susie Hobson, and don't you forget it!"' Daisy shuddered, as if Germans were hideous apparitions from the underworld.

'But Johann is nice, Daisy, don't you think so?'

'Miss Dorothea's young man, do you mean? Well, yes, *he's* alright, I suppose. He don't say much, but when he does speak he's very civil. But that name of his! I can't get my tongue round it! And as for his brother, huh, what an uppity package!'

'He's only seems uppity because he doesn't speak much English: that's what Doro says. And his name is Siegfried.' Eliza was proud, having the foreign names off pat.

'Don't speak English? That's no excuse! A smile's the same in any language.' Daisy sighed, putting her cap back on and stuffing her hair inside. 'I must go. I only come up for—' She stopped, clapped a hand to her forehead. 'What *did* I come up for? It's gone right out my head. Oh lawks, I shall be for it now, with Bossy Bourne up in arms and the whole place in an uproar. If it weren't all for Miss Dorothea's sake, I'd have handed in my notice days ago, I swear I would.'

Daisy went lurching off, still complaining about the heat. The nursery lapsed into a soporific silence. Eliza, who'd been toying with the idea of venturing downstairs, now decided against it. If the place really was in an uproar — if Daisy wasn't simply exaggerating (it had been known) — then it would be wise to keep out of the way. Mrs Bourne up in arms was always best avoided. And then there was Mama. Eliza was still in Mama's bad books after running away to London back in April.

Dangling her legs over the arm of her chair, Eliza turned her thoughts to the terrible Germans who weren't so terrible really (another of Daisy's exaggerations). Four Germans were in residence at Clifton: Johann; and Johann's father, brother and cousin. In Switzerland two years ago, there'd been Johann and a different cousin, a man named Heinrich who Eliza had rather liked, who'd taken time to talk to her, who hadn't been at all arrogant whatever Roderick might have said. But Heinrich's wife was expecting a child and couldn't travel. Heinrich had not wanted to leave her and had stayed in Hamburg. Heinrich's younger brother Gerhard had come instead. He was a pale imitation of Heinrich, not worth bothering with.

Johann's brother Siegfried was not worth much either. Daisy in this instance was quite right: not being able to speak English was no excuse. Siegfried was full of himself, worse than Roderick in his most bombastic mood. Siegfried was quite humourless too. His father, however, was completely different, a jolly man with a white beard and white whiskers, a doctor. He wore spectacles on the end of his nose when he read the newspaper.

But it was Johann who was most important, the man Dorothea was to marry. He was rather quiet, as Daisy had said, so it was difficult to make up one's mind about him. Certainly he had none of Roderick's swagger, nor was he rough round the edges like Young Stan. Johann's teeth were perfect, there was no hint of any spots. His eyes were very blue, his nose slightly snub, his blond hair swept back in a side parting. In Switzerland he'd been rather pasty-faced, convalescing, but there was a healthy glow about him now. The housemaid, Susie Hobson — never backward in coming forward when it came to giving her opinion — was most impressed. 'Oh, miss, have you ever seen the like? If he only had wings he'd be an angel out of heaven. Fancy a Plain Jane like Miss Dorothea catching a man like that!'

His full name was Johann Kaufmann. The Kaufmanns lived in Hamburg. Eliza, sitting sideways in her chair, closed her eyes and told herself once more the story of the Kaufmanns that she'd learned from Dorothea. Many years ago in Hamburg there'd been two beautiful sisters. Eliza pictured them as Snow White and Cinderella, illustrations in a book. Dr Kaufmann's brother had married Snow White. Eventually, after much prevarication which the family had often later laughed about, Dr Kaufmann and Cinderella had got married too.

It was a satisfyingly symmetrical story, two brothers marrying two sisters and each couple having two children, all boys. If it had been a fairy tale it would have ended there. They would all have lived happily ever after. But real life was not like that, as Eliza now knew. Real life was full of tragedy and despair.

'Tragedy and despair!' Roderick had rolled his eyes. 'You do talk bilge, Eliza. I can't imagine where you get it from. Why are you so interested in these Teutons, in any case?'

She was interested because the story was so sad it was impossible to forget. Dr Kaufmann's brother had died of a terrible cancer in his throat. The cancer before he died had taken away his voice. This seemed particularly cruel, to be denied a few last words with one's dying breath. ('I forgive you, Roddy. I forgive you now I'm dying. I forgive you even though you have been absolutely beastly to me so many times and have never stopped chaffing me about my *overactive imagination*.')

The cancer was not the end of it. Some years later cholera had come to Hamburg (cholera?) and both Snow White and Cinderella had died, leaving Dr Kaufmann to bring up on his own not just his two boys, but his two nephews as well.

This was all true. It came from Dorothea. But when Eliza had tried to tell the tale to Roderick (she had, admittedly, added a few embellishments), he had accused her of 'making up stories which bear no relation to the facts'.

Facts? What did facts matter! They were nothing but an encumbrance!

Footsteps sounded, interrupting Eliza's reverie. Someone was coming. The someone turned aside, went into Dorothea's room. Eliza made the effort to get to her feet. She went to see who it was.

Dorothea's room was still Dorothea's room, just about. There were trunks and cases all over the floor, some for the holiday, some for Hamburg, labels affixed to each but most of them open and only half-full. On the bed, on the chairs, on the dressing table were piles of clothes, and hats in boxes, and pairs of shoes in bags. Dorothea was standing in the midst of it all, looking round with a perplexed expression on her face.

'I need to finish packing but—' She spread her arms as if to say *Where do I start?*

'I will help,' said Eliza. But she made no move to begin. It would have seemed somehow like speeding Dorothea on her way, which was the last thing she wanted.

'Mr Antipov has just arrived,' said Dorothea at length. 'Yet another man. The house is full of men.'

'Mama likes it when there are lots of men,' said Eliza. 'She shines brighter for men. They reflect her, like mirrors. What is happening downstairs, Doro?'

'Everyone is in the drawing room. Dr Kaufmann has made himself popular by admiring the view.'

'And I suppose Mama told him that the landscaping was never finished, that the money ran out, that the present gardens belonged to the old manor before it was demolished.'

Dorothea smiled. 'Of course. All the usual things. Dr Kaufmann asked who the Massinghams were. Aunt Eloise told him they were her forebears, the people who built Clifton Park, a somewhat impecunious family. Mr Antipov said that "impecunious" is an interesting word and that he likes to learn new words. But he then rather blotted his copybook by suggesting that the Royal Family are more German than English.'

'And Mama said, "That is a despicable thing to say! You are a despicable scoundrel, Mr Antipov!"'

'Oh, Eliza, of course she didn't! As if Aunt Eloise would ever say a thing like that!'

'What, then, *did* she say?'

'She asked about the Russian Royal Family and Mr Antipov told her that *they* are German too. And Dr Kaufmann said, "Royalty is obviously one of our more successful exports!" Everyone laughed.'

'Everyone laughed,' echoed Eliza. She sighed. 'Oh Doro! Who will tell me these things when you are gone? Who will tell me anything? Why must you go? Why must you go so soon?'

'There didn't seem much point in waiting, once I'd made up my mind. After all, time doesn't stand still.'

Time, thought Eliza. Time had never seemed to matter much before. It had merely been a convenient way of knowing when to get up, when to have lunch, when to take a walk in the gardens. But time wasn't just a clock on the mantelpiece. It was like cancer and cholera, it killed, it destroyed, it changed things forever. First Father, now this.

'Oh Doro! You'll get married and go away and I'll never see you again!'

Dorothea put her arms round Eliza, stroked her hair. 'I will miss you too: of course I will.'

They stood in the stifling heat, their arms round each other, staring at the trunks and cases; and Eliza wished that time would come to an end right then and there so that she'd never have to find out what life was like in a Clifton Park without Dorothea.

* * *

'Sleep, sleep,' murmured Eliza. 'Why can't I sleep?'

Lying in bed in the dark, Eliza craved sleep but feared it too, feared what it would bring, the nightmares that had stalked her since coming back from London all those months ago. She craved sleep, she invited it; she had even blown out her night light to welcome it. But still she tossed and turned, still she was wide awake.

It was the wedding tomorrow. The wedding would be spoilt for her if she spent all day yawning.

She decided to get up. She might feel more like sleep after a turn around the room. She thought it rather daring, getting up. Once you'd said your prayers, once you'd been tucked in, you should stay in bed until morning. But tonight was out of the ordinary. Tonight had a special character all of its own. Tonight was Dorothea's last night at Clifton.

Eliza slipped from under the bed covers and made her way to the window. She pulled the curtains a little aside. Her toes curled into the Turkey carpet as she leant out of the open casement. It was a quiet, breathless evening. Cool air washed against her face. Stars in the deep-vaulted darkness glinted like cold, white eyes. The trees of the Pheasantry and the evergreens along the drive were sharp black silhouettes against the paler sky. The spreading bows of the cedar tree in front of the house seemed almost close enough to touch. To the left, the gardens were wreathed in shadow. Beyond, in the distance, the dim mass of Rookery Hill was crowned with a bank of grey-dark cloud. There was a faint sound of voices, of laughter, which must be spilling out from the french windows and carrying in the stillness right round to this side of the house.

Crunching footsteps made Eliza jump. Her eyes picked out a hunched figure in the gloom below. Billy Turner, was it, walking with his hands in his pockets, heading towards the drive: Billy Turner the stable hand? Going to visit his mother, perhaps, in the village; or more likely sloping off to the Barley Mow. His 'second home', Daisy called it, disparaging her brother and his taste for a pint of ale.

Turner disappeared into the dark. The sound of his footsteps faded. *A man of few words*, Young Stan had said of him, *but a fine fellow underneath.* Yet what did it matter anymore what Stan thought? He had taken his leave, he was back in Coventry, his brother Jeff was now the chauffeur, a rather prickly, monosyllabic sort of boy. *Shy*, Dorothea said, *still finding his feet.* Dear Dorothea! She always saw the best in everyone. She convinced you of it, too. No one else could do this in quite the same way. And soon, like Stan, she'd be gone.

The thought gave Eliza a pain in her chest as if a shard of the sorcerer's mirror from *The Snow Queen* had pierced her heart and turned it to ice. One word, one smile from Dorothea would warm it back to life. Dorothea would be in her room. She had eaten dinner in the nursery this evening one last time. She still had packing to do. There was every chance she'd be awake.

Eliza opened her bedroom door, crossed the big shadowy day room, barefooted, silent. As she reached for the handle of the main door she heard someone in the lobby beyond. There came a soft tap on Dorothea's door. The door squeaked as it opened. It always squeaked.

'So you are still up, then,' said a voice. It was Roderick's voice. His voice sounded different heard through the panels of the day room door: muffled and mellow and resonant.

Eliza pressed her ear against the wood, listening. 'It was absurd of you, Doro, not to come down to dinner on your last night.'

'The bride and groom mustn't meet on the eve of the wedding, it's tradition.'

'It's superstitious rot. But it wouldn't be a problem if that bevy of Teutons had stayed in a hotel. There are hotels in Lawham.'

'But Aunt Eloise invited them here. She insisted.'

'She can't do enough, just as I predicted.'

'She's been more than kind. I can't imagine why.'

'You don't know why? You are a goose, Doro!'

'Oh, Roddy! What if I'm making a mistake? Is it too late to change my mind?'

'That's nerves talking, Doro. Nerves are quite usual in this situation, or so I'm given to believe. Your intended is just the same, white as a sheet and quiet as a mouse, quieter even than normal. He ought to prescribe himself a cure.'

'He's not a doctor yet.'

'Then it's highly presumptuous of him, to imagine he could ever be good enough, a mere medical student.'

'It's the other way round. I am not good enough for him. What will his friends think, back in Germany? They will hate me. I know they will!'

'Of course they won't, don't be absurd! No one could ever hate you, Doro. You'll always fit in wherever you are. The Germans, I'm sure, will grow to like you just as much as we do.'

'Like?'

'Alright, love, if you must be pedantic about it. We love you, Doro.'

'You used to say love only exists in the minds of idle girls.'

'I used to say a lot of things. I was an odious little tick. I can't think why you put up with me.'

'Because I like you.'

'Like?'

'Alright, love. I love you, Roddy. But you already know that.'

'Doro, Doro! What on earth will I do without you? Nobody keeps me on my toes the way you do! But tell me honestly. Are you quite ready for connubial bliss? Are you ready for . . . for all that comes with it?'

'I don't know what you mean.'

'I am alluding to the act of union — and I don't mean 1707.'

'Trust you, Roddy. Trust you to bring that up. I am not entirely ignorant, believe it or not. I know where Pandora's kittens came from and how they got there.'

'Pandora is not a person, she's a cat.'

'The principle is the same. Dearest Roddy, there's no point in your looking all superior. I know you're trying to shock me but you forget that I lived in Stepnall Street. It's an education in itself, Stepnall Street.'

'Evidently. Eliza only went there once and she's not been the same since.'

'There's something different about you, too, Roddy. Do you know what I think? I think you're in love with Miss Halsted.'

'Absolute rot! I've never heard anything so ridiculous. Love has nothing whatever to do with it. We've nothing in common, for one thing, me and Miss Hasted. We never stop arguing. She gets in my head and nearly drives me mad!'

'What did I tell you? Love.'

'Then all I can say is, love is hell. You have my heartfelt sympathies, Doro, if you're afflicted in that way too.'

'*Afflicted*? You say the most ridiculous things, Roddy, you really do!'

'So you keep telling me. So you've told me every day since you first arrived.'

'Just keeping you on your toes.'

'I pity your poor Teuton. He's no idea what he's letting himself in for. If, that is, you decide to go through with all this. I told him I was coming up to talk you out of it.'

'You didn't!'

'He seemed to think I was joking.'

'Honestly, Roddy. You're hopeless, you really are!'

'I know. I'm quite beyond redemption.'

They were laughing. Happy. But Eliza in her nightdress in the dark of the day room felt the shard of glass in her heart again. A sob worked its way up her throat, threatening to burst out of her. She put a hand over her mouth to keep it in. Why did she feel so lonely and left out?

A thin breeze, almost indiscernible, began to whisper through the open window. Polly's eye was suddenly unlidded, glinting in the shadows.

'Oh Polly! Oh Polly, why, why, why?'

But Polly, uninterested, closed her eye again. Eliza, rejected, her heart pierced to the core, ran back to bed and pulled the covers up to her chin. Tears slowly oozed from her eyes. One-by-one they slid across her cheeks. The curtains began to billow as the breeze strengthened. In the distance, on the edge of hearing, thunder rumbled in the silence of the night.

* * *

'I can't eat,' said Eliza. 'There are too many butterflies in my tummy.'

'You must have some breakfast.' Dorothea stood over her, calm and sensible as if this was any other morning. 'Try a little of this scrambled egg.'

'You must eat too, Miss Dorothea,' said Daisy, easing Dorothea into a chair. 'We can't have you fainting at the altar.'

Eliza picked at her plateful of eggs. A storm had passed in the night. The sound of thunder had permeated her dreams, mixed with the helpless mewling of a kitten before turning inexplicably into the sound of the sea. She had felt as if she was floating on water, her bed rising and falling with the motion of the waves, gulls on the wing wailing above her, the grey sea stretching vast and empty to a distant dark horizon. All at once the sky had cracked open and a blinding light had poured in. With that she had woken to a bright and sunny morning, the sky a washed blue, the air fresh after rain.

Time was marching on. Breakfast was soon abandoned. More and more people came crowding into the nursery. Mama was there, tall, elegant, unruffled. Miss Cecily Somersby, Eliza's fellow bridesmaid, stood still and silent in one corner. Daisy darted in and out, fetching and carrying, running errands. Mama's maid appeared to do Dorothea's hair. Mrs Turner arrived from the village with a vast bunch of flowers and her two grandsons. Little Dick, Dorothea's favourite, was ten years old now and not so little anymore. He and his younger brother Sid were to be page boys. They ran around the room getting under everyone's feet and exclaiming in shrill voices at such a cornucopia of toys and games.

Mrs Carter from Coventry — the one who wrote the letters — was the next to arrive. 'And this must be Miss Eliza. Bless me, how you've grown! I'd never have known you for the baby you were.' Eliza went red with embarrassment at being singled out.

The clock ticked. It was time to get ready. Eliza in her room struggled with her frock as the hubbub next door began to subside.

Daisy came hurrying in. 'Now, now, miss, you'll have that dress in shreds if you keep pulling it about like that.'

'It won't do up. It doesn't fit. I look silly.'

'Of course it fits. Let me. You'll look as pretty as a picture.'

'I won't. I'm ugly, so ugly.'

'My, you *are* a narky thing this morning! There, that's all done. Now come and see Miss Dorothea. You won't recognise her!'

The day room had emptied. Even Mama had gone. Only Dorothea remained. Daisy was right. The transformation was remarkable. Dorothea's dress was white with a low-cut neckline draped over a lace chemise. The bodice was pouched at the waist. Skirts flared out to float and trail across the floor. Dorothea sparkled. She looked ethereal. The white of her dress was offset by her black hair and the pink of her cheeks.

Dorothea took hold of Eliza's hands. 'Well, Eliza? How do I look?'

But Eliza was too choked to speak.

They were alone. Daisy had gone running, she had a million and one things to do, the house must be got ready for when they all came back. But they were not alone for long. A chink of glasses sounded in the corridor and suddenly Roderick was there, a bottle in his hand, glasses dangling from his fingers. He stopped and stared. Eliza watched his eyes widen, his pupils dilate, as he took it in, Dorothea in all her splendour. A smile played on his lips. He was very tall and handsome. He was scrubbed and tidy and decisive, all neat lines from the creases in his trousers to the cut of his jaw. His dark hair was shiny with oil. He smelled of aftershave and Euchrisma.

He held up the bottle. 'Champagne,' he said to Dorothea, 'to steady your nerves.'

'Oh, Roddy, I hate champagne, I always have.'

'All the more for me, to settle *my* nerves.'

'You will make yourself drunk. And we don't have time.'

'Yes we do. You must keep him waiting: another tradition.' He poured champagne, put the bottle and the spare glass aside on the big nursery table. 'Mother has gone. There's only Cecily now. She's being dosed with smelling salts by the Dreadnought.'

'Oh, poor thing! I must go to her!'

'Leave her. She'll be fine. I'll make sure of it. If the smelling salts don't work, I shall tell her exactly what I think of her. That will smarten her up.' He grinned.

'You mustn't be horrible to poor Cecily, Roddy, I absolutely forbid it!'

His grin grew wider and wider, his eyes glinted, he looked happy, devilish, different — so much so that Eliza blushed as he turned to look her.

'Well, well! My little sister. Who'd have thought.'

They were together, just the three of them, as they'd always been, growing up in the nursery. They looked at each other, smiling, harking back, and it seemed to Eliza that for one brief moment the sense of occasion and all their fine clothes were forgotten. They'd called her 'Baby' until she was nearly seven. She'd never thought to mind. She wished she could go back in time and be Baby again.

Roderick's smile faded. 'My head is throbbing like Hades,' he said. 'Antipov's fault. He never wants to go to bed and he drinks like a fish. All Russians do, I expect. They've nothing else to occupy them on those long winter nights.' He took a sip of his champagne, grimaced. 'I don't really want this. I say, Doro. Shall we get it over with?'

Dorothea nodded. They were solemn now, the two of them, as Roderick took her arm. They walked side-by-side out of the day room without a backward glance. Eliza, motionless, watched them go. She felt she was being deserted. Would she always be left behind, a fixture like Polly in her cage?

She roused herself, was about to follow them when she noticed Roderick's abandoned glass. She reached for it on impulse, tasted the champagne, gulped it. Strange. Quite nice. Cool and fizzing in her mouth. Why did Dorothea dislike it so much?

She was seized by a sudden panic that they might leave without her. She flew down the stairs. But there they were on the last half-landing waiting beneath the portrait of the man in the white wig whose name was Sir George, an ancestor. They were looking back up the stairs. They had not forgotten her.

Roderick said, 'Ready?' and she nodded vigorously, her heart swelling within her.

Down they went. Cecily Somersby was waiting in the hall. Basford opened the front door. Mr Ordish handed Roderick his top hat. They stepped out into the sunshine. At the foot of the steps was the motor car, the all-modern

Mark IV, sleek and black, wonderfully elegant with its simple lines and square edges, shining as if it had just this moment issued from the factory at Allibone Road.

The chauffeur opened the doors and doffed his cap — and suddenly Dorothea was laughing and reaching up to kiss his cheek. 'Stan! It's you! What a wonderful surprise! But I thought you'd given up chauffeuring for good?'

'I couldn't resist, miss: one last opportunity to drive you. I wouldn't have passed it up for the world.'

The motor accelerated down the drive. They turned onto the road. The hedgerows were in full leaf. The wheat in Corner Field was ripening in the sun. Breasting the rise, they swept down into the village. Dorothea held Roderick's hand the whole way.

In the blink of an eye they were pulling up by the lych-gate. A crowd had gathered here, outside the churchyard. More people were watching from the Green. Eliza stepped down, self-conscious, from the motor. She could see Johnnie Cheeseman standing tiptoe, peering over someone's shoulder, looking at her with his mouth agape as if he couldn't believe his eyes.

An old woman detached herself from the crowd and tottered forward: Mother Franklin from down Back Lane, toothless and wrinkled and holding in her gnarled hand a little bunch of hedgerow flowers. Dorothea had tears in her eyes took the flowers. She kissed the old lady, first one cheek, then the other.

The lychgate was open. As Dorothea passed under the little roof on Roderick's arm, applause broke out amongst the crowd. There were cries of, 'Good luck, Miss Dorothea! Best wishes!'

Eliza with Cecily brought up the rear as they walked up the little path. By the church porch, they came to a halt.

Roderick turned to Dorothea. His dark eyes were like deep wells. 'Suppose I decide not to give you away? Suppose I decide to keep you for myself?'

Eliza could not always tell when Roderick was teasing. His deadpan expression gave nothing away. Dorothea

116

searched his face as if she too wasn't sure. Certainly she looked in no mood for jokes. *Green about the gills*, Daisy would have said.

'Oh, Roddy! I wish it was all over!'

'Nearly there now. The last lap. Come on.'

They arranged themselves. Eliza felt giddy as she took her place behind Dorothea and Roderick. Cecily next to her was red as a beetroot. The church door was open wide, ready to receive them. In they went.

It took a moment for Eliza's eyes to adjust. The church was always gloomy, always bone-chillingly cold, never more than half-full. But as the deep, melodious sound of the organ washed around her, she gazed in wonder at the sight before her. Sunshine slanted in rainbow colours through the stained glass windows. Every seat was taken. The mellow air was richly scented with an abundance of flowers.

There came a collective sigh from the congregation as Dorothea began her walk up the aisle. People were packed together in rows. The clothes grew ever more opulent nearer the front. Men had their hair combed and cut and brilliantined. Women wore hats with ribbons and with veils, with flowers and fake fruit. There was one vast hat like a galleon in full sail that could only belong to Mrs Somersby.

The genial old vicar was waiting by the chancel, a beaming smile on his face. There, too, was Johann with his brother, both facing away, Johann spotless and elegant in his frock coat. Rainbow sunshine glinted on his golden hair as he turned to look over his shoulder, grave and modest and well-proportioned. *The consummate man*, said Eliza to herself. She was not sure what the words meant, whether she'd overheard someone using them or whether she'd made them up herself. Somehow they seemed to fit: the consummate man.

She felt she should hate him for taking Dorothea away but that wasn't possible. *He is too nice and kind and noble*, she told herself. *But I won't ever know him properly, I won't get the chance. How I wish that . . .*

But what did she wish for? Words piled up higgledy-piggledy inside her head and she could no longer sort the wheat from the chaff.

They are going to be married. They are going to be married in this magical palace — for this is not a church but a palace in the sky, a palace perched on high white clouds far, far above the earth. They will get married and then set off. They will set sail in Mrs Somersby's hat. They will sail off into the wide blue yonder in Mrs Somersby's galleon-hat while I, I, I will be left alone here to fade and wither with all these flowers . . .

She wanted to laugh at such silliness. She wanted to laugh out loud. She wanted to cry too. She was brimming over. She couldn't breathe.

Dorothea took the place on Johann's left. The music suddenly stopped. The echoes died away. There was an expectant hush. Eliza felt the sorcerer's glass slicing into her heart: slicing and slicing and slicing.

She wondered how she would ever be able to bear it.

* * *

The house had come alive. Every door, every window was open. Eliza drifted from room to room. There were people wherever she turned. There were a hundred different conversations all taking place at once.

'My dear! Isn't it extraordinary? Clifton can't have seen such a gathering since Old Harry's day. But of course, you won't remember Old Harry, Mrs Brannan's father. You're too young. He was a gentleman of the old school. Famous for his parties. This was — oh — thirty years ago and more.'

'Wonderful situation for a house. Splendid view. The canal, I suppose, must be over there somewhere. And is that — yes — Ingleby Wood. A glorious afternoon. They've been so lucky with the weather, given the summer we've had: so disappointing after last year. Imagine leaving all this behind! Imagine leaving England! The colonies are one thing — but Germany!'

'That's Miss Ryan for you. A singular sort of girl. Always has been. Even so, one has really grown rather fond of her.'

'She certainly seems popular. So many people have come! But tell me, do: who is that gentleman over by the pianoforte?'

'Wait one second . . . my spectacles . . . ah, yes, now that's the bridegroom's father. A doctor, I'm told. Quite charming, for a German. That boy with him is his younger son.'

'Not nearly as handsome as his brother but I can see the family resemblance. But what about that young man over to the right? There seems something odd about him. Is it his eyes, perhaps . . . ?'

'It's no wonder you think him odd, my dear. He's Russian. A friend of the family. Mrs Brannan's son met him at Oxford, I believe — Oxford, of all places!'

'He met him where? I didn't quite hear, with all this noise, and with Colonel Harding talking at the top of his voice: I am sure one could hear him halfway to Lawham. Isn't that his youngest daughter over there by the fire screen?'

'By the fire screen . . . ah, yes, you're right, that's Miss Eileen Harding. And that's Mrs Somersby's son she is talking to. They *do* seem engrossed. But you see the gentleman to their left? That's Mr Smith. He designs motor vehicles. He and the late Mr Brannan were in partnership. There's a factory, I understand, in Coventry. I don't care for motors myself — noisy, smelly things — but they are quite the rage just now. The family business, so the rumours go, is worth a small fortune.'

'Isn't Henry Fitzwilliam involved in all that, the Brannan motor business? I'm surprised he isn't here today.'

'Oh, but my dear, hush! Didn't you know? Henry Fitzwilliam was quite besotted with Miss Ryan at one time, made a proposal of marriage which was refused. I expect he can't bear to see her happy with another. Not many people know all this, of course, but as you know, I'm intimately acquainted with the family.'

'Perhaps then, as an intimate acquaintance, you could tell me about the — ahem — how to put this delicately?

— the *certain people* I've seen about the place, the people who look as if they are wearing their slightly shabby Sunday best? Who, for instance, is that woman over by the french doors?'

'Ah, well, *she* used to be a maidservant here at Clifton, so I'm reliably informed. Miss Ryan invited her. You know Miss Ryan. Her endearing little ways.'

'All the same, there are limits, or there ought to be. People of that sort — maidservants — are not really cut out for an occasion like this. They don't know how to behave in polite society. They are not born with the social graces. One has only to look at her hat; and as for the man with her . . .'

* * *

'They're talking about us, Nora, I'm sure they are.'

'Get on with you, Arnie. Who'd want to talk about *you*?'

'Like that, is it? Time was you thought me rather a handsome chap.'

'If you're fishing for compliments, Arnold Carter, you can fish elsewhere. I've a bone to pick with you. I was relying on you to get that misery guts of a brother of yours up to the big house. Miss Dorothea was most upset not to see him.'

'You know our Nibs, Nora. Stubborn as a mule. "Too many posh toffs all in one place," he said.'

'I'll give him "posh toffs" when I see him! But never mind that now. Here's Miss Dorothea coming down the stairs in her going-away clothes. We must see her off.'

* * *

Tides of people flowed into the hallway and out down the steps. Eliza was swept along with them, following in the wake Mrs Somersby's hat which sailed serenely above the sea of faces. The servants were lined up on the gravel. Dorothea was taking her leave of them. Cook was in floods of tears, Basford standing on his dignity biting his lip, Mr Ordish — but no one ever noticed Mr Ordish. Mrs Bourne was misty-eyed as she watched Dorothea go along the line. (The Dreadnought, shedding a tear? Was it possible?)

The old gardener Becket, white-haired and weather-worn, pressed Dorothea's hand between his own gnarled hands. 'Place won't be the same without you, Miss Dorothea. No one else takes such an interest in the gardens as you do. But by gum, you've had a good send-off! All this to-do puts me in mind of Christmas in the old days. We'd stand in a line just like this and old Mr Rycroft would give out presents. There'd be dancing after, and a barrel of beer. We had a rum old time. It all stopped, though, when Master Frederick became master. There were no more presents, no more beer. I don't think his missus approved on it.'

'Oh Becket!' said Dorothea, crying, laughing. 'What will I do without you and all your stories of the old days?'

There were goodbyes and goodbyes and goodbyes. Last of all the family stepped forward: Roderick, then Mama, and Eliza after everyone else. She couldn't see for the tears that were falling. She couldn't think what to say. And already it was too late. Young Stan had the motor ready under the cedar tree. Johann handed Dorothea in, got in beside her. The door slammed. The car began to move. It's slow, heavy tyres crunched on the gravel. The crowd surged forward in the July sunshine. There was a chorus of goodbyes and good lucks. Rice was thrown, and confetti, and satin slippers. People were waving. They were crying.

Eliza in the crush found herself next to Daisy and Daisy's elder sister, the sister who had once been Nora the nursery maid but who was now Mrs Arnold Carter of Coventry, rather plump and amiable and bred with none of the social graces. She was crying unabashed in her second-hand hat as the motor disappeared down the drive and waving her hand-kerchief like a mad thing.

'To think what a scarecrow she looked when she first came and nothing to wear but rags!' sobbed Mrs Carter. 'I had to get our Billy to fetch up an old frock of mine for something to put her in. She was never any trouble. Good as gold, she was.'

Po-faced Daisy wrinkled her nose. 'You know the old saying, Nora. "Married in July with flowers ablaze, bitter-sweet memories in after days."'

'Oh Daisy, really!' cried Mrs Carter, dabbing her cheeks with her handkerchief. 'What a thing to think of at a moment like this!'

The sound of the motor had long faded. Everyone had made their way back indoors. Eliza was left standing alone on the gravel. She felt her heart had been torn out. She was sure she would never get over it.

* * *

'How very vexing!' exclaimed Mama over lunch two days later. Mr Ordish had just brought in a telegram. Mama was reading it. 'The new governess says she can't now take the position after all.'

Since the house was now empty of guests (except Mr Antipov), Eliza had been permitted to eat downstairs. The new governess would once have been of considerable interest to her but nothing mattered now that Dorothea had gone.

Mama put the telegram aside, returned her attention to her red mullet. 'I do wish people wouldn't let one down. And to leave it to the last moment — so *very* inconvenient. I shall have to leave you in charge of your sister this afternoon, Roderick. I'm due at the vicarage about the church fête and it's Turner's half-day, so there won't be anyone in the nursery.'

'Sorry, Mother.' Roderick, chewing his fish, spoke out of the corner of his mouth. 'Sorry, I can't, not this afternoon. Miss Halsted is arriving by train. I have to be at Welby to meet her.'

'Miss Halsted. Of course. I'd forgotten.'

'Don't worry, Mother. Antipov can keep an eye on Eliza. He was going to come to the station but there's really no need. He can make himself useful instead.'

Mama looked rather dubious. Nor did Mr Antipov seem entirely happy. He said, however, 'Is great pleasure, Mrs Brannan. I am glad to be of service.'

And so it was settled.

* * *

Eliza looked at her reflection in the mirror. With Daisy on her half-day, it had been necessary to dress herself. In her new embroidered skirt and with an old parasol of Dorothea's held at a rakish angle, she looked every inch a young lady.

She was going on a walk with Mr Antipov: his own suggestion. Ordinarily she might have resented being parcelled out by Mama and Roderick but when it was Mr Antipov . . . ! Her heart was beating fast. She was excited and apprehensive in equal measure.

There was one big problem. What would they talk about? The problem grew ever more acute as they made their way down the drive and emerged from the shade of the evergreens into the heat and sunshine of the Lawham Road. Mr Antipov was no help. He was strangely quiet and kept looking over his shoulder as if he would rather be back at the house. Or was it . . . could it be . . . was he thinking of Miss Halsted arriving by train at Welby station?

They went on in silence. The hedgerows were running riot. Windrows of hay were drying in the fields. The canal glinted in the bright sunlight. The long road stretched ahead, dusty and deserted. Of all the places to walk! They could have been strolling across the meadows on their way to the village; they could have been leisurely climbing Rookery Hill. What had she been thinking, coming this way? She hadn't been thinking, that was the trouble. Oh, misery! Misery!

They came after what seemed an age to the place where the road dipped down under the railway, the branch line to Leamington. Mr Antipov halted in the shade of the brick-built bridge.

'Perhaps we go back now, Miss Brannan? You are tired, yes?'

'Oh no! Not yet!' She couldn't bear it, to go back to Clifton with the walk having come to nothing. She would feel such a failure.

In her desperation she thought of Lawham, she tried to interest him in Lawham with its shops and Market Place and the ruins of the old priory.

'I would like to see these ruins,' said Mr Antipov. 'I have interest in your English history. But you look a little pale. This town is too far, perhaps? The heat is too much?'

'I'm not hot at all! I'm cool, quite cool! And Lawham's very near! We're almost there!' If she could just show him the ruins she would have accomplished something, the walk would have been saved from disaster.

They went on. They toiled up the rise into Lawham. They came to Market Place. The town was quiet and somnolent in the afternoon heat. The tall, pointed spire of the church was sharply delineated against the blue of the sky.

Disappointment awaited. The ruins had vanished, along with the grassy space around them. All that was left was a piece of churned up earth and some wooden stakes hammered into the ground.

'The old priory, miss?' said a passing woman when appealed to. 'Oh, that was knocked down months ago and the stones carted off. The old school is being demolished too and we're to have a new one where the priory ruins used to be. A brand new school: imagine that!'

The sense of failure was crushing. She had brought Mr Antipov all this way for nothing. How different this place had been only last summer, on a rare visit to Lawham so that Roderick could see his tailor. Eliza remembered playing amongst the crumbling walls of the priory. Dorothea had sat on the old stump of an arch reading a letter.

The thought of Dorothea made her heart lurch and she suddenly found she was crying — crying in front of Mr Antipov! This was appalling. The ultimate humiliation.

But, oh, what did it matter? She had been fooling herself to think she could look like a lady. She hated her silly skirt, the preposterous parasol. She covered her face with her hands and sobbed.

'Please! Miss Brannan! Do not cry!' He prised her hands away. He was squatting on his haunches. His grey eyes peered anxiously up at her. 'What is wrong? What is it that has made you so unhappy?' He wiped her tears very gently with his fingers.

To her complete surprise and almost before she was aware, Eliza found herself telling him everything: how much she missed Dorothea; how the nursery was a lonely place now; how she was nothing but a nuisance, in the way, nobody wanted her. She told him all about London and how it haunted her, how she couldn't forget what she'd seen. She even told him about the kitten, the poor, dead kitten, and how she dreamt about it night after night: she'd told no one this, not even Dorothea. She was not sure quite what else she said or if it made any sense. She was not sure that Mr Antipov understood any of it. 'I can't . . . I don't . . . everything is . . . why do I feel so . . . oh, I wish, I wish . . .'

It seemed like madness to be pouring her heart out in the middle of Market Place. But he didn't seem to mind. He listened, he wiped her tears, his eyes never left hers, he didn't seem to care that people might be watching.

At length she had nothing left. She was empty. She gave one last sob, shuddered, fell silent.

'Well, Miss Brannan — or may I call you Elizabeth? That is your name, yes? In Russian is *Elizaveta*, *Leeza* for short. And I am *Nikolai*: you say *Nicholas* in English. My friends call me *Kolya*. You must call me Kolya too.'

'M-m-may I? May I really?' Such privilege!

He stood up. 'We go back now, yes? We talk as we go. Is good, I think, to walk and talk.'

He took her hand in his. She held it shyly, a man's hand, a Russian hand; he had long, bony fingers. They walked down the hill leaving the town behind. The sun warmed her. The countryside was green and quiet. She listened to Mr Antipov talking. She listened to his low-pitched voice, his strange accent. The meaning of his words only slowly sank in: she was always one step behind, trying to catch up. But she didn't worry about that. Somehow she knew she was storing it all up for later.

It seemed incongruous to be walking along the familiar Lawham Road with this stranger from another land. Why was he here? She felt bold enough now to ask.

'I have interest in England. Is most advanced country. I wish to see for myself. Since coming here, I am liking England and English people. I have become *Anglophile*. My father was eager for me to study in England. I will behave myself in England, he thinks. In Russia I get into trouble. My name is perhaps known to the secret police.'

'Why? Are . . . are you a . . . a *criminal*?'

'In Russia, is a crime to express your opinion.'

'But you are safe in England — safe from the secret police?'

'I do not know. Maybe the Okhrana has agents even in Oxford.'

They had reached Ingleby Wood which stretched away on their left in the angle of land between the road and the canal. Were there perhaps secret police spies lurking in the shadow of the trees, peering out at them? But even her imagination couldn't conjure up such things in the peace of the golden afternoon.

She stumbled, weary, and Mr Antipov immediately halted. 'We will rest a while, I think, here in the shade.'

He took off his jacket and spread it for her under the eaves of the wood. He sat down on the grass next to her, removing his cap and pulling from his pocket a ubiquitous book. Drawing up his knees, balancing the book on them, he began to read.

The dusty road sloped gently here down to the canal bridge. The hedge on the opposite side was lush with leaves and tangled with blossom. Grass grew thickly on the verge.

Above, thin, ragged clouds were smeared across the sky. The sun glowed brightly through them in the peace of the afternoon. The peace soaked into her. A fragile calm took hold.

Yawning, she lay back looking up at the trees and the sky through the twisted branches of an old blackthorn. A spider's web shimmered in the sunlight. Eliza picked out the spider who'd made it, sheltering in the lee of a leaf, one tiny leg poised against a silken thread. She watched the spider as it waited with infinite patience, unmoving; she watched and her eyelids grew heavy, her head grew muzzy.

Before long she was fast asleep.

* * *

An angry buzzing pervaded her dreams. The sound drew her slowly to the surface. She passed imperceptibly from sleeping to waking.

The buzzing grew more frenzied. She opened her eyes. Above her, a wasp was trapped in the web. It was struggling to free itself but only to become ever more tangled. Swift and agile, the spider came running along the stretched-out threads and set upon the wasp. A fierce battle was joined.

The wasp was doomed, thought Eliza. Or was it? As she watched, somehow the wasp found a way to break free. The spider turned suddenly from predator to prey. Bundling it up, the wasp flexed its wings and took off, swooping up and quickly away, carrying the spider to an unknown fate. The buzzing sound faded. The web remained, torn, tattered, abandoned.

Eliza lay still, shaken by such savagery. What would become of the poor spider? Where was it being taken? And to think that at first she had felt sorry for the wasp, helplessly meshed in the web!

She thought of the kitten, she had felt sorry for the kitten too. And yet, earlier, Mr Antipov had said — she frowned, trying to remember — he had said that she ought also to feel sorry for the boys who'd tormented it to death.

But that couldn't be right. The kitten was not like the wasp. The kitten hadn't been able to turn the tables. So what did Mr Antipov mean?

She sat up. Mr Antipov was asleep, stretched out on the grass. Dappled shade shimmered over him, over his threadbare clothes, his round, ordinary face, his tumbled, flaxen hair. Who was he? What did she really know about him?

His name was Nikolai. He came from Russia. He was twenty-two, younger than Johann, older than Roderick, not as handsome as either — and different, so very different. She'd never met anyone like him. Almost she wanted to pinch herself, to be sure she wasn't dreaming, to be sure he was real. Almost she wanted to touch him, to brush back the lock of hair that had fallen across his forehead, to hold again his hand as she'd held it in walking from Lawham.

She touched instead his well-worn cap lying on the grass. She picked up his book where it had fallen from his outstretched hand. A piece of torn newspaper fell out that he used as a bookmark. There was a news story ringed in red ink, something about the Lena goldfields. It sounded so picturesque — the *goldfields* — but the article was all about death: *107 shot dead . . . 84 have since died . . . 210 wounded . . .*

She tucked the piece of paper back inside the book then began to turn the pages. She'd expected to see those strange Russian hieroglyphs that were impossible to decipher but she found that the book was actually in English. Mr Antipov as usual had been writing in the margins, had underlined words and passages. Slowly she began to read.

'. . . *there are those who still insist in telling us that the conquest of power in the state, by the people, will suffice to accomplish the social revolution! — that the old machine, the old organisation, slowly developed in the course of history to crush freedom, to crush the individual, to establish oppression on a legal basis, to create monopolists, to lead minds astray by accustoming them to servitude — will lend itself perfectly to its new function: that it will become the instrument, the framework for the germination of new life, to found freedom and equality on economic bases, the destruction of monopolies, the awakening of society*

128

and towards the achievement of a future freedom and equality! What a sad and tragic mistake!

'"What a sad and tragic mistake",' she murmured. What did it all mean? Was Mr Antipov so clever he could understand it? She wished she was clever too. She wished she could understand things. But she was just a girl who nobody wanted, a girl trapped forever in the nursery at Clifton Park.

'I do not think, Leeza, that your mother would approve of your reading Kropotkin.'

She started and looked up. He was awake. He was lying there and watching.

Hurriedly she put the book aside. She was almost as embarrassed as if she'd been caught touching him as she'd wanted. She could feel herself colouring up under the gaze of his intense eyes. And yet were they really so terrible, his eyes? Pale grey and shining, keen and clear, there was a transparency about them that was disturbing but not alarming — as if, could you only learn how to read what was written there, you'd know him completely.

'What is it, Leeza? Why are you frowning?'

'I . . . I don't understand you. What you said about those boys. *They* should have died, not the kitten. They were horrible — evil!'

'No one is truly evil, Leeza.' He sat up, took hold of the book, opened it, searching. 'Listen: "The defeated, the incurious, the bellicose, the spiteful: these are examples of social pathology caused by prisons, slums, armies, insidious class distinction, want, and demeaning toil." Now do you understand? If you, Leeza, lived like those boys, if you had none of your nice things around you—'

'I could never be like them, never!'

'Cruelty lurks in the heart of everyone, Leeza. We are all animals. We have animal instincts. Is how we rise above our instincts that makes us different. This is battle each of us must fight alone. We must fight tyranny of our own natures before we fight the tyrannies of the world. We must learn to be heroes in our own lives.'

'But ordinary people aren't heroes! Heroes are people like . . . like Wellington and Nelson and General Gordon.' These were names that had been constantly on Roderick's lips once-upon-a-time.

'Those men are not real heroes, Leeza. They are not men who have built the British Empire. Your Empire was built by coal miners, by iron smelters, by factory workers, by able seamen.'

'Coal miners!' She looked at him in wonder. Miners were a national disgrace, everyone knew that. They had been on strike earlier in the year, they had made the trains run late. They weren't *heroes*.

'Just think, Leeza. Think. Every day from age of twelve or thirteen, every day for fifty years, miners go down into the dark. They work by candlelight. They choke on dust. They are killed in pit falls. How often do they see sun and grass? How often do they breathe fresh air and listen to birds sing? And yet without them — without the coal they dig — factories would not work, trains and ships would not go, there would be no winter fire in your nursery. Is it not a brave and noble sacrifice that they make? Yet all the reward they get is a few shillings a week as their health is slowly destroyed. Meanwhile, mine owners live off profits and never do day's work in their lives! Is this good? Is this right? Is this the spirit of fellowship and cooperation?'

Eliza stared at him. Coal, ordinary coal, which Daisy brought up from the cellar as a matter of course: was it really the stuff of heroism?

Mr Antipov broke into a grin. 'I am sorry, Leeza. I am carried away. Is that correct idiom, *carried away*? I can never keep opinions to myself. You see now why secret police take interest.' He jumped up, jamming on his cap, pocketing his book. 'Now I think we must go or we will be late for your English tea time.'

He held out his hand, he helped her to her feet, he picked up his jacket and slung it over his shoulder.

Eliza sighed as they took to the road again. 'Clifton won't be the same when you've all gone away. Doro's gone, you will go soon, Roddy will go back to Oxford. Life will be so dull.'

But Kolya squeezed her hand and said, 'Life is never dull, Leeza, unless you make it that way. Life is never dull. You will see!'

CHAPTER SIX

Miss Halsted arrived at Clifton, stayed a week, departed. Mr Antipov — Kolya — also took his leave. 'Life is never dull,' he'd said. For him maybe. For Eliza the days dragged and the weeks stretched on, interminable. Nothing happened. The nursery was silent, lonely; there was only Polly for company, and Daisy when she wasn't busy elsewhere. The beautiful weather during the week of Dorothea's wedding now seemed almost unreal as a cold, miserable August gave way to a cold, miserable September.

Roderick was next to go, heading back to Oxford. The day after, the new governess arrived: a grey-haired, pinch-faced, humourless woman. She was a poor substitute for Dorothea but the best Mama could do.

'It is becoming impossible to get hold of good servants,' Mama complained. 'I am still a maid short. Heaven knows where I will find one.'

Dorothea herself now existed only in letters and post-cards. Eliza used them to track her cousin's progress as the newlyweds retraced the steps of the continental holiday two years ago. Eliza and Roderick had been Dorothea's companions back then. Now she was with Johann. The happy couple went first to France, to the village where Mlle Lacroix lived, Dorothea's old governess. (If only it was possible to find another governess as nice as the Mam'zelle!) Johann was introduced to Mlle Lacroix and approved of, and several blissful days were spent in the heart of the French country-side, after which the newlyweds went on to Switzerland to stay in the very same Gasthaus (or pension) where they had first met. Finally they made the journey to Hamburg and Dorothea's new home. Here, as the only woman, Dorothea took up a new role as mistress of the house. She had not only Johann to look after, but Dr Kaufmann, Siegfried and cousin Gerhard too. The other cousin, Heinrich — the one Eliza remembered from Switzerland — was a frequent vis-itor along with his wife, two daughters and new baby son. The two little girls, Dorothea reported, were lovely creatures, clever and charming and adorable. 'Her new favourites,' said Eliza bitterly. When would Dorothea give her old friends a thought and come back on a visit?

'Goodness, miss, she's only just left!' said Daisy. 'She'll want to settle in, I expect, and get used to her new home. Besides, it must be a fair step from here to Hamburg. It takes long enough to get to Northampton. Heaven knows what it's like to travel all the way to Germany!' Daisy, in fact, was quite well aware of what it was to travel. She had accompa-nied them on the continental holiday two years ago. But she had hated it so much that she liked now to pretend that it had never happened.

Distance was one thing. There were dangers too. The world was a perilous place. There were icebergs, earthquakes and epidemics; there were train smashes and motor accidents; there was the threat of distant war. A new war began that autumn in which Bulgarians, Greeks, Serbians and Turks fought one another in places called Thrace, Salonika and Kumanovo. Eliza was not sure who was on whose side nor where the places were. Nowhere near Northamptonshire, she knew that much, but perhaps near Hamburg? She couldn't look it up because the map book had been confiscated. Soon *The Times* was forbidden too — forbidden apart from carefully selected clippings which the new governess cut out neatly with scissors. The new governess was of the opinion that Eliza's education up to now had been decidedly lax and far too haphazard. There had been an excess of history and geography at the expense of more suitable subjects such as sewing, embroidery, table manners, polite conversation and deportment. Gone were the days when Eliza could while away a lazy afternoon bent over the map book looking for places with exotic names (Timbuktu). Now she had to sit up straight and read the clippings out loud, taking particular care with her diction (whatever that might be).

'"The British motor manufacturer",,' Eliza read, '"will lose a valuable market to foreign imports unless he produces small cars as good and cheap as those from abroad. "'

'This article has a bearing on the family business,' said the governess crisply. 'One should always be able to converse on the subject of the family business.'

Or again, '"It has been announced that George Pelham Huntley, Seventh Earl of Denecote, passed away yesterday at the age of ninety-seven."'

'Lord Denecote was a relative of the family.' The governess sounded most prim, as if Lord Denecote had been a relative of *hers*. Eliza was sure that she herself had never heard of such a person.

Eliza at first did her best to be friendly and obliging in a way that Dorothea would have approved of. As *The Times* was considered unsuitable, might they not take the *Daily Mirror* instead? (The *Daily Mirror* was in any case preferable as it had pictures.) But the governess looked down her nose and said that the *Daily Mirror* was a publication for the semi-literate and would never be found in a respectable home. Besides, it was not *seemly* for a young lady to be seen reading a newspaper. It gave quite the wrong impression. Now, would Miss Elizabeth *please* sit still and finish her sampler? It ought to have been finished years ago if there'd been any sort of structure to her development.

'I don't want to make a sampler!' cried Eliza, venting her frustrations at Daisy when the governess was safely out of the way. 'I don't want to be developed, I don't want to be seemly, I just want to be me!'

'It's all for your own good, I'm sure, miss,' said Daisy as she emptied the ashes and swept the grate, behindhand as always these days because they were still missing a maid downstairs and Daisy had to double up.

'Everything is forbidden, Daisy, everything! And I have to practice curtsying over and over, and walk around with books on my head, and learn Barnet and Tewkesbury and boring Bosworth in the right order!'

'What's Barnet and Bosworth got to do with the price of butter?'

'It's the Wars of the Roses. Proper history, *she* calls it. She's a—'

'Now, now, miss. Don't take on so. There's worse things happen at sea. If it's roses you're learning about, you'd best ask Becket. He knows more about roses than anyone.'

'Servitude, Daisy! That's what it is. Servitude and oppression. I want freedom and . . . and equality!'

'Do you, indeed!' Daisy cocked an eye at her. 'If I was you, miss, I'd spend less time flouncing about the place and more time minding my tongue.'

'I can't, Daisy, I can't! I do have opinions, you know! When you have opinions, you can't always keep them to yourself even if the secret police try to stop you!'

'I've never heard of no secret police in Hayton,' said Daisy. But she didn't realise what it was like. She didn't have to undergo the indignity of being summoned downstairs to perform like a circus animal for Mrs Somersby or Lady Fitzwilliam or whoever else had happened to call. Eliza was made to recite poetry or play the piano or show off her other 'accomplishments' (as the governess called them). Eliza hated playing the piano. She was all fingers and thumbs. Nothing she attempted to play ever sounded quite right. 'If you would only *apply* yourself, Miss Elizabeth,' the governess scolded, 'you might come to perform the pianoforte tolerably well.'

'*Apply yourself . . . pianoforte . . .*' Eliza mimicked the tyrant and the tyrant's habit of over-emphasising her words. The mimicry made Daisy giggle. But Eliza felt there was nothing to laugh about. She wondered how she could ever have found Clifton dull. The summer months after Dorothea's wedding had dragged at the time but now seemed like an oasis of peace and freedom. As for her life before Easter — before Johann's proposal, before Stepnall Street, before the kitten — it was a golden age that Eliza could scarcely believe in. She had never realised how lucky she was. And now it was all gone.

* * *

The governess decided that Eliza did not *mix* enough. She needed to mix with young ladies her own age. A series of visits was arranged. Eliza was dragged miles and miles across country to different houses and forced to socialize with dull, lumpy girls in various nurseries, while their governesses and nannies sat around gossiping and eating copious amounts of cake. Eliza despised the lumpy girls and all their stupid talk about frocks and ponies and whose mama said what and when. None of the girls were the least interested in hearing why coal miners were heroes and how cruelty lurked in the heart of everyone.

In the motor on the way home, the governess scolded Eliza for being aloof and told her she must make more of an effort. 'And,' she added sharply, pursing her lips, 'we'll have no more talk of miners, *if* you please!'

A sigh worked its way up from deep inside but Eliza swallowed it back: sighing was forbidden too.

* * *

The weeks dragged by. December came. Roderick arrived from Oxford, bringing Kolya and Miss Halsted. Eliza was permitted to go down to the drawing room to see them. She sat there with a feeling of dread, terrified lest the governess demand she display her *accomplishments*. Nothing would be more mortifying than to show herself up in front of the Russian and Miss Halsted.

Miss Halsted had a cold. It served her right, Roderick said, for standing in the rain all day at that by-election. (What was a by-election? Eliza didn't dare show her ignorance in such company by asking.)

'The by-election was weeks ago,' said Miss Halsted. 'In any case, a few sniffles would be a small price to pay in the cause of women's suffrage.'

'But all your efforts came to nothing,' said Roderick. 'Lansbury lost. People voted for the Tory standing on a ticket of Women Do Not Want The Vote.'

'Not people, Mr Brannan, men. Only men voted. It's typical of men that they should decide what women want without bothering to ask women themselves. But whatever the outcome, the by-election advanced our cause by bringing it to the attention of the public.'

'What about smashing windows and setting fire to pillar boxes?' said Roderick. 'Does that also advance your cause? Or is it just mindless destruction?'

Kolya broke in. 'Any method is justified that brings about downfall of rotten system. But by-election was mistake, I think.'

'How can you say that!' cried Miss Halsted, rounding on him. 'After all the hard work people put in, after all the public interest it aroused.'

'You are being particularist,' said Kolya. 'Women's suffrage is only part of problem. We must address whole problem. Only way is to change society. Miss Pankhurst — Miss Sylvia Pankhurst — she says this too. She understands.'

The argument raged. Miss Halsted was attacked from both sides, by Kolya for putting women's suffrage first, by Roderick for bothering with women's suffrage at all. Finally Mama said, 'For goodness sake, leave the poor girl alone! It's

bad enough that she feels unwell without you two tormenting her.'

Eliza was rather surprised by Mama's intervention.
Could it be that Mama felt sorry for Miss Halsted?

Later, in bed, lying sleepless, Eliza came round to thinking there might be more to it. Mama that afternoon had not
reigned over the drawing room in her usual sure-handed way.
She had lost control of the conversation as the argument
progressed. All attention had been on Miss Halsted instead
of the Perfect Hostess. Perhaps Mama knew as little about
by-elections and 'the cause' as Eliza. Perhaps she had been
out of her depth.

Eliza turned over and over, unable to get comforta-
ble. She wondered if she would get an opportunity to talk
to Kolya alone as she had in the summer. Kolya explained
things. He made you see differently. The nameless horror
that had haunted her after her return from London had
somehow been tamed by his words. The nightmare about
the kitten had stopped coming. She had been able to sleep
peacefully again.

She desperately wanted to tell him about the governess
— the tyrant. 'We must fight tyrannies,' he had said. But
how? Her only worry was, if she did speak to him, how could
she be sure she would not end up sounding like one of those
lumpy girls, bleating about their ponies being lame and their
lack of new frocks? If only she knew enough about society
and the rotten system to be able to talk with him the way
Miss Halsted did! It was impossible, however, at Clifton, to
learn anything of importance. The library had no books that
could help and when she'd asked if she might be permitted
to read Kropotkin, the governess had said that she'd never
heard of Kropotkin, that he sounded foreign, that foreign
authors were markedly inferior to English writers such as
Shakespeare and Dickens. However, it would be much better
if Miss Elizabeth did not get into the habit of *reading*. Being
bookish was a grave defect in a young lady. Young gentlemen
did not care for girls who were bookish.

Eliza ground her teeth in the dark of her room. Why should she care what young gentlemen thought? Why shouldn't women read books if they wanted? Why, for that matter, shouldn't they have the vote?

But this thought was rather disturbing. Somehow she'd reached a point where she was in sympathy with some of Miss Halsted's ideas. She was not at all sure that she wanted to be in sympathy with Miss Halsted.

Eliza shut her eyes and tried to sleep, counting sheep in her head. But the sheep all ran off in different directions and they refused to come back be counted no matter how much she shouted and stamped her feet.

* * *

When the governess's back was turned, Eliza ran off and went downstairs in the hope of finding Kolya. She found instead Roderick and Miss Halsted talking in the billiard room. She lingered outside the billiard room door, listening.

'Why won't you stay?' Roderick was saying. 'I want you to stay!'

'I stayed last year,' said Miss Halsted. 'This year I must spend Christmas with my family.'

'Your family!' sneered Roderick. 'Those aunts you despise.'

'I don't *despise* them. You are putting words in my mouth. Please leave me alone. I don't feel well. Having you bully me is not helping at all.'

'Leave you alone? Yes, you'd like that, wouldn't you!' There was a nastiness in Roderick's voice which was rather unpleasant to hear and made Eliza think of all the times when she too had been bullied by her brother. She found herself almost feeling sorry for Miss Halsted. 'I suppose you're saving yourself for Antipov now,' he added harshly.

'I don't know what you mean.'

'You must know that Antipov is in love with you.'

'I . . . *ah* . . . *ahh* . . . *atchoo*! I know nothing of the sort. Kolya and I are friends, nothing more.'

'Perhaps we should tell him about last Thursday.'

'That was a mistake.'

'So I'm a mistake, now, am I?'

'I didn't say that. All I meant was — oh, I don't know what I meant. I can't think when my head is aching like this. I wish you'd go away — you, Kolya, everybody. Men are all the same, making demands, riding roughshod.'

'If *that's* how you feel—'

'There's no need to—'

' — then I won't bother you again!'

'Roderick, please, wait—'

But he didn't wait. He came storming out of the billiard room taking Eliza completely by surprise. He paused, looked at her with blazing eyes.

'You! What are you doing here?'

'I — I—'

He brushed past her, stalked out of the drawing room, slammed the door behind him.

A moment later, Miss Halsted emerged from the billiard room, slow and hesitant as if unsure of herself — and who wouldn't be after being shouted at by Roderick! She looked in her highly-coloured clothes rather like a bright-plumed tropical bird: there was even a feather in her hair. Dark-haired, olive-skinned, she presented a rather exotic appearance when compared with the staid surroundings of the drawing room. If she was surprised to see Eliza, she didn't show it.

'Your brother can be so overbearing.' She sneezed. She seemed in that instant very fragile, laid low by her cold and by Roderick's bullying. But then she managed a smile. 'Are you looking forward to Christmas? I'm sure you will have a jolly time of it!'

As if speaking to a little girl, thought Eliza resentfully. Any compassion she had felt for Miss Halsted drained away. She drew herself up. 'I am not a child,' she said coldly.

Miss Halsted appeared taken aback. Her eyes met Eliza's. Her expression slowly changed. 'No,' she said slowly as if feeling her way toward some new discovery. 'No, you're not. I see that now. I'm sorry. I should have known better.'

She was talking now as if to an equal. But in what way were they equals, Eliza wondered: equal in enmity?

Eliza turned away, confused, finding it impossible to hate Miss Halsted but finding it impossible to like her either. 'I'm . . . I'm going upstairs,' she said.

She left Miss Halsted alone in the drawing room.

* * *

Miss Halsted departed, heading for Tonbridge and her aunts. On Christmas Eve, the governess packed her case too and went off to spend Christmas with her brother and his family (they were welcome to her). That evening, Eliza ate dinner alone with only Polly for company. There were guests downstairs and she was not wanted. She found herself envying the lumpy girls who at least had each other. The nursery seemed very drab and silent. The fire was a mess of glowing coals. Clothes were drying on the fender.

Eliza pushed her plate away. She had no appetite.

Daisy came at length to take the tray away. She'd been working downstairs most of the day on Mrs Bourne's orders.

'Goodness, miss, you *are* an old misery this evening! You've a face like a wet blanket and you've not even touched your steamed pudding.'

'I don't want it. You have it.'

'Well . . .' Daisy eyed the steamed pudding and custard. 'It *does* seem a shame to waste it.' Quickly she sat at the table and pulled the bowl towards her. 'Ooh, miss, this is heaven! There's nothing can beat Cook's steamed pudding! Are you sure you don't want some?'

Eliza shook her head and gave a heartfelt sigh. She was free to sigh now that the governess was out of the way, just as Daisy was free to sit and eat steamed pudding.

'I don't want pudding. I don't know what I want, Daisy.'

Daisy looked at her shrewdly, licking the spoon. 'It gets you like that sometimes, miss.'

'Like what?'

'Like you're all at sea. Like you don't know what you're looking for. Then, out the blue, you find that what you wanted was right under your nose the whole time.'

Something in Daisy's words aroused Eliza's interest. 'Have *you* found something under your nose, Daisy?' she asked curiously.

Daisy looked smug. 'That's for me to know and you to find out.' She stood up, wiping a blob of custard off her chin. 'If you're sure you've finished, miss, I'll take these crocks down to the kitchen.'

* * *

'We are rather diminished this year,' said Mama as they sat down to Christmas luncheon, just the four of them: Eliza, Mama, Roderick and Kolya. It was mild and miserable outside, the sky grey, spots of rain on the window.

'Is delicious food, Mrs Brannan,' said Kolya. 'I enjoy immensely. Is that correct word, *immensely*?'

Eliza looked sidelong at Kolya as she spread bread sauce over her slices of turkey. She had been rather wary of him these last few days. She had begun to wonder if she really knew him at all. Was it true that he was in love with Miss Halsted as Roderick claimed? Surely he was too sensible for that! And Miss Halsted was so off-putting, so very serious and self-sufficient, not lovable at all.

Pushing her Brussels sprouts from one side of the plate to the other, Eliza was reminded of last Easter, seeing Roderick kiss Miss Halsted in the hallway at 28 Essex Square. She had not expected that, either. She had thought that Roderick would scoff at something as soft and silly as love.

'More plum pudding, Mr Antipov?' said Mama. The dinner was drawing to a close. 'I am so sorry,' she added, 'that you must leave us tomorrow. The house is beginning to feel rather empty.'

* * *

Love! How she hated love!

Eliza in the day room sat slumped in the chair by the window (her posture would have scandalised the governess), twisting a lock of hair round her finger. Love was a disease just like Miss Halsted's cold. Those under its spell obviously saw Miss Halsted as someone mysterious, alluring, desirable. Love made Kolya seem a stranger. Love drove Roderick to kiss Miss Halsted in the hallway at 28 Essex Square, and to bully her in the billiard room here at Clifton. Was there any cure for love?

It was love, too, that had taken Dorothea away.

'People can't help falling in love,' said Daisy. 'It's just one of those things.' She paused, blew out her cheeks, began swinging her shoulders from side to side. Suddenly, as if it was bursting out of her, a smile wreathed her face and her eyes shone. She said in a breathless rush, 'Oh, miss, you mustn't breathe a word, but I'm stuck on Susie Hobson's brother: I've fallen for Zack Hobson!' She ended on a dramatic flourish as if confessing to some unspeakable crime.

'Is it bad, then, to be in love with Zack Hobson?'

'Terrible bad, miss! I don't know what I'm to do! Those Hobsons, they're the ones everyone looks down on. They're poor as poor. Their dad's out of work as often as not. Their mum borrows bits and pieces all round the village — a pinch of tea or a screw of sugar — and she never pays it back. My dad would string me up if he knew. He'd rather die than have a daughter in company with a Hobson. But — oh — miss: *Zack*!' She was all goo-eyed over him as if he was the last word in boys.

Even the nursery, it seemed, was not safe from the ravages of love.

Who was Zack Hobson? Eliza had a vague recollection of a boy a few years older than herself, a rather thin and scrawny boy, a boy with bare feet, a snotty nose and a tattered shirt — a bit like the boys she'd seen in Stepnall Street. But she'd not seen Zack Hobson in quite a while. Perhaps he'd changed since then. But could he really be so wonderful?

'You mustn't breathe a word of this to anyone, miss.'

'Of course I won't, Daisy!'

'You mustn't even mention it to Susie, his sister. She'll only go blabbing, if I know Susie.' Daisy gave a heartfelt sigh. 'She don't know when she's well off, that Susie Hobson. Nibs Carter worships the ground she walks on. I know he's a bit of a grump, and he's ever so touchy, but nobody would ever say that a Carter weren't good enough. Nobody looks down on the Carters, for all that they're poor. But instead of counting her blessings, Susie's holding out for something better. I don't know who she thinks she is. Perhaps she's waiting for the Prince of Wales to come calling.' Daisy sniffed then sighed again. 'Well, I must get on. The governess is back tomorrow and if this place isn't spic-and-span she'll go running to Mrs Bourne and then it'll be who'd-have-thought-it.'

This reminder of the governess plunged Eliza into despair. So much for a happy New Year. The life of slavery would shortly resume with no end in sight. She'd be better off if 1913 was cancelled from the outset.

* * *

'Miss Eliza! What do you think? You'll never guess!'

Eliza struggled to sit up in bed, rubbing sleep from her eyes. Daisy had come bursting into her room at a ridiculous hour. It was barely light.

'What is it, Daisy? Must you make so much noise? I was having the nicest dream before you came stampeding in.'

'Grumpy guts. But wait till you hear! This'll put a smile on your face. She's gone! She's packed her bags and gone!'

'Who's gone? What are you talking about?'

'The governess, miss: she's gone!'

Eliza could scarcely believe her luck. She had never dared hope the day would come. She had expected the life of tyranny and oppression to go on forever. (It was barely February, the governess had been at Clifton less than six months, but it seemed like *years*.)

The governess had gone. Just *why* she'd gone was not clear. Everyone had a different theory.

'She had a set-to with Mrs Bourne,' said Daisy. 'Bossy Bourne is the last person you want to pick a fight with. No one gets the better of *her*!'

'The governess was making eyes at Mr Ordish,' said Susie Hobson. 'He was swooning from the shock of it. She had to be sacked for the sake of his health.'

'She was caught filching the silver,' said Sally Kirkham. 'The police came and hauled her off to jail.'

'I am not discussing it, Elizabeth,' said Mama. 'It has nothing to do with you.'

'But she was my governess, she was—'

'Please don't shout! I have the most dreadful head this morning.' Mama did indeed look unusually ruffled. She was sitting on the stool by her bureau in the parlour, rubbing her temples, her brow furrowed. 'Why must people let one down? This couldn't have come at a worse moment, when I've the christening today and now a funeral tomorrow.'

Eliza knew about the christening. It was Colonel Harding's first grandson who was being christened: not a child of Charles's (Charles Harding still wasn't married. Some people said he never would be. No woman would put up with him.) but of the younger son, Julian. Julian Harding had got married last year only a few months before Dorothea. Roderick called Julian 'the housemaid's son', a reference to the local rumour that for his second wife the Colonel had chosen one of his own servants. Mama told Roderick not to be so silly. Of course Colonel Harding wouldn't marry a housemaid!

So that was the christening. What of the funeral?

'It doesn't concern you, Elizabeth,' said Mama. 'Now do please at least *try* to behave yourself over the next few days — if it's not too much to ask.'

Dismissed from the parlour, Eliza trailed back to the nursery, resentful. Nobody these days had any time for her. She was told nothing. She was ignored. She had always to stay at home and be good. But where did it ever get her?

Slowly climbing the stairs, she thought of Dorothea, who had believed in looking on the bright side. Was there a bright side in this situation? Well, the governess had gone. That was something. And Mama would be out most of today and tomorrow too.

Eliza's spirits rose. She would have the run of the house. She would be able to do whatever she wanted. She could please herself for a change.

There was a lot to be said for looking on the bright side, it turned out.

* * *

Next morning, as soon as Mama had set off for the funeral, Eliza went downstairs in search of the newspaper which had been forbidden in the days of the tyranny. She felt most grown up sitting in the drawing room with *The Times* open on her lap. Dare she ring for a glass of milk and maybe a slice of cake?

But then she turned a page and the headlines made her blood run cold. *ANTARCTIC DISASTER — LOSS OF CAPTAIN SCOTT AND HIS PARTY — OVERWHELMED BY A BLIZZARD.*

There had been no news of Captain Scott for ages and ages. Roderick had said that he must be dead. Eliza had refused to believe it. Now here it was in black and white. Captain Scott, so brave, so intrepid, had been killed by the snow.

She was still trying to take it in when, without warning, the door flew open and Mrs Bourne swept in with a jangle of keys and a forbidding frown. Roderick's name for her—'the Dreadnought' — was for good reason.

'And just *what* are you doing in the drawing room, Miss Elizabeth?'

'I was—' Eliza pointed mutely to the terrible headlines. Surely even Mrs Bourne's heart must be touched.

But no, the housekeeper was unimpressed. 'Go back to the nursery where you belong. Go back at once. And leave the newspaper. I do like everything to be kept in its proper place!'

Eliza obeyed.

Back in the day room she walked up and down and began to feel ashamed. Why be such a milksop? Why allow herself to be bossed around by the Dreadnought, a mere servant? She wished a blizzard would overwhelm Mrs Bourne and good riddance.

She leant against the bars on the window. There was no sign of any snow. There was no sign of anything. The world was shrouded in fog.

There was no bright side in a fog.

* * *

Daisy came running. 'The mistress is back. You're to go down, Miss Eliza, and have tea.'

'Me? Have tea? But why?'

Daisy was in a fluster and no wonder. Mama hated to be kept waiting. 'She has a gentleman with her,' Daisy added as she searched for a clean frock in Eliza's wardrobe.

'A gentleman? What gentleman?'

'The gentleman whose daughter has died: Mr Simcox.'

To sit in the same room as a man whose daughter had died: it made Eliza shudder to think of it. Death seemed to be stalking her today. First Captain Scott, now Mr Simcox's daughter. She thought of death as a tall, grim man all in black lurking in the fog.

'Daisy, I can't go downstairs, I can't, please don't make me!'

'What a daft ha'porth you are, miss! Mr Simcox is not a monster. Now do hold still and let me get the lugs out your hair.'

Wild ideas crowded into Eliza's head as she made her way down the stairs. What if Mama wanted to offer her up as a replacement for the man's dead daughter? Mama would only be too glad to get rid of her!

But when Eliza arrived at last in the drawing room she found there was nothing alarming or intimidating about Mr Simcox — just the opposite, in fact. Bowed, haggard, with a balding head and a straggly grey moustache, he looked insignificant and rather brittle. He was not a complete stranger. She had a vague idea she had seen him before. She'd certainly heard of him, Mr Bradley Simcox, a friend of Daddy's. He'd worked for Daddy in Coventry. It had been just the two of them in the beginning when Daddy first set up his bicycle business. The bicycle business had grown apace in the years since then. Daddy in his will had left Mr Simcox shares in it (whatever *shares* were) and Mr Simcox was now general manager. But as she listened to Mama and Mr Simcox talking, Eliza came to understand that the bicycle business no longer made bicycles.

'Such a shame,' said Mama. 'Albert was always rather partial to bicycles. They were his first success when he came to branch out on his own. Not that he didn't do well with watches. But he always thought of that as his father's affair, not his own. The watch-making business was something he'd inherited; he hadn't built it up himself. Albert liked to be his own man.'

Mama was in black today as was Mr Simcox. Black had always made Mama look cross in the days of her mourning after Daddy died. But she seemed different this afternoon, gentle almost, leading Mr Simcox in conversation. She was a match for this situation as for any other.

'It's a shame, Mrs Brannan, about the bicycles, a real shame. But there's no money in them anymore: not in ordinary bicycles, anyway. It's a different story with the motorised variety. They started off as a sideline but have become something of a money-spinner. However, we've passed the patents on to our sister company, the BFS: they are better placed for that sort of thing. We at the Crown Street works now only make motor components, for the BFS and for other companies: demand is growing. That is why we have changed our name, from Brannan Bicycles to Brannan Engineering. It seemed the sensible thing to do.'

'I am sure that Albert would have approved, Mr Simcox. He was nothing if not pragmatic.'

'You're quite right, Mrs Brannan. He was very pragmatic. Forward-thinking, too. He believed that invention and innovation were not only good for business but improved people's lives, too. All the latest trends — standardisation, batch production, conveyer belts and the like — would have interested him a great deal. He would have been asking himself how these techniques could be applied to the BFS factory at Allibone Road. Not that Allibone Road is behindhand. Mr Smith, of course, has always prized quality over quantity but he learned a lot from Mr Brannan, he'd learned to move with the times. He's been keeping a close eye, I believe, on that new factory built in Manchester by Ford's and the methods they are using there.'

Mr Smith, Eliza remembered, was the father of Young Stan and of Jeff, Stan's brother, who was now chauffeur at Clifton. She wondered how Stan was getting on at the motor factory. She shrank from asking, still rather in awe of Mr Simcox and the weight of his grief. Mr Simcox, loquacious one minute, would fall silent the next, staring at the carpet, lost in thought. But Mama nudged the conversation along and there were no awkward silences. Effortless, it seemed to Eliza. Enviable, too. Mama could talk sensibly on any subject, always asked the right questions, whether the talk was about bicycles or motor cars or motor components or manufacturing techniques. Mention was made of motor racing, too. The BFS, it appeared, gained much public notice thanks to its competitions department which was headed by their neighbour Henry Fitzwilliam — the man who, so it was said, had once wanted to marry Dorothea (was this true?). Henry was much involved in racing, whether on the track or in hill climbs. He was making quite a name for himself, Mr Simcox said.

Afternoon tea came to an end. Mr Simcox got to his feet. Mama pulled the cord.

'You will want to rest before dinner, I expect, Mr Simcox. Ah, here is John. John will show you to your room.' (*John* was the name Mama used for the footman, Basford.)

Mr Simcox paused in the doorway, looked back, looked for the first time at Eliza. He seemed as shy of her as she was of him.

'What a lovely girl you've got, Mrs Brannan. So quiet and polite. Reminds me of my Peggy at that age. A very studious girl, my Peggy. Devoted to her old dad. Everybody loved my Peggy. But there. She's gone. She's with her mother now, God rest 'em.'

He went out. Basford closed the door.

'Such a tragic loss,' sighed Mama after a pause. 'She was only twenty-five.'

'Is . . . is Mr Simcox staying with us, Mama?'

'For a few days, yes. It is what your father would have wanted. I expect you to be on your best behaviour, Elizabeth. Mr Simcox needs peace and quiet at this difficult time.'

Back in the nursery, Eliza returned to her place by the window. The fog had cleared a little, was tattered and shredded. Indistinct dark shapes had appeared along with the ghostly silhouettes of naked trees. But a thick mist still lay along the line of the canal and the horizon was veiled in a white pall.

Eliza found herself thinking of Daddy. He'd had a whole separate life in Coventry, a life that Mr Simcox and Mr Smith knew all about but which she had never given much thought to. He'd been a big man, her Daddy, a gruff man. She'd been frightened of him at times though he'd never been nasty or cruel. What would he thought of her as she was now? Would he have loved her the way Mr Simcox had loved his Peggy?

Staring into the swirling fog, she remembered the unkept promise to take her to the Crystal Palace; she remembered walking with him on occasion hand-in-hand in the gardens; she remembered once, long ago when she'd been very little, he'd lifted her up in the drawing room and sat her on top of the piano. He'd been happy that day, he'd been excited about something: the motors, perhaps? There had often been great excitement at Clifton in the early days of the motors, when Daddy was first building the business.

Eliza could not now recall what Daddy had said to her that day. Had it been something along the lines of 'What a wonderful family we are' or 'What wonderful times we shall have'? But she remembered clearly the timbre of his voice, the way his eyes had shone; she remembered his smile half-hidden by his greying, bushy moustache; she remembered his big strong hands on her bare arms, lifting her effortlessly. She had thought Daddy would always be there. She had thought he would go on forever. Then, one day, out of the blue, his heart had stopped working.

Looking out at the world shrouded in fog, Eliza decided that next time she was in the village she would go to Daddy's grave in the churchyard. She would go to his grave, she would visit him, she would not be afraid, she would never go out of her way to avoid him again.

She might even take flowers.

CHAPTER SEVEN

Mama came unlooked-for to the day room. 'Here you are, Elizabeth.'

Where else would I be, said Eliza silently, mutinously, as she sat at the table picking the threads from her unfinished sampler. *Where else?* But her heart sank. It must be about the new governess. Why otherwise would Mama have come up here? One governess had already come and gone since February, a prim and rather fussy woman who'd decided after a month-and-a-half that the climate didn't suit her and the location was not propitious. She was used to the modern amenities of a town; life in the countryside was positively medieval. And the people, so unfriendly. The way they looked at you in the village. She couldn't, she really couldn't.

But Mama had not come about the new governess. There was no new governess. 'I haven't had time, what with one thing and another, and these headaches. I keep getting headaches. Colonel Harding's daughter — one of his married daughters — has been so kind as to invite me to Scarborough for a few days. The sea air may do me some good. It can't hurt. I shall be away a week, two at the most.'

Eliza experienced a sudden surge of excitement. A week, a whole week, to do as she pleased, to enjoy herself! With

Mama away and Roderick not home, the house would be *hers*. *She* would be mistress.

Mama gave her a sharp look. 'Now, Elizabeth, you must be a good girl while I'm away. I don't like to leave you really but there's a house full of servants and Roderick is due back any day from his friend's.'

Eliza did her best to look as if butter wouldn't melt. 'I will be good as gold, Mama, I promise.'

* * *

Mama departed. The sense of freedom was exhilarating. Eliza waltzed around the house, walking on air.

That first morning she found Basford in the dining room polishing the table. She stopped to speak to him. They'd hardly exchanged two words when the door flew open and Mrs Bourne swooped in. She glared at them. What was all this giggling and gossiping? Why hadn't Basford finished with the table yet? She couldn't abide idling and sloppiness. She would be having words with Mr Ordish. As for Miss Elizabeth, she must *not* distract the servants from their work, she must *not* get under their feet. She would confine herself to the nursery — her proper place — and do her lessons as Mrs Brannan had instructed.

'I shan't and you can't make me!'

The words were out before Eliza realised. She had no idea where they'd come from. Mrs Bourne flushed bright red, her eyes grew wider and wider, her hand twitched: she was obviously resisting the urge to slap. It was terrifying, the Dreadnought at action stations bearing down at her, but Eliza knew she had to stand her ground or lose all the advantages of Mama's absence.

Something stirred within her. Courage?

'I shan't do what you say, I shan't!'

Mrs Bourne bristled. 'Your mother will hear of this!'

'I don't care! You can do what you like! I'm not scared of you!'

'You brassy-faced madam! I've never come across such impertinence in all my life!'

Mrs Bourne's fury lashed over her. Eliza found fortitude in the sight of Basford who was standing behind the housekeeper with his cloth in his hand and grinning from ear to ear.

Mrs Bourne abruptly turned away. Basford's grin snapped off at once and he began assiduously polishing the table. Mrs Bourne barely gave him a glance. She swept out of the room, slamming the door behind her.

Basford stopped polishing. He and Eliza looked at each other, rather breathless. They could hear voices in the corridor, Mrs Bourne and Mr Ordish. It was impossible to make out Mr Ordish's words but the housekeeper's shrill voice carried clearly.

'. . . never been spoken to in such a way . . . a mere *girl* . . . in all my years in service, no one has ever, *ever* . . .'

Eliza could not have endured another clash with Mrs Bourne. Her reserves for the moment were depleted. Even Mr Ordish would have been too much for her and he was no more terrifying than a fly. Leaving Basford to his polishing, she ran along the passage to the back door and ran down the steps outside, seeking sanctuary away from the house.

Round the side of the house, and past the stable block, she climbed a fence and jumped down into the meadow known as the Old Close. Washing was drying on the grass, white in the sun. There was no sign of the laundry maid.

As she wandered between the spread-out sheets and pillowcases, Eliza reached the conclusion that she did not like arguments, not even when it was Mrs Bourne. She tried to remember what it was that Kolya had once said about a spirit of fellowship and cooperation. Was it too much to hope that this spirit of fellowship and cooperation might blossom at Clifton Park?

In the vegetable garden she found Becket the old gardener thinning out carrots, stooped over. He seemed less than delighted to see her.

'Just stay out of my road today, Miss Eliza. I've no time for chopsing. There's too much to do, and my arthritis playing up, and that boy is next to useless.'

That boy was Jack Britten, one of the baker's sons from the village, almost the same age as Eliza. She made a note of the fact that he was useless. She could chaff him about it later.

'Don't worry, Becket. I will help you.'

'Eh? What's that?' He was growing a little deaf.

'I said, I'll *help* you. I'll help with the garden.'

'Now, why ever would you want to do that?'

'Because of the spirit of fellowship and cooperation.'

'Oh, aye.' He eyed her dubiously. 'Well, you *could* do a little weeding, I suppose.'

'I'll start right away!'

'Mind it's weeds you pull up and naught else!'

But it proved impossible to avoid pulling up several cabbages and a good handful of young lettuce along with the weeds. Becket muttered darkly and shook his head and seemed disappointingly relieved when she said she had to go now, it was time for luncheon.

'I'll do better this afternoon, I promise!' said Eliza, wiping her muddy hands down her frock. 'I shall come back this afternoon!'

'If you must, miss.'

Back in the nursery, Eliza found that news of her collision with Mrs Bourne had spread throughout the house. Daisy was full of admiration.

'I wish I had your pluck, Miss Eliza! I'd like to tell that sour-faced old crow exactly what I think of her!'

'Why don't you, Daisy?'

'I'd be out on my ear, that's why. I'd have no job and no money and I'd end up in the Spike. We can't all be as free-and-easy as you, miss.'

Eliza chewed this over while she was chewing her cutlet. Fight against tyranny, Kolya had said. But how could Daisy fight against tyranny when to do so would land her in the

Spike? The Spike was the name Daisy had for the work-house in Lawham: a terrible place, she said, where the old and unwanted were ground up and used as manure, while surplus children were killed and made into pies. Dorothea had suggested that Daisy might perhaps be exaggerating a little, but even Dorothea had not had a good world to say about the workhouse.

Perhaps the tyranny of the workhouse was even worse that the tyranny of Mrs Bourne.

* * *

After luncheon, Eliza hurried to keep her promise to Becket. She let herself out by the side door. In the stable yard she stumbled unexpectedly on the tail end of what had obviously been a protracted and rather violent tussle between Billy Turner and Jeff Smith. Turner had Smith in a headlock and was dragging him across to the water trough. Both young men were dusty and dishevelled and breathing heavily.

As Eliza watched, Billy Turner ducked Smith's head under the water and held it there. There was an explosion of bubbles. Smith kicked his legs wildly but he couldn't break free.

Eliza ran across the yard. 'Stop it, stop it, he'll drown! How could you, how dare you, you're nothing but a . . . a . . . a *tyrant*!'

Billy Turner looked round in some consternation. He also loosened his grip. Jeff Smith wriggled free. He was bedraggled and dripping and his hair was plastered to his head, but his eyes were glaring and he looked ready to resume the fisticuffs. Seeing Eliza, however, he seemed to think better of it. Casting a last louring look at Billy Turner, he slunk away across the yard.

Eliza in high dudgeon turned her back on Turner and went marching off towards the gardens.

* * *

'That don't sound like our Billy,' said Daisy as she served tea in the nursery. 'He's a lummakin great lad but he'd never pick on someone for no reason.'

'I did ask him later,' Eliza admitted, 'and he said that Jeff had been *chelping away* at him all morning.'

'Well, that explains it. He's a lippy one, that Jeff Smith. Thinks he's it, he does. I daresay he only got what he deserved. You oughtn't to be so quick to judge, Miss Eliza!'

'I'm sorry, Daisy.'

'It's not me who needs to hear it.'

'I'll tell Billy, too. I'll tell him straight after tea.'

'As you like, miss.'

'Why are you being so horrid, Daisy? I've said I'm sorry!'

'Oh, don't mind me, miss. I'm in a narky mood. It's Zack. I never get to see him. I'm always late finishing since I started filling in downstairs, and Zack's working all hours down Manor Farm haymaking. It's enough to make anyone down in the dumps!'

'Why not write him a letter? It's the next best thing.'

Daisy wrinkled her nose and looked shifty.

'What's the matter, Daisy? You *can* write, can't you?'

'Of course I can write! What a thing to say! I'm just not much good at it, that's all. I never could get the hang of all those fiddly bits. It didn't help that our Nora — our Billy, too, for that matter — could write like clerks from the day they was born. And oh my, weren't they smug about it!'

'Let me write the letter for you, Daisy! Tell me what you want to say and I'll put it down.'

Daisy brightened. 'That would be something, if I could send Zack a proper letter!'

Eliza pushed aside the remains of her cake. 'We'll start now!'

* * *

Once the letter was finished, Eliza went to look for Billy Turner as she'd promised. She found him, of course, in the stable block. He was cleaning out one of the loose boxes. Two interested horses were watching, heads jutting over their half-doors. Eliza watched too, hanging back. It took some nerve to approach Billy Turner in cold blood.

He was working with his cap on and his jacket off and his shirt open at the collar. He had a tanned face and neck, a dimple on his chin, cuts and bruises from the fight earlier, bandy legs ('Our Billy couldn't stop a pig in an entry,' was how Daisy put it). Jeff Smith was perhaps a head taller than Turner but he didn't have Turner's muscles. Billy was throwing great bales of hay around as if they were nothing. He was also scowling ferociously. Eliza shrank from approaching him.

Billy paused in his work to have a word with one of the horses: Roderick's Conquest, it was, an aristocratic beast. Billy tickled Conquest under the chin, muttering softly all the while. The horse snorted and deigned to lower its head, allowing Billy to stroke its neck, nuzzling Billy's shoulder. Billy's expression changed. He looked almost good-natured now. But when, a moment later, he caught sight of Eliza loitering in the doorway, his scowl came back at once. He stepped away from the horse, touched his cap.

'Miss.'

Eliza took a deep breath. She proceeded to make her apology. Billy listened, scratching his neck and glowering. It was quite alright, he muttered. It was all forgotten. And he'd do his best to get on with Jeff Smith in future if that was what Miss Eliza wanted. He hadn't got anything against Jeff Smith. He hadn't got anything against anyone.

'Not even Zack Hobson?' Eliza bit her lip. It was a mistake to mention Zack Hobson.

'Who's been talking to you about Zack Hobson?' said Billy gruffly. 'Weren't our Daisy, were it, miss?'

Eliza sidestepped the question. 'Who *is* Zack Hobson?' Could he really be the ragamuffin boy she remembered?

'He's a good-for-nothing sort of chap, that's what he is, but our Daisy thinks the sun shines out his arse.'

'Out his *what?*'

'Out his — never you mind, miss.' Billy peered at her, suspicious. 'Has our Daisy been talking to you about him? Has our Daisy been talking *to* him?'

'No, of course not, she hasn't said a word to him.' A letter, after all, was not the same as *talking*.

'Aye, well, that's good. But just you steer clear of Zack Hobson, miss, and tell our Daisy too and all. They're a bad lot, those Hobsons.'

Eliza began to feel guilty about the letter. She had wanted to be helpful, she had wanted to get on Daisy's right, but she wondered now if it might be better to be on *Billy's* right side. This was a rather surprising thought. She had never paid much attention to Billy Turner. She had always found him rather daunting.

Billy scratched his neck once more, shuffling his feet. If Miss Eliza had finished, then he ought to be getting on. There were a dozen and one things needed doing and the afternoon half over. He had to go to the village later, too. His ma expected him on a Tuesday. And while he was in the village his granddad, no doubt, would want him to go traipsing down to his bit of land to help with the pigs and the hens and whatnot. A chap's time was not his own. It was a dog's life and no mistake.

Eliza was rather taken aback. She had never heard him say so much all in one go. 'Isn't there anyone to help you?' she asked. 'Mr Ordish has Basford, Cook has Merrells, and Becket has Jack Britten.'

'When I started here, miss, a dozen or so years back, there was three of us in the stables and I were the lowest of the lot. Now there's only me — unless you count Jeff Smith. But he's no help, polishing his motors all day long. He's not like his brother. His brother used to lend a hand. He was a good mate, was Stan. But never mind, miss. Take no notice of me. A bit of hard work never hurt anyone.'

It didn't seem fair, all the same, that so much should be heaped on his shoulders, broad though those shoulders were.

'I shall help you, Billy. I've been helping Becket today. Tomorrow I will help you. It's my new idea, to be helpful. It's because of the spirit of fellowship and cooperation.'

He didn't really understand about the fellowship and cooperation but at least he'd stopped scowling quite so hard. She wished she could get him to look at her the way he'd looked at Conquest. But perhaps it was only horses he looked at that way.

How busy she would be in the coming days! Her heart swelled at the thought as she made her way back to the nursery. The spirit of fellowship and cooperation was blossoming already.

* * *

There was a magnificent view from the summit of Rookery Hill. Rolling countryside stretched away on every side, an endless patchwork of fields and trees and hedgerows to the far-off horizon. Hayton was spread out below, its houses like child's toys; in the other direction, there was a glimpse of distant Brockmorton. Eliza had spent some time admiring the view, she had gathered handfuls of foxgloves, too. Now she was lying on her back in the grass. The tall poplars swayed and hissed in the breeze. White fluffy clouds sailed across the blue summer sky forever changing shape. They reminded her one moment of a face in profile, a fire-breathing dragon the next.

She had taken some time for herself this morning. She felt she deserved it after all her hard work. Not only had she been helping in the garden and in the stables, she'd found time to lend a hand in the house, too. She'd polished the silver with Basford, carried coals for Kirkham, dusted with Daisy; and she'd helped the laundry maid as well, working the mangle, and folding and squaring the freshly clean tablecloths. Days passed in a blur of activity. Eliza had lost count of time. At least a week had gone by, probably two. Mama had not come home. What could she be *doing* in Scarborough all this time?

Eliza's tummy rumbled, reminding her about lunch. She jumped up. Running helter-skelter down the steep grassy slopes of the hill, she left a trail of foxgloves behind her. Oh well. She could always pick more another day. Tossing the rest of the flowers into the air, she joined the bridleway from Brockmorton and was speeding past Becket's cottage before she knew it. She leapt up the front steps of the house and flung open the door with a crash.

'Miss Eliza! Do be careful! You nearly had me over!'

'Sorry, Basford, sorry!' She made a dash for the stairs — and lunch — but Basford's next words stopped her in her tracks.

'Wait, miss! Master Roderick's been asking for you. He said to tell you that—'

'Roddy's here? He's back?'

'Yes, miss, in the drawing room. He said—'

Eliza spun on her heels on the stairs and headed full pelt for the drawing room, suffused with sudden joy. She found her brother spread on the couch. He was not alone. Kolya was with him.

'I'm so glad you've come!' Eliza's smile expanded to take in the Russian as well as Roderick.

Roderick looked her up and down. 'What on earth have you been doing? You're out of breath, your face is bright red, and your clothes—'

'I've been up Rookery Hill.'

'And through a hedge backwards by the look of you. Now, what's all this I hear about you running wild? Shouldn't you be doing your lessons? What is your governess thinking of?'

'The governess has gone. She's left.'

'Another governess gone? What do you do to them? I see now why Mother was so keen for me to hurry home. She needs someone here to keep you in line. Which is all very well, but she can't expect me to alter my plans merely for your sake.'

Eliza looked at him with sudden suspicion. 'What plans? Aren't you home for the rest of the summer?'

It appeared not. Roderick and Kolya were off next day to Wales where they were to join Miss Halsted and her friends.

'It's not fair!' cried Eliza, throwing herself onto the settee. 'Everyone is leaving me! First Doro, then Mama, now you!'

'Don't be absurd! I'm only going to Wales for a week, not emigrating.'

'That's what Mama said. She went away for a week but it's been ages!'

'In which case she can hardly complain if I go away as well. As for you, kiddo, it's high time you were taken in hand. A finishing school was mentioned, I believe.'

Eliza shrank from the idea of school, especially if it meant being sent away, but just then there were more pressing matters to attend to. 'I'm hungry! What's for lunch?'

'We've already eaten ours.'

'Oh, Roddy, you could have waited!'

Roderick raised his eyebrows, said loftily, 'I suppose you could, if you wanted, have dinner with us this evening.'

Eliza jumped to her feet. 'Oh, Roddy, yes please!' Dinner with just her brother and Kolya! How thrilling! She wished it was evening already.

* * *

Daisy helped her dress for dinner, to put her hair up and fasten all the hooks-and-eyes on her best frock and arrange her beads around her neck. Eliza looked anxiously at her reflection.

'Do I look alright, Daisy? Do I look nice?'

'It's only dinner, miss. Why all this fuss? Are you thinking of making eyes at Master Roderick's friend?'

'Of course not, don't be silly, I'm not going to *make eyes*, or whatever you call it, at anyone. I'm mistress tonight. It's my *duty* to look nice.'

'If you say so.' Daisy twisted a stray lock of Eliza's hair and fastened it with a hair pin. 'I suppose I'd want to look nice if I was having dinner with two young gentlemen — and Master Roderick and all.'

'Roddy? What's so special about Roddy?'

'Now, don't get me wrong, miss. I'm not one to go mooning over him like that Susie Hobson. But he *is* rather handsome.'

Twisting from side to side to inspect herself in the mirror, Eliza said, 'What is it, Daisy, that makes a man handsome? Do . . . do you think Billy is handsome?'

'Our Billy? Handsome? He's nothing but a great ham-fisted lump! But if you were to ask me about Zack . . .' Daisy rolled her eyes, a great soppy smile on her face. She stepped back to admire her handiwork. 'There. You look good enough for anyone. And now, miss, I'll be off, as you're not having dinner upstairs. Don't you go telling Mrs Bourne that I left early!'

Eliza watched in the mirror as Daisy hurried out of the room. Was she off to see Zack? What about the things Billy had said? But there were more important matters at hand. It was time to go downstairs.

She joined Roderick in the drawing room where they waited for Kolya.

'He will be deciding which of his two and only jackets to wear,' said Roderick with something of a sneer.

Eliza was offended on Kolya's behalf. What did it matter if the Russian had only two jackets? Jackets were not the measure of a man.

It was enough to make her wish she had a different sort of brother, one who didn't sneer or ride roughshod, one who told her how nice she looked, one who didn't go gallivanting off to Wales.

'Must you go, Roddy? It's not as if you like Miss Halsted's friends. You call them cranks.'

'They *are* cranks. They eat foreign food in cheap restaurants, they go to endless meetings, they sit on the floor and read poetry — but not Victorian poetry: they disdain the Victorians. They like to be *modern*.'

'So why do you want to go with them to Wales?'

'You wouldn't understand, a child of your age.'

'I am *not* a child! I am thirteen!'

She was ready to argue the point but Kolya came in just then and almost immediately Mr Ordish announced dinner. Eliza had made up her mind as the (temporary) mistress of Clifton to sit in Mama's place at the table but when it came to it she didn't have the nerve. She went to her usual place. She was rather disgusted at her own timidity.

Dinner tonight was not a decorous and orderly affair as when Mama was at home. Roderick and Kolya seemed bent on quarrelling over everything, whether it was lectures at their university or the war in the Balkans. Their arguments grew more heated as the courses came and went. They drank a lot of wine, their faces grew flushed, they raised their voices and pointed at each other with their knives. There was no mention of how nice it had turned out today and what a delicious sauce Cook had prepared for the fish: those were the sort of things Mama would have said.

'Russia is a *backward* country!' cried Roderick, filling up his glass, not waiting for Basford to fill it for him. 'Russia will never amount to anything!'

Kolya shook his head. 'Russia by her very size will be greatest power in world.'

'But never as great as England. The Royal Navy rules the waves. Most of Russia's navy is at the bottom of the China Sea.'

'All empires reach their end. Rome—'

'Rome lasted for centuries. The British Empire will, too.'

'But world changes. Capitalist system will fail. Revolution will sweep away old order.'

'So you keep saying. But it's complete hogwash!'

When the food was all eaten and the wine all gone, the argument continued in the drawing room. Eliza curled up in the rocking chair. Roderick and Kolya set about the brandy.

Kolya began talking as he'd talked on the Lawham Road last summer about ordinary people being heroes and how one man could change the world. Or one woman, for women were now beginning to play their part.

Roderick scoffed. One woman? A woman like that lunatic at the Derby last month, getting herself trampled to death? What had that achieved?

Emily Davison, said Kolya, had proved her commitment to the cause, she had made the ultimate sacrifice as all good revolutionaries must be willing to do. Her heroic action had brought the emancipation of women one step closer.

Roderick asked mockingly if Kolya was also ready for the ultimate sacrifice — to give up his youth, his joy and all he had, to be paid back with earth and dust? But in any case, Roderick continued, all this talk about emancipation was so much bunkum. Women did not want to be emancipated. They wanted marriage, a family, a home. It was in their nature. You couldn't go against nature. All those troublemakers — throwing themselves under horses, chaining themselves to railings — needed to be brought to heel. They had to be shown that they couldn't break the law and get away with it.

Laws were made by the rich to protect their ill-gotten gains, exclaimed Kolya. The rich were thieves and parasites and the rule of law under the capitalist system nothing short of despotism!

Eliza had sat silent and forgotten all this time, but Roderick got up now to pour more brandy and noticed her at last.

'Time you were in bed!' he growled.

She didn't dare disobey when he was in this mood. Out in the passage, however — away from his glaring eyes and fierce frown — she changed her mind. She was not ready for bed. She did not feel the least bit sleepy. She felt instead rather stifled, after the heated atmosphere in the drawing room. The back door was to her left at the end of the passage. She turned towards it.

It was cool outside and quiet. She stood on the terrace looking out from the parapet as if from the deck of a ship.

The moon, near full, hung bright and round in the black sky. A cold white light spilled across the landscape. Clouds banked on the horizon were touched with silver. All was still and silent and colourless, like an engraving.

The sound of voices brought her back to herself. She turned to face the house, crept along the terrace. The french windows were ajar, there was a chink in the curtains; she could see into the drawing room where Roderick and Kolya were both on their feet. There had been a lull as she left the room but now the argument had resumed and had grown in intensity. They were talking for some reason about Miss Halsted who they called *Rosa* with what Eliza thought of as a disturbing familiarity.

'You do now own her! She is not serf! She is free!'

'All that rot she comes out with — all that man-hating rot — she has learned it all from you!'

'Is you who talk the rot! She has own opinions. Not my opinions. But you — she will never agree with you!'

'Is that right? Is that so? We don't have the same outlook on life, it's true, but that has not prevented us from becoming intimate. There's no one knows her as intimately as I!'

'Rosa — and man like you? Is not true!'

'Believe what you like. It won't change the facts.'

They were standing in the middle of the room squaring up to each other. It was worse, far worse, than what had happened between Billy Turner and Jeff Smith. Fighting on the muddy cobbles of the stable yard was one thing, but two young gentlemen dressed for dinner in the sanctity of Mama's drawing room? It was unthinkable!

Kolya stepped back. Eliza breathed again.

'What?' jeered Roderick. 'Don't you want to fight me? Haven't you got the *guts* for it?'

'To fight will solve nothing.'

Kolya's words were innocuous enough. Eliza could only imagine it was something in his eyes — those intense, unnerving eyes — which made Roderick see red. It happened in an instant. Roderick swung his fist as Kolya was turning away. Roderick's fist connected with Kolya's jaw. There was a sickening sound like ice cracking. Kolya was caught off balance and fell heavily across the low table. There was a noise of crunching wood and breaking glass followed by a heavy thud. Eliza watched in agony. Kolya seemed to lie unmoving for what seemed an age. Had Roderick killed him?

But no, Kolya was picking himself up, he was shaking himself down. He was rather dishevelled, his lip was bleeding, but he seemed otherwise unharmed. He looked at Roderick, reproachful, angry. Roderick's face was stony.

At this point, Mr Ordish walked in without knocking.

'I thought I heard a noise, sir. Is everything alright?' His bland air of clam poured oil on troubled waters. Eliza was mightily glad to see him. She'd never been glad of Mr Ordish before.

'Yes, yes, everything's perfectly alright,' said Roderick shortly.

Mr Ordish's eyes swivelled towards the mess on the floor. 'Oh dear, sir. There seems to be broken glass. I'll get it cleaned up right away.'

'Leave it, Ordish. Just go. Go.'

There was a short pause, then Mr Ordish said, 'Very good, sir.'

He backed out of the room but Eliza sensed that his intervention had changed things, the danger was over. Roderick and Kolya moved around, not looking at each other. When would they speak?

Just then she heard a muffled click. She ran quickly to the back door only to find it locked. Through the glass panels she could see Mr Ordish retreating along the passage. He had shut her out. She could, of course, go back in through the french windows but Roderick and Kolya were there and she couldn't face them, she daren't.

What did it matter, though? Nothing mattered!

She ran down the stone steps and out across the trimmed meadow known as the Park. She was seized by a sudden, wild exuberance. Leaping and skipping across the grass, she danced in the moonlight, throwing her arms out, throwing her head back, spinning round and round. She was a primeval spirit of nature; she had tangled hair and tattered skirts; she whirled across the face of the world, no one could tame her.

At last, dizzy and breathless, she tripped and fell, tumbling onto the ground, rolling over and over, coming to rest on her back. Her chest was heaving, her heart beating. She looked up with wide eyes at the moon. In the sudden hush after the havoc of her dance, she heard faintly the harsh, croaking call of a corncrake. The call was repeated again and again. It seemed to come from every direction at once.

After a time she got slowly to her feet. In the nursery the dark always seemed thick and clinging like a veil. Out here the veil was drawn back. The night had opened up around her. She had come a long way as she danced, almost as far as the hedge that marked the periphery of the Park. The house was dim and distant, looming like a shadow at the top of the gentle rise. Lights palely gleamed in one or two windows. The chimneys stuck up like spines on a dragon's back.

She did not want to go back — not yet — so she went on instead. There was a gap in the hedge. The field beyond was disused and overgrown. She made her way through the tall grass and the brambles, stumbling over the uneven ground which sloped steeply down for a distance before flattening out. The call of the corncrake faded. All she could hear now was the rustle of the grass and the sound of her own breathing. Her wild exuberance was spent, but her every nerve tingled with a solemn sense of adventure.

She pushed through a bed of nettles with her arms raised so that her hands didn't get stung. The overgrown meadow came to an end. She had reached the canal. It curved towards her out of the shadows on either side, moonlight glinting on its black, glassy surface, strands of mist curling and drifting above the water. The tow path was like a pale ribbon stretched along the opposite bank. Beyond, the impenetrable dark of Ingleby Wood stood like a wall. High and remote, clouds were moving mysteriously, silently in the night sky, etched in cold, white moonlight.

She heard a trampling behind her. Someone was coming. She turned, feeling as smooth and calm as the canal. She waited to see who it was.

'Leeza. I have found you at last.' Kolya was wading through the nettles towards her. His low-pitched voice splintered the silence. 'I saw you from the window. I saw you dancing on the grass. I followed.' He joined her where she stood by the canal, a few feet from the brink. 'What are you doing here? Are you not afraid?'

'I'm not afraid at all. It doesn't seem . . . seem real, somehow. It's like being in a dream, or in a picture. It's like magic.'

'The silence of the English night,' he said, and he sighed. 'I did not expect England to be like this. I thought in England revolution would come — in England first, before anywhere. But I look, I listen. I see how little has changed, English countryside least of all. Peasants still toil in the fields. Gentry still live off fat of the land. Nights are steeped in the peace of ages. England goes on and on. England endures. Forever and ever, amen.'

His thick Russian accent gave these ordinary English words a different texture. They seemed to fall from his lips new-minted. Eliza found her mouth moving, repeating each word soundlessly as if trying to wring from it every last drop of meaning. She glanced at him curiously, shyly. He had no jacket, not even a waistcoat. There was blood on his white shirt. The shirt ought to be soaking in water, she said to herself. That was what the laundry maid had taught her, how to get the stains out of clothes by soaking them in cold water with washing soda. Eliza had learned this. She'd learned so much, these last few weeks.

As well as blood on his shirt, there was blood congealing on Kolya's lip.

'Your poor face . . . your lip.'

He touched it gingerly. 'I hit lip on table. It grows — how do you say — fat?'

'Swollen.'

'Swollen. Ah. Yes. Swollen.'

'Roddy is a brute, hitting you.'

'We got drunk. We were foolish. I am ashamed, losing my temper. Now I cool off. Is that correct idiom, *cool off*? I cool off in canal.'

'You're going to swim? Here? In the dark?'

He began undoing his shirt buttons. 'Sometimes when moon was bright I used to swim in lake by our *dacha*.'

'Are there lakes, then, in your city? You said you lived in a city.'

'In Petersburg, yes. But we have also house in country-side called *dacha*. Is my mother's house. We used to go there in summer: in summer long ago.' He took off his collar, untucked his shirt tails. 'Do not wait for me, Leeza, if you wish to go back. It is late. You must be tired. But look away now, for modesty.' He walked towards the canal edge, shrugging free of his shirt.

She covered her face with her hands but the temptation to take a peek was too strong. Parting her fingers, she saw in the gap between them Kolya dip down as he removed his underwear. He straightened up, his back to her. He stretched, his hands reaching for the sky. He was white and naked in the moonlight like a marble statue; or like a picture of Jesus hanging on the cross, lean and slender and stainless.

She shut her eyes. She screwed them tight. It was improper to look at a naked man. It was wicked to compare him to Jesus.

But who would know if she broke the rules out here in this moonlit night so far from civilisation?

She opened her eyes. Kolya had gone. There was a pile of clothes on the bank. Out on the dark water she saw his head bobbing, she saw the white flicker of his arm as he swam. But he seemed a long way off and she was alone. The night had lost its magic. It was vast and empty, the moonlight cold and austere. Her thoughts turned longingly to the comfort of her bed.

A breeze got up as he made her way across the Park. Clouds scudded across the moon. It grew colder, darker. She climbed up to the terrace. The french windows were wide open, the curtains billowing in the breeze. The electric light seemed incredibly bright, showing up the squalor of the broken table and the broken glass. *The Times* that had been thrown carelessly over the arm of the couch was scattered by the gusting wind, its pages flapping round the room. There was no sign of Roderick.

She turned off the lights but left the window open for Kolya. Quietly, sleepily, she took the stairs.

* * *

Eliza woke late to a grey sky and rain. The wind was rattling the windows. Thunder rumbled. Daisy in the day room was busy covering the mirrors as she always did when there was thunder. She had disappointing news. Roderick and Kolya had been up with the lark. They had gone already.

'They made a right mess of the drawing room last night, by all accounts. Broken glass on the floor and the table leg snapped off and bits of newspaper all over.'

'They had a fight, Daisy, I saw them.'

'Lads! They're all the same, nothing but trouble. Zack's just as bad. It's Hayton lads against Broadstone lads, that's the latest. I've never heard anything so daft.' But Eliza sensed that for all Daisy's head shaking and tutting, she was actually rather proud of Zack Hobson and his scrapes.

Eliza said nothing about her moonlit meeting with Kolya by the canal. It really did seem like a dream in the broad daylight of the grey morning. She wondered if she would she ever see Kolya again now that he and Roderick had fallen out.

'I wouldn't worry, miss. They were best of friends again this morning, from what I've heard. There's no accounting for boys and their bust-ups.'

Billy also said the fight was nothing to worry about when Eliza sought him out in the stable yard. Lads often got into fights, he said, especially when they'd a drink inside them. More often than not, it was all forgiven and forgotten next day.

'Do you fight, Billy, when you've a drink inside you?' She knew he liked his ale.

'Beer don't act on me like that. I don't have much of a temper. I'm an easy-going chap, or so they say. Too easy-going, if you listen to our ma. She goes on: "Ask for more wages, Bill, now you're doing all that extra; smarten yourself up, too, it wouldn't hurt; and get yourself a girl: you're twenty-four, it's about time." I says to her, "Don't fuss, Ma, I'm alright as I am." But she won't have it.'

'Why can't Roddy be more like you! Why can't *he* be easy-going!'

'We're all on us made the way we're made, miss, and there's no changing it. Master Roderick's not a bad sort. We used to have a lot to do with each other at one time, back when we was kids, playing cricket and rabbiting and whatnot. But he's got no time for the likes of me now. He's got bigger fish to fry, has Master Roderick.'

* * *

Haymaking was over, the harvest was beginning. A letter came from Mama. She was putting off her return yet again. The sea air at Scarborough was working wonders. Mrs Varney (the Colonel's married daughter) had pressed her to stay a little longer. *I trust that you are behaving yourself, Elizabeth,* Mama wrote, *and are not being a nuisance to your brother.* But Roderick was not at home. Nothing had been heard from him in weeks. It was as if he'd vanished off the face of the earth. There would be hell to pay (as Daisy put it) when Mama came home and found out what had been going on. In the meantime, Eliza was bent on making the most of her liberty. The whole summer, it seemed, was to be hers to do as she pleased.

* * *

Walking back from the village late one afternoon, swinging her straw hat by the ribbons, Eliza came across some men working on the Lawham Road not far from the turning to Clifton. There were laden carts parked up. There were unhitched horses cropping the grass of the verge. A fire was burning in a metal drum. Most interesting of all, a big machine with a funnel belching smoke was being driven back and forth across the surface of the road. It looked like a larger version of the roller that Becket used on the lawns at home (or Jack Britten used it now: it was too heavy for Becket these days). The men told her they were 'making up' the road: macadamizing it. There'd be no more ruts or holes. It would be as smooth as silk from now on.

As she stood watching, a familiar figure came plodding from the direction of the canal, hollow-eyed and dusty, dragging his heels.

'Johnnie Cheeseman! Where have you been?'

'Working, miss.'

'Working? But what about school?'

'School's on holiday, miss, it's August. Any road, I don't go to school no more. I made up my times and I left. Grandad said I could work for him at the Barley Mow but me dad said it's time I learned what a proper job's like, so I been helping with the harvest down Manor Farm.' He yawned, rubbing his eyes. 'What's to do here then, miss? What's this monster machine?'

'They're making the road as smooth as silk.'

'It'll still be as hard on your feet.' He gave another vast yawn. 'I should get on, miss. I'm about done in.'

'Before you go, Johnnie Cheeseman, help me over this wall. I'll go back home by the Spinney and cut the corner.'

He gave her a leg up and she scrambled to the top of the crumbling sandstone wall. She looked down at him as he stood on the verge, screwing his cap in his hands and squinting at her, a rather skinny boy, whey-faced and worn out. He was the boy she'd always known best of all the village children. He lived at the Barley Mow with his mother and father and his grandfather the publican, and was related to the Turners in some complicated way typical of the village. In days gone by Eliza had sometimes played fox-and-hounds with him and they'd gone mushrooming together. He was the same age as her, almost to the day, not yet fourteen. But playtime was over for him.

'Well, goodbye, Johnnie Cheeseman.'

'Goodbye, miss.'

She jumped down from the wall and set off across the field. Not ten minutes ago she'd been happy and at ease, rambling along the Lawham Road in the late afternoon sunshine; but now she felt — well, she was not quite sure how she felt or what had brought it on. Was it seeing the familiar Lawham Road being transformed? Was it meeting Johnnie Cheeseman, now a working man? Or was it something else entirely?

She wondered if Johnnie Cheeseman had been one of the men she'd seen earlier working in the field called Nate's Piece, right down by the canal. She'd been on her way to the village after lunch and had stopped at the end of the drive to look. She'd been surprised to see as she stood there one of the distant figures go sloping off to the edge of the field before ducking down behind the hedge and making his way onto the road. She'd hidden behind a tree as he'd come running swiftly towards her, booted feet raising the dust. At the Clifton turning he'd stopped and looked all around. He'd not seen her; there'd been no one else in sight apart from the distant workers he'd left behind. He'd whistled softly. There'd been an answering whistle from amongst the trees by the empty round cottage known as the Gatehouse.

It was an odd, rather forlorn place, the Gatehouse. An odd name, too. 'There's never been no gates at Clifton,' Becket had told her. 'Leastways, none that I can remember — and I've worked here sixty year and more.' At one time the gamekeeper had lived in the Gatehouse. But he was gone now and the old place after two years was falling into disrepair, ivy crawling all over it and trees crowding round. It had been in the shadow of the Gatehouse doorway that

Daisy had been waiting for the young man with the ragged waistcoat and rolled-up sleeves who was as dark and swarthy as a gypsy. As Eliza watched, he'd put his arms round Daisy and kissed her. Eliza had realised that it must be none other than Zack Hobson, the boy Daisy was so stuck on. She had been shocked by their both playing truant, by their shameless unconcern. She had shuddered to think what would happen if they were caught.

Making her way now across Corner Field towards the Spinney, she tried to put all these disturbing thoughts aside. The round, red sun was sinking slowly towards the horizon on her right. The shorn field was bathed in golden light. Stooks cast long shadows across the stubble. She did her best to perk herself up. The stooks, she said, were great, lumpish troll-creatures who'd crept out to feed on the gleanings now that the workers had gone. She turned back to look at them, to tell herself their story. But the story fell flat. Somehow she couldn't spark any enthusiasm. The field, empty and silent, and the setting sun, made her lonely, made her sad. So many different feelings ached inside her. She longed for — what? She had no idea. Yet she felt that she might break into pieces from wanting it.

At length she turned away. Beneath the tangled branches of the Spinney it was dusk already. She crept silent as a cat through the gloom. As she did so, sudden fear took hold of her. The stook-trolls came to life in her mind. But they were not the friendly, lumbering giants she'd imagined. They were silent, they were deadly, they were pursuing her into the wood. They would do anything to stop her revealing the secret of their existence.

A pheasant squawked. She nearly jumped out of her skin. She stood frozen, wide-eyed, listening. Nothing. Not a sound. Turning slowly in a circle, she peered all round. There were no trolls, no sign of life, not even the pheasant. She was completely alone.

She set off once more. The trees seemed to press in around her. It grew murkier and murkier. The snapping of twigs and the rustling of last year's leaves beneath her feet was painfully loud. Surely the driveway must be close by now?

Suddenly, without any warning, a great burly figure lunged out from behind the bole of a tree. White eyes rolled in a craggy, hairy face. A gaping mouth uttered brute, guttural sounds. Gnarled hands reached towards her.

She screamed and she ran.

The peace of the Spinney was shattered. The alarm calls of birds set up a raucous chorus. Eliza plunged through the undergrowth. She expected at any moment a groping hand to grab her from behind. She sobbed with fear. She tripped, stumbled, forced herself on. The Spinney seemed never-ending.

Her lungs were fit to burst. Her legs were giving way. With her last ounce of energy she threw herself forward. And suddenly the trees vanished. She had left the Spinney, she was out on the drive — and she ran smack into Billy Turner.

She had never been so glad to see anyone. She clung to him, spent.

'Miss Eliza? What's up, what's wrong?'

She managed between sobs and gulps of air to tell him about the man in the Spinney: the mad, terrifying man who'd been chasing her.

'A man, is it?' said Billy grimly. 'A poacher, I'll be bound. It's not dark yet but they've got bold as brass since the old keeper passed on. What did he look like, miss, this man?'

'His face was wrinkled, like bark. He had a beard, green—'

'*Green*?' Billy's eyes widened.

'I . . . I think it was green. It might have been grey. It was all straggly, like moss. He was like a . . . like a troll, all raggedy.'

'Sounds more like a turnpike sailor than a poacher. That's good. It'll save me a job, any road. I'd have to take a look if it was a poacher.'

'A . . . a what did you say?'

'A turnpike sailor, miss. A tramp. Asleep on a nice bed of leaves, as like as not. I daresay you frit him just as much as he frit you.'

She tried to believe this but she couldn't convince herself. What if the tramp had caught her? She pictured herself stretched out cold and lifeless amongst the brambles and pale leaves.

What did it mean to be dead?

She shuddered, tightening her grip on Billy, pressing her head against his chest. He was warm and alive, he was comforting. She could feel the coarse fabric of his shirt against her cheek, she could hear his heart beating, she could smell a certain smell, half horse and half something else, the sweaty smell of Billy himself. She closed her eyes and breathed in, a long steadying breath.

'Alright now, miss?'

'I . . . I think so. I will be. In a minute.' She was safe with Billy. She didn't want to let go. And it was nice, having his arms round her, having him hold her. She would never have guessed just how nice.

The terror of the tramp began to fade.

'Let's get you up to the house, miss.'

He helped her up the drive. She leant against him, feeling weak. But she didn't want him to think she was completely helpless. She wanted to show that she could be brave. She began to talk, trying to keep her voice steady, trying to sound blithe and unconcerned. She told him about the stooks in Corner Field, about Johnnie Cheeseman working at Manor Farm, about the men making up the Lawham Road. Before she knew it she was recounting how she'd watched Zack Hobson sneaking off from Nate's Piece.

She heard her words, was horrified, clamped her lips together. But Billy turned to her, his slow brown eyes searching her face. 'What's that about Zack Hobson? Miss Eliza, you would tell me, wouldn't you, if you knew summat?'

She felt just then, with his eyes on her and his arm round her waist, that she would have told him anything, everything, whatever he wanted. She couldn't help herself. 'I saw them. I saw them by the Gatehouse, Zack and Daisy. They were kissing.'

He scowled. He took away his arm. She felt bereft. She was appalled, too, by what she'd done, betraying Daisy. Her frock was torn, her hands scratched, her hair hanging loose, she had lost her hat: she felt utterly wretched.

She turned and ran. She ran full pelt. She didn't stop until she reached the nursery and had closed the green baize door behind her.

* * *

She still felt shaky later on, lying in her bath. Wiping herself with her flannel, she tried to wipe away all memory of the tramp and of her betrayal of Daisy. She thought of Billy instead. She thought of his gruff, gravelly voice and the dimple in his chin, she thought of her head on his chest and his heart beating, she thought of his smell and the feel of his muscular arm round her waist. Remembering how he'd rescued her from the terror of the tramp gave her a warm feeling inside. She dropped the flannel into the water and hugged her knees against her chest, holding on to this feeling and blotting out everything else.

CHAPTER EIGHT

Daisy marched into the day room with a face like thunder. 'Well, miss, I hope you're pleased with yourself! I never had you down for a tell-tale-tit — and to go clacking to our Billy of all people! You know very well he and Zack don't see eye-to-eye. And now Billy's gone and told our dad and there's been the biggest row you ever saw and I'm not to talk to Zack Hobson ever again!'

Eliza blenched in the face of such fury. 'I'm sorry, Daisy! I didn't mean to say anything. It just slipped out.'

'Spite, that's what it is. Pure spite,' said Daisy nastily. 'You think you're it, don't you. You think you're so high-and-mighty. But you weren't so clever when you started your monthlies and you thought you were dying!'

'Oh, Daisy, you beast!'

Eliza turned crimson with embarrassment. The memory was horribly fresh in her mind. With all the blood and the pain in her tummy, she really had thought she was dying. She had sat up in bed and screamed. But when Daisy came running and saw what it was, she'd been quite unconcerned. 'It's perfectly normal, miss. Hasn't anyone told you?' But nobody told her anything.

'You beast, Daisy, you beast! That's private, you mustn't talk about it, you mustn't!'

'Now you know how it feels, miss. Me and Zack, that was private too!'

But it wasn't the same. It wasn't the same at all. Daisy didn't understand the shame of it, having a body that played tricks, a body that was so much a mystery. There was no one to answer her questions, even if she'd known what to ask. She daren't ask Daisy who always laughed when you got things wrong.

'You beast, Daisy! You're hateful!'

Eliza ran to her room and slammed the door. Face down on her bed, she sobbed. She'd been having such fun as mistress of Clifton Park, able to do whatever she liked, but now it was all going wrong. She didn't dare leave the house in case the tramp was waiting for her. She pictured him creeping round outside, trying the doors and windows, hunting for a way in. Even the nursery no longer seemed quite safe. If she didn't have Daisy on her side — Daisy, the only one who ever came up here under the eaves of the house — well, it didn't bear thinking.

Contrite, Eliza crept out of her room. Daisy was dusting the toy shelves.

'I'm sorry, Daisy, I really am. Please say you'll forgive me.'

Daisy stuck her nose in the air. 'Well I shan't. And you can't make me, for all you're a miss and I'm just a plain nursery maid!'

* * *

But if there was one thing Daisy was *not*, it was consistent, and it wasn't long before she heard some news which quite eclipsed her quarrel with Eliza.

'It's the King and Queen, miss! They're coming to Lawham! Our Jem says it's the talk of the town. They've come to watch the army manoeuvres. They're staying tonight at one of the big houses nearby, tomorrow they'll pass through Lawham itself! Oh, miss, just think! If we could go, if we could *see* them! You could arrange it, miss. You could tell Mrs Bourne you need me, we could set off early. It's not far to walk, not really. Our Jem does it every day, going to the shoe factory.'

Eliza, anxious to get back in Daisy's good books, was sure she could do better than that. Bypassing Mrs Bourne, she went herself to see Jeff Smith and ordered him to have the motor ready next morning. He looked rather sulky about it but he couldn't exactly say no.

Sure enough, the motor was waiting by the front door after breakfast the following day.

'Don't go in the front seat, Daisy,' said Eliza. 'Get in the back with me.'

'What larks! I shall feel like a real lady!'

Daisy didn't notice, as Eliza did, Jeff Smith rolling his eyes at her words. As she climbed into the motor, Eliza found herself regretting that she hadn't let Billy Turner duck Jeff's head a few more times in the water trough.

There was quite a crowd gathered by the crossroads at the top of London Road in Lawham. It was the best place, general opinion had it, from which to see the royal party pass by — though no one seemed quite sure of the direction they'd be coming nor when they might be expected. The morning wore away. The expectant buzz faded. People began to mutter. Perhaps the King wasn't coming, perhaps he never had been, it was probably someone's idea of a joke. The crowd began to thin.

'We should go, miss,' said Daisy, disappointed. 'Mrs Bourne'll be having kittens.'

They began to walk along Cow Street back towards Market Place where they'd left motor. Eliza dragged her heels. She felt somehow responsible, as if she'd promised Daisy a treat and failed to deliver.

They had just reached the narrowest part of Cow Street and could see Market Place ahead when Daisy suddenly stopped.

'Listen, miss.'

They heard faintly the sound of cheering but, when they looked back, the junction with London Road was out of sight round a bend and the street behind them quiet and empty. They were about to carry on when the droning and humming of motor engines stopped them in their tracks. Two motorcycles came sweeping majestically round the curve of Cow Street. Behind them was a black limousine, polished to perfection.

Daisy gripped Eliza's arm. 'Oh, miss, it's them! It must be! I can't look!'

Eliza had no time to answer. The limousine was already gliding past before her very eyes. And there, sitting on the nearside, framed in the window, was the Queen in a feathered hat and high collar looking just as she did in her portraits. The rather severe expression on her face reminded Eliza of Mama. Daisy, for all her protestations that she couldn't look, was jumping up and down at Eliza's side, waving like mad. Eliza remembered just in time to wave too.

The Queen turned her head. She saw them. She spoke to a figure sitting next to her, pointed. The figure leant forward, a man in uniform with a beard and sweeping moustache and rather bulging eyes, unmistakably the King. Both the King and the Queen were now looking and smiling and, as the limousine slipped away, they waved: such slow, regal, dignified waves that Eliza was quite overcome by the magnificence of it.

It had all happened in the blink of an eye. The motorcade swept on. It skirted Market Place, turned into Priory Street, disappeared round a corner. The sound of the engines faded.

'Oh, miss, it was them, it really was! I couldn't believe my eyes! And we had them all to ourselves!'

She was right, for Cow Street was now empty again and silent.

It seemed to Eliza as she looked up and down that there was something rather sinister about the emptiness and the silence. A sense of dread crept over her. It put her in mind of the feeling she had experienced on the day of the eclipse over a year ago. There was no sign or portent this time. The sun was shining, the day was bright and clear, she was in Lawham: sleepy, dreary, ordinary Lawham. Yet this somehow made the feeling worse, more frightening. She was sure that something unspeakable was about to happen, or maybe was happening already, unseen, unsuspected but inexorable, inescapable. She was for a moment paralyzed with fear.

Daisy, wrapped up in her own excitement, didn't notice anything amiss. Eliza was relieved about that. She felt incapable of describing what it was that had engulfed her. As the first shock of it faded a little, Eliza was able to follow Daisy along the street, to drag herself across Market Place, to climb into the motor. Here she sat curled up on the back seat while Daisy went to root out Jeff Smith from the Peacock or the Lion and Lamb (he was not interested in seeing no boring king or queen, he'd insisted, striking a pose).

Eliza cocooned in the motor looked out at Market Place and the wide High Street trailing away between terraced buildings. Sunshine glinted on the shop windows. There was a scattering of people going about their business. A horse and cart made leisurely progress. A dog with its tail in the air zigzagged across the road. Here in Lawham a little over a year ago — here on Market Place — she'd poured her heart out to Kolya. How long ago it seemed now!

She saw out of the window Daisy walking towards her with Jeff at her side. Daisy, who wouldn't normally have given Jeff Smith the time of day, was talking nineteen to the dozen and waving her arms about, reliving the moment when she'd seen the King and Queen. But Eliza was no longer interested in the King and Queen. She thought longingly of home and lunch and the sanctuary of the nursery.

* * *

Eliza leaned out of her bedroom window. The day was breezy and overcast. There was an autumnal feel to it. Spots of rain were in the air.

183

From her high vantage point she watched as the motor came into view, the sound of its engine fading in and out as the wind gusted in the trees. The motor circled the cedar tree and drew up by the front steps. After a week in Scarborough that had turned into a stay of three months, Mama was home at last.

Jeff Smith jumped down and ran to open the door. Mama got out of the motor smoothly, majestically. She was wearing a large hat with a green bow; she held onto it as the wind caught the wide brim and made it flap up and down. Foreshortened from Eliza's perspective, elegant in her long coat, Mama paused at the bottom of the steps to look up at the house as if to remind herself what it was like. Eliza held her breath. Would Mama see her? Her heart swelled with — was it pride, was it love: what was it?

The moment passed. Mama climbed the steps and entered the house. Jeff got back into the motor and drove it round to the stable block.

The breeze gusted. Dead leaves swirled on the gravel.

* * *

The expected summons came. Eliza made her way slowly, reluctantly to the parlour. Now she must begin to pay the price for all her weeks of liberty.

Mama was seated on the stool by her bureau, her face impassive. Eliza felt clumsy and awkward by comparison. Her hands moved of their own accord, twitching and picking at the lace decoration on her dress.

Mama sighed. 'Where to begin. As if I hadn't enough to do, with the accounts behindhand and so much waste and inefficiency. The maids *will* use too many cloths and dusters. One needs eyes in the back of one's head.' She sighed again, an ominous sign. 'I am most displeased, Elizabeth. To come back to reports of your running wild — frolicking in the fields. *Frolicking* was the word used. Mrs Bourne tells me you were extraordinarily rude to her and—'

'Oh, Mrs Bourne!' said Eliza dismissively.

'Mrs Bourne does a difficult job with considerable ability. We couldn't manage without her. You might remember that in future.' Mama pursed her lips, patted her coiffure. 'It's my own fault, of course. I stayed away far too long. I don't know what I was thinking. But Mrs Varney was so very hospitable, and Colonel Harding—'

'Colonel Harding was there? Colonel Harding was in Scarborough?'

'Yes, he was there for a time. He was visiting his daughter. He is quite entitled to visit his daughter. But that is neither here nor there. We are not talking about Colonel Harding. We are talking about you and your . . . behaviour. If I'd had the slightest idea of what was going on . . . But I thought Roderick would be here. I was relying on Roderick. I am really quite cross with him. I have no idea where he is. He seems hardly to have been at home all summer.'

But Roderick wouldn't get summoned to the parlour, thought Eliza. He wouldn't have to pay the price for *his* liberty. Roderick would always be forgiven.

'Do stop *fidgeting*, Elizabeth! Now, what is all this about your being overfamiliar with the groom, Turner? You were seen *talking* to him on more than one occasion. You were seen — if one can believe it — with his *arm* around you.'

'But he had to put his arm around me! I was so frightened I nearly fainted! A tramp chased me through the Spinney and—' She stopped abruptly, gulped back the rest of her words. The look on Mama's face was enough to silence anyone.

After a pause, Mama said, 'Well, the matter is closed. I have spoken to Turner and—'

'But that's not fair! It wasn't *his* fault!'

'The matter is *closed*, Elizabeth. Really, this has to stop! All this running about, all these flights of fancy. You are old enough to know better. It is time you started acting your age. You will begin by apologising to Mrs Bourne—'

'Apologize to the Dreadnought? I won't, I shan't, she's a tyrant!'

'*Enough*! You will do as you are told! You will apologize to Mrs Bourne. You will, in future, not be rude to any of the servants. You will, in fact, not speak to the servants at all. It is beneath one's dignity to keep company with servants.'

'But Doro—'

'Dorothea was different. Dorothea was a special case. She had her own way of doing things. But at least one could say of Dorothea that she never made herself look ridiculous. You need taking in hand, Elizabeth, that is patently obvious. Since it has proved impossible to find you a suitable governess, I have decided to send you to school. Viola Somersby has mentioned a good boarding school. Or there is an academy for young ladies in Northampton: you could go there as a day girl.'

Go to school? Roderick had mentioned the possibility. Eliza had not taken him seriously. But now the moment had come. It would be terrible. A disaster. She would turn into one of those lumpy girls whose parties she had attended. It was all part of a plot. Mama wanted to punish her. Mrs Bourne wanted revenge.

'We will start as we mean to go on,' Mama continued. 'Arthur Camborne is coming to dinner tomorrow. It will be just the three of us, a chance for you to behave like a proper young lady.'

There was no arguing with Mama. Eliza bowed to the inevitable, dinner with Dr Camborne and then school. She didn't like to think what would become of her.

* * *

Eliza did her best to behave at dinner. She did her best to acquit herself like a lady. But before she'd even finished her soup, her hair had come loose, then she dipped her sleeve in the oyster sauce, and when Basford poured her some wine by mistake, she gulped it back so quickly — before Mama could notice — that it made her feel quite funny. Her hand shook as she put the empty glass down. Dr Camborne, in full flow as usual, glanced at her across the table and smiled, as if he knew everything she was doing and thinking. His smile made her skin crawl. He was so ugly with his bald head, his parchment skin, the attenuated wrinkles. She couldn't bear to look at him.

She looked at her plate instead, pushing the salmi of duck aside so she could see the design, blue on white. There were strange-looking birds with their heads thrown back and their beaks open; there were patterns like knotted ropes or rows of fishes' scales; there were plants with many leaves and massive, drooping flowers. It was exotic, extraordinary, like looking through a window into another world, a world in which—

Eliza stopped herself just in time. What was it Mama had said about flights of fancy? Hurriedly she covered up the pictures with her uneaten food and put her knife and fork down.

The doctor was still working his way through a large helping of the salmi. 'Such wonderful food, this. So clever of you, Eloise, to find a good cook and to keep her. Good cooks are a dying breed. I was at the Grange last Tuesday and the beef, quite frankly, was inedible. Lady Fitzwilliam used to be so meticulous, too, when it came to her victuals. It is really rather sad to see how her standards have fallen. But I expect, under the circumstances . . .'

'Circumstances?' said Mama enquiringly.

'But of course, you won't have heard, you've been away.' Dr Camborne perked up, having news to impart. 'It's been the talk of the neighbourhood. Lady Fitzwilliam's son, young Henry, crashed his motor car in some sort of race. Sport, they call it. Dicing with death, I say.'

'Was he very much hurt?'

'Eh? What?' The doctor had his mouth full, intent on doing justice to the duck.

'Henry Fitzwilliam: was he hurt?' Mama prompted.

'Oh, yes, yes, I'm afraid he was. Got rather smashed up. Broke his back. He'll never walk again. I've examined him myself, there can be no doubt about it.' Dr Camborne pointed to his plate with his knife. 'I must say, this is a very fine salmi of duck, very fine indeed.'

Eliza, the portentous words *never walk again* echoing in her head, burst out, 'I knew it, I felt it! I could tell that something terrible was going to happen!'

There was a sudden silence at the table. Mama and Dr Camborne stopped eating, stared at her in astonishment. Going bright red, Eliza gabbled, 'I went to Lawham with Daisy Turner, we saw the King and Queen, they passed us in a motor, they waved, then the street was empty and . . . it was like there was something waiting, something dreadful—' She broke off, staring with wide eyes, the fear she had felt in Cow Street coming back to her.

Dr Camborne regarded her with interest. 'Prescience?' he suggested.

'Hysteria,' said Mama firmly, bursting the doctor's bubble. 'Elizabeth has a rather vivid imagination, I'm afraid. This, you see, is what we mothers have to put up with. But poor Alice! How is Henry now?'

'Oh, the boy's bearing up. Bearing up. *Nihil cuiquam accidit ad quod ferendum natura non sit comparatus.*'

Eliza wrinkled her nose. The 'boy' Henry Fitzwilliam must be well into his thirties. But perhaps that seemed young to a man as old as Dr Camborne. How old was he, exactly, the village doctor? He never seemed to change. He was ageless. Roderick called him 'the wrinkled gnome'. Roderick also derided the doctor's habit of quoting Latin. What did it mean, *nihil cuiquam wotsit wotsit*? Eliza bit her tongue, determined not to give the doctor the satisfaction of asking him to translate.

Dr Camborne swallowed the last of his salmi and put his knife and fork down with a self-satisfied air. 'I am very much afraid that misadventures such as young Fitzwilliam's are only to be expected if one starts messing around with modern machinery. A case in point. I was called out a few weeks ago to an emergency in the fields. Boy from the village, one of the Carters it was, Edmund, just a child really. Got his arm caught in a harvesting contraption. Tore his hand right off at the wrist.'

For Eliza, this was too much. After the wine — after the news that Henry Fitzwilliam would never walk again — the sudden, vivid image of Edmund Carter's severed hand was more than she could take. Everything grew fuzzy one moment, went entirely black the next. She fainted across the table.

* * *

Dr Camborne prescribed an early night. Too much excitement, he said, was not good for young girls. Their constitutions could not cope. They got overwrought. The weaker vessel required wrapping in cotton wool.

But Eliza could not settle in bed. She got up and went into the day room, sat in the chair by the empty fireplace in the soft glow of the table lamp. The nursery was silent, Polly asleep, the rest of the house remote. Eliza felt forlorn and forgotten.

She had disgraced herself again. She had tried so hard but it had all come to nothing. Why was it so impossible to get things right?

The severed hand had been her downfall. She couldn't get it out of her head. Had it been sliced off cleanly the way Mr Lines the village butcher cut meat with his cleaver? Or had it been mangled in the machine? It made her feel queasy to think of it. Poor Edmund! *Edmund* the doctor had called him, one of the younger brothers of Dorothea's friend Nibs Carter. In the village he was known as Ned. He was only sixteen.

Eliza drew her feet up, huddled in her chair. Ned and his hand, Henry Fitzwilliam and his paralysed legs, Captain Scott in the snow, the sunken liner in the cold Atlantic. The world was fraught with danger. She wondered that she'd ever found the courage to venture out of the nursery. It made her

189

blood run cold to think of all the days and weeks and months when Mama had been away. She'd wandered by herself in the woods and fields and byways without a thought as to what might be lurking in wait. She'd gone out in the dark, she'd walked all the way to the canal in the moonlight. What if it hadn't been Kolya she'd met there, but the turnpike sailor — or someone even worse? What if she'd fallen (or been pushed) into the canal and drowned? She wished that Clifton was a castle. She wished it had cyclopean walls and a drawbridge. But would she be safe even then? No one was safe from God.

God is love, the vicar said. But Eliza in the gloom of the nursery pictured God as a Colonel Harding figure, blotchy-faced and bombastic, enthroned in high heaven, the world spread at his feet. On a whim, God with one vindictive finger could reach down and inflict any number of calamities: Captain Scott perished, thousands drowned, Ned Carter lost his hand.

There was no defence against God.

* * *

She went in search of Billy Turner despite Mama's strictures. She felt it her duty to beg Billy's pardon as it was her fault he'd got into trouble. But Billy seemed quite unconcerned, as if being *spoken to* by Mama was neither here nor there. 'It's in one ear and out the other with me. That's what our ma says, any road.'

To be quite sure there were no hard feelings, Eliza insisted on shaking hands. Billy's hand was much larger than hers. It was brown and calloused with big stubby fingers and dirt ingrained. Eliza wondered what Ned Carter's hand had been like. Billy, of course, knew all about Ned's accident, for the Turners and Carters lived almost opposite each other and, although Billy mostly slept in the stable block at night, barely a day went by when he wasn't in the village at one point or another. He did not seem to think there was any use in weeping and wailing over Ned's misfortune. What was done was done, Billy said with a shrug of his broad shoulders. All Ned could do now was make the best of it. Ned must learn to cope with one hand instead of two: his left hand, not his right.

Eliza wished she could shrug things off the way Billy did. But no one, not even Billy, could save her from school. Mama had finally decided on the academy for young ladies in Northampton. It was better than being sent away — but not much better. Roderick had survived school, however. So must she. She could not be found wanting.

* * *

Lady Fitzwilliam had once been a frequent visitor at Clifton, often accompanied by her son Henry, but when she called towards the end of October, alone, it occurred to Eliza that such visits were now few and far between.

It was a Saturday. Eliza did not go to the academy on Saturdays. During the reign of the pinch-faced governess she would have been expected in the drawing room to play the piano or recite poetry or in some other way show off her 'accomplishments'. Thankfully, those days were gone. She could sit quiet and still, watching and listening.

Mama raised the subject of Henry. Eliza would not have dared. Mama was fearless.

Henry, Lady Fitzwilliam reported, was as well as could be expected. There were days when he was a little despondent but it soon passed: he'd always been an optimistic sort of boy (Lady Fitzwilliam, like Dr Camborne, called Henry a boy). People were kind. So many took the trouble to call. Only the other day, Giles Milton had stopped by: Giles and his wife and their two little boys, the younger of whom was Henry's godson. Henry and Giles, of course, had been friends for years, united by a shared obsession with motor cars. They had often raced together. These days one saw less of Giles at the Grange. He had given up racing and was kept busy running the BFS showroom in London.

'If Henry had only given up racing too. But racing was his passion.' Lady Fitzwilliam shuddered. 'I don't like to talk about motors since Henry's accident. I don't like to *think* about them. I refuse to get in one. I use the old brougham instead. It needed some work — the floor had fallen out — but it's almost as good as new now.'

Lady Fitzwilliam at first sight looked and sounded the same as ever but Eliza on closer inspection wondered if perhaps her hair was a little greyer, if there weren't perhaps a few more wrinkles. She was thinner, too, and her eyes had lost some of their old sparkle. Despite Mama's best efforts, the conversation lagged at times. This would never have happened in the old days. Lady Fitzwilliam had been almost as adept in the drawing room as Mama.

Eliza noted that although several different subjects were essayed, the talk always came round in the end to Henry. He had been getting a little stout of late, Lady Fitzwilliam said, apropos of nothing. He would get stouter still now he was confined to a wheelchair. Then again, he would be thirty-six next February. Putting on a little weight was to be expected at that age.

'Thirty-six! Imagine!' Lady Fitzwilliam gazed wistfully out of the french windows: she was not looking at the view. 'It seems only yesterday he was a babe in arms. Do you remember, Eloise, when he was born? There was all that agitation for war at the time. Everyone was for the Turks and against the Russians. There were demonstrations in Hyde Park. Joseph still had his seat in those days. He was often in the House until late. He was very anti-Russian. "If we let the Russians get their hands on Constantinople," he said, "there will be no stopping them! It will be India next!" It's all changed these days. We are friends with the Russians now, or so I'm given to understand. Not that I've ever met a Russian, or even a Turk for that matter — although now I come to think about it, there was that friend of Roderick's. Wasn't he from Russia? A most peculiar boy. Very earnest. He'd got eyes that looked right through you. What became of him, that boy? Have you seen him lately?'

No, thought Eliza. Not for ages and ages. Not since that night in August, the night when Roderick and Kolya had fought, the night of Kolya's moonlight swim.

'I am sorry not to have seen Roderick,' Lady Fitzwilliam continued. (Mama was content now just to listen. She seemed to know by instinct exactly what was required.) 'It's been so long since I saw him last. He's grown into such a fine young boy, so very handsome, and so like his grandfather! Dear Old Harry. He was anti-Russian too. Do you remember, Eloise — well, of course you do, he was your father: do you remember how he disliked the Russians? Gladstone, too. He detested Gladstone. And the railways. He had an aversion to anything modern. He'd have had no time for motor cars. Perhaps he was right all along. Progress, we used to call it, us younger generation. Progress. We thought it a good thing, we mocked our parents for not keeping up. But now, I wonder. Yes, I wonder.'

She sighed, looking round the room, her eyes not focusing on anything. Finally her gaze came to rest on her hands in her lap.

'Isn't it odd that Henry was crippled by a motor car, one of the very machines that are making him rich. *Ironic*, Joseph would have called it. That was one of his words, *ironic*. What a blessing Joseph didn't live to see his own son . . . But there. Never mind. And now I must go. I mustn't take up any more of your time. I don't like to leave Henry too long. Where did I put my stick . . . ? Ah, thank you, Ordish. And my hat too. Bless you. Well, goodbye, Eloise, my dear. Goodbye Elizabeth. But my word, how you've grown! And you're attending school now, I hear! What interesting lives you lead, you youngsters, always on the go. Henry was just the same. Just the same.'

Off she went, stooping, shuffling, leaning on her stick—

But that was complete nonsense, Eliza told herself sternly. It was her imagination running away with her. Lady Fitzwilliam was straight-backed, proud and hale, didn't really need a stick. She was only a dozen years older than Mama.

What was it about her, then, that made her seem so ancient?

With Lady Fitzwilliam gone, Mama got up to return to the parlour. She hesitated, however, by the breakfast room door and looked back. Her lips were slightly parted. Eliza felt for a split second that Mama was about to say something different to anything she had said before, something profound, something that would change things between them forever.

But all she did say, after a pause, was, 'Back to the nursery now, please, Elizabeth.'

* * *

December rolled round at last. The Michaelmas term was over and Roderick arrived from Oxford. On his first morning back he came up to the nursery as he'd always done. Perhaps he'd forgotten that Dorothea wasn't there. Perhaps he'd come up from habit. Eliza hardly dared presume that he'd come to see her.

'Mother's being reading the riot act,' he said gloomily, pacing up and down. 'I neglected my responsibilities. I let you run wild all summer. It's a bit rich, I must say! I wasn't the one who spent three months in Scarborough!'

He flung himself, frowning, into the chair by the fire. He surely knew, thought Eliza, that Mama would not stay mad at him for long. She never did. Perhaps, then, there was another reason for his air of gloom.

'Well, kiddo, and what have you been doing with yourself? You've started school, Mother says. A bit late in the day, I would have thought. What's it like, this school of yours?'

But she couldn't bring herself to tell him about the academy, how dull it was, how she could *feel* herself getting lumpier and lumpier every passing day. Already it seemed as if she'd spent half her life there. She asked him instead about Wales. He had been going to Wales when he left Clifton in August.

Roderick wrinkled his nose. Wales was a gruesome place, barely civilized, the people savages. He and Kolya had stayed with Miss Halsted and her friends in a primitive sort of cottage half way up what the Welsh had the temerity to call a mountain. It had rained most of the time. There'd been nothing to do but listen to the pointless conversations of his companions, who had talked endlessly about politics and philosophy. They had also taken up *country crafts* (Roderick sneered at the words). They had tried their hands at spinning and weaving and dying cloth, without much success. They had made items of wooden furniture which fell apart as soon as they were finished. What the point of it all was, he didn't like to guess.

From Wales, Roderick continued, getting up and resuming his pacing around the room, he'd followed Miss Halsted to London where he'd had the misfortune to attend a meeting of her infamous Thursday Evening Club. It had proved a ghastly experience. The so-called club was an unholy hotchpotch of upstart cockneys, muddle-headed artists and frightful bluestockings, not to mention the foreigners — there was even an Irishman. They had endless debates, talked the most incredible drivel. How in the modern world could one best advance the cause of women's suffrage? Was a socialist elite a contradiction in terms? What, if any, were the artistic merits of French post-impressionism? They wouldn't listen when he tried to talk sense, they shouted him down and called him a chauvinist and a reactionary. They were nothing but a load of cranks and charlatans. He was sorry he'd ever met them.

'And . . . and Kolya?' Eliza ventured to say, anxious for news of the Russian.

'Oh, they all think Antipov a fine fellow! He talks as much bosh as they do. It impresses them no end.'

'Roddy, do you hate Kolya now? I saw you hit him!'

Roderick glanced at her keenly. 'So you know about that, do you? We both got a bit hot under the collar that night. It's nothing new. We never agree on anything. That's half the fun. He has the most hare-brained ideas I've ever heard but he's . . . he's a very *honest* sort of fellow. There's not an ounce of affectation in him. I suppose that's why I like him. If I do like him. There *are* limits to what a chap can take,' he added darkly.

He gave a huge sigh and threw himself back into the chair. Antipov had graduated, he went on. Antipov had left Oxford. One hardly saw him now from one month to the next. It was the same with Miss Halsted. It was so long since he'd seen Miss Halsted he'd all but forgotten what she looked like. Lord, what a wretched business life was, absolutely beastly! He might as well drop Miss Halsted altogether. He might as well. What was the use if he never got to see her?

A moment later he sprang to his feet once more. There was no point in sitting round moping. He'd be better off taking his dog out. He'd take a gun, too, shoot a few wild animals. That would make him feel better.

The nursery seemed more than usually silent and empty once Roderick had gone. Whatever else you said about him, he certainly livened a place up. In her bedroom, Eliza looked out of the window, her elbows resting on the sill. It was a still, overcast morning. Rooks flapped lethargically in the sky. After a while she saw below Roderick emerge from the house. He strode across the gravel in his long overcoat, a gun on his arm, Hecate at his heels. Circling the cedar tree, he disappeared into the Pheasantry to reappear after a time in the big ploughed field called Horselands where the path to the village was like a pale brown ribbon dwindling towards the distant crenulated tower of St Adeline's, grey and austere. Hecate, a black spot at Roderick's feet, was never still.

Roderick raised his gun. The report from his shot came a moment later, muffled by the window. A rook fell from the sky.

* * *

The hunt was to meet at Newbolt Hall. There was nothing like a spot of hunting, Roderick said, to blow the cobwebs away. He would ride over to Colonel Harding's house and join them.

Eliza went downstairs to see him off, stood side-by-side with Mama on the doorstep. It was a crisp, bright morning with the promise of sunshine later. Roderick was astride his restive horse, which was jigging about, kicking up the gravel. He pulled on the reins impatiently, looking round for Billy Turner and the spare horse.

'Where is he, the useless clot?'

With Roderick watching for Turner and Mama watching Roderick, it was Eliza who was first to see a solitary figure emerge from behind the evergreens at the head of the drive: a woman wearing a beige coat with big buttons, a hat with a turned-up brim and shiny black boots. Eliza at first did not recognise her as she hesitantly approached them.

'Rosa!' Roderick leapt down from his horse, went striding to meet her, pleasure and puzzlement written over his face in equal measure. 'What are you doing here? Have you walked all the way from the station? You should have let me know!'

Miss Halsted gave a timid smile. For Miss Halsted to be timid was most out of character.

'Good morning, Miss Halsted. How very nice to see you again.' Mama pitched her words perfectly as only Mama could, polite good manners layered over a soupçon of surprise, with just the merest hint of reproach at such an unexpected — not to say unorthodox — arrival. She turned back to Roderick. 'You really ought to go or you will miss the start at Newbolt Hall.'

'Never mind that.' Roderick shrugged off all suggestion of the hunt. He took Miss Halsted's bag, ushered her towards the house, his hand on her back. 'Come in out of the cold, Rosa. Some tea, perhaps? You've had breakfast, I suppose.'

At that moment Billy Turner appeared leading Roderick's second horse, which trotted meekly behind him, behaving itself as all horses did for Billy.

'Here, Turner,' said Roderick. 'Look after Conquest a moment, would you? I shan't be long.'

Mama, bowing to the inevitable, led the way into the house. Eliza on the threshold stepped aside to let Roderick and Miss Halsted pass. She caught a glimpse of Miss Halsted pausing in the hallway to grip Roderick's arm; she heard Miss Halsted's urgent whisper: 'Roderick, I must speak to you! I must speak to you right away! It's incredibly important.'

Mama, looking back, interrupted. 'This way, Miss Halsted. The morning room. I will ring for tea. And you will want to sit down after your long walk.'

* * *

They sat in the morning room, the four of them, and drank tea, while Billy Turner waited outside with the horses: Eliza could see him from where she was sitting by the window. Miss Halsted did not say why she had come. She did not say much at all. She looked — as Daisy would have said — white as a sheet. Mama in due course extended an invitation to luncheon. Miss Halsted accepted.

The little party broke up. Back in the day room of the nursery, Eliza sat down then got up, picked toys off the shelves, put them back. With one finger she traced the chalked words on the blackboard where she'd been trying to help Daisy with her writing. Daisy had drawn the D of her own name back-to-front as she always did. She could never seem to get it right.

Turning away, Eliza met the parrot's eye. 'Oh, Polly! Something's happened!' But what? What was so important that Miss Halsted had come all this way, had walked the three miles or so from Welby station?

Polly looked at Eliza cryptically then, losing interest, began to preen her feathers.

In no time at all, or so it seemed, the gong sounded for luncheon. Eliza ran to her room, dipped her hands in the water in the basin on her washstand, splashed her face.

Half way down to the next floor she heard voices on the landing below and stopped to listen. Roderick and Miss Halsted were talking in whispers.

'Are you sure? Are you absolutely *certain*?' Roderick sounded tense, almost angry.

'Of course I'm not *certain*,' hissed Miss Halsted. 'I may have got it wrong. I'm not sure. I don't think so.'

'I don't understand. How has this happened?'

'I would have thought that was self-evident.'

'But I've seen you once in all these weeks! I've been going out of my mind, wanting you, and you always finding excuses. Once, Rosa, once!'

'Once is all it takes, it seems.'

'Thanks for that statement of the blindingly obvious.'

'There's no need to take that tone. I wanted you to know, that's all. There's no need to bother yourself further.'

'Rosa, wait, I'm sorry. Rosa, where are you going? Come back, Rosa!'

Footsteps sounded. The voices faded.

Eliza made her way down, one step at a time. She was shaking, she didn't know why.

Luncheon was a rather awkward affair, the atmosphere strained. Even the Perfect Hostess seemed at a loss.

'What are your plans, Miss Halsted? You are welcome, of course, to stay the night — to stay as long as you like. But I must let Cook know about dinner.'

'She's staying,' said Roderick shortly. 'She's staying to dinner, she's staying the night.'

Rosa gave him a look as cryptic as Polly's.

* * *

Having dressed for dinner with Daisy's help, Eliza went through to the day room and found Roderick there already changed, impeccable and debonair as he paced up and down. She was rather taken aback, couldn't account for his being there.

As soon as Daisy had gone he burst out, 'I wish Doro were here! Doro would know what to do!' He frowned. He was very tall and grim. Eliza remembered how he'd tugged at the reins of his horse. She remembered the rook falling from the sky. She was almost frightened of him.

He stopped his pacing and stood right in front of her, chewing his lip. 'Oh, God, kiddo. Oh Lord.' He sounded as if he was in pain.

'Roddy, what is it? What's the matter? I do wish you'd tell me!'

'It's . . . it's Rosa. She's going to have a child. My child.' He went silent, chewing his lip ever more feverishly, looking at her dubiously. He said at length, 'You do know what that means, I suppose? You do know about babies?'

She nodded. But she didn't know, she didn't know at all. She knew that babies came in the midwife's bag — or did they? It didn't quite ring true. There was something strange about babies, something sly and secret, something she hadn't got to the bottom of.

'She thinks she can raise it on her own! That's her idea, anyway. That's her plan. She's mad as a hatter. But why should I care? Let her get on with it! I don't want a child. I'm only twenty-one, still at Oxford. And I couldn't very well marry her even if I wanted to. Mother would—' He stopped abruptly, pulled out a chair, sat down at the big table. He tapped the scrubbed wood with his fingers.

Her back to the wall, Eliza ventured to say, 'Do . . . do you like Miss Halsted very much?'

'No, I don't! I don't like her at all! She's monstrous!' His hands on the tabletop bunched into fists. He glared at them as if deciding how best he might use them. Then his expression changed. Slowly he uncurled his hands and flattened them against the scrubbed surface of the table, his fingers twitching. 'I'm talking rot. I do . . . I do like . . . But, hang it all, *like* is such an insipid word!' He gave a little laugh: a hollow, rather disparaging laugh. 'Lord, I'm such a fool! Ask Doro, she'll tell you. Or . . . well . . . you can't ask her. She's gone. I keep forgetting.'

He got up abruptly, knocking his chair over. Crossing to the shelves, he began rummaging amongst the toys that Eliza herself had rearranged only that morning.

'Rosa makes me feel . . . I'm not sure . . . as if I can be *myself* when I'm with her.' He was muttering under his breath

200

as if talking to himself, picked up a wooden box distractedly and turned it over and over in his hands. 'She's not the sort of girl I ever thought I'd like. We're so very different. And yet . . . she seems to like me, too. And sometimes I think it's the parts of me no one else likes that she likes best of all. It's . . . it's . . . I don't know . . . I can't explain.' He suddenly swung round, dark eyes flashing. 'Why should I need to explain? Why should I explain myself to *you*?'

He took a step towards her. Eliza flinched, pressing herself against the wall. But at that moment he noticed the box in his hands. He seemed suddenly to recognise it. He opened it. It was full of toy soldiers. He sorted through them. A distant look came into his eyes. 'Doro bought me these. I told her she needn't. As usual, she didn't listen. Lord, she'd have some things to say now! I've got my just desserts, she'd say.'

He replaced the lid on the box and put it aside. 'She has her head in the clouds,' he muttered, and Eliza, listening, understood he wasn't talking about Dorothea now but Miss Halsted again. 'She hasn't a penny and her saintly aunts will disown her. She listens too much to those friends of hers. Those half-baked cranks fill her head with nonsense. And Antipov—' He broke off, began pacing up and down once more. A new fire kindled in his eyes. 'Antipov, that snake! I can see it all now! This is the opportunity he's been waiting for. He can step in and save her! Well, I shan't let him. If the child is mine, why shouldn't I own it? I don't care what Mother thinks. Mother can't tell me what to do. If I want to marry Rosa—' He broke off, cocking an ear. 'Listen! There's the gong. We have to go down.' He swung round, glared at her. 'Not a word! Not a word to anyone! Do you understand?'

She nodded, not trusting herself to speak. She watched him smooth his hair and pull down his shirt cuffs. He looked at her and smiled: a rather savage smile, but a smile nonetheless. He held out his hand. 'Come on, kiddo. Let's go.'

* * *

It seemed to Eliza at dinner that of the four of them only Mama was her usual self. She didn't seem to notice there was anything amiss. Eliza found herself feeling sorry for her, so ignorant of the facts when normally she was mistress of every situation, sensitive to every nuance. It was as if her omniscience had been shown up as a cheap trick.

It seemed wrong, feeling sorry for Mama.

* * *

A feeling of oppression seemed to weigh down the whole house next morning. Or was it her imagination? Eliza could not decide. She tried to remember everything Roderick had said in the day room yesterday. It was all such a terrible muddle in her head. Did he think Miss Halsted a fool, or did he think her the only person in the world who liked him? Was he going to marry her, or wasn't he? It was impossible to sit quietly and work it all out. Daisy was being at her most annoying, 'clatterbanging round the place', as she herself might have put it, and grumbling too. Miss Eliza was in the way; it was the devil's own job trying to get the place clean without Miss Eliza under her feet; why couldn't Miss Eliza just keep out her road?

But when Eliza retreated to her room, Daisy after a moment followed. The sheets needed changing, the room must be aired. Why didn't Miss Eliza find herself something to do instead of moping around with a face as long as a gasman's mackintosh?

There was no talking to Daisy in this mood. She still harboured a grudge over the Zack Hobson affair and was making Eliza pay. It was best to get right away.

Downstairs in the hallway as Eliza tried to make up her mind what to do she became aware of voices in the parlour — loud voices. They had to be loud to carry all across the breakfast room and out here into the hall. Mama and Roderick were arguing. They were actually *shouting* at one another.

Eliza clapped her hands over her ears. She didn't want to listen. She didn't want to know. It was all very well for

Roderick to say that he wouldn't let Mama tell him what to do, but no one went against Mama and got away with it. Most people were too sensible even to try. It sounded, however, as if Mama and Roderick wouldn't stop until they had torn each other to pieces.

Hounded out of the nursery and now out of the house itself, Eliza took refuge outside. The wintry gardens were bleak and withered. Frost lingered in patches. The sky was gunmetal grey. In the old summer house she sat on a creaky wicker chair amongst the dust and the cobwebs and the mouse droppings. She thought of Mama and Roderick arguing in the parlour. She thought of Daisy clatterbanging round the nursery. She thought of Miss Halsted and the baby. It seemed to her that everything was falling apart. The whole world was as grubby and decayed as the summerhouse.

She sat there in silence, unmoving, all alone.

CHAPTER NINE

The wedding was arranged for the end of January, to take place in Tonbridge. It had to be done in a hurry because of the baby. Eliza wished she could ask Daisy about the baby but she baulked at showing herself up again as she'd done with the monthlies (if *monthly* was even the right word: Daisy did not always use the right word for things).

The baby was causing all sorts of trouble and it hadn't even arrived yet.

'Mother was absolutely furious,' said Roderick cheerfully. All his doubts appeared forgotten. He was smiling his cat-with-the-cream smile. 'You should have heard her, kiddo! You wouldn't believe what a scoundrel you have for a brother. I'm a stain on the family name, we shall be the talk of the neighbourhood, I've ruined our reputation forever. There was a lot more. I can't remember half of it. I'm surprised she didn't have me horsewhipped.'

But this was overplaying his hand. Mama would never have hurt a hair on his head, no matter how much in disgrace he was. All the same, Eliza looked at him with a new respect. He had stood up to Mama and he had won. She would never have believed it possible.

Mama did not waste time with wailing or beating her breast. As Billy Turner might have said, what was done was done and now it was a case of making the best of things.

'But I do wish Dorothea were here,' Mama sighed. 'Dorothea was such a help at times like this. There is so much to do.'

What exactly needed to be done wasn't clear. When Eliza offered her services, Mama merely told her to stop making a nuisance of herself: she had enough to cope with already. Eliza muttered to herself darkly: 'Mama would rather have Dorothea as a daughter than me. I am just a changeling who nobody wants!'

Like Mama, Eliza had doubts about Roderick's wedding. To marry Miss Halsted seemed rather rash. Eliza couldn't imagine Roderick married. Would he change? Would he be different?

Doubts aside, there was plenty to look forward to: a new frock, a trip to Tonbridge, a stay in a hotel. Nothing so exciting had happened since the continental holiday and that seemed an age ago now. Best of all, the wedding meant that Eliza would be free of the hated academy for an entire week. That really *would* be a treat.

She began counting the days.

* * *

The big day drew steadily nearer. It made Eliza go hot and then cold to think of it. It made her head throb and sent her dizzy.

'It sounds to me like you're sickening for summat,' said Daisy. She felt Eliza's forehead. 'I was right, miss. You're burning up.'

The doctor was sent for.

'There's nothing wrong with me. I feel quite well.'

'Let me be the judge of that,' said Dr Camborne, opening his bag.

'But the wedding!' Eliza was ready to beg and plead. 'I must go to the wedding!'

'We'll see.' He checked his thermometer. 'You are running a temperature. Probably a touch of flu. Bed for you, young lady. Plenty of rest. I shall call back tomorrow to see how you are.'

* * *

'I'm well, quite well!' Eliza announced when Daisy came into her room next morning. 'I don't feel ill at all.'

She had done everything in her power to see off her sickness. She had prayed fervently to God for half the night. But as she slipped out of bed while Daisy was opening the curtains, spots appeared before her eyes and her legs gave way. Before she knew it, she was in a heap on the floor.

At once the room was full of people. Basford lifted her up, placed her gently back in bed.

'Send for Dr Camborne,' Mama ordered.

'At once, ma'am,' said Mrs Bourne.

'No, no, no!' Eliza turned, twisted, fighting thin air. 'Not the doctor, I don't want the doctor!' It was a plot, Mama and Mrs Bourne together. And to have Dr Camborne examine her again: the thought was unbearable, his clammy hands sliding over her skin.

'Stop this at once, Elizabeth!' Mama used the tone of voice that everyone invariably obeyed. 'You are ill. You need the doctor. That's an end to it.'

And so Dr Camborne came. It seemed to Eliza that he took great pleasure in pronouncing her doom. She was much worse today. She would need at least a week in bed. Eliza wanted to protest. She wanted to scream and shout, to *demand* to be taken to Tonbridge. But when it came to it she found she was too weak even to speak. She burst into tears instead.

'There, there, my dear, it can't be helped.' Dr Camborne patted her as if she was a dog — as if she was Roderick's Hecate. 'It's only a wedding, not the end of the world.'

Eliza glared up at him through her tears. How she hated him! She hated him with a passion that seemed to burn her up inside. Everything about him was repulsive: his smarmy smile, his prying hands, the sinister way he knew every detail of one's body. Perhaps he even knew about the monthlies. Perhaps he could tell just by looking. It was too demeaning for words.

When he'd gone, Eliza lay in bed silent and still. Her head ached, her nose ran, she felt weak and watery, the daylight hurt her eyes even with the curtains closed. How spiteful of God! How unutterably spiteful, and after she had prayed so hard! She could just picture him — God/Colonel Harding — laughing and sneering, pointing at her with his vindictive finger, pressing down and down on her, squashing her to nothing.

* * *

Mama came up to the nursery in her travelling clothes. She looked incredibly upright and elegant, a match for any-one, even Mrs Somersby. Unlike Mrs Somersby, however, there was never anything showy about Mama. Her hat, for instance, was quite plain. But the way wide brim was poised at a perfect angle made your heart swell to see it.

'Now, Elizabeth,' she began crisply, looking down at Eliza. Then she paused. Her expression softened. She took Eliza's hand. 'Such a shame, to be ill at a time like this.'

But to be pitied by Mama was awful, far worse than being chastised. Eliza found herself wishing that Mama would just go, go, go.

Alone in her room, Eliza heard the sound of the motor's engine fading down the drive. Mama was off to Oxford. She was going to meet Roderick, they would travel together to Tonbridge, and then—

Oh, but what was the use in thinking about it? It made her head hurt. It made her chest hurt. It made her heart hurt most of all. Her heart was aching and aching. To miss her brother's wedding, to miss the only bright spot in all the long dull months: it was unbearable.

She curled up shivering, awash with misery.

* * *

She woke from a deep, deep sleep. She was not sure what day it was or how long she'd been sleeping. The curtains were half shut. A cold grey light came into the room. Was it morning or afternoon? She couldn't tell.

She raised her head. Daisy had been peeking in, was about to close the door. It must have been the sound of it opening, Eliza realised, that had woken her.

'Daisy, wait!'

'So you're awake, miss. I wasn't sure. There's a visitor. I can send him away if you like — if you don't feel well enough.'

'Don't send him away! Show him up! I feel quite well enough for visitors.'

Eliza sat up, straightened her hair, tucked the bed covers round her. She'd forgotten to ask who the visitor was. Daisy hadn't said. An unreasoning fear took hold of her. What if it was the turnpike sailor? What if he'd tricked his way into the house and was coming to get her? Rigid with fear, she gripped the blankets in her fists and waited.

The visitor walked in.

'Oh, Kolya, it's you, it's really you! How lovely!'

It was like seeing a vision. She feasted her eyes on him. Almost half a year had passed since his last visit to Clifton but he was just as she remembered — unless he was perhaps a little more dishevelled even than usual. He had his overcoat on. His hat was in his hands.

'If you are poorly, I shall go away.'

'Don't go, please stay!' She held out her hand. 'I feel so much better now. It was only influenza.'

He took hold of her hand, allowed himself to be drawn towards the bed, sat down on the edge. His cheeks were flushed and his eyes bright, as if he'd been walking in the cold. But his hand was warm, his grip firm.

'I've been so sleepy,' she said. 'I feel like I've slept for days and days. I've lost track of time. Is it morning or afternoon? Is the wedding over?'

Instead of answering her questions, he said softly, '"Sleep is a gentle thing, beloved from pole to pole." One of your English poets wrote that. I cannot remember which one.'

'I don't know about poetry. They don't teach us things like that at the academy. I go to an academy now, an academy for young ladies.'

'What *do* they teach you at this academy?'

'Dull things, boring things. How to behave at dinner. How to cultivate the art of listening — *cultivate*, as if it was a plant! I get into trouble because I always say, "I ride in the train to school," when I ought to say, "I *drive* in the train." Oh Kolya, you don't know how silly it all is, how pointless. I spend all day looking out of the window. I watch the children in the charity school opposite. I watch men digging up the road to lay tram tracks. The tram wires are already in place. They look like a giant spider's web.'

'I also *ride* in a train. I ride from Tonbridge to see you.'

'To see me? You came all that way for me?'

'Mrs Brannan was most anxious. She thought you might be worse. I came to put her mind at rest.'

Was it really possible that Mama had been *anxious* about her? 'I am not worse. I feel much better. But what about the wedding? Won't you miss the wedding?'

'The wedding . . .' He glanced at his pocket watch. 'The wedding happens just about now.'

He let go of her hand and turned away but not before she'd seen a spasm cross his face. She understood then why he'd volunteered to come and see her. He'd not wanted to stay. He'd not been able to bear it.

'I set out early. No one was awake. I did not wait for breakfast. I did not even shave.' He rubbed his chin, his face in profile.

She reached out. She touched his cheek. His bristles were very fair and almost invisible but they felt prickly against her fingers. What made the hairs grow, she wondered: what were they for?

She drew her hand back. He caught hold of it and turned to look at her. His questing eyes made her catch her breath. What wild impulse had made her touch him? And now her hand was snared and he was very close with only the bed covers between them. All she had on was her nightdress.

But she didn't feel as she did with Dr Camborne, that he had a hold over her. There was no sly smile. Her skin didn't crawl as it did when the doctor prodded and poked her. She felt instead that nothing bad could ever happen to her while Kolya was there. There was something unsettling about him, it was true, but not in a bad way. His strangeness, his foreignness, only served to round him off. Kolya would not have been Kolya otherwise.

'Will . . . will you grow a beard?'

'No. I will not grow beard. Beards are not . . . *fashion*: is this correct word? Beards once were fashion in Russia but the Tsar put tax on them.'

'A tax on beards? How funny!' She couldn't stop herself from giggling. Hysteria, Mama would have called it. She was afraid he would think her silly.

He smiled. 'Is funny, yes. But also is unfair.' His smile faded. He looked at her solemnly. 'There have been taxes on many different things, on salt, on windows, even on people, but is always the poor who pay most. To a rich man, a rouble is nothing. He has others. A rouble to a poor man may be all he has.'

'I wish I knew about beards and about roubles! Why must I go to that hateful academy where I learn nothing?'

'Every experience has value, Leeza, even your academy. Perhaps what they teach is no good but you learn all the same. You learn what is important and what is not. You learn about human nature. You learn about tram tracks in the road. And you see the tram wires as a spider's web. That is poetry, Leeza. You are a poet.'

He wasn't mocking her. He was quite serious. Nobody took her as seriously as he did. 'Oh, Kolya, I'm so glad you've come! You always make me see things differently. I do feel better now!'

'Good. Is good.' His smiled briefly then got up, went over to the window. He stood with his back to her, framed against the timeless grey day. 'Desolation,' he murmured, as if trying out a new word, testing it. Yet somehow she sensed he knew exactly what it meant, had chosen it expressly.

The desolation of this winter's day, she wondered, or the desolation in his heart? She could feel his sadness like a sharp pain inside her. It *wasn't* just her imagination, it wasn't!

He sighed, turned away from the window, came back to the bed, picked up his hat. 'Now I will go. I will leave you to get well.'

'But you mustn't, you can't, you've only just arrived!'

'I cannot stay. There is no one to invite me.'

'Yes there is! I shall invite you! Mama is away, I am mistress. You must stay to dinner, you must stay the night. I shall tell Mrs Bourne to make a room ready. I shall *order* her. She is a terrible tyrant but I'm not afraid of her. I shall *make* her obey me!'

Kolya suddenly laughed. It was enough to dispel all the desolation from the room. 'And me?' he said. 'Shall I obey you too?'

'Of course!' said Eliza, joining in with his laughter. 'You have no choice.'

* * *

Time passed quickly in Kolya's company. It was afternoon before she knew it. She sent him off so she could get dressed. It felt good to be getting up in defiance of Dr Camborne's orders.

She found Mrs Bourne in the basement. Despite the early hour, electric lights were on in the gloomy white-tiled passage. Eliza demanded a room for Mr Antipov and dinner straight away.

'Dinner?' Mrs Bourne looked askance.

'Well, of course dinner. We've missed luncheon.'

'But dinner at half past three? I've never heard the like!'

'What's this about dinner?' Cook appeared just then, bustling out of the larder with a covered tray in her hand. 'You can have dinner, my love, any time you want. I've half a chicken put by that will do nicely.'

Mrs Bourne passed no further comment. She put her nose in the air and swept off. The sound of jangling keys faded up the basement stairs.

'Well,' said Cook with satisfaction. 'That showed *her*!' She disappeared into the kitchen.

They were half way through dinner when Kolya suddenly remembered he'd left his bag at the station. He'd not been expecting to stay and had seen no point in lugging it with him.

'I will send someone to fetch it,' said Eliza imperiously. But who? Jeff Smith had gone off with Mama and there was no one else who could drive.

'If I might make a suggestion, miss . . .' Basford, waiting on, would never have dared speak if Mama had been there, or Roderick. But he was an obliging fellow, when he wasn't being put in his place. 'There's the old governess cart, miss. Turner could get it out, drive to Welby, fetch the gentleman's bag.'

And so it was arranged. When dinner was over, Kolya went off with Billy Turner while Eliza retreated to the drawing room and curled up on the settee to await their return. Basford had drawn the curtains and made up the fire. It was warm and snug. Before long she was fast asleep.

* * *

She woke up hours later. The fire had died down. One glance at the clock told her it was long past bedtime. Kolya had just come in. A smell of beer came in with him.

212

'I have drunk much of your English ale,' he said, swaying where he stood. He put his hand on the piano to steady himself. 'I have drunk your English ale and now I am *intoxicated*. This is good word, yes? I have never used this word before. *Intoxicated*.' He savoured the sound as well as slurring it, his Russian accent more pronounced now he was drunk.

She was worried that he might fall over but after a moment he got down on his hands and knees and crawled towards the fire place. He stretched out on the Turkey carpet. Eliza looked on astonished. Had anyone ever done such a thing in the decorous drawing room? How extraordinary to have a grown man lying at her feet!

Something stirred within her, a sense of adventure, perhaps. *Every experience has value*, Kolya had said. And here were lots of new experiences all at once.

She sat up on the settee. Sleep fell away.

'I have been to what you English call *a pub*,' said Kolya, addressing the plain painted ceiling. 'Vilyam Turner took me. That is his name: *Vilyam*. We are now best of friends. I drink much ale. I try to forget. I do not forget. Wedding is real. Wedding has happened.'

'But it *had* to happen, don't you see? It had to happen because of the . . . the baby.' She blushed at the whispered word *baby*. She was beginning now to guess where babies came from and it was nasty, loathsome, unthinkable. But the sense of adventure stirred within her once more and she blurted out, 'Where do babies really come from?'

He turned his head to look at her. 'You do not know?'

'Nobody tells me anything!' The blood was throbbing in her cheeks. He would think her such a child, the way she had giggled earlier over beards and now showing her shameful ignorance.

But he did not laugh as Daisy would have, he did not mock like Roderick. His bony fingers picked at the carpet as he carefully picked his words. 'Baby grows inside woman.'

'But how does it *get* there?'

'Is — is — I forget word. My head is all jumble. Is something that happens between man and woman. Is nothing to be afraid of, Leeza.' And indeed, the way he went on to explain it made it sound not nasty or loathsome but plain and simple — if rather improbable. 'Is not mystery. Is instinct, is nature — is beautiful. You will see.'

'Is . . . is it *love?*'

'Love is part of it, yes.'

'But love is such a nuisance! Love makes people do silly things. Love makes *you* unhappy, because of Miss Halsted.'

'Yes. I do love Rosa. I cannot help this. She is strong woman, she is intelligent woman, she is — but how do you say . . . ?' Growing animated, he made an effort to sit up but immediately sank back down with a groan. 'Room is going round. I must stay on floor.'

He looked rather helpless, spread-eagled on the carpet, like a fish washed up on a beach. His boots were scuffed, the heels worn; his trousers were rather shapeless and baggy; the middle buttons of his waistcoat were missing. She felt sorry for him, so drunk and down-at-heel and disconsolate. Sliding off the settee, she sat beside him on the carpet and took his hand: the hand that didn't make her skin crawl, the bony fingers that had been picking at the carpet.

He stared up at the ceiling through narrowed eyes, grey as flint. With Rosa by his side, he said, there was no knowing what he might have achieved. Without her, he was nothing. But this was wrong. It was weak. A man could not be a true revolutionary if he was swayed by love. A revolutionary must renounce love, must renounce *all* ties of affection. A revolutionary lived only for the destruction of society.

She didn't understand. Why did he want to destroy things?

'Urge to destroy can also be creative urge, Leeza. Society must be destroyed to its roots before we can build better world. This is what I want — what I dream of, what I long for: better world. While some men remain slaves, I cannot truly be free.'

'Sometimes I think that . . . that God wants to destroy us. That is why he makes bad things happen.'

Kolya looked at her with unguarded eyes. 'Leeza, there is no God.'

'But there is! There is! There must be!'

'You want God to be real because you are afraid. But we cannot make things real by just wishing. God is superstition. I believe in science. I have faith, yes, but my faith is in people, in human spirit.'

'How can you have faith in people when so many of them are horrid and wicked!'

'No one is born wicked, Leeza. It is society that makes us so. We do not need God to tell us what is right. We know in our hearts what is right.' With an effort, he sat up. 'Now I must go to bed before I fall asleep on floor.'

She watched him walk unsteadily out of the room. He left the door open. A draught came in. It made the dying embers glow with renewed life. Eliza sat on the floor hugging her knees. *There is no God.* Was Kolya right? Dorothea would never agree! But Dorothea believed in a God with a kindly smile, not God with the vindictive finger.

Eliza hugged her knees ever tighter. A cold, sharp, shivery feeling took hold of her. She would never go against Dorothea. But just imagine if it was true, if there was no God, no vindictive finger. Just imagine!

The cold, sharp, shivery feeling surged through her so that she came up in goose pimples.

* * *

'*Moya golova*! *Moya golova*!' Kolya in the breakfast room sat slumped over the table holding his head in his hands. 'Never shall I drink your English ale again. I shall drink only Russian vodka.'

'Bacon, sir?' said Basford, hovering.

'No. No bacon. No anything. You eat bacon.'

'Beg pardon, sir?'

215

'I see you looking at bacon as if you are hungry. If you are hungry, eat. Sit. Eat.'

Eliza paused with her fork halfway to her mouth, uncertain if Kolya was being serious or not. Basford looked affronted at the very idea but couldn't stop his eyes sliding round to take another peek at the dish of bacon on the sideboard.

Eliza jumped up. 'Why don't you sit with us, John? You ought to!' It would be rather funny, rather naughty, to eat breakfast with the footman. She would never have thought of it. It was always Kolya who came up with these interesting notions.

'Sit at the table, miss? ' Basford spoke rather stiffly. 'I couldn't possibly, it wouldn't be right! What would Mr Ordish say? And *Mrs Bourne!*'

'Fiddlesticks to Mrs Bourne! You know I'm not afraid of Mrs Bourne. Neither should you be, a big, tall man like you!' Eliza pulled out a chair. 'Sit here! *Do* please sit!'

'Well, miss, if you insist . . .'

'That's it. Pull your chair in. Now, what would you like? Bacon? Eggs? Coffee?'

'You mustn't make fun of me, Miss Eliza. It's not fair.'

'I'm not making fun, John. *I* shall serve *you* for a change, instead of the other way round. But I can't keep calling you *John.* What's your real name?'

'Basford, miss.'

'I know that! Your *first* name, silly!'

'Well . . . er . . . it's . . . Herbert, miss. My name's Herbert.'

'Herbert. That's a nice name. Like the Prime Minister. Much better than John. Here's your breakfast, Herbert, a bit of everything. And here's your coffee.'

Basford eyes his plate greedily. 'I shall get my marching orders if anyone catches me like this!'

'No you shan't, I shan't let them,' said Eliza as she returned to her own breakfast. She noted that Kolya had stopped clutching his head and was now watching them closely. She felt pleased to have done something that had aroused his interest. 'You are not doing anything wrong, Herbert, because . . . because . . . I don't know what it's because. Kolya will explain.'

Kolya broke into a grin. 'All men are created equal,' he said in a rather throaty voice.

'There! Do you see, Herbert? We are all equal.'

'If you say so, miss.' Basford glanced once more at the door before giving in to temptation. He took off his gloves, picked up his knife and fork, tucked in. 'This is first-rate bacon,' he said with his mouth full. 'We don't get nothing like it downstairs. Cook's a right skinflint, I can't tell you. Like being on holiday, this is.'

'Yes, you're quite right, that's just what it's like, with everyone away and with Kolya here. What a shame Mama is coming back so soon to spoil it! Why can't she stay away like Roddy? He won't be back until Easter!'

'Thank heavens for that!' exclaimed Basford, forgetting himself. But then he froze with his mouth full and went bright red.

'What's the matter, Herbert? Don't you like Roddy?'

'It's not that, miss. The thing is, I know he's your brother and all, but by jiminy Master Roderick is hard work! He likes all his clothes laid out just so, shirt on the left, trousers on the right, and woe betide if you get it wrong. He shaves sitting in his bath and all, which I think is downright dirty. But what do I know? I'm just the footman.'

'No man is a hero to his valet,' said Kolya.

'Ain't that the truth, Mr Anpitov!'

'Mr Antipov, Herbert: it's Antipov,' said Eliza, laughing.

Kolya was laughing too, his hangover in abeyance, and Basford was grinning all over his face in true Basford style, chewing all the while. His breakfast was disappearing like frost in the sun. Eliza had never known anyone eat so quickly. She had never known, either, breakfast to be such fun. This was just the right way to start the day.

* * *

The holiday spirit was short-lived. Kolya announced after breakfast that he had to leave.

'Oh, must you? I wish you could stay!'

'I have appointment. I must visit acquaintance of my father in Hampstead: cultured man, rich man. He translates into English the works of Tolstoy, Chekhov, Dostoevsky: Russian writers. I help.'

'Can't the man do without you just this once?'

'Perhaps he can do without me. But I cannot do without him. He gives me money. I need money for living in England. What my father sends from Petersburg is not enough.'

Eliza was surprised how disappointed she was. But with Kolya gone and Mama coming back, life would take a turn for the worse. The academy was waiting to claim her and there was all the uncertainty of having Roderick's new wife at Clifton: for while Roderick would be heading back to Oxford, Miss Halsted — Mrs Roderick Brannan — would be arriving with Mama.

'Miss Halsted doesn't like me. She thinks me a child.'

'You do not know each other yet, that is all. You will be friends, I think. You are much alike. Rosa has made her own way, as you do.'

In the hallway, Kolya kissed Eliza's hand, put on his battered hat, picked up his Gladstone bag. Basford had the door ready.

'*Do svidanye*, Leeza.'

'Good bye!' When would she see him again? Not knowing was torture.

Kolya shook Basford's hand then ran down the steps, calling a greeting to Billy Turner — Vilyam — who had the old governess cart ready. The sky was white and pale grey as if draped in muslin. The horse's breath steamed in the cold air. Eliza stood on the doorstep waving until the creaking cart disappeared down the drive.

Basford closed the door. 'Well, miss, he's a caution right enough,' he began. But his words were cut short. There came a sound of jangling keys getting rapidly nearer. Both Eliza and Basford turned and fled.

In the day room Daisy viewed her with concern. 'You look peaky, miss.' She felt Eliza's forehead. 'Yes, you're running a temperature again. All this gadding about. Well, back to bed with you.'

Eliza was too weak to argue. She really did feel quite poorly though she would never have admitted it. As she lay in bed she thought of Kolya, who'd stayed such a short time. A large portion had been spent with Billy Turner in the pub. What had they talked about, what had they done? Only Billy would know.

'Daisy, will you fetch Billy up when he gets back from Welby station?'

'What do you want with a useless lump like him?'

'Please, Daisy!'

'Oh, very well, miss, if that's what you want. But get some rest first. You look like death warmed up.'

* * *

Billy Turner came clomping in his hobnailed boots, cap in hand. His face was bruised and grazed.

'Mind where you're going, you lubbering great lump!' Daisy scolded him. 'Look at the mess you've made with those dirty great boots of yours, treading muck everywhere! As if I hadn't enough to do without cleaning up after you. I'll need the dust pan and brush, I can see.' She paused on her way out, raised an eyebrow at him. 'You want to watch it, giving me those dirty looks. If the wind changes, you'll stay like that.'

Sitting in bed cushioned by her pillows, Eliza questioned him. Yes, said Billy, he and Mr Nicholas had stopped off in the village on the way back from the station. Mr Nicholas had caused quite a stir. They weren't used to foreigners in the Barley Mow. He had some queer ideas, too. But he'd stood his round, whether or no, and he'd told some rum stories of Russia and the like. They'd had quite a time of it.

They'd had quite a time of it. It didn't seem fair. Why couldn't *she* go to the Barley Mow? Would she always be left out? It made her feel quite angry and she took it out on Billy, asking him sharply about the cuts and bruises on his face. Had he been fighting with Jeff Smith again when she'd specially asked him not to?

'I done me best, miss, to keep the peace. But he'd argue with an echo, that Jeff Smith.'

'What do you argue *about*?'

Billy scratched his neck. 'Motor cars. Horses. Which is best out the two of them. He lords it about the place because he was born in the city and I wasn't. He calls me a yokel. And he was so cock-a-hoop about going to Tonbridge that I couldn't help but—'

He trailed off in a mumble, avoiding her eyes. He looked rather shamefaced. He looked rather awkward and cumbersome, standing there. Her anger evaporated. It wasn't Billy's fault that she couldn't go to the Barley Mow. Whose fault was it, then? Who made the rules? Perhaps Kolya would have been able to explain. Certainly Kolya would not approve of her shouting at Billy. Kolya never shouted. He spoke to servants as he spoke to anyone. She'd only really noticed it on this latest visit when he'd made friends with Vilyam and had told Basford to eat the bacon. Oddly, Kolya's attitude reminded her of Dorothea, who'd also had her own way of speaking to the servants. Yet in every other way Dorothea and Kolya could not have been more different.

'I'm sorry, Billy. I shouldn't have shouted.'

'Never mind, miss. In one ear—'

' — and out the other: yes, I remember!' She laughed and he dared to look at her face for a second, smiling one of his rare, fleeting smiles. He flushed. The colour rose up his neck and flared in his cheeks. He looked very out of place in her bedroom just as Basford had looked out of place sitting at the breakfast table. Would she be equally out of place in the Barley Mow?

Billy had been up to the nursery once before, he admitted, but a long time ago when he was just a lad. It had been Miss Dorothea's birthday. His mother had sent him from the village with some flowers. 'A stack of folks was up here, Mrs Brannan and all. I dint know where to put meself.'

Only when Billy had gone did Eliza remember she had been in the nursery that day too. Billy had not mentioned it. Perhaps he'd forgotten. Or perhaps at the time he'd never even noticed her.

A wave of misery washed over her. The academy was waiting to claim her as soon as she was well again. Now that the wedding was over there was nothing to look forward to. Days, weeks, months stretched ahead; the whole of 1914 was a desert. And after 1914 would come 1915, then 1916, and her bleak existence would go on and on, no end in sight.

She rolled onto her side, biting her lip. She would not cry. She was determined not to cry. Kolya had gone, and Billy no doubt thought more of his ferrets than he did of her, but she could at least pretend to make them proud.

She was not a child anymore.

* * *

Mama was back. Eliza was still in bed, unwell. She thought this might stir some sympathy. Not a bit of it.

'How many times must I tell you, Elizabeth, about consorting with the servants? I have made myself quite clear. But I come home to find — well, where do I begin? Mrs Bourne and Cook have been quarrelling again after all I've done to keep the peace, Turner was seen in the nursery where he's no business being, and John, by all accounts, sat and had breakfast with you!'

'His name is Herbert Basford! He's a person just like anyone else! It's rude to call him John!'

'His name in this house is John, Elizabeth. It is *John*.'

221

Mama was standing tall and straight by the bedside. No fault would be found at the academy with Mama's deportment. Her blue eyes were icy, her skin clear and smooth. The few lines on her face only served to give her an added dignity. There was a timeless quality to Mama which could not fail to impress.

Mama sighed. 'For the last time. Servants are people one employs. One cannot be friends with them. It does no good on *either* side to be overfamiliar. You must learn to find companionship amongst your own kind.'

Eliza found she was crying. She'd promised herself not to, never again, and she knew it would do nothing to raise her standing with Mama, but she simply couldn't help it. She wasn't even sure what she was crying about. Everything or nothing.

'Why can't things turn out *nice* for once?' she sobbed.

'It does no good crying about it,' said Mama crisply. 'If I'd taken your line, Elizabeth, sighing over castles in the air, I'd still be waiting now, after forty-nine years, for things to *turn out nice*. You must learn to make the best of things as they are. I say this for your own good. Now,' she added, leaning down to straighten the counterpane, her manicured hands working quickly, efficiently, 'no more tears. No more wishing for the impossible. Remember that God's purpose is worked out in all our lives. You must trust to Him to know what's right for you.'

But there was no God, thought Eliza as Mama left the room, closing the door quietly but firmly behind her. There was no God and there was no hope. She wished she could believe, as Kolya did, in the possibility of a better world. She wished she could believe that people were good and noble. She wanted so much for it to be true. But it just didn't seem that way to her. Without God, what was there to stop people running riot and revelling in their wickedness? Without God, what purpose would her life have?

* * *

It had been easy up until then to forget that Roderick was married, but now his wife had arrived to take up permanent residence. Mama took the trouble to show the erstwhile Miss Halsted to her room. Eliza trailed after them, not sure if her presence was required.

Opening a door, Mama said, 'I thought you'd like this room, a room of your own.' It was at the opposite end of the corridor to Roderick's. 'I will leave you to settle in and to dress for dinner. The gong will sound when it's time.'

Mama swept off. Eliza was about to follow when Miss Halsted put a hand out and touched her gently on the arm.

'Won't you stay and help me, Elizabeth? There's so much I have to do, so much to learn. And I would like to get to know you better.'

Eliza was in two minds. She rather resented Miss Halsted for all the upheaval over the baby and the wedding, and for Kolya's unhappiness, too; she had always been rather intimidated by her. But Mrs Roderick Brannan seemed a different sort of woman, quieter and less sure of herself. And Eliza was sure that Kolya would be disappointed if she didn't at least make an effort.

'I'll help you.'

'Thank you, Elizabeth. You must call me Rosa, of course, for we are sisters now.'

'And I'm Eliza.'

'Very well, Eliza. Let's take a look at this room, shall we?'

It was a nice room with a view over the Park and the shallow valley beyond where the canal lay hidden. But Rosa did not seem interested in the view.

'Someone's unpacked my things.' A few of her belongings had been sent on ahead including a large number of books and a box of brightly coloured clothes that Mama had called *cheap things*.

'The servants will have done that,' Eliza explained.

'I don't like to think of people going through my things.' Rosa began to rearrange some books that had been stacked higgledy-piggledy on a shelf but then suddenly stopped. 'My trunk. I'll need my trunk if I'm to dress for dinner. Can you see it anywhere?'

As Eliza turned to look for it, she found herself face-to-face with Susie Hobson lounging in the doorway.

Rosa noticed her too. 'Hello! I wonder, could you find my trunk? Now I come to think of it, it may be downstairs in the hallway.'

Susie Hobson sniffed. 'It's not *my* job, miss, to lug trunks up and down the stairs. You'll need to get John for that.' She tossed her head and flounced away.

Eliza blushed with embarrassment. Susie Hobson was well known for what Daisy called *sauce*, but this was astonishing even by her standards. Whatever would Rosa think, a house where the servants were as rude as that?

But Rosa didn't seem to notice. Instead of ringing for Basford, she went off to find her trunk for herself.

* * *

At the end of February, Rosa's friend Miss Ward arrived on a visit.

'Most inconvenient!' Mama complained. 'Rosa really should have consulted me before inviting people to stay. I shall have to go all through the week's menus again now.'

At dinner on the first evening, Miss Ward — usually so solemn and starchy — grew almost animated as she talked about the recent thrilling 'action' against the Rokeby Venus. Wasn't it *wonderfully* symbolic, to single out that particular painting, the one men stared at?

Rosa agreed.

Mama looked at Rosa and Miss Ward with reproof. 'I'm sorry, but what that foolish woman did is simply deplorable. The painting was slashed to pieces.'

There was a sudden hush. Rosa exchanged a look with Miss Ward, then said hesitantly, 'But surely you see, Mrs Brannan, that when the government is so intransigent, the only way to further our cause is to shock people out of their complacency? Until men acknowledge how much women are oppressed, nothing will ever change.'

'I don't know anything about that,' said Mama frostily. 'All I know is that nothing can ever justify breaking the law. If everyone took that attitude, where would it all end?'

The two younger women did not reply. Dinner continued in silence.

* * *

On her way home from the academy after another soul-sapping day, Eliza got off the train at Welby station, surrendered her ticket and walked down the steps. In the forecourt, Billy Turner and the old governess cart were waiting for her instead of Jeff Smith and the motor. Billy reported that the mistress had gone out in the motor and he had been detailed to fetch Miss Eliza.

Eliza was glad. It was much better to be rattling along the Hayton Road in the governess cart than to be sat in the back of the motor with only taciturn Jeff Smith for company. Eliza sat on one side of the cart, Billy on the other. She watched him drive, the reins slack in his hands, the horse clip-clopping complaisantly along the smooth-surfaced road. There were snowdrops scattered on the verges and leaf buds showing in the hedges. The sun was low in the sky away beyond Windmill Hill. The air was cool but not cold. February on the whole had been a mild month that year. Now it was all but over and there was a definite hint of spring in the air.

They crested a rise. The village came into sight. Eliza's imagination galloped ahead. What if they didn't stop at Clifton? What if they passed the turning and went on, into Lawham and out the other side, following the road wherever it led them?

The idea delighted her and she laughed out loud. Billy darted a glance in her direction then quickly looked away. His cheeks were flushed — the fresh air, of course — and there were dark bristles on his chin and on his upper lip, much more noticeable than Kolya's bristles. She wondered if they'd be equally prickly to the touch. Not that she would dare touch Billy's cheek, the way he was scowling, the way he was flicking the reins and making the horse pick up the pace. And yet she rather liked his scowl — she rather liked him altogether. She laughed again. It seemed strange that she should be so happy when she'd been miserable all day at the academy.

The house was quiet. There was no one in the hallway to greet her. It was as if the whole place was deserted. Eliza dropped her bag, hat and coat, and made her way upstairs.

Pausing on the first floor landing, she heard voices along the corridor. Curiosity got the better of her. She tiptoed nearer. Rosa and Miss Ward were talking softly together in Rosa's room. Miss Ward was speaking.

'. . . a ghastly place, I've always said as much, so cluttered and old-fashioned, all this satin and damask, so very *Victorian*. But it's your own fault you've ended up here, Rosa. You chose to get married, against all our principles.'

'I had no alternative, Maggie. There was the baby to think of. I know we've always said that the outmoded conventions shouldn't matter, but it wouldn't be right the ways things are to saddle a child with the stigma of illegitimacy. I was thinking of the child, not of myself. But you can't see that, none of you. Tom says I've become a brood mare for the landed gentry!'

'Oh, well, Tom! Tom is a hypocrite. They all are, the men we know. All their high principles are just so much talk. Tom decries the monied classes but he's only too quick to take advantage of them when it suits him. As for Leo, he's in a panic because the Aunts are threatening to take up residence in Bloomsbury to look after him and Carla. I know that Leo is your brother, Rosa, but he can be very selfish at times, even you must admit it.'

'What about Kolya? Kolya's not a hypocrite! He offered to marry me, Maggie. He offered to take on my child, never mind who the father is.'

'Very noble! And how would he have supported you and your child? He's a dreamer! He has his head in the clouds! In any case, sooner or later he'll go home. You wouldn't want to live in Russia, would you? Face it, Rosa. Men can't be relied on. Christabel Pankhurst has it right. Men are riddled with disease and only oppose the suffrage because it would put a stop to their promiscuous behaviour!'

'Do you really believe that, Maggie? Do you really believe it of Kolya and Aidan and Erik? Of Tom and Leo? It's far too simplistic in my view. I would suggest that — What? Why are you laughing like that?'

'Oh, Rosa! How I've missed you! Our Thursday evenings aren't the same. The other girls are so silly. Only you and I ever made sense. Only you and I ever stood up to the men. That's why I can't understand you choosing a man like Roderick Brannan. To have married a man your aunts *approve* of: it's grotesque!'

'They do approve of him, don't they! He's better than anything they dared hope for. Somehow he charmed them by not being charming — by being his usual, arrogant self! You see? I do admit he can be arrogant and overbearing and insufferable. But there's more to him than that. And — oh Maggie — I do love him, I really do!'

'Is it love, though?' Miss Ward sounded sceptical. 'You used to say you loved Kolya.'

'I did — I do. But as you said, what could Kolya offer me? He doesn't even believe in marriage! I had to make a choice, Maggie. And I had to choose Roderick.'

'I just wish you hadn't shackled yourself like this!'

'We are going round in circles, Maggie. I've explained why I had to get married: because of the child.'

'And so here you are, trapped in this ghastly house in the middle of nowhere, while *he* enjoys himself at Oxford!'

'He has to complete his studies. We both agreed on that.'

'Much good will it do him. He has a closed mind, Rosa.'

A silence fell. Eliza outside the door didn't dare breathe in case they heard her.

Rosa suddenly burst out in a wail of remorse. 'Oh Maggie, you're right, I know you are! I've betrayed everything we believe in! We said we'd blaze a trail, not succumb to convention!'

'Now don't start getting maudlin,' said Miss Ward emphatically. 'You've done what you've done, and you had your reasons, and I respect that. What I won't accept is the way you let yourself be terrorized by that old witch Mrs Brannan. You've always stuck up for yourself, Rosa. It's always one of the things I most admire about you. So why let yourself be walked over now?'

'What can I do, Maggie? I used to think that changing society would be a challenge, but this place . . . ! It's as if nothing's altered in a hundred years!'

'There's one thing you can do right away. You can move into your husband's room. It's ridiculous being at the other end of the corridor! She's done it deliberately, you must see that. But Roderick is yours now and you must show her.'

'Oh, Maggie, I can't! I *daren't*!'

'Yes you can! We'll do it now, right away, whilst she's out. We'll present her with a fait accompli.'

There were sounds of movement inside the room and to Eliza's alarm the door at once began to open. Caught so far from the main stairs, she had no choice but to scramble through the servants' door. She closed it softly behind her, catching a glimpse as she did so of the two women coming out of Rosa's room with armfuls of books, Miss Ward leading the way.

Miss Ward! What a horrible person she was, so pompous and hard-nosed, calling Mama 'a witch'! But as Eliza dawdled up the back stairs, she found herself harbouring a grudging admiration for both Rosa *and* Miss Ward. Whatever else one said about them, they were not afraid of the world. They were spirited, intelligent, independent. They held themselves the equals of any man — or superior, as Miss Ward would have it.

Why shouldn't women be superior, Eliza asked herself: why *shouldn't* they?

It was not the sort of outlook that would be encouraged at the academy — and that in itself was a glowing recommendation.

* * *

'I feel quite faint!' cried Mama, appearing without warning in the day room and collapsing into the chair by the fire. 'I've never seen anything like it, never!'

It was Sunday, a dull day: no academy and nothing to do after church but sit around in one's Sunday best and be 'good'. Idling away the hours, Eliza had hitched up her skirts and had sat on the old rocking horse, simply for the sake of it. She felt now at a decided disadvantage with her skirts tucked up and her calves showing. Mama might actually think she'd been *playing* with the rocking horse!

But Mama did not seem to notice. She seemed, indeed, rather flustered — if such a word could ever be used of Mama.

'It was bad enough when she moved all her things into Roderick's room without even *asking*. But this — *this*!'

She was obviously Rosa but what was *this*: what had Rosa done this time that was so terrible?

'She has painted all the walls. She has quite spoilt the print wallpaper. And the colours! Orange and purple and emerald green! It's enough to make one giddy!'

That wasn't all. Rosa, it seemed, had painted swirls and doodles all over the chairs, the dressing table, the wardrobe and the headboard. All the bedroom furniture was ruined.

It was the last straw. Rosa had simply been impossible ever since the visit of that friend of hers. Why must she meddle in everything? Why mix up the flower displays, for instance, so there were *different* types of flower in the *same* vase? And those clothes of hers, like a gypsy's, coloured headscarves, ragged skirts — a *red* petticoat, if you please! Thank goodness Roderick would soon be home for Easter. He would have to deal with his wife. He would have to make her see there were certain standards.

Mama's unexpected visit ended as abruptly as it had begun. She sailed off, her skirts sweeping across the floor, closing the door firmly behind her.

* * *

Eliza, who had no interest in the flower arrangements and who had grown over the last couple of months to quite like Rosa's unusual clothes, wondered if orange and purple might not suit Roderick's bedroom walls. She had to wait until the following Saturday for a chance to see for herself.

There was no academy on Saturdays and Mama had gone to call on Mrs Somersby. Rosa too was out: Eliza had watched her from the bedroom window setting off for the village. Slipping down one flight of stairs, Eliza went along to Roderick's room, opened the door, and let herself in.

Her heart stopped. She froze. There was someone sitting at the dressing table. Rosa must have come back. She hadn't gone to the village after all.

Then came a rush of relief. It *wasn't* Rosa. It was Susie Hobson sitting at the dressing table bold as brass, her dusters and polish laid aside. She had been arranging Rosa's pearls around her neck and admiring herself in the mirror.

'Oh, miss, it's only you, thank goodness! But you *did* give me a turn, creeping up on me like that!'

It's only you: this stung. Because of it — or for some other reason which she couldn't fathom — Eliza experienced a surge of irritation.

'You shouldn't mess with Rosa's things!'

'I'm only looking.' Still seated, Susie put the pearls down, picked up her feather duster. 'I do wish Miss Rosa wouldn't leave so many bits and pieces out! It makes it ever so difficult to dust. Who does she think she is, anyway? I expect those pearls are made of paste. Master Roderick ought never to have taken up with a girl of her sort. He ought to have waited for a nice girl to come along. But she caught him good and proper. My word, didn't she!'

'What do you mean?' asked Eliza rather stiffly, feeling at a disadvantage, as she often did with Susie Hobson.

'That baby of hers: that weren't no accident!' Susie flicked her duster, knocking over a bottle of scent. 'She's made a right mess in here with her tins of paint. It looks like a stuck pig's innards. Master Roderick won't like it.'

'I think it looks nice. Cheerful. And you don't know anything about what Roddy likes.'

'That's what you think!'

Susie looked so very smug and pleased with herself that Eliza wanted to hit her. It was rather shocking, to feel like this. It put her even more on a back foot. Angry, she said, 'Don't let me catch you messing with Rosa's things again, do you hear?' She winced. This sounded just like Mama. But there was something in Susie Hobson's manner that made one *feel* like Mama, wanting everything proper and correct.

Eliza drew herself up, gave Susie a look she imagined Mama might have given. 'You are not to mess with Rosa's things,' she repeated. 'Do I make myself clear, Hobson?'

'*Hobson*, now, is it? What happened to *Susie*? It used to be Susie.'

'*Miss*. You must call me *miss*.'

'Yes — *miss*.' Susie ladled the word with sarcasm.

Eliza stuck her nose in the air as if she didn't care, as if it was water off a duck's back. She made her way, slow and dignified, out of the room.

Her heart was beating. She had to pause in the corridor to catch her breath. It had shaken her, the sudden dislike for Susie, wanting to *hit* her. But even more unexpected was the way she had felt protective of Rosa's things. She had taken Rosa's side against Susie.

She remembered Kolya's words. *You do not know each other yet . . . you will become friends . . .* She would never have believed it. But as she retraced her steps back to the nursery Eliza began to wonder if Kolya had perhaps got it right yet again.

CHAPTER TEN

'I admit I am disappointed, young Roderick,' said Dr Camborne, slicing cheese and eating it off his knife. 'I quite expected you to get a first.'

Roderick at one end of the table helped himself to more claret. 'I rather think, sir, that a first is only necessary if one is angling for a fellowship.'

'And you don't fancy being a don, eh? Well, it's not for everyone. *Ut quod ali cibus est aliis fuat acre venenum.*' The doctor looked round with a self-satisfied smile at five blank faces. Turning his attention back to the cheese, he continued, 'In the good old days a young gentleman chose between army, navy, church and law. If we consider first the law: now the law is always . . .'

Eliza stifled a yawn. This conversation was pointless as well as boring. Roderick's future was already mapped out. Starting next month, he'd be going to Coventry each day to learn about Daddy's businesses. 'I may as well,' he'd said. 'I've nothing else to do. No doubt I'll be running the whole show by Christmas.' Why didn't he explain this to Dr Camborne?

'. . . and then, of course, there's the church.' The doctor eyed Roderick rather dubiously. 'Perhaps not the church. Which leaves us with . . .'

Dr Camborne might be able to quote Latin, thought Eliza, but he didn't know how to behave. She had learned at the academy that on no account should one ever raise one's knife to one's mouth at the dinner table. It was the height of bad manners, she'd learned.

'. . . and so we come to the army. The army would be just the ticket for a vigorous young man like you. I remember saying to—'

Roderick interrupted. This also was on the academy's list of social faux pas but it was, in the circumstances, excusable. 'Isn't the army rather redundant these days, sir? If there's trouble anywhere in the world we simply send the Royal Navy and that soon settles it.'

'An interesting point, young man, and I might be inclined to agree with you were it not for recent events.'

'Recent events, sir?'

'This business in Ireland.'

'Ireland soon will be free.' Kolya spoke up. He'd arrived at Clifton only that afternoon after an absence of many months. 'Ireland will be free. Is inevitable.'

'Free?' Dr Camborne looked at him, puzzled. 'Free? No, no, you've quite missed the point. You wouldn't understand, being foreign. The Irish are a feckless race. They need firm government. Only England can provide it. This farrago of Home Rule—'

It was Rosa this time who interrupted. 'Home Rule is a reality, Doctor. The Bill has been passed under the provisions of the Parliament Act. Kolya and I have a friend from Ireland, Mr O'Connor, who says that the Irish will never accept anything less than Home Rule, and if Ulster won't accede, there will be civil war.'

'I'm not sure if . . . it's a rather complex . . . but you young people see everything in black and white. When you get to my age . . . as Lucretius said . . . or was it Cicero . . . and who can fathom the Irish, rebellious as they are?'

The doctor's eyes ranged round the table as if seeking a way out. Perhaps there were no pearls of Latin wisdom about

Ireland, thought Eliza. Or was Dr Camborne simply out of his depth? Was it possible that Rosa was just too clever for him?

Eliza was intrigued by this idea but just then, rather alarmingly, the doctor's gaze came to rest on her.

'Well, now, young lady, and what do you have to say for yourself? You are looking forward, I'm sure, to Frau Kaufmann's visit. A plucky girl, Frau Kaufmann. How she nagged me about that boy Richard. There was one occasion when—'

Dr Camborne was cut short once more, this time by Mama who began to get to her feet, the signal that dinner was over. Kolya jumped up to pull out Mama's chair, a characteristically unexpected gesture which made Eliza smile. Roderick, meanwhile, lent Rosa a hand in getting up, even though he knew it would irritate her. 'Women are not flimsy, helpless creatures, Roderick. We can fend for ourselves, you know.' Which was just as well, thought Eliza, for there was no one to help *her*. She had to get out of her seat by herself.

In the drawing room Mama took up her cross-stitch and Rosa opened the newspaper as they waited for the gentlemen to join them. Eliza was restless, wandering around the room. She wasn't sure she wanted to sit with the gentlemen when they came through. She didn't mind Kolya — just the opposite — but she couldn't bear to listen to anything more from Dr Camborne. It was utterly disheartening, the way he summarised life in a few short Latin phrases.

When Mama became absorbed in a particularly fiddly bit of needlework, Eliza took the opportunity to slip behind the curtains and silently open the french windows. She stepped onto the terrace. She breathed in, smelling grass and pollen and the faint scent of flowers. She breathed out, expelling the miasma of a long, boring dinner.

Leaning over the parapet, she surveyed the summer twilight. On the far horizon to her right, a fading residue of the vivid sunset was sliding slowly beneath the rim of the world. The first faint stars were glimmering high above. She tried to gauge her state of mind — not an easy task these days. She was happy of course to have Roderick home now that he'd finished with Oxford; she was happy that Kolya had come and that Dorothea would soon be on her way. So why did she feel that — oh, what was it she felt?

A faint sound wailed through the gathering dusk like the cry of some plaintive animal calling in answer to her mood. It was the hoot of a far-off locomotive. A train must be passing on the Lawham branch line. She could see it in her mind's eye steaming through the gloaming, lights showing in the long carriages. She populated it with passengers invented off the top of her head: a woman with a covered basket on her knees; a stately man with a top hat and a cane; a boy in school uniform. The basket held a live chicken. The cane was shod with silver. In the boy's pocket nestled a sling. Where were they going, these people, so late and so lonely? To Broadstone or Leamington or Timbuktu? How she longed to go with them. How she long to share in all the excitement of other people's lives.

Discontent stirred within her. Why go back into the stuffy drawing room? Why not rebel, like the rebellious Irish?

She took off her shoes and her stockings, rebelling. She ran down the steps. The grass was cool and damp and strange against her bare feet. There were probably all sorts of creepy-crawlies, worms oozing in the mire, beetles scuttling. She outfaced them. She was not afraid.

She climbed the fence into the Old Close. The last dregs of daylight were draining from the sky. Everything was mysterious and half-known as the dusk deepened. Here was the gate leading onto the bridleway. There — there was Becket's little cottage, one dim light showing in a downstairs window. The archway leading into the stable yard was like a yawning mouth opening onto a black pit. In the brick wall opposite was a rickety wooden door which gave access to the gardens. She pushed it open. She plunged headlong through.

The darkness was thick and black beyond the wall. She felt her way, treading gingerly, her toes curling. The scent of rosemary and of sage rose to greet her: Becket's herb garden. There was lavender, too, rich and fragrant, the log stems brushing against her. But of course, she said to herself, this must be the notorious lavender jungle. She was a bold and fearless explorer, stepping off the edge of the map. And what was this, looming in the shadows? Ah, the potting shed, I presume!

No. Not a potting shed. A gilded palace. A gilded palace long forgotten, lost in the depths of the jungle. She was the first to rediscover it — she, the bold explorer. (Could girls *be* explorers? But girls could do anything, everything. That was what Rosa said.)

The gardens were a whole world, measureless in the dark. Rookery Hill was lost in the night, a myth on the border of knowledge; the village was as remote as the stars. The faint sound of the church bell striking the quarter hour was a message from the far-flung reaches of the universe, from the infinite deeps of time. What did it say, this message? *The nights are steeped in the peace of ages. England lives on. England endures. Forever and ever, amen.*

The sound of the chimes faded. There was a rustle in the dark. Something moved, a sliver of blackness. A lion, perhaps, or a tiger. She tracked it across the flower beds, she stopped to sniff a rose, she ran on, bent double. It was in her sights now, the lion, the tiger. She leapt forward. She scooped it into her arms. It writhed against her, a bundle of warm fur.

Pressing her face into the cat's soft body, she whispered, 'Oh Whisky, Whisky! My how you've grown!' *My how you've grown*: it was what grown-ups always said. It was what Dorothea would say the day after tomorrow. Eliza tingled all over at the thought of Dorothea at Clifton.

With the cat in her arms, Eliza paced the cinder paths until she reached another doorway. She looked out. She saw the house framed against the dark, she saw the spreading boughs of the cedar tree reaching out like supplicating arms towards the bright lights of the windows.

The front door opened. Yellow light spilled down the steps and pooled on the gravel. At the same moment Billy

Turner appeared out of the shadows to the right with Dr Camborne's old horse and gig. The gig creaked and rattled. The horse plodded. A wise old beast, Billy called it. 'He's had to find his own way home on many a night, haven't you, boy!' Dr Camborne now emerged, tottering down the steps as Basford looked on, silhouetted in the doorway. Billy helped the doctor into the gig, handed him the reins, stepped back.

'Gee up!' The doctor's voice sounded sharp and savage in the wide silence. The gig moved off. It turned into the drive. It disappeared from view. The sound of it slowly faded into the night.

Billy and Basford exchanged a few words, chaffing each other, amiable and careless, so different from how they usually spoke. Or maybe, thought Eliza with a pang: maybe *this* was how they really were and what she knew of them was false, all false. If only . . . oh, if only . . .

Billy went lumbering off towards the stables. Basford for a moment paused with one hand on the door, looking up at the stars meshed in the branches of the cedar tree.

'I have to go now, Whisky. I have to go.' Eliza let the cat leap from her arms. 'Goodbye, Whisky! Goodbye!'

Eliza ran. The gravel hurt her feet. But this was her last hope: she must reach the house before the door shut or she'd be lost in the dark forever! Already Basford was turning to go.

'Basford, wait!' She flew up the steps, she slipped breathlessly through the narrow gap. 'Oh Basford — Herbert — thank goodness! I was about to be marooned on a dark continent, the prey of lions and tigers and nameless savages!'

Basford broke into a grin as he shut and locked the door, eyeing her bare feet. 'You're a wild one, Miss Eliza, no two ways about it!'

'I'm an explorer, Herbert. An adventurer. Girls can do anything now, didn't you know?'

* * *

'She's here! She's arrived!'

Eliza flew down the stairs. The front door was open, Mr Ordish and Mrs Bourne in attendance. Eliza hung back, inexplicably shy. She could see through the doorway Mama standing statuesque on the steps. Kolya was there with a book in his hand. Roderick and Rosa were side-by-side. As the motor appeared at the head of the drive and turned towards them, rounding the cedar tree, Roderick put his arm round Rosa as if staking his claim — or could it be that he was nervous too? Was this possible in someone as dauntless as Roderick? Rosa, who might have been expected to begrudge such a proprietorial gesture, seemed to acquiesce instead, leaning against him a little as she had leant against him in the hallway at 28 Essex Square all that time ago. Eliza wished that she had someone to lean on, someone's hand to hold.

The motor come to a halt at the foot of the steps. Jeff Smith opened the door. A lady in a cream travelling coat and a feathered hat got out. Was this really Dorothea?

The lady stood for a moment looking up at the front of the house just as Mama had done last September on returning from Scarborough. Then she turned to Jeff Smith. She touched his arm. She spoke a few words. She raised a smile even on the pokerface of the self-important chauffeur. So it really was Dorothea, the same Dorothea, working her magic as of old.

Up the steps she came. As she crossed the threshold, she was thronged about with people. She espied Eliza loitering in the hall.

'Here you are, Eliza! I couldn't see you at first. Let me kiss you, dear Eliza. Goodness, how you've grown! You must be taller than me now.'

'Come, Elizabeth, let Dorothea get by.' Mama eased Eliza aside. 'Tea is ready in the drawing room.'

Cook had done them proud. There was a mountain of sandwiches. There were innumerable cakes. Mama poured tea, presiding.

Dorothea was the centre of attention. Her journey had been long and tiring, she said, but to be back again made it all worthwhile, it was so lovely to see them again. Her only regret was that Johann at the last moment had been unable to come because of something to do with his medical training. He'd missed a lot of time when he was ill and now wanted to qualify as soon as he could. But he'd pressed his wife to go ahead with her plans, which was very much in keeping with how he was. No one could be kinder, more thoughtful, so selfless. They'd see for themselves when they came to Hamburg. They must all come to Hamburg. Why not next summer? Hamburg was at its best in summer.

Clifton was just as Dorothea remembered, the village too from what she'd seen of it, driving through. But there were some changes, of course. Roderick had finished with Oxford and was now a married man: what a surprise that had been! Rosa, naturally, was a most welcome addition to the family. And they were expecting a child. How lucky they were! A baby was such a blessing!

'What else have I missed? What have you all been doing?'

'I have been taking my life in my hands teaching Antipov to drive,' said Roderick. 'Yesterday we drove right through a hedge and over a flock of sheep.'

'After the baby is born,' said Rosa, 'you must teach me to drive too, Roderick.'

'Oh, I must, must I?' Roderick's dark eyes flashed as he looked at his wife in a way that would have made most people quail but Rosa seemed quite unconcerned. Was it possible, Eliza wondered, that Roderick had met his match?

Roderick turned back to Dorothea. 'Are there motor cars in Hamburg, Doro? I expect it's a beastly place, still in the Middle Ages. No wonder you have come hurrying home.'

'Dear Roddy, still the same as ever! How I have missed your teasing! But I've been married two years. I have hardly come hurrying back. Hamburg now is home for me.'

Mama brought tea time to an end. 'We have a room ready for you, Dorothea.'

'I was thinking, Aunt. If I may, I would like my old room in the nursery.'

By all means, Mama said. Whatever Dorothea wanted.

Dorothea smiled at Eliza. 'It will be just like the old days,' she said.

* * *

'I am taking my dog out,' said Roderick next morning after breakfast, 'if you'd like to come, Doro.'

'There's nothing I'd like more. And you must come too, Eliza.'

But Eliza felt rather a spare part trotting at their heels with Hecate as they strolled past Becket's cottage and turned right, passing through the kissing gate and taking the path that led up Rookery Hill.

Roderick flung a stick for Hecate. 'You have arranged things very nicely, Doro. You will be here for my birthday.'

'The eighth. I haven't forgotten.' Dorothea held up her skirts to negotiate a steep section of the path, taking it in her stride. 'You will be twenty-two, all grown up. From what I hear, you are planning to take the helm at Uncle Albert's businesses.'

'Perhaps not quite yet. I've a lot to learn. No good trying to run before I can walk.'

'Goodness! I was wrong about you, Roddy. You are *not* the same. You used to know it all.'

'I shall ignore that remark. I shall rise above it. I shall tell you instead about the estate. I've been looking into the estate. I daresay it hasn't been properly run since Grandfather's day in the 1880s. The estate agent is too busy with his own allocation at Home Farm to worry about the rest. Things drift. Nothing gets done. That's where I come in. Land can't be made to pay, I'm told. But it's worth a try. Rents need reviewing, there are repairs to be done, everything must be put on a proper footing.'

Dorothea glanced at him curiously. 'You have never bothered with the estate before.'

'Ah, well, now that my son and heir is on the way—'

'What if your son and heir turns out to be a girl?'

'I shall sell her into white slavery and try again. Girls — as I've often told you in the past, Doro — are a waste of space.'

They were laughing together as they toiled up the last green slope. Eliza followed them to the brow of the hill. The tall poplars rose behind them, the view was spread out before them, vast and clear under a cloudy yet bright sky. There was haymaking going on in the fields beyond the Lawham Road, the workers like matchsticks. Nearer at hand, Eliza could see the gables and chimneys of Home Farm where the agent lived who was too busy to bother with the estate.

As Roderick wrestled a stick out of Hecate's mouth, Dorothea murmured, 'There is so much to do, so many people I want to see, the village . . .' But, shading her eyes with her hand, she was gazing out not at the village but at the rounded summit of Windmill Hill in the distance with the green smudge of Grange Holt at its foot. The house of Hayton Grange, home to the Fitzwilliams, was invisible from this angle.

Roderick threw the stick. It traced a great arc through the air. Hecate, barking, went bounding after it down the hill. Shoving his hands in his pockets, Roderick frowned as he stared at the wide panorama. 'Is this all there is?'

'What do you mean?' said Dorothea. 'What more could you want, the heart of England in high summer? And you've a wife now, and a baby on the way, and the factories and the estate: plenty to be getting on with.'

'Yes, I know, my cup runneth over. I ought to be glad. But there are times when I feel . . . I don't know . . . as if I want to *do* something. You've had your big adventure, Doro: your Teuton, and Hamburg. What is there for me? Nothing.'

'I didn't *want* to leave. I would have lived happily at Clifton forever if Johann hadn't happened along. It was love that changed things.'

'I want more, Doro: more than this.' Roderick wrinkled his nose, kicking at the grass. 'Oh, don't mind me. It's just talk. It doesn't mean anything. I'll buckle down when it comes to it, you'll see.'

'I know you will,' said Dorothea. 'I've always believed in you, Roddy.'

She threaded her arm through his and they turned away, Roderick whistling for Hecate as they made their way between the poplars. They had slipped easily into their old intimacy as if Dorothea had never been away.

Left on her own, Eliza looked down at the grey house, her home, half-hidden by the trees: firmly fixed, a lasting part of the landscape. *It will be like the old days*, Dorothea had said. But it wasn't. Eliza in the old days had never imagined that the old days would end whereas she knew that this was just a passing moment. All too soon, Dorothea would be gone again. What would happen after that? Roderick had Daddy's factories, had the estate, his future was mapped out. What was her portion, what did the future hold for her? She must sit, she supposed, and be decorous, twiddling her thumbs until the time came when she was required to get married. And who would she marry? She couldn't think of anyone she liked even half enough to marry them.

She had been so pleased with herself the other evening, stirred by the sound of the distant train, imagining herself an explorer. But the dark continent had not been real and the half-heard train had steamed off without her. A year ago in the moonlight she had walked as far as the canal without giving it a thought. Now she didn't dare leave the gardens unless someone went with her.

Girls could do anything. But how to begin? She felt as if she was set on a course that couldn't be altered. She lacked the courage to do so. It would take an upheaval as big as an earthquake to make a difference. But nothing would ever shake the foundations of Clifton Park that were so deep-rooted and enduring.

* * *

'Here is a note from Colonel Harding,' said Mama, unfolding a piece of paper brought in on a tray by Mr Ordish, as they sat in the morning room after breakfast. Another Wednesday was upon them. The days of Dorothea's visit were passing all too quickly.

Roderick looked over the top of the newspaper. 'A note from Colonel Harding? Oh Lord, what does *he* want?'

'He suggests an expedition,' said Mama, her eyes scanning the piece of paper.

'An *expedition*,' scoffed Roderick.

'An expedition,' repeated Mama, not looking up, 'to the Eidur Stones. To mark the bank holiday. And — oh — in honour of your visit, Dorothea.'

'It has taken him long enough to realise she is here.' Roderick was scathing, went back to *The Times*.

'The Colonel,' Mama continued, still reading, 'is looking forward to — to what? Really, his handwriting is atrocious! Ah, I have it: "I am very much looking forward to trying out my new motor — "'

'His new *what*!' Roderick dropped the newspaper in astonishment. 'That can't be right, Mother! The Colonel detests motor cars.'

'It does seem unlikely, I admit, but it's here in black and white.'

'How nice of the Colonel to go to so much trouble,' said Dorothea.

'So much trouble, my eye!' said Roderick. 'He won't lift a finger, you can be sure. He'll expect everyone else to make the arrangements.'

'In any case,' said Mama, putting the note aside, 'I'm not at all sure we can fit it in. There's dinner at Brockmorton Manor, there's the church fête: we are so very busy.' She glanced out at the cedar tree and the grey sky beyond. 'The weather does not look exactly promising, either.'

'The weather may change by Monday,' said Dorothea. 'Oh, Aunt, we simply *must* go, if only to see the Colonel in a motor car.'

'Very well, Dorothea, if that is what you wish. But we shall need to get organised. I shall reply to the Colonel at once.'

Roderick, too, got to his feet, tossing the newspaper aside. 'And I must get back to the estate records. The sooner I get through them, the better. They are too dull for words.'

There was a general exodus, Dorothea, Rosa and Kolya following Mama and Roderick out of the room. The newspaper was lying on the chaise longue where Roderick had left it. Eliza picked it up. She read a bold, black headline: *WAR DECLARED BY AUSTRIA*. The Austrians, it seemed, were making war on Serbia. But Serbia — where was Serbia?

She knew so little of the world. The academy did little to enlighten her. But the academy could not be ignored. Come September the dreary routine would begin again.

She pressed her face against the window, looking out at the space of gravel, the heavy dipping boughs of the cedar tree, the garden wall with its neat rows of red bricks. She sighed. Her breath misted the glass. The world outside melted away.

* * *

'I really must,' said Mama at luncheon next day, 'go to Lawham this afternoon. I can't put it off any longer.'

She had a list of things to do. The Colonel's picnic had only served to make that list even longer.

'Let me help, Aunt,' said Dorothea. 'I shall go to Lawham with you.'

Roderick announced that he would go too. There were papers he wished to consult lodged with the family solicitor. And so after luncheon Mama, Roderick and Dorothea got in the motor and were driven away by Jeff Smith. Eliza stood on the front steps and watched them go. The sound of the motor faded. Silence descended. Another long, languid afternoon had come to Clifton.

It was warm, hazy. The gardens were green and verdant, everything growing apace. In the broad daylight they looked nothing like a jungle: they were far too ordered and homely. Bees were busy about the lavender. Becket pottered short-sightedly amongst his onions, leeks and carrots. On the lawn, the shadow of the mulberry tree faded in and out in the fitful sunshine. Eliza, acting on impulse, climbed unladylike (Mama was safely in Lawham) up into the branches to perch amid the leaves like an exotic bird, a . . .

But she didn't know the names of any exotic birds, only parrots like Polly. Polly was not a good example, caged as she was, a captive.

The lawn was a secluded corner, bounded by crumbling brick walls and a tall privet hedge and the raised patio with the old summerhouse. Eliza lay along a knobbly branch balanced by her dangling legs, drowsy, lethargic. When Kolya appeared, rambling across the grass, it was too much of an effort to hail him. She watched through half-closed eyes as he sat down on the time-worn swing, stretching his legs out. He had no jacket and no hat. His flaxen hair flopped forward as he leant over his book. She expected him at any moment to notice her but when at length he looked up he was so deep in thought that he hardly seemed aware of his surroundings.

He went back to his book. Eliza closed her eyes. She could hear the soft creak of the swing as it rocked gently back and forth. She could hear the faint *chuck-chuck-chuck* of a blackbird. Remote on the edge of hearing there was a sound like the wind in the trees — or was it more like waves on a distant shore?

Lulled by the peace of the gardens, she was all but nodding off when new sounds raised her from her torpor, a rustling and a laboured breathing. She opened her eyes to see Rosa walking across the grass, slow and ponderous in a loose blouse and a bright, flowing skirt, her hair tucked into a headscarf. Rosa's distended belly was both intriguing and disturbing.

Kolya jumped up and helped her lower herself onto the swing. She sighed as she settled herself. 'I grow weary with waiting. I have swollen ankles. My back aches. I am enormously fat.'

'You are not fat,' said Kolya. 'You are *pulchritudinous*.'

She smiled up at him. 'Your word of the day? Do you still learn a new English word every day?'

'I learn many words. You are fulsome and fecund and fertile: three new words. You look like pagan mother goddess.'

'I don't feel like a goddess. I don't feel fertile and fecund. I am a fraud. I'm not cut out to be a mother. Frau Kaufmann, childless though she is, has an air of matronly respectability which puts me to shame.'

'You will be new sort of mother, progressive mother. You will lead the way.'

'With your help.'

'I will not be here.'

'Why not? Where will you go? Back to London?'

'Back to Russia.'

'Don't say that!' Rosa reached out, took his hand. 'What would I do without you?'

'You have *him* now. You belong to him. He will not invite me to Clifton again. This is last time, to — what is phrase? *Rub my nose in it*.'

'Oh, Kolya! He's not like that! He could never be so petty!' Rosa struggled to her feet. 'What can I do — what would it take — to get you to stay?'

'You know what I want,' said Kolya hoarsely. He drew her hand to his lips, kissed it. 'I long for you, yearn for you, hunger for you: there are not words enough in your English language. *Ya tebya lyublyu*.'

'Don't, Kolya, please don't — you mustn't be so cruel. I am a married woman.'

'Marriage is bourgeois despotism.'

'We live in a bourgeois society.'

'Bourgeois society will soon come to end.'

'Do you believe that? Do you really believe it? After living here at Clifton these last six months, I'm beginning to think that nothing will ever change. Oh, Kolya, I wish I knew — I wish I *knew*!' Rosa flung her arms round him and he held her, stroking her gently.

246

What was it Rosa wished she knew? Eliza could not guess. She watched them standing on the lawn with their arms round each other. She watched Rosa rest her head on Kolya's shoulder.

Eliza in the tree went cold all over. Kolya was looking over the top of Rosa's head, he was looking directly at the mulberry tree. Eliza knew that he'd seen her. His pale eyes seemed to pierce her to the bone. He said nothing, his face impassive, and she couldn't stand it. She shut her own eyes tight, clinging to the branch.

When, after a time, she opened her eyes again, the lawn was green and empty. It was as if Kolya and Rosa had never been there. Had it all been a dream? But as she jumped down from the tree she saw in the grass Kolya's book where he must have dropped it. It had a plain cover with the word *Chernyshevsky* embossed on it. Eliza for a moment hesitated then quickly reached down and picked it up, tucking it in her pocket.

She reached the house just as the motor returned, Mama, Dorothea and Roderick back from Lawham. More time had passed than she realised. Dorothea took her hand. They walked up the steps.

'Tomorrow,' said Dorothea, 'I will visit Hayton Grange. I have been putting it off and putting it off but now the time has come. I should have made my peace with Henry long ago. Will you come with me?'

'Yes,' said Eliza.

* * *

Hayton Grange. The name was so familiar. It was so near: just off the Newbolt Road, the other side of the village. Yet as Eliza walked hand-in-hand with Dorothea up the drive in the dappled shade of the overhanging trees of Grange Holt, she could not remember ever being here before. It was absurd. In all her fourteen-and-a-half years, she must have been to Hayton Grange at least *once*. But the memory wouldn't come.

The house itself nestled beneath the steep green slopes of Windmill Hill. It was a neat, compact, brick-built structure with tall chimneys and many latticed windows. Here Lady Fitzwilliam lived with her son.

'Henry is a recluse,' Roderick had said at luncheon. 'He's a cripple, hideously disfigured after his accident.'

'Don't be so silly, Roderick,' Mama had reproved him. 'Henry damaged his spine. He is unable to walk. That is all.'

That was all. But that was enough. Eliza did not know quite what to expect as Dorothea rang the bell.

They were shown into a rather gloomy, wood-panelled room. A fire glowed in the hearth even though it was July. Lady Fitzwilliam rose to greet them. She was wearing a simple, old-fashioned dress. Her hair looked a little dishevelled. But when you were used to Mama, anyone's hair would look dishevelled.

'My dears, what a lovely surprise, so kind of you to call! Dear Dorothea — Mrs Kaufmann, I should say: it's been too long. How well you look — and such lovely clothes! You will want to see Henry, of course. He is in the conservatory. He likes to sit there these days. I will show you. Follow me. This way. Mind the step. I'm sure you know, Mrs Kaufmann — or may I still call you Dorothea? I'm sure you know that Henry can't walk. Such a tragedy, for a young man in particular. But his spine, his legs . . . Arthur Camborne says that if you stabbed Henry's knee with a knitting needle, he wouldn't feel a thing, not a thing.' The unexpected violence of the image coming from the lips of a courtly old lady was rather disconcerting. 'You may,' Lady Fitzwilliam continued, one hand on a door handle, 'find Henry has changed. He is not as . . . jolly . . . as he once was.'

Jolly. Had Henry been jolly? Well, yes, he had. He had possessed a sense of fun. Eliza had rather liked him. But it had been a long time since she'd last seen him. Would he recognise her now she was so grown up? And what would Henry himself be like? Disfigured, Roderick had said.

She experienced a catch of fear as Lady Fitzwilliam opened the door.

The conservatory was a riot of greenery, crowded with potted plants of all shapes and sizes, steeped in bright daylight yet somehow cut off, the outside world invisible. Henry Fitzwilliam was sitting in a bath chair in the midst of it all. There was a rug over his knees, his shoulders were hunched. He was fatter in the face than Eliza remembered and his chestnut hair was greying at the temples, but his thin moustache was exactly the same, he was instantly recognisable, not disfigured in any way. He did not seem to hear them come in. There was a vacant expression on his face.

His mother touched him lightly on the arm. 'Mrs Kaufmann, dear, come from Germany. And Elizabeth Brannan.'

'Hello, Henry.' Dorothea drew up a chair quite naturally as if there was no question of any awkwardness. She raised on Henry's face a wintry smile.

Eliza sat a little apart as the conversation stuttered a little before it got going, an ordinary drawing room conversation about the weather and the village fête, with polite enquiries after their health and Dorothea's journey. Sitting back and observing, speaking only when spoken to, Eliza could not help but wonder if it would have been easier — less disturbing — if Henry *had* been disfigured. He looked so much the same and yet he was an empty shell. Or perhaps not quite empty. It was as if (Eliza fumbled for the right words) something inside him — his spirit, his essence — had not so much died as fallen out of sight, like sinking into a deep, deep well. This was the man Dorothea might have married. He had been, so the story went, quite besotted with her. And now? Did he feel the same? Did he feel *anything*? Or was his heart paralysed too? If you stabbed it with a knitting needle, would he even notice?

'My dears!' Lady Fitzwilliam groped for the arms of her chair. 'I haven't offered you any tea! Where are my manners? I will see to it at once. Where is that girl when she's needed?'

Watching her disappear amongst the foliage, Henry said, 'Poor Mother. She has such a lot to cope with. I have proved something of a disappointment. Father made a success of his life — he was an MP, he was knighted — whereas now I can't even give her grandchildren, something any man could do.'

'You too have been a success, Henry,' Dorothea insisted. 'There would be no BFS motors but for you. It was you who persuaded Uncle Albert that motors had a future. And what about your racing? You were quite the celebrity.'

'But now—'

'Now you must turn your mind to other things, your next achievement.'

'That is what people tell me: Mother, Camborne. It's a case of adjusting, they say, of getting used to things. But it's been a year now and . . . Well, I know now how that boy Richard felt.'

'Richard was awfully fond of you, Henry. So many people are. That won't change. I have never forgotten how kind you were to me the night I arrived at Clifton — you, before anyone else.'

'You sat on my knee. You were so small and thin. There were holes in your boots. I gave you champagne.'

There was a flicker in Henry's eyes as if dying embers had briefly flamed into life. But at that moment Lady Fitzwilliam returned and the talk turned to other matters.

The tea arrived. Balancing a cup and saucer on her knee, Eliza noted that Henry had gradually fallen out of the conversation. Was he even listening now?

'These goings-on in Europe,' said Lady Fitzwilliam, 'the archduke, the Austrians. "Gravest apprehensions", it said in the newspaper this morning. I don't understand it. I don't understand it at all. If only Joseph were still alive. Joseph knew how to explain things.' Her husband Sir Joseph Fitzwilliam had been dead twenty-six years.

The visit came to an end. Dorothea getting to her feet kissed Henry on the cheek. Henry, Eliza told herself, would shed a single tear that would leave a glistening track down his cheek. But when she looked his cheeks were dry and the flicker in his eyes had gone out.

Lady Fitzwilliam saw them to the door. 'God bless you, my dears. Do call again soon. But what am I saying? Why not stay for luncheon? There's no need to rush off!'

Dorothea smiled gently. 'Dear Lady Fitzwilliam, luncheon was hours ago, it is nearly teatime now.'

'Teatime? Well, yes, so it is. How time flies. How time flies, never to return.'

The door was shut. They turned away. Eliza was assailed by a keen sense of sadness. For Henry of all people to have been singled out, Henry who had never hurt a fly. *A tragedy for a young man*, Lady Fitzwilliam had called it and she was right. Thank goodness, then, that such terrible injuries were so rare. But how bright the world looked after the seclusion of Hayton Grange!

Dorothea took Eliza's hand. Together they set off up the drive towards the Newbolt Road.

* * *

'Are we to wait for Mr Antipov?' said Mama in the drawing room before lunch the following day, a Saturday.

'Antipov is prostrate,' said Roderick cheerfully. He and Kolya had been out that morning for another driving lesson. Their motor had broken down the other side of Bodford. They'd had to trek back across country. 'Our little stroll has left him worn out and his feet are covered in blisters. It's what comes of wearing second-hand boots that don't fit properly.'

'And Rosa?' said Mama. 'Is she coming down?'

'Rosa says she has a headache,' said Roderick. 'I told her to rest.'

Mama pursed her lips and Eliza wondered if she was thinking of the orange, purple and emerald green walls of Roderick's bedroom, enough to give anyone a headache. That was Mama's opinion, anyway. Roderick was more blasé.

He had mocked the colour scheme when he first saw it but had not had the room repainted. As for the ruined furniture, he said, well, not everything that was old needed to be preserved in amber. The whole house could do with a good clear-out. (He had not said any of this in Mama's hearing). If Rosa wanted to waste her time doodling, he'd added, then it was her lookout, but it was a whole lot better than smashing windows or setting fire to pillar boxes. Eliza couldn't help feeling that Roderick was secretly rather pleased by what Mama called Rosa's *eccentricity*. He'd certainly always been scathing of girls who were the opposite of eccentric, the dull sisters of some of his Oxford friends.

'Very well,' said Mama, 'if we are all here, we may as well go through to luncheon.'

As they took their places in the dining room, Mr Ordish appeared with another note from Colonel Harding. Should the picnic be cancelled in light of the grave news?

Mama looked up from the note. 'What news? Does anyone know what he's talking about?'

'I expect he's referring to the European crisis, Mother.' Roderick shook out his napkin. '*The Times* was positively lugubrious about it this morning. How did it go? "The prospects of a general war have become more imminent", something in that line.'

'Oh, that.' Mama laid the note aside, dismissive, as the soup was served. 'I thought the silly man had heard something important. All this fuss over nothing won't have any bearing on the picnic. If we don't have a motor, however, Roderick—'

'I told you, Mother, Antipov and I were using the old landaulet. We've two other motors in perfect working order. I would be more worried about the weather if I were you.'

Taking up her spoon, Mama glanced out of the window. It had been a dull, rather close morning with rain in the air. 'I do hope it stays fine for the fête tomorrow.'

Dorothea had not started on her soup. 'Does the Colonel really think there may be a war?'

'The Colonel always thinks there's going to be a war,' said Roderick. 'He's been predicting the next one ever since we finished giving the Boers a good drubbing. There won't be a war. Even if there is, it won't affect us. Why should we care about Serbia?'

'But Roddy—'

'We've been here before, Doro. Remember that commotion over Morocco a couple of years back? You asked me then if there'd be a war. I said no. I was right.'

Stirring her soup, Eliza wondered if it was her imagination or if there really was a note of disappointment in Roderick's voice. She remembered his air of discontent on Rookery Hill last week. Was he thinking of Wellington and Nelson and General Gordon, his old martial heroes? Was he dreaming as he used to of following in their footsteps? But he never talked of them now and he'd long given up playing with his toy soldiers.

'I shall reply to the Colonel directly after luncheon,' Mama asserted. 'I shall tell him on no account to cancel. Now. Who would like some more soup? Ordish, if you would.'

* * *

'I don't want to go to the fête, I shan't go to the fête, the fête is too boring for words! Something is bound to go wrong, it always does. It will rain or the vicar will lose the tombola tickets or the tea stall will fall apart.'

'Why must you be so *awkward*, Elizabeth?' said Mama as she adjusted her hat in the hallway. 'I really don't have time for this — not today. The vicar is expecting me. We have so much to organise for this afternoon.'

Eliza dug in her heels. She would *not* go to the fête, she absolutely refused. She would not go on the picnic tomorrow, either. She could think of nothing worse than spending the whole day in the company of Colonel Harding.

'Very well, Elizabeth, I shall take you at your word. Don't think you can change your mind later. It is time you learned to live with the consequences of your ill-conceived outbursts. Let this be a lesson to you.'

* * *

'Talk about cutting off your nose to spite your face!' exclaimed Daisy in due course as she came belatedly to make Eliza's bed. 'Fancy not wanting to go to the fête! I wish I could go! But Bossy Bourne says it's not my turn. It's never my turn for nothing, if you ask me.'

Wild horses could not have dragged from Eliza the admission that there was now nothing she wanted more than to go to the fête. Apart from anything else, Dorothea was there: Dorothea, whose days at Clifton were numbered. Why lose any opportunity to be with her?

Daisy smoothed the counterpane and stepped back, hurriedly tucking strands of hair back inside her cap. 'That's your bed done, miss. And now I'd better get back downstairs before old Bossy Boots sends a search party.'

Alone in her room, Eliza hung out of the window gazing towards the village of which only the top of the grey church tower was visible. What was happening there? Was that music she could hear? She leaned further out, listening, but there was nothing, not even birdsong, just the breeze amongst the trees.

She flung herself onto the bed that Daisy had just made. Why, why, why did she do this to herself? Why must she be so contrary? Daisy was correct, it was cutting off her nose to spite her face. Mentioning the picnic in her outburst had been another mistake. Now she would miss that too. Mama, once her made was made up, was implacable. Why, Eliza asked, could she never get it right with Mama?

She got up and went into the day room. There she saw on the heavy table Kolya's book that she'd picked up off the grass three days ago. She felt guilty. She ought to have given it back by now. But she'd been too shy to face him since that afternoon in the gardens. Had he gone to the fête with the others or was he still suffering with his blisters? Like Dorothea, he too would soon be gone.

Why, then, waste time being shy?

She grabbed the book. She ran along the corridor and down the stairs, before her resolve could crumble. Knocking on his door, she walked in without waiting for an answer.

It was one of the smaller guest rooms on the same side of the house as her bedroom, overlooking the cedar tree and the space of gravel. The curtains were half-closed. It was like entering a grotto, dim and secluded. Kolya was sat on the bed with his legs drawn up, writing in a notebook that was resting on his knees. His shirt had no collar and the top buttons were undone. He had no waistcoat on, no shoes or socks. His jacket was draped over a chair. His scuffed second-hand boots that didn't quite fit lay on their sides on the floor. The bedside table was piled with books and sheaves of paper. Over by the wardrobe, his Gladstone bag was open a little, giving a glimpse of a jumble of clothes inside and yet more books. The sight of the books reminded her of her purpose.

'Your book.' She held it out to him. 'You dropped it in the garden.'

He looked at her for a moment with those pale and hypnotic eyes. Then he smiled, putting his notebook aside, taking the book out of her hands. 'Do you remember,' he said, 'you found my book once before, the first time I came to Clifton?'

More than two-and-a-half years ago. She had been a child then. She was too old at fifteen to be tongue-tied.

She forced herself to speak. 'Do . . . do you still have blisters?'

'They are starting to heal.' He showed her. The blisters were red and raw on his slim, white, bony feet.

She wondered if it was perhaps unseemly to be looking at his naked feet. Mama would surely think so. She could see too inside his shirt, she could see the hollow of his throat and the ridge of his collar bone. Yet he seemed to think nothing of it, her being alone with him in his room when he was half-dressed. He did not care what was seemly or unseemly.

He never put on airs. He always — as she put it to herself — wore the same face for everyone.

She wondered if she was perhaps in love with him. Certainly she liked him better than almost anyone. But if it had been love, wouldn't she have known it? Wouldn't it have taken hold of her, wouldn't she have felt it inside — wouldn't it have *hurt* more?

What did hurt was the thought of him leaving, of never seeing him again. He had said that Roderick wouldn't invite him to Clifton anymore. And if he went back to Russia he'd be lost to her forever.

Must he go? She asked him.

Yes, he said, he had to go back sooner or later. He liked England immensely but Russia was home and he missed his family. 'But when I go, is not the end of our friendship, Leeza. I may return. And you must come and visit me.'

'Me? Go to Russia?' She looked at him in disbelief.

'Of course! Why not? I shall be waiting for you!' He picked up his notebook, turned the pages, wrote something with his pencil, tore out the leaf. Handing it to her, he said, 'My address in Petersburg, so you will be able to find me.'

He smiled at her then turned away, getting up off the bed and crossing to the window. He pulled back the curtains and looked out at the bright but overcast afternoon. The room was now flooded with light.

She went to join him. She tried to explain that she would never go to Russia, she wasn't brave enough. She hardly dared leave Clifton. She was afraid of a world without God. There was so much she didn't know, she added, so much she hadn't done. She had no idea where Russia was, she had no idea about love — she had never even been kissed.

He listened, watching her with his grey eyes. Then, when she came to a breathless stop, instead of speaking, he leaned down and kissed her.

It was brief, it was gentle, his lips on hers: unexpected, indescribable, like nothing she'd ever imagined. Her heart was thumping. The blood roared in her ears.

'There,' he said softly. 'Now you have been kissed.' He tucked a strand of her fair hair behind her ear. 'You remind me a little of my sister. I have sister, Annushka. She is quiet girl, shy girl, but she also has passionate heart, she also is beautiful.'

'But I'm not — I'm not—'

'You are beautiful, Leeza. Do you not know? You are brave, too. All you need is to have faith in yourself.' He turned his head and looked out of the window again. A change was coming, he said. The world would soon be different. For women in particular it would be a new dawn. At long last women's lives would start to be their own.

Eliza took her leave of him. She skipped up the stairs on her way back to the nursery. She was brave, she was beautiful, she'd been kissed. A change was coming, her life would be her own, Kolya had said so. He sounded so sure that she felt he must be right.

The day room was deserted, the windows open. The metal bars were like stark black lines inked across the grey sky. The lush green countryside was basked in a breathless Sunday hush. Gazing out, Eliza was beset by sudden doubts. Roderick said that Kolya talked hogwash. What if Roderick was right?

She had the piece of paper still, Kolya's address in his spidery hand, his name in bold letters *N. P. ANTIPOV*. But Russia seemed impossibly remote, change seemed so improbable. Brave as she was and beautiful (beautiful?), it would take more than words to alter her course. She needed someone or something, a helping hand, the way Johnnie Cheeseman had helped her over the sandstone wall.

She pressed her face against the bars, staring at the vague horizon. Without warning, it started to rain. Rain poured out of the sky. It fell with a soft sound like a long and heartfelt sigh.

* * *

Bang!

Eliza jerked awake to a sound like a gun shot. Befuddled by sleep, for a second she could not think where she was. She looked around. She was lying on piles of cushions on the terrace, the remains of afternoon tea spread about her. How long had she been sleeping?

Bang! The sound came again: not a gun but the french windows blowing in the breeze. The curtains billowed out, twisting and flapping as if they were alive. The sky was streaked with cloud. The sun, round and yellow, was dipping down towards far-off Hambury Hill.

Eliza lay back. She rubbed sleep from her eyes. It was Bank Holiday Monday, the day of the picnic. It had been a day as long as years.

It had begun early, everyone rushing to get ready. Mama, Roderick and Dorothea had set out, Kolya too, his blisters much better. Jeff Smith had driven them. They were headed for the crossroads at Welby where they were to meet the contingents from Newbolt and Brockmorton before proceeding in convoy to the far-flung Eidur Stones. They were a party of twelve, not counting Colonel Harding's little grandson, but including in the number Mrs Somersby with her son and daughter. Mrs Somersby could never be left out of anyone's calculations.

Eliza had watched them go with a deep regret but had shunned all idea of begging Mama to change her mind: she had not demeaned herself. (Rosa too had been left behind but she had stayed in her room all day so it was as if she wasn't there.)

After eating breakfast alone, Eliza had wandered list-lessly from room to room until, in the library, she had taken a book off a shelf and lain on the floor to read it. She had read it from cover to cover. True, she had skipped the boring bits, but she had read the first words and the last and felt justified in saying that she had completed *Nicholas Nickleby*.

It had been lunchtime by then. She had eaten lunch, against the rules, in the kitchen. Cook had made a fuss of her, had been in holiday mood because Mrs Bourne was out on an errand.

'I shall sit and rest my legs for five minutes, my love. What a difference it makes, not having Old Misery-guts breathing down my neck!'

'We call her the Dreadnought.'

'The Dreadnought. I shall remember that. It's just the name for her.'

But after a time Cook had sighed and hauled herself out of her chair. She had to make a start on dinner. There was no rest for the wicked. Now, where had Evie got to, that sad excuse for a kitchen maid?

Eliza had resumed her listless wandering. There'd been no sign of Pandora or of Whisky in the stable yard. Jeff Smith, of course, had gone out with the motor, but Billy Turner was missing too. He'd taken a day's leave. He'd gone to Northampton with Harry Keech from the village. 'You'd think it was the ends of the earth to hear them go on,' Daisy had sniffed. 'What's a great lummock like our Billy want with a place like Northampton, any road?'

Eliza had fed sugar to the horses. Roderick's Conquest had gobbled greedily, his lips rough against her palm.

Back in the house, Eliza had stood in the hallway. All had seemed silent and sleepy. Except, when you came to listen, the house was never entirely quiet. The tick-tock of the grandfather clock measured the long slow minutes. Muted voices floated up from the basement. There had been a faint chink of cutlery, too, as Basford laid the table in the dining room. The unending routine of the house, reassuring and yet somehow stifling too. In order to escape it — to do something different — Eliza had carried out armfuls of cushions onto the terrace. She had taken afternoon tea in the sunshine. She had fallen asleep.

Bang! The french windows blew in the breeze. The last rim of the sun slipped below the horizon. The picnickers would be on their way home by now. An air of expectancy was growing. How soon before they arrived?

Eliza got to her feet. Indoors it was already gloomy. She made her way to the breakfast room. The window was open. Outside, deep shadows had gathered beneath the flat-sweeping boughs of the cedar tree. The space of gravel was empty, waiting.

How far were the Eidur Stones? Five miles, ten miles, twenty? Eliza drifted round the room. She circled the satin-wood table. She counted the japanned chairs. She ran her hand along the polished surface of the sideboard. She could hear next door Basford bringing in the cushions, closing the french windows, turning on the lights. A yellow glow seeped under the connecting door.

On the side table, where Mrs Bourne would have been most displeased to find it, the newspaper lay folded up next to the Kiangsi vase. No doubt it had been cast aside during that morning's rush, had lain forgotten all day. Eliza took it to the window where there was still just enough daylight to read by. The pages rustled as she turned them.

FIVE NATIONS AT WAR
FIGHTING ON THREE FRONTIERS
GERMAN DECLARATION TO RUSSIA
INVASION OF FRANCE
BRITISH NAVAL RESERVES MOBILIZED

The series of headlines leapt out at her. She tilted the page, straining her eyes to read the smaller print.

The great catastrophe has come upon Europe—

'The great catastrophe . . .' A shiver went up her spine as she repeated the ominous words. But at that moment she heard a faint sound through the open window. It was them, it had to be them. Mama and Roderick and Dorothea and Kolya were back at last.

Eliza abandoned the newspaper, went running to the hallway where the electric lights were on. Opening the front door, she stepped out into the twilight. She stood listening.

It was not the sound of the motor. It was altogether a quieter, more solitary sound, running footsteps getting ever nearer. A lone figure emerged from between the evergreens at the head of the drive. Booted feet crunched on the gravel. The figure came to a halt in the pool of light at the bottom of the steps.

'Billy Turner.'

He took his cap off, held it in both hands. He was out of breath from running. 'Have you seen our Daisy, Miss Eliza? I wanted to tell her — to tell her—'

'Tell her *what*?'

'I'm just back from Northampton, miss. You should hear what people are saying.' He gulped air, his chest heaving. His clean shirt showed up white in the V of his waistcoat. As he looked up at her, his eyes glinted in the light spilling from the hall. 'If the Germans don't back down, then England will fight, that's what people are saying. It means war, miss: war! And we shall be in it!'

She had never seen him so animated. Her heart stirred within her. She had the strangest illusion that she'd been waiting all this time not for the return of the picnickers but for Billy Turner, this husky lad done up in his Sunday best looking suddenly so young and so eager and bursting with momentous news.

The August dusk was deepening, veiling the world in shadow. But to Eliza it seemed there was a different veil and it was dissolving around her, as if she was beginning to see her way clear at last. But what was it that lay in store for her?

She was tingling all over. She was afraid but she didn't let that daunt her. She was brave, she was beautiful, she had faith: she had faith in herself. Whatever was coming, she was ready. She would meet it head-on. And — oh! — she couldn't wait for it to begin!

THE END

ALSO BY DOMINIC LUKE

THE BRANNANS FAMILY TRILOGY
Book 1: AUTUMN SOFTLY FELL
Book 2: NOTHING UNDONE REMAINED
Book 3: DREAMS THAT VEIL

Thank you for reading this book.

If you enjoyed it please leave feedback on Amazon or Goodreads, and if there is anything we missed or you have a question about, then please get in touch. We appreciate you choosing our book.

Founded in 2014 in Shoreditch, London, we at Joffe Books pride ourselves on our history of innovative publishing. We were thrilled to be shortlisted for Independent Publisher of the Year at the British Book Awards.

www.joffebooks.com

We're very grateful to eagle-eyed readers who take the time to contact us. Please send any errors you find to corrections@joffebooks.com. We'll get them fixed ASAP.

Printed in Great Britain
by Amazon

83467879R00154